SARD HARKER

THE WORKS OF JOHN MASEFIELD

PLAYS:

THE FAITHFUL
GOOD FRIDAY
ESTHER. (*From the French of Jean Racine*)
BERENICE. (*From the French of Jean Racine*)
MELLONEY HOLTSPUR

A KING'S DAUGHTER
THE TRIAL OF JESUS
THE TRAGEDY OF NAN
TRISTAN AND ISOLT
THE COMING OF CHRIST
EASTER
END AND BEGINNING

POETRY:

DAUBER
THE DAFFODIL FIELDS
PHILIP THE KING
LOLLINGDON DOWNS
A POEM AND TWO PLAYS
REYNARD THE FOX WITH SELECTED SONNETS AND LYRICS
ENSLAVED
RIGHT ROYAL
SELECTED POEMS (new edn.)
KING COLE

POEMS (collected)
MIDSUMMER NIGHT
MINNIE MAYLOW'S STORY
A TALE OF TROY
A LETTER FROM PONTUS
SOME VERSES TO SOME GERMANS
GAUTAMA THE ENLIGHTENED
WONDERINGS
NATALIE MAISIE AND PAVILASTUKAY
ON THE HILL

FICTION:

SARD HARKER
ODTAA
THE MIDNIGHT FOLK
THE HAWBUCKS
THE BIRD OF DAWNING
THE TAKING OF THE GRY
THE BOX OF DELIGHTS

VICTORIOUS TROY
EGGS AND BAKER
THE SQUARE PEG
DEAD NED
LIVE AND KICKING NED
BASILISSA
CONQUER

GENERAL:

GALLIPOLI
THE OLD FRONT LINE
ST. GEORGE AND THE DRAGON
THE BATTLE OF THE SOMME
RECENT PROSE
WITH THE LIVING VOICE
THE WANDERER OF LIVERPOOL
POETRY: A LECTURE

THE CONWAY
THE NINE DAYS WONDER
IN THE MILL
NEW CHUM
THANKS BEFORE GOING and A MACBETH PRODUCTION
A BOOK OF BOTH SORTS

SARD HARKER

A NOVEL

BY
JOHN MASEFIELD

WILLIAM HEINEMANN LTD
MELBOURNE :: LONDON :: TORONTO

FIRST PUBLISHED OCTOBER 1924
REPRINTED (TWICE) OCT. 1924, NOV. AND DEC. 1924,
1926, 1928, 1931, 1934, 1935, 1936, 1939
NEW EDITION 1938
REPRINTED 1949

PRINTED IN GREAT BRITAIN
AT THE WINDMILL PRESS
KINGSWOOD, SURREY

To
Isaline and Henry Philpot

SARD HARKER

Part ONE

SANTA BARBARA lies far to leeward, with a coast facing to the north and east. It is the richest of the sugar countries. Plantations cover all the lowland along its seven hundred miles of seaboard, then above the lowland is foothill, covered with forest, rising to the Sierras of the Three Kings, which make the country's frontier.

The city of Santa Barbara lies at the angle of the coast in the bight of a bay. The Old Town covers the southern, the New Town the northern horn of the bay: in between are the docks and quays.

In the northern or New Town there is a plaza or square, called Of the Martyrdoms. Until about thirty years ago, there was a block of dwelling-houses on the western side of this square, which attracted the notice of visitors. Though the other buildings in the square were gay or smart, with flowers, colours and lights, these were always dingy, by decree. If any asked why they were dingy, they were told that those were the houses of the last sighs, "las casas de los sospiros ultimos," and that they dated from the time of the Troubles under Don Lopez, who was Dictator de Santa Barbara from 1875 till 1887.

This Don Lopez de Meruel, called The Terrible, after nine years of murder and cruelty, began a year of madness by decreeing that he should be given divine honours in all the churches of the State. Finding himself opposed by some of the clergy and by many of the hidalgos, he seized the daughter of one of his richest land-owners, Señorita Carlotta de Leyva de San Jacinto, then on a visit to the capital, and ordered her to pray to him while he sat throned in public on the high altar of the mission church. On her refusal, he ordered her to be enclosed in a house of common prostitutes.

The mistress of this house, an Englishwoman known as Aunt

1

Jennings, refused to obey the order to receive her. "Miss Carlotta is a lady," she said, "and she does not come in here. And none but a dirty dog would have thought of sending her. And as for praying to the dirty dog, Miss Carlotta has done quite right. If he wants folk to pray to him, let him come here, and my little Sunday School will give him all the pray he wants with a wet rag off the dresser."

When this was reported to Don Lopez, he ordered that Carlotta and Aunt Jennings should be taken along the water front by the hangman as far as the Plaza in the New Town, and that there their throats should be publicly cut against the walls of the houses on the west side, then used as houses of charity. This deed was at once done. The two women were killed by Don Lopez' son, Don José, then a lad of twenty, assisted by a negro (Jorge) and two half breeds (Zarzas and Don Livio).

Don Manuel San Substantio Encinitas, the betrothed lover of Carlotta, was then at his estate of Las Mancinillas, two hundred miles away. When the news of the crime was brought to him, he gathered his friends, sympathisers, and estate servants, some seven hundred in all, and marched to unseat Don Lopez and avenge the murder.

His army was routed by Don Lopez in a green savannah near the city; many of his friends, not killed in the fighting, were hunted down and killed; he himself, with about forty horsemen, rode from the battlefield, then swerved and made a dash for the city. They appeared at the Old Town at sunset and summoned the fortress to surrender.

Don Livio, who commanded in the fortress, recognised Don Manuel and determined to outwit him. While parleying at the gate as though for terms, he sent a lad, one Pablo de Chaco-Chaco, to some Republican troops quartered outside the fortress in a sugar warehouse. These troops, being warned by Pablo, took up their positions in windows commanding Don Manuel's troop and suddenly fired in among them. In the skirmish which followed, Don Manuel's men fell back along the water front, and were shot down as they went. As darkness closed in, the last six of them, including Don Manuel, gathered at what is known in the ballads as the

2

Bajel Verde, a green boat or lighter drawn up on the beach. Here they made a stand till their ammunition failed. They then took to the water, swimming, in the hope of reaching some English ship in the harbour. But by this time Don Livio had sent out soldiers in boats to patrol the water front. All of the six except Don Manel, were shot or clubbed, as they swam, by these patrols. Don Manuel, through fortune, and because he took to the water some minutes after the others, managed to reach the English barque Venturer, whose captain (Cary) took him aboard, and brought him a few days later to safety in Port Matoche.

Eighteen months later, having laid his plans with care, Don Manuel sailed from Calinche with another company, in a tramp steamer. He landed unexpectedly at Santa Barbara, shot Don Lopez with his own hand and made himself Dictator.

In spite of frequent risings of the Lopez faction, most of them led or inspired by Don José, who had escaped Don Manuel's justice, the rule of the New Dictator was the most fruitful of modern times.

Lopez had caused a rhyme to be carven over the door of the cathedral of Santa Barbara. In translation it runs:

> Lopez found me brick
> And left me stone.

When the new cathedral was built upon the site of the old, men remembered this rhyme, and pled that it should be recarven:

> Lopez found me brick and left me stone,
> Manuel made me like an angel's throne.

For indeed Don Manuel, in his rebuilding of the city, made the cathedral the marvel of the New World. That and the chapel of Carlotta at his palace, were the chief of his works in his own mind; but in truth he made Santa Barbara as eminent for the arts and sciences as for religion. He founded, built and endowed four big universities, three opera-houses, nineteen theatres. He discovered, encouraged, helped, and at last employed through the years of their power, all the architects, sculptors, painters,

A*

musicians and poets who have made Santa Barbara the glory of Spanish-speaking America.

In his person Don Manuel was as glorious as his mind. He has been described in a sonnet:

> A calm like Jove's beneath a fiery air.
> His hands most beautiful and full of force,
> Able to kill the wolf and tame the horse
> Or carve the granite into angels' hair.
> His brow most noble over eyes that burn
> At thought of truth or knowledge wanting aid.
> His mind a very sword to make afraid,
> A very fire to beacon at the turn.
>
> His step swift as a panther's, his will fierce
> To be about the beauty of some deed,
> Since beauty's being is his spirit's food.
> His voice caressing where it does not pierce;
> His wrath like lightning: he is King: indeed
> He is much more, a King with gratitude.

*   *   *   *   *   *

Chisholm Harker, rector of Windlesham, in Berkshire, wrote a pamphlet on English Mediæval Mystical Romances, and died young, leaving a widow and one son, Chisholm, the "Sard" Harker of these pages, who was thirteen at his father's death.

Mrs. Harker married again two years later. Sard, at his own request, went to sea, sailing first in the barque *Venturer*, Captain Cary, mentioned a page or two back. He was on his first voyage in her when Don Manuel took refuge in her. She was one of Messrs. Wrattson & Willis's sugar-clippers, then regularly trading to the ports of Santa Barbara. Later in his time Sard followed Captain Cary into the *Pathfinder* and remained with him in her as third, second and at last as chief mate. He was mate of the *Pathfinder* and had been for ten years at sea when this tale begins. He was called "Sard" Harker (though seldom to his face) because he was judged to be sardonic. He, too, has been described in a sonnet:

4

A lean man, silent, behind triple bars
    Of pride, fastidiousness and secret life.
His thought an austere commune with the stars,
    His speech a probing with a surgeon's knife.

His style a chastity whose acid burns
    All slack false formlessness in man or thing;
His face a record of the truth man learns
    Fighting bare-knuckled Nature in the ring.

His self (unseen until a danger breaks)
    Serves as a man, but when the peril comes
And weak souls turn to water, his awakes
    Like bright salvation among martyrdoms.

Then, with the danger mastered, once again
He goes behind his doors and draws the chain.

Captain Cary, who had made the *Pathfinder* a famous ship,
thought him the best officer he had ever had.

The *Pathfinder* was the last and finest of Messrs. Wrattson &
Willis's sugar clippers. She made some famous passages in the
sugar and wool trades before she went the way of her kind. She
has been mentioned in several sonnets:

She lies at grace, at anchor, head to tide,
    The wind blows by in vain: she lets it be.
Gurgles of water run along her side,
    She does not heed them: they are not the sea.
She is at peace from all her wanderings now,
    Quiet is in the very bones of her;
The glad thrust of the leaning of her bow
    Blows bubbles from the ebb but does not stir.

Rust stains her side, her sails are furled, the smoke
Streams from her galley funnel and is gone;
A gull is settled on her skysail truck.
Some dingy seamen, by her deckhouse, joke;
The river loiters by her with its muck,
And takes her image as a benison.

*   *   *   *   *   *

5

How shall a man describe this resting ship,
  Her heavenly power of lying down at grace,
This quiet bird by whom the bubbles slip,
  This iron home where prisoned seamen pace?

Three slenderest pinnacles, three sloping spires,
  Climbing the sky, supported but by strings
Which whine in the sea wind from all their wires,
  Yet stand the strain however hard it dings.

Then, underneath, the long lean fiery sweep
  Of a proud hull exulting in her sheer,
That rushes like a diver to the leap,
  And is all beauty without spot or peer.

Built on the Clyde, by men, of strips of steel
That once was ore trod by the asses' heel.

A Clyde-built ship of fifteen hundred tons,
  Black-sided, with a tier of painted ports,
Red lead just showing where the water runs,
  Her bow a leaping grace where beauty sports.
Keen as a hawk above the water line
  Though full below it: an elliptic stern:
Her attitude a racer's, stripped and fine,
  Tense to be rushing under spires that yearn.

She crosses a main skysail: her jibboom
Is one steel pike: her mainsail has a spread
Of eighty-seven feet, earring to earring.
Her wind is a fresh gale, her joy careering
Some two points free before it, nought ahead
But sea, and the gale roaring, and blown spume.

*   *   *   *   *   *

Las Palomas, where this story begins, is far away to windward
on the sea-coast of the Tierra Firme. It has grown to be an
important city since the northern railway was completed. It has
been a frequented port since the days of the Conquistadores,
because it is a safe harbour in all winds save the north, with good
holding ground and an abundance of pure water for the filling.

6

In the years 1879-80 it had an evil name, for it was then the nearest seaport to the newly discovered goldfields at Entre las Montanas in the province of Palo Seco, three hundred miles inland. Many diggers returning with gold from the fields were knocked on the head at Las Palomas.

Las Palomas means the Doves. It got its name from the blue rock-pigeons which used to haunt the cliffs just south of the old (or Spanish) town. The cliffs are now covered with buildings and the pigeons are gone. The only doves thereabouts now are the Little Doves of Santa Clara in a Convent school so named.

Las Palomas was formerly mainly a coffee and sugar port, but of late years it has become a great place for the exportation of copper-ore from the mine at Tloatlucan, only seven miles inland.

Nearly thirty years ago, when this story begins, there was open savannah to the north and north-west of Las Palomas city. In those days you could walk (in that direction) in less than an hour from the heart of the city into primeval forest. If you walked due north along the beach, from Jib and Foresail Quay on the water front, you could reach a part of the forest in two miles. This was a clump of pines which came right down to the sea on a tongue of red earth.

If, in those days, you walked through those pines, still northward over the tongue, you came to a little beach, edged with a low bank of shrubbery. There, between the forest and the sea, was the mansion known as Los Xicales, where old General Martinez, the last descendant of one who came there with Cortés, lived to his end in faith, poverty and style.

Los Xicales.—Nobody knew at a first hearing what the xicales were. They were not jicales nor jicaras, as many thought, but trumpet-shaped flowers, with blue and white stripes, which General Martinez had brought there from the Indian territory. They were neither convolvuluses, petunias, nor hermositas, though like all three. They were just "xicales," which is as near as the Spaniards could come to the Indian name for them, which means, simply, "flowers." The house might have been called "the flowers" without loss of time.

*   *   *   *   *   *

On the evening of the 18th March, 1887, just ten years before my story begins, Sard Harker, then on his first voyage to sea, lay in the barque Venturer, in Las Palomas harbour, expecting to sail at daybreak for Santa Barbara, "to complete with sugar for home."

During the day, while bending sails aloft, he had seen the white walls of Los Xicales and had been struck by their likeness to a house in England, near the sea, where he had stayed as a child. He had taken a good look at the place, while waiting for the sail to come up to him, with the thought that it was either a coast-guard station or a lighthouse. After that, work occupied him until dusk, so that he put the house out of his mind.

For some weeks he had been training himself to be "a hard case," that is, able to stand exposure, by sleeping on the top of the deckhouse, between the mizen staysail and one of the boats. Here, with one blanket between himself and the deck, one blanket over him, and a coil of boat's falls for a pillow, he went to bed that night as usual, thinking the thoughts which meant much to him. These thoughts were not about the house, but about a girl, whose idea filled his inner life intensely.

He had thought his thoughts of this girl, as he always did, when putting the day from him, and had then turned over, to sleep as usual. He saw the stars overhead, through a maze of the main-rigging: he heard the water go crooning and gurgling by, and a man in the deckhouse beneath him knock out his pipe; then instantly he was asleep, in a sea-sleep, a depth of sleep, a million miles from this world.

Out of his sleep he started up, an hour before dawn, with that mansion by the sea lit up in his brain and words ringing like prophecy in his ears:

"You will meet her again in that house, for the second of the three times. It will be very, very important, so be ready."

He had risen up in the cold and dew of before dawn to stare towards the house, almost expecting to see it lit with angels; but it lay among its trees, barely visible. The dew was dripping, the water crooning and the watchman humming a song between his teeth. The cook was up making coffee, for there was a light in the galley; everything was as usual, except himself.

8

He was so shaken with excitement that he gripped the mizen stay to keep himself from leaping overboard to swim to that lone beach. Then caution had come back upon him, with the thought, "It will not be to-day; we are sailing to-day; 'it will be,' the message said, not 'it is'; I am to stand by; it is all for the future, not for now."

At that moment the order came to call all hands; and by daylight the Venturer was standing out from the northern channel, while Sard cut loose the gaskets and shouted "All gone the mainroyal" to those on deck. For more than nine years he saw no more of Las Palomas, but the memory of his dream remained intense. The "first" of the "three times" was the deepest thing in his life: it made him shake, even to think of it: the hope of the second time kept him alive.

Then in February, 1897, he came again to Las Palomas, this time as mate in the Pathfinder. Again he looked out on Los Xicales, this time through a strong telescope from the main topgallant crosstrees. He saw the house unchanged in all those years, save that it looked more battered. When he could he went ashore, and walked northward along the beach, over the tongue of red earth with the pine trees, to the house itself.

He found no barrier to his entrance to the grounds on that side, save the close-growing thorny mita-shrubs which covered the low bank above the beach. Beyond the bank, they had spread beach-shingle as a drive; the house rose up out of the shingle white and withered against the blackness of pines and the gloom of Spanish moss. It was a pleasant, Southern mansion, less than twenty years old, the worse for wear. It had a look of having come down in the world, or rather, that staring look of having come past its best, which houses share with men and flowers:

> "This neither is its courage nor its choice
> But its necessity, in being old."

It had a look of having no heir, and of being the last of the family. It had not been painted since its builders left it nineteen years before.

It was shuttered up tight, throughout; no smoke rose from it;

9

plainly everybody was away. He noticed big leaden urns near the blistered green verandah. They were filled with a sprawling trailer about to blossom. He thought, "These are probably rare flowers, brought here when the house was new, when the owner thought that he would be a success."

He stared at the house, thinking that there he was at last, after all those years, there at the house of his dream, where he was to meet her for the second time.

And now, on the excitement of being there, after all those years, after his mind had gone alone so often to where he stood, came the disappointment, of finding the house shut up, with no one there. He had half-expected and wholly hoped to have found her outside the house, looking for his coming. Hope and expectation were dashed. The house was empty.

Feeling that he was trespassing, he walked to the western side of the house, climbed the stone steps and rang the bell, which gave forth a jangle far away to his left. No one answered the bell, though he rang a second time. Little scraps of plaster were scaling off the wall by the bell-pull; the forest behind the house needed cutting back: it was coming too close with its evil and its darkness. The noise of its sighing was like the whispering of heirs about a death-bed.

"I am not to meet her here this time," he said to himself; "but since she may live here or have been here, I will go all round it, so that I may know what she has known."

He found that it ran, roughly, north and south, parallel with the beach. It had an old green verandah on the sides looking on the sea; the stone perron and steps on the west, and outhouses, on which the jungle was encroaching, to the north. On the north side was a path, which seemed to be still in use: it led through an iron gate, which was open, as though to invite him on. He passed through it, into a jungle of evergreens, in which he heard the noise of water. In a few minutes he came out on to a causeway of stone which led over swampy ground to a pier or quay, on the bank of a river which curved out into the sea there. The pavement continued inland upstream along the bank of the river till the forest hid it from sight.

As all water interests a sailor, Sard stopped on the bank to watch this river. It came round a curve out of the forest, broadened suddenly to a width of thirty yards, and went babbling in a shallow over the sands into the sea. It was like listening to poetry to hear it.

"They had this place a harbour once," Sard thought, "and boats loaded produce here. Then, in some flood, the other side of the harbour was washed away: there is a bit of a pier of masonry still standing: and they were never able to afford to repair it. This river makes the northern boundary of the estate, I suppose."

He stayed, watching the water so intently that he never saw the approach of a woman, coming from the forest along the path by the riverside. He looked up suddenly and found a tall old proud-looking negress within a few feet of him. She was dressed in black, she wore a mantilla over her shoulders, and a big straw Gainsborough hat upon her head. She wore very heavy old silver earrings in her ears, which were small. Her nose was small; her face was sharply and cleanly cut; she walked like an empress; she had race in every line of her. She carried a small basket, which Sard judged to contain eggs or meat. She seemed at once both to resent and to ignore Sard's presence there. Sard saluted her, and asked her whether he could reach a road to Las Palomas by continuing along the river.

"Yes," she said. "But if you will come with me by the house, it will be a shorter way."

She led Sard back along his path; presently they were in sight of the house.

"Madam," Sard said, "who lives in this house?"

"It is closed at present. I live here with my husband. I am Tia Eusebia, the caretaker."

"Whose house is it?"

"It is the house of General Martinez, who is away in the South."

"It has been a beautiful house. Is General Martinez married? Has he children?"

"God has willed that the General should be alone."

"When will he return?"

"Who knows?"

11

By this time they were at the northern end of the house where there was a small door. Tia Eusebia brought out her door-key.

"See," she said, "since you want the road to Las Palomas, continue past the house; turn to the right near the front door, up the drive to the lodge. The gates are locked, but you can pass. If you then turn to the left, you will be upon the road to the North Gate of Las Palomas, which is distant, by the savannah, a league; but, by the seashore, less."

"Thank you indeed, Madam, for your guidance," Sard said. "And now will you tell me yet one thing more? Do you know of one, Señorita de la Torre, who has been to this house, or is now here or to come here?"

"De la Torre?"

"Yes. Señorita Juanita de la Torre."

"God has neither brought nor promised such," she said. "It is thought that some English may come here, but of no such name."

"This lady is not English, but Spanish."

"If she be young and beautiful, she will not come here, Señor, where youth died long ago and beauty withered. This is the house of the xicale flowers, brought from the Indian country by the General, for his love, who died before she saw them, and for his son, who died before they flowered."

"They flower for others, Señora," Sard said.

"Others do not taste with my tongue," she said. "But since God favours others, it is enough. Vaya con Dios, Señor."

"Adios, Señora."

He went, as she had told him, up the drive to the lodge, which was ruinous but inhabited, since a negro child was crying in it. The gates were locked, as she had said, but he could pass by a gap in the fence into the road. The fence was mainly gap: it might have been said that the gaps had fence in them. The forest shut in the road, which went on the right hand (as he judged) to a bridge over the river, and on the left hand to the savannah and Las Palomas. Sard walked back to Las Palomas and went on board his ship to his cabin.

Sitting there, on his red velvet settle, he wondered what it all meant. On an unforgettable day fourteen years before, when he was a boy, he had met a girl, who had changed his life for him. He had met her by a succession of chances and had never seen her since. Four years later, he had been told in a dream, such as no one could neglect, that he would meet the girl again at Los Xicales.

After the dream, life had kept him away from following his fancy; he had had to serve his time and make his way. Five years after the dream, he had been free for a while: he had gone to Spain to look for the girl, but had found no trace of her.

"And now that I come to Los Xicales," he said, "I find the house shut up and her name not known. Whenever I hope to make this more than a dream, it goes to nothing."

He looked from his ports upon the deck of the ship. He told himself that he was a grown man who ought not to let himself be swayed by a dream. "As for the girl," he told himself, "she is dead or has forgotten, or is where I shall never see her."

"I will put her right out of my mind," he said. He tried to interest himself in a book, but found it impossible. "I cannot put her out of my mind," he said. "She is all twined into it and part of it. And the dream tells truth. Probably she is at Los Xicales now and needs my help."

As this thought was unbearable, he went ashore again to make sure. "She will be there this time," he told himself. "Beyond all doubt she will be there this time." Presently he was at the lodge gates, making sure.

At the lodge, a negro child was still crying. A very tall, lean, pale negro was sitting on the edge of the lodge's verandah-stoop, plaiting a withy-basket. Sard hailed him.

"Has a Spanish lady come to this house to-day?"

"Yes, sir."

"Is she at the house now?"

"Yes, sir."

"What is her name, do you know?"

"Yes, sir."

"What is her name?"

"What is her name?"

"Yes," Sard said, "what is her name?"

"What name?"

"The name she is called by: her surname."

"Whose name?"

"The lady's name."

"Which name? There's so many names."

"The name of the Spanish lady who came to this house to-day."

"Oh," the man said, "the name of the lady who came to this house to-day?"

"Yes, that is what I want to know; what is her name?"

"Yes, sir," the negro said; "now I know what you want. I didn't know for the first moment what you asked me about, but now I know. Oh, yes, sir. Look, sir, I'm making a basket:

> Put the withy there,
> Cross the withy there,
> Jesus in the air . . .

Sir, forgive my asking, but have you a little bit of tobacco or a goddam cigarette?"

"No," Sard said, "I have not."

"What do you want here, sir?" the man asked. "What do you come to this house for? This is General Martinez' house."

"So I understand," Sard said. "I want to know the name of the lady who came to this house to-day."

"Oh, Lord, are you American?"

"No."

"I thought you were an American, because you talked such funny language."

"What is the name of the lady?"

"There is no lady here, sir; the lady died a hundred years ago. Oh, say, the lovely yellow candles, and the priest he go Do diddy diddy oh do."

"Then there is no lady?"

"All put into the grave: ring a bell: Do."

"Is anyone at the house at all?"

"All in the grave. Do. Ring the bell. Do."

A square-faced man, riding sideways on a heavily-laden mule, stopped in the road.

14

"Sir," he said to Sard, "can I be of service to you?"

"Yes, sir," Sard said. "Can you tell me if any Spanish lady came, or is coming, to this house to-day?"

"The house is shut up, sir. No one will come to this house for some weeks. I, who am Paco, know this, since I have this day talked with Ramón, the caretaker of the General. It may be that in some weeks' time, when the English, who are to be here, have come, Tio Ramón may know more."

Sard thanked him and walked on; he came to a little bridge over the river, crossed it, and continued through the forest for half a mile, when he came to a cleared patch where a forge stood beside the road with an inn (of sorts) alongside it. Here a grey old Italian, who said that his name was Enobbio, confirmed what Paco had said: the house of Los Xicales was shut up, in the care of Tio Ramón and his wife Eusebia: no visitor would come there for some weeks.

Sard thanked him and returned to his ship.

"There it is," he said, when he stood once more in his cabin. "This thing has no foundation in fact, but it has the power to make me do stupid things. I will not go ashore again, unless I have some certain tidings to take me there. This love has led me elsewhere in the past: it must not lead to folly now."

His room was light enough to show how little his love had led him to folly in the past. He was a tall lean muscular man in hard condition, sunburnt to the colour of a Red Indian. His hair was black, very fine and worn a little long (to shore eyes). He was clean-shaven and his face was a clear brown with blood in it. Wind and sun puckers made his look hawklike. His hands were big and fine. He was always choicely and subtly well-dressed. Everything about him was fastidious, to the point of keeping people aloof and afraid.

His room contained many books, for he was deeply read in his profession and in the sciences allied to it. He spoke the four languages which he reckoned to be necessary in his profession. French, German and Norwegian he had learned from intelligent shipmates as a lad: Spanish he had learned more thoroughly, since it was "her" native tongue. He had read not widely but choicely in all these tongues. In English he cared deeply for only one literary period, from the coming of Dryden to the death of Doctor Johnson. A flute and the music of that time amused his odd moments. He had taught himself to make accurate drawings of things which interested him. His sketch books contained much that would be valuable now to historians of that old way of life:

"The forepeak of the *Venturer* at 3 a.m., March 3rd, 1889, after collision with the *Tuggranong*."

"The main·top gallant parral goes."

"The following sea. June 16th, 1891," etc., etc.

On the bulkheads of his room were standard and aneroid barometers given to him by the Meteorological Society, with other instruments, for the excellence of his meteorological records.

He looked round these things, with the thought that they were not life, but the solace of loneliness. He felt as lonely as a captain. "I'll go no more ashore," he thought, "I'll spend my time teaching the boys Spanish. Huskisson has a gift for languages: he ought not to be at sea."

He did not go ashore again, but thought, day after day, that before he sailed he would perhaps go. As the time passed, the thought that he was a fool to be swayed thus by dreams kept him on board. In five more weeks the *Pathfinder* got her hatches on, although light, ready to drop down to leeward to Santa Barbara to complete with sugar for home. It was the evening of the 18th March, 1897: the tug was to be alongside early the next morning, to tow her clear of the Rip-Raps.

"It will be just ten years to a day," Sard said, "at five to-morrow morning, since that dream was a fire in my soul; but all the same, I will not go ashore; this inner life of mine shall fool me no longer."

He passed the evening making his room all ready for sea-fight, for the *Pathfinder* was a lively ship when not loaded down to her marks. When all was stowed and chocked, he took his flute and played some of the airs printed in D'Urfey's "Pills to Purge Melancholy." He was not more than a competent player, but the night and the water gave a magic to his fluting. The men came aft as far as the waist and hung in a body there,

16

At about ten o'clock, knowing that he was to be on deck at day-break, he turned in. He heard Captain Cary, in the chart-house on deck, call the steward for his nightcap; he heard the steward go, and the spoon chink in the glass. Then the watchman went shuffling forward from the main hatch, tapping out his pipe. The sea gurgled down the side, then life was shut off as by the turning of a tap, he was asleep in a sea-sleep, dead to the world.

Out of his sleep he started up, an hour before dawn, with the knowledge that a gigantic cock of fire was bursting out of clouds and crowing:

"To-day, to-day, to-day, for the second of the three times, O be ready, O be ready, O be ready; at the house of the xicale flowers; to-day, to-day, to-day."

Instantly the crowing of the cock and the image of the house were merged in the memory of the first time, so that all was burning with the idea of her. He leaped up, for all these things were real, in his room, there, as it seemed, to be touched and caught. He saw them slowly fade from him, die away, not as it seemed, into his brain, but out of his three forward ports into the greyness of morning. He followed them till his brow was pressed on the brass rim of one of the ports. There was nothing beyond but the deck, the hatch, the bulk of the mainmast made darker by the mizen staysail, and the noise of the dropping of dew.

"To-day," he said, "to-day. Why, we sail to-day. We shall be gone in two hours, far out of this, and God knows if I shall ever be here again.

"Very well, then. I will go ashore. I will leave ship and sea, so as not to fail her.

"I cannot do that," he added, "I am tied, both to Captain Cary and to the ship. I shall sail at daybreak. I must get on deck."

It was but a step from his cabin door to the deck. He stood beneath the break of the poop, looking out upon the dimness; he heard the cocks crowing ashore.

"I'll put these dreams in their place," he said to himself. "But when they come, they are shaking experiences. As long as I know

17

that they mean nothing, I can steer a compass course."

He brought a towel to the waist, stripped and called the watchman to pour some buckets of salt water over him. As he dressed in his cabin afterwards, the steward brought him some coffee; he carried it out on deck, and heard the cocks crowing far inland in clearings of the forest. "It is a marvellous noise," he muttered; "they shout for the sun before there is a glimmer, and the sun comes. To-day, to-day, to-day."

The deck was wet with dew, which was dripping from the eaves of the deckhouses. The port was not yet awake, though lights were burning. The ship was awake: there was a light at the galley door; the boatswain was standing there, yarning with the cook; and from time to time a drowsy man shambled into the light from forward to fetch coffee or to ask a light.

Sard put his cup between two pins and stared at the line of the coast to the north of the town, some two or three miles from him. There, in the dimness of the dawn, the white of Los Xicales just showed against the blackness of the forest. He looked at it intently. It was one small patch of paleness, becoming clearer from minute to minute.

"That is it," he said to himself. "I've thought of it every day for ten years, and stared at it ever since we moored, and been to it twice; and now that I am sailing I am warned again that I am to meet her there again. I am warned just as I was warned ten years ago, on this very day of the year, at this very time of the day, in this very berth of Las Palomas, just as I was sailing as I am to-day, for Santa Barbara, on that cruise when we saved Don Manuel. The second of the three times is to be to-day and I am to be ready."

Looking over the water at the house, the emotion which had woken him surged back upon him, so that he had to grip the pins.

"It is all madness," he said. "A man must go by intellect and will. These dreams fight against both. Life has settled the matter: I am not to meet her. My task here is to sail this ship wherever the old man bids me. Now I will do my task."

He walked forward to the port half-deck door where the boys stood waiting for a call.

"On deck; turn-to here. Get the colours up, ready for bending, two of you," he said. "Huskisson, get the Blue Peter." As they came trooping out behind him, he turned to the boatswain, who was hanging about in the waist waiting for the word.

"Rig the head-pump," he said.

"Rig the head-pump, sir," the boatswain said. "Head-pump there, two of you. Beg pardon, sir, shall we be heaving in, after washing down?"

"Yes."

Mr. Dorney, the third mate, drove some of the boys forward with an accent from the northern midlands. "Now, choom Jelly-bags," he said, "get tha boockets; and Nibs and Woolfram get tha scroobers. We want a good harbour scroob for sailing."

Mr. Dorney was a rougher customer than the other mates, but a faultless practical seaman. He would have made a perfect boat-swain. Anything to be done with hands (especially a dangerous thing) was Mr. Dorney's delight. He had a heavy, loutish, expressionless face, which seemed to have been badly carved out of pale wood. He had only scraped through his navigation examinations after three attempts. "Ah haate all this fooss of sights," he said. "Ah can foodge a day's work." In any emergency he was as swift as Sard himself, but his excellence stopped at seamanship: he was a coastwise seaman who had strayed into blue water.

In a minute or two Sard was forward with his watch, setting the pace in washing decks against the second mate. He had rolled up his trousers to the knee and worked barefooted in advance of the scrubbers, scattering sand for them to scrub with, then snatching buckets from the water-carriers to sluice the portion scrubbed. By the time his watch had worked aft to the main hatch, he was five yards ahead of the second mate. There came a hail from a water-boat going past them to the outer anchorage.

"Pathfinders ahoy!"

Sard went to the rail to take the hail. The water-boat was going dead slow, as though only half awake. She still carried her navigation lights, but men were taking them in and blowing them out as she paused to speak.

"Pathfinder ahoy!"

"Hullo, the water-boat."

"Your tug won't be alongside till six this evening."

"At six this evening! Why not this morning?"

"She's blown some of her goddam guts out."

"Where is she?"

"Having her guts done at Ytá-Ytá."

"Right."

"Will you tell Captain Cary?"

"Right, Mister."

"The *Otoque* will be in. You'll get your mail before you sail. So long, Mister."

"So long, Mister."

Sard slipped on shoes, unrolled his trousers and went to report to Captain Cary, who was sitting bolt upright in a chair in his chart-room, being shaved by his steward.

"The tug has broken down, sir. She can't be alongside till six this evening."

"Who said this?"

"The skipper of the water-boat, sir."

"Thank you, Mr. Harker. Mr. Harker."

"Sir."

"I shall wait for her. I won't try the Rip Raps without a tug. Carry on with your brass work and bright work. Stay one moment, I've got something to say to you, Mr. Harker. I believe you used to be fond of boxing?"

"Yes, sir."

"The agents gave me some tickets the other night, for a sort of an assault-at-arms this afternoon. Since we are not to sail, perhaps you would like to take them, and go, after dinner this afternoon. Would you like to go?"

"Thank you, sir. Yes; very much."

"Then oblige me by taking the tickets. Steward, find the tickets for Mr. Harker."

"Where are they, Captain Cary?"

"I told you to find them."

"Very good, Captain Cary."

They were in the pocket of the Captain's go-ashore coat. They were handed over to Sard.

"You can take your own time, or course, Mr. Harker," the captain said. "Let me see, you never got ashore here in the Venturer?"

"No, sir."

"And I think you were only ashore once this time since the anchors were down. You ought to see the place; not that there's anything to see: so stay out of the ship if you wish, till the tug's alongside. I have always gone by the maxim, Mr. Harker, that one ought to see everything that one has the chance of seeing; because in life not many have one chance and none has two."

"Thank you, Captain Cary. Are we to heave in, sir?"

"Not till this afternoon, Mr. Harker."

"Thank you, Captain Cary."

Sard returned to the deck to finish the washing down. He had the running rigging thrown from the pins and recoiled: he had the men to the brasswork; saw the colours up and the house flag and Blue Peter hoisted. Captain Cary was on deck by a quarter to eight with an eye like a hawk for a spot or a started rope yarn. Sard at that moment was at the windlass with the carpenter. Coming out, he cast a glance aft and a glance aloft, with the thought that for all that magnificent thing, the ship, he was the man responsible, and that she would stand even Captain Cary's eye. "She is in good order," he thought, "she can stand anything that the sea can send. There's nothing wrong with her."

She was indeed beautiful, even from forward, looking aft. The power of her sheer made a sailor catch his breath. She was not very lofty, but her yards were very square: her spread was huge. She was in lovely order; yards squared, harbour-stowed, all the chafing gear bran-new, and the decks already sea-shape. He sent a boy aloft to dip a rope clear, and then went aft, with an eye for everything and the knowledge that the ship was fit.

As he went aft, he stopped just abaft the fo'c's'le (the forward deckhouse) to have another look at her. He never realised how much he liked his work until just before it was tested. He looked up at her great steel masts with the enormous yards (the fore and main yards together, end for end, as long as three cricket pitches) with the thought that this was art, this iron shell, with her gear, and that he was the master of this art. "It's a good framework," he

21

thought, "a good foundation. Building a steeple is only going a little further in the same direction, and building a steeple is the finest thing a man can do. But a steeple is based on rock and this flies along water. This thing works for her living."

He stopped abreast of the main-rigging to have a word with "Pompey" Hopkins, the second mate, a fair-haired, snub-nosed man of twenty-three, whose sea career he had watched from its beginning. He was called "Pompey" because he came from Portsmouth.

"Any chance of a Liverpool leave, Mr. Harker, since we are not to sail?"

"None, Mister," Sard said; "you know the old man by this time, don't you?"

"What shall we be doing, then?"

"After breakfast he will have a look-see and decide to trim her by the head."

"I used to think sugar was a food," Pompey said, "but now I know that it's a poison."

Sard left the deck in charge of Pompey and went below to make ready for breakfast. He had been too busy ever since dawn to think of his own affairs, but down in his cabin the words of the warnings rang again in his brain: "You will meet her again in that house: it will be . . . very, very important." And deep within his mind a voice seemed speaking: "You, who did not believe, see what has been done for you. The way has been cleared for you to go ashore."

"Yes," he thought, "I shall be ashore by two bells. I could go to the house before the boxing. I shall be free here for five hours, when I expected to be out at sea. All the same, I am not ashore yet. Captain Cary may change his mind."

For the last two years he had noticed old age, "with crawling clutch," laying hold of Captain Cary. One of its results was an old-maidish inquisitiveness about his officers' doings ashore; a desire to screen them from "temptation." This was easily to be understood, since he had himself trained all his officers from their first coming to sea, but it was trying to grown men. Sard knew that Captain Cary looked upon him partly as a favourite chick, a prize hatching from a clutch who had become "my mate," or "my chief officer," or "my Mr. Harker," but that mainly Captain Cary still thought of him as a boy in the half deck, whose morals must be watched in port. "I know," he muttered, "the old man will say something at breakfast that will check my movements ashore. He won't give me absolute liberty on the day of sailing."

He went into the long narrow cabin, that was painted white fore and aft; little shields painted with blue and white stripes were on all the doors opening into this cabin. A clock and a tell-tale compass were under the skylight, set into coamings. All round the after bulkhead were stands of arms, old Snider rifles, bayonets, boarding pikes, tomahawks and cutlasses, all shining like stars. On the table were six red geraniums in pots. The table shone with electro-plated ware, for Captain Cary kept a style. He was at the head of the table in clean white drills. The old steward stood at attention beside him. Sard took his seat.

At breakfast, Captain Cary, after feeding his canaries, talked of the pleasure of getting away to sea with a full crew. "When my brother was here in the *Lolita* in '79, in the beginning of the gold rush, everybody left her, except his boatswain, and none of them came back, except one of the boys, a lad of the name of Jenkins, who had a lump of gold as big as one hand, done up in a handkerchief."

"I hope, sir, that your brother charged Jenkins bullion-rates for freightage."

"No, Mr. Harker; he gave him the end of a brace for going out of the ship. And Jenkins went ashore in the ship's dinghy that night and never went aboard again. He started one of these low dance-and-cigar divans; there used to be too many of them. He married one of these greaser women after, but I never heard that he did much good."

"Did your brother get a crew, sir?"

"Yes; when some of the gold-diggers had had enough of it; or too much, as often happened, for there were Indians, then, in the foothill country, seventy miles from here. When I was here myself, in '74 or '75, you could see the Indian bucks riding their ponies. You could get your hair cut for nothing outside the walls after nightfall in those days. You can get your throat cut for nothing inside the walls in these days, for the matter of that."

"Yes, sir. I hear, sir, that that is because the rum-smugglers have been landing their cargoes along the coast here."

"There's a great deal too much lawlessness all along this coast, Mr. Harker, and it is all coming here from outside. Your Occidental is a quiet, hard-working man, or used to be, as I remember, but a breed of hard cases has got loose here out of some jail, or every jail in Europe by the look of them, and Las Palomas is not Occidental any longer. You couldn't give the people liberty here, even on Sunday, not even just to go to the church ship and back. The place is a sink of iniquity. Mr. Hopkins, have you seen the Mission Church here? It is very remarkable; that is, it is said to be by those who know, for its paintings of the Last Judgment. I was thinking of sending you ashore this morning, to see them—since we are not to sail."

"Thank you, sir; thank you very much, sir," the second mate answered. The captain turned up his eyes as though he were watching a bird through the skylight: he reddened and gurgled in his throat.

Sard, who knew the symptoms, stole a glance at Pompey Hopkins, caught his eye and gave him the flutter of a smile. Pompey was another lad who had served all his seven years at sea under Captain Cary; he, too, was still a boy, in the captain's eyes, to be guarded from the sins of a seaport town. Sard and he both saw the thought slowly crystallising in their captain's mind:

"If I send this boy to one of these foreign churches, he may be caught by this foreign way of worship and fall into all kinds of sin: it is just devil-worship by what I understand of it. He had better stay on board and do some useful work." In a few seconds the captain's voice was heard again.

"I was thinking that, Mr. Hopkins; that I would send you ashore this morning; but I'm not at all satisfied with her trim. When we are riding light, as we shall be this time, I like her to be more by the head. I will just have a look-see, as the Chinese say, from the dinghy after breakfast, and if it's as I think, Mr. Harker, you will have the power down and see if we can get her down more. She lies a much better course in a light wind when she is by the head.

24

"I think, too, Mr. Harker, that since we are so light, we'll have the main-royal mast down on deck. And let the boys do it all, will you, with yourself and old Birkett. Since ships became big, they do not get the practice in these things which we used to have. I remember when people came down to the water-front to see a ship of seven hundred tons."

"Yes, sir: do you indeed, sir?"

"Yes, sir, and ships of the line sent down top-gallant yards at dusk."

Pompey Hopkins' face expressed due wonder, with the inner reservation that "this kind of thing was the old man's perk."

"A little more kedgeree, Mr. Hopkins?"

"Thank you, sir."

"Steward, have the goodness to give Mr. Hopkins a little more kedgeree. About this kedgeree, Mr. Harker: they call the fish Pompano ashore here at Las Palomas, but it is not the true Pompano, which is the great delicacy at New Orleans, but more of a salt-water shad."

"What's in a name, Captain Cary? It is a credit to any name. What is the true Pompano like, sir?"

"Do you know, Mr. Harker, I never tasted it. I saw it in the boats at the levees, when I was there, but I was there in a fever season, and many people thought that the fever was spread by the fish; for it seemed to hang about the water-front. It is difficult to account for the fever in any other way. We lost seven men of the fever. They went ashore one night to bring down some scantlings we were in need of, and they all partook of this Pompano in one of these negro fish-joints, and they all afterwards sickened and died. I tell you these things, gentlemen, because you will one day command ship's companies, and it is right that you should know to what you may expose them, when you send them on shore, even upon necessary duty."

"Yes, sir, indeed," Sard said, knowing that his turn was now come.

"Since the tug will not be alongside until six, Mr. Harker, I think that if you have no objection, I will accompany you ashore myself. I understand that this boxing contest is something more

25

than one of these low-class fighting-den affairs; it is an affair of two athletes in a real gymnasium."

"I shall be very proud, sir, if you will come with me," Sard said. His heart had sunk at the thought, for it meant that he would have no chance whatever of going out to the house as he had hoped; but he was sincere when he said that he would be proud if the captain would come with him. Captain Cary was not only famous but most eminent in his profession. He was

"John Craig Cary of the ship *Petrella*,
Thunder-ship and Stand-from-under fella.
John Craig Cary when he makes a passage,
Treats his owners just as so much sassage,"

of the song of thirty years before.

"In the old *Petrella*, when I had her," Captain Cary said, "we had two athletes forward. I felt that they took an undue position in the fo'c's'le. When we reached Sydney, I bought some sets of boxing-gloves and caused them to teach boxing to all hands for a plug of tobacco a hand. By the time we left China, there were six or seven men in each watch able to deal with them. I shall be glad to see some boxing again. I understand that you box, Mr. Harker? I think that I used to see you box when we went to Auckland that time."

"Yes, sir, I used to box a little."

"Steward, will you have the goodness to set out my shore-suit presently? I shall go ashore after coffee after dinner with Mr. Harker."

"Very good, Captain Cary."

"You will explain the different blows to me, Mr. Harker. I have never boxed, myself, but I have sometimes had to hit men. The principle I have always gone upon is, to be first."

"It is a very sound principle, sir."

After breakfast, Captain Cary had his look-see from the dinghy, and as a result of it Mr. Hopkins went below with the hands to trim her by the head. Sard, with the third mate and the best of the boys, got the main-royal mast down on deck. He himself went to the top-gallant cross-trees at the beginning of the work.

26

Up there in the wind he had a good view of Los Xicales. There it was, white, shining and mysterious. "You are mixed up with my life," Sard muttered, "and as far as I can foresee, I shall not find out why even this time."

While he was aloft, he saw a big barquentine-rigged steam yacht come smartly in to the steamship anchorage and let go her anchor. She was of about six hundred tons, and this and the fact that she was flying the blue ensign, told him that she was the *Yuba*. He pointed her out to Borleigh, one of the boys there. "There is the *Yuba*, Sir James's yacht, that went round the world, and then went back the other way to take the turn out."

At dinner Captain Cary was uneasy about the weather.

"I think we're in for a norther," he said. "The air's got that bright look and the glass is falling."

"I was thinking that, sir," Sard said. "It's a bit plumy and whitish over El Cobre."

"Eh? Whitish, is it?"

"Yes, sir."

"I don't like the idea of a norther in Las Palomas," Captain Cary said. "I'd like to be out of it and clear of the Rip-Raps before it comes on."

"We ought to be well clear of the Rip-Raps, sir, by eight bells."

"I shall be glad of it, Mr. Harker," Captain Cary said, "because I was here in the big norther of '74—or was it '75?—perhaps it was '75. Seven ships went ashore: they drove, as we used to say, from Hell to Hackney. We did not go ashore, but we lost all three topmasts, and the sea made a clean breach on deck.

"In this shallow Golfe the sea gets up very quick, and is very short and very dangerous.

"However," he added, "it seems to be coming on slowly. I dare say we shall be gone in plenty of time."

After dinner, Captain Cary took Sard to the boxing-match. He took him in style, going first to the agents, then to the gymnasium, in a one-horse caleche hired on the water-front.

The gymnasium lay at a little distance from that part of Las Palomas to be seen from the ships. It was in the Ciudad Neuva, or New Town, on the slopes of savannah which led to the moun-

B

tains, in a garden of palm, cactus and plumbago. In itself, it was remarkable, being an arena, a Circo Romano, as the Greek who kept it called it, built of lime-washed adobe. When Sard had entered in with his captain, they both felt that they were in an arena of old Rome about to watch some gladiators.

There was, of course, no roof to it. It looked like a small circus ring surrounded by tiers of wooden seats. Inside the circus ring was a square platform on which a boxing-ring was pitched. The two sailors were shown to seats near the ring, but with one row of vacant seats between them and it. Their seats, being White Men's Seats, were screened from the sun by an old green-and-white striped awning. From under this awning they could see the sky, intensely blue, the Coloured Men in the opposite seats, some palms rattling the metal of their leaves, and grasses, sprouted in the tiles on the adobe top, being hovered over by black and scarlet butterflies.

"Now, Mr. Harker," Captain Cary said, "we seem to be in plenty of time. Since you know Spanish so well, here's one of their programmes or bills of fare. You might read it over and let me know what it is that we are to expect."

Sard took the sheet of coarse yellowish paper printed in blunt old type which had once printed praise of Maximilian. He read from it as follows:

"Feast of Pugilism.
At three o'clock punctually.
Grand display of the Antique Athletic.
Contests with the gloves for the decisions.
The Light-Weights, the Middle-Weights,
The World Famous Heavy-Weights.
At three o'clock, punctually.
At three o'clock, punctually.
Six contests of the three rounds for the Champions
Of Las Palomas
For the Belt of the Victor.
To be followed by a Contest Supreme.
Twenty Rounds. Twenty Rounds.

Twenty Three-Minute Rounds.
Between
El Chico, Champion Caribe de la Tierra Firme,
And
Ben Hordano, Champion, of Mexico City.
Grand Feast of Pugilism.
At three o'clock punctually."

"H'm!" Captain Cary said, "it's nearly three now. They evidently won't begin very punctually, for we are almost the only white people here. We might have had time to go down the south end of the water-front to see that new floating dock they've got there."

"Shall we go, then, sir?"

"No. It's too late now. We're here now. We may as well stay here now we are here. It's a dock badly needed in Las Palomas and I wanted to see it. It's like the one they have at San Agostino."

They sat talking while they waited, but there was always a professional restraint about their talk. Captain Cary ashore was still "the old man," Sard Harker, the mate, was still, in the captain's eyes, the boy whom he had taught to steer. Both found themselves staring ahead over the further wall of the arena, at the old Spanish fortifications as white as spray beyond.

There came a pounce and squeal in the air just over the open ring. There were excited cries from the negroes, the wail died out and a few feathers drifted down into the ring.

"What is it?" Captain Cary asked.

"A hawk, sir; it came down and struck and carried away a little bird just over the ring."

"That is what they call an omen of something."

"An omen that the better fighter is going to win, sir."

They were still almost the only whites in the arena. They chatted or were silent while the other side of the arena filled up with negroes and half-breeds who had come to cheer the Carib. Many of these, being young men, were dressed in what was then the extreme fashion among the coloured peoples. This fashion was based on the belief that youth is irresistible: it dressed men to look young. That there might be no doubt about it, the costumes chosen were those of little boys of six or seven years of age. About a hundred of the young bloods of Las Palomas were wearing little round straw sailor hats, with ribbons hanging from the bands over their faces. On their bodies they wore little sailor suits, with flopping collars and very short knickerbockers. Their legs were mostly bare from above the knee to the ankle. Little white socks and tennis shoes covered their feet. Had they carried little spades and buckets, they would have looked like little boys dressed for the sea-shore. As it was, they carried little parasols of red and blue stuff: many of them had opened these and sat beneath them in their places: the rest carried fans or handkerchiefs of bright colours. They were exceedingly noisy and merry: they seemed to make the arena-side to flash with their teeth. Until about twenty minutes past three, many of them shouted insults at the two whites, who sat unmoved, not knowing the debased dialect of the Occidental. After twenty minutes past three, many white men entered: the insults stopped, a drummer, a zither-player and a bone-rattler struck up a jig to which the negroes kept time with Hues and stamping.

"Very late in beginning," Captain Cary complained. "It is half-past three now. If they mention a time, they ought to keep to it. They used not to be like this in the Occidental. They used to be people of their words, like the Chinese. But they have lost their religion since they began to make their fortunes, and now they are regular hasta mañana people."

"They will not be long now, Captain Cary."

"I ought to have known that they would be thoroughly late. We could have gone to the dock and then we could have gone to the cutting and seen the new steam-shovel that they talk about. That would have done us more good than sitting here all this time."

"Things seem to be beginning to move now, sir."

Indeed, things were beginning to move, for the bone-rattler had roused two negroes to leap into the ring to step-dance. This they did with extraordinary skill and invention against each other, among Hues and laughter. All the negroes present kept time with their feet to the slap and rattle of the dancers' feet. The little boy bloods sang songs. Lemonade-sellers came round with drinks; cake-and-sweetmeat men, each in a cloud of flies, sold sticky messes for pennies. Then two men standing at the ringside with guitars, began to sing in falsetto about the cruelty of love; and a littleish skilly-faced man, whose head, having been clipped for ringworm, had a look of prison, offered to reveal the result of the big fight for a half peseta down. The Angel Gabriel had revealed the matter to him in a vision, so he said.

Captain Cary became silent as was his way when vexed. Sard was left with his own thoughts, which were of "her" and of his chances of getting to the house, as he meant, before he left the shore. His mind went over various schemes for getting rid of Captain Cary, but none seemed very hopeful. "He will have to come along," he thought, "and at half-past four at the latest, I shall go from here."

Then the hope of meeting her merged in his mind into an expectation of meeting her, in perhaps less than two hours. All his life, since he had met her as a boy, when sex was beginning to be powerful in him, had been a hope of meeting her again by some divine appointment. He was weary of waiting and waiting.

He was also weary of loneliness, for he was as lonely as a captain, although he had not yet come into command. He was the most hated, feared, and respected man he knew: men were afraid and boys terrified of him. He knew what was said of him: "He is not a companion ashore and sets too high a standard afloat." "He's a damned sardonic devil with a damned sardonic way." "He may be a good sailor, but he's an ass with it, staying on in sail, and he hasn't a friend between Hull and Hades."

He had, however, two friends, an Australian surgeon, whom he had met in Sydney, and a friar whom he had met in the Church of Saint John Lateran in Rome, during his one real holiday. That gaunt and burning soul, the friar, was the likest to himself in all the world.

Women he hardly spoke with from year's end to year's end. He had not been six months ashore in eleven years. His mother was alive, but they had not been good friends since her second marriage; he disliked his stepfather. The second marriage had been much of a shock to him in many ways. His only woman friend was an austere old lady with a gaunt and glittering mind, of whom he had been fond ever since his childhood. This was Agatha, Lady Crowmarsh, who lived in Berkshire. She was very proud of Sard and was ambitious for him in her own way and world, which were not his. They used to spar when they met, because he would not give up his power for her advantages. She wished him to be a part of her world of ruling families and permanent officials. He wanted to be himself, pitted against the forces which he understood, in a world of elements.

Sitting in the arena waiting for these boxers, he asked himself what his future held for him. How long was he going to be "an ass with it, staying on in sail?" He had indeed "passed in steam," but there was something hateful to him in the thought of steam. It meant being subject to an engine-room: it came down to that: which seemed a fall after being a master of two elements on the deck of a clipper-ship. He knew very well that the sailing ship was doomed. He had watched the struggle for ten years, and had seen line after line give up the fight and "go into steam." The tea-clippers had gone before he came to sea: the wool-clippers and big four-masters were being squeezed out: they were starved and pinched and sent to sea hungry, but even so they did not pay. "They can't pay," he said to himself, "they ought not to pay: they are anachronisms. The steamship is cheaper, bigger, safer, surer, pleasanter, and wiser. The sailing-ship is doomed and has to go."

He knew that his own owners, Wrattson and Willis, were feeling the pinch acutely, and that they were both too old to change the habits of a lifetime in time to avail. He had watched their struggle at close quarters, for their struggle was passed on to their ships without delay. They had been pinching their ships for some years; cutting down the crews to danger-point; cutting their officers' wages; making old gear serve till it was junk, and grudging even a pint of oil for the decks. He had seen them become mean. When he first went to sea, the *Pathfinder* had carried four boys

32

in the half deck: now she carried eleven. Each paid twenty or thirty pounds for their three or four years' service; each did the work of an ordinary seaman, and the better trained of them worked with the sailmaker and made every sail they set. Yet all this would not serve. The steamship was beating them in spite of it all, and Wrattson and Willis were being squeezed out. There was no doubt of it; the fleet was going. The *Venturer* had been wrecked; the *Voyager* was being broken up; the *Wayfarer* had been sold to the Norwegians; the *Loiterer* had been sold to the Italians; the *Intruder* had been sold to the Portuguese; the *Scatterer* was up for sale; the *Messenger* and the *Roysterer* had been barque-rigged and sent to the West Coast; the *Endeavourer* and *Discoverer* were said to be going the same road; the *Pathfinder*, the glory of the fleet, would surely follow before long: the line would "go into steam," or into liquidation.

Captain Cary spoke suddenly from the depths of his silence, as though he had followed the same lines of thought to another conclusion.

"Did you ever see the *Petrella*, Mr. Harker?"

"Yes, sir, I did; when she was lying for sale in the George's Dock, in 1885. I went all over her and over her masthead."

"Yes, yes. I think you have told me that. What did you think of her, Mr. Harker?"

"She was a very sweet little ship, sir."

"We did not think her little, in the sixties, Mr. Harker. She was 891 tons. We carried a crew of 43 men and boys: sixteen hands to a watch: we could shorten her down to her lower top-sails, which we were the first to set, or among the first, with the watch alone; or, if we had all the stunsails set, and it happened to be daylight, with the watch and the idlers. That is different from the *Pathfinder*, Mr. Harker."

"Well, sir, we have a harder time to compete with."

"A harder time," Captain Cary said. "There is no such thing as an easy time; but in life you are wanted or not wanted; and the *Pathfinder* is not wanted."

"Don't say that, Captain Cary, a crack ship and captain will always be wanted."

"Don't you believe it, boy"; Captain Cary always called him a boy when he wished to silence all opposition. "Don't you believe it. What is passing out of this world is the business of personal relations. Captain Wrattson is a master mariner, Mr. Willis is a ship-designer with a second mate's ticket. When you go into their office you see that they know you and the worth of your efforts for them, and the difficulties you have faced for them. It is all friend to friend, man to man, sailor to sailor, if you understand what I mean."

"Yes, sir."

"So it was when I had the *Petrella*. Pennington and Foster were like that: Fremantle and Henry: Waltham and Binfields', Shurlock Brothers, Richard Oakleys', all the old firms were like that: the Green Sleeves Line: they were family affairs; an officer was a friend of the firm and could marry the employer's daughter. But that is gone, or going: ships have become too big: they are not owned by "firms" now: nothing's firm in the business: they are owned by companies; who don't know one hand on their pay-sheets. A company, as we say, has neither a stern to be kicked nor a soul to be saved. It is a damned abstraction, Mr. Harker, without either a mind to understand or an eye to see: it has neither guts to scare nor hands to shake."

"Yes, but, Captain Cary . . ."

"Don't answer me, boy: it is as I say."

The bearings were plainly running hot, but luckily at this instant there came wild Hues as the whole negro audience rose to welcome the beginning of the boxing. The old negro boxers, who were seconding the early bouts, came to the ringside, pitched some much tattered gloves into the ring and hoisted two back-less chairs into opposite corners. A couple of lanky lads, shivering in serapes, climbed through the ropes to the chairs, were gloved and introduced; then the gong struck and the bouts began.

The boxing, when it did begin, was fast and very skilful: it roused the partisans in the coloured men's benches to fight with banana skins and half-sucked oranges. There were five, not six "contests of the three rounds," and only one of the six went to the end of the third round.

"These lads are good at their business," Captain Cary said.

"Yes, sir; there are two or three fine clever lads among those. That whitish-looking lad who beat the merry one, would be a dangerous boxer if he were fit."

"Well, I enjoyed that. It was like an English summer; good when it came; but a long time on the road. Now I suppose we shall have to wait again, for the big fight."

After the bouts of the boys, in the pause before the coming of the heavy-weights, the better seats, which had not been crowded, filled up with whites. Two men came down the gangway and sidled into the vacant ring seats just in front of the two sailors. One of them, who was powerfully built, Sard judged (from his back) to be a likely man, but when he saw his face he changed his mind: it was a rotten face: the muscle had all gone to brothel with the man's soul.

His companion was a little, grey-bearded man, whose neck was swathed with a rag which partly hid a boil. The boil made him keep his head forward as he spoke. Both men spoke English as they entered. They looked hard at the two sailors for an instant before they sat down; then, having made up their minds that they were just a couple of English sailors, they sat and began to talk in Spanish, which Sard knew very well. The little man talked rapidly and much, using slang. Some of his front teeth were gone. He had a way of drawing his breath sharply through the gaps with a noise of relish. Sard reckoned that the bigger man was a flash townee, the other, probably, a fence. The little man was a spiteful little devil (perhaps the boil was touching him up) with a way of rising in his excitement to a kind of song. Sard thought him a horrid little man, but likely to be clever in his own rather dirty little way.

"Yes, these negroes," the little man said, in Spanish, "they need to be fed into the hopper and be taught the way again. They are getting too uppish to my liking. I love my black brother, but I love him best with the toe of a boot, to show him he's got to go. Yes, sir, he's got to go. This is God's country: it ain't going to be any black man's not while little 'Arry Wiskey is on the tapis.

O yes, it is God's country,
For no black man's effrontery.

How long are these Dagoes going to keep us waiting? We're twenty minutes late as it is. Hasta mañana; that's always the way with these Dagoes. They got no sense of the value of time, even the good ones. That's singing to their guitars instead of sound commercial competition. We shall be late, setting out."

"Here's El Chico, anyway," the other said. "And even if it goes the twenty rounds, we shall have time enough for Mr. Bloody Kingsborough."

The little man seemed scared at the mention of the name, and glanced back, over his shoulder, to see whether either Sard or Captain Cary had noticed.

"Hush, Sumecta," he said. "No names."

"He doesn't understand Spanish," Sumecta replied, meaning Sard. "And if he does, what odds?" He glanced back at Sard, whose face seemed intent upon the Carib, then just entering the ring. Sumecta's eyes followed Sard's to the Carib: he spat, turned to Mr. Wiskey and said, in a low voice:

"He won't have much show."

"Who, El Chico or Mr. K.?"

"I meant El Chico; but Mr. K. won't have much."

"Have much!" Mr. Wiskey answered; "he'll have about as much show as a cat in hell without claws. When it's peace, he has a show, but when it's war, he's got to go."

The Carib pitched off his green wrapping, sat down upon his chair and stretched out his legs for his seconds to massage them. His reddish-brown skin moved with the play of healthy muscle: he shone with health and oil.

"Yes," Mr. Wiskey muttered, staring at the Carib, "you may listen and you may glisten, but you'll go where the nightshade twineth if you put the cross on little 'Arry Wiskey."

"So this is Chico," the Captain said. "Well. Mr. Harker, he looks to me liker a panther than a human being. I must say that I do not like to see these cannibals pitted against Christians. I am in two minds about staying."

36

"Sir, I expect he is as good a Christian as the other. And he may not be nearly so good a fighter."

"True," the Captain said. "The Church has lost its hold here, as I was saying, but still I don't think that even these modern Occidentales would let a Carib fight a Christian, if they thought that he stood a chance of winning. Where is this other, the Christian? I think, Mr. Harker, I will go get a cigar at the office, while this other man is being made ready, if you will keep my seat."

"I will keep your seat, Captain Cary."

After Captain Cary had edged away to buy a cigar, Sard waited for the two men in front to go on with their talk, for what they had said had interested him. He had not liked to be ranked with any other mate who knew no Spanish, and he wondered why Mr. Bloody Kingsborough was to have no show. Who was Mr. Bloody Kingsborough? He did not know the name. The tone in which the name was pronounced suggested that Mr. Kingsborough was judged to give himself airs. Sard judged that if Mr. Kingsborough did not take good heed, he would be a bloodier Mr. Kingsborough before dawn. Chico was not to have much show in any case, but to have none if he disappointed Mr. Wiskey. Sard hoped that the talk would go on, but it did not. Mr. Wiskey began to eat a pomegranate by tearing off the skin with his teeth and spitting it out into the ring.

"He's a dirty shining yellow snake," he said at last in English, meaning Chico; "Palm-oil all over him. It's that that gives them leprosy in their old age. Yah, you dirty Carib.

> Knocky, knocky neethy
> On your big front teethy.

That's what's coming to you in one dollar's worth. The royal order of the K.O., or else a boot you'll feel for as long as you can sit. Yet he looks a treat. If he could have the yellow bleached out of him, he'd make a bit for a manager, sparring exhibition bouts up West."

"He would that," Sumecta said, also in English.

37

"He's got the torso of a Greek god, as they say, though which his torso is I never rightly understood."

"It's like you would say his physique."

"The slimy yellow ounce-cat."

"Heya, Chico," Sumecta called, "Chico!"

The Carib caught Sumecta's eye. Sard was watching him at the moment and saw a strange look of fear, or at least anxiety, pass over the savage face. Sumecta opened his mouth and tapped his teeth with his fingers: whatever the sign may have meant, it made Chico smile uneasily.

"Yes," Sard said to himself, "these two ruffians have bought El Chico to lose the bout, and now that it comes to the point, El Chico is scared of these buck negroes with their razors. The whites will shoot him if he wins, and the coloured men will skin him if he doesn't. And who is this Mr. Kingsborough who will not have much show, and for whom there will be time enough? I wish that they would say some more about Mr. Bloody Kingsborough."

Mr. Wiskey suddenly turned round upon Sard. He had his head ducked down so as to avoid giving pain to his boil, and the ducked-down dart of the skull gave the movement something deadly, like the strike of a snake or ferret.

"He's a treat, sir, for looks, and a beautiful boxer, this Chico, the Carib here," he said to Sard. "Would you like to have a friendly dollar on him, just to give an interest to the proceedings?"

"Thank you. I do not bet," Sard said.

Mr. Wiskey looked at him, but thought it better to be quiet.

"Quite right, sir," he said. "I respect your feelings. I'm a gentleman myself and can appreciate them. They do you credit, sir." He turned round to the ring again, took another wrench and spit from his pomegranate, bit into the seeds and said something in a low voice, with a full mouth in Spanish, to Sumecta, about "one of nature's bloody caballeros." There was a chill upon the talk for nearly a minute; then Sumecta turned round, had a look at Sard, and surveyed the benches behind him.

"There's old Abner," he said.

"Where?"

"In the back row, about seven from the end."

38

Mr. Wiskey burst into song, parodying a familiar advertisement:

> "He's one of the party,
> Old Abner MacCarty,
> On the day of St. Patrick, at ten."

"I don't see Mr. Sagrado B.," Sumecta said.

"He's not staying for the party: he's off: out of it: going by the briny."

"The sort of thing he would do; mind his own skin."

"Sound sense, too," Mr. Wiskey said. "If a man won't mind his own skin, there's darned little he will mind, and no one else will mind it for him."

Presently Sumecta turned again to Mr. Wiskey.

"What is Mr. Sagrado B.'s game with Mr. Kingsborough?" he asked in Spanish. "Besides the bit of skirt in the case, what is he out for?"

"You've seen the bit of skirt?" Mr. Wiskey asked.

"Yes. She's it."

"That's what he is out for: just the woman in the case."

"He's getting to be too old for that kind of game," Sumecta objected.

"He's got a bit of needle against this one and so she's got to go."

"What was the needle?"

"Something that touched him where he lives. But Mr. B. has a long arm and a way of getting his own back."

"Then she's to be Mrs. Sagrado B.," Sumecta said in English. "And what is Mr. K. to be?"

"He's going to be beef-stoo," Mr. Wiskey said in the same tongue. "And if he don't like being in the soup, he can go in the cold meat cart."

"I wonder at Mr. B. starting this," Sumecta said, "just at this time, when the other thing is getting ready. This woman business will make a stir."

"Naturally, and while the stir is on, we'll be visiting friends in Santa Barb. But here comes Ben. Viva Ben!

We want only Ben
Ben, Ben and white men."

The white men present joined in the cry of "Long live the Christian." Captain Cary, edging back to his seat with his cigar, was doubtful for a moment if they meant him.

Ben, the hope both of his colour and his creed, came slouching into the ring with his back turned to the coloured men's seats. He was a pale, very evil-looking man, with oblique eyes that were downcast: nothing short of an execution would have brought a smile on his mouth. He slipped off his shabby clothes and appeared in boxing tights. With his clothes on, he looked mean, but when stripped to fight, he looked dangerous. His arms and shoulders were knotted with muscles: he had a fine chest and magnificent pectoral muscles. When he had been gloved, he stood up to shake himself down: a more villainous looking ruffian never entered a ring.

"Will Ben be at Mr. K.'s party?" Sumecta asked.

"He will stir the beef-stoo," Mr. Wiskey said.

Captain Cary took his seat beside Sard.

"You are just in time, sir," Sard said. "What do you think of the Christian champion?"

"He's like a man I saw hanged once at Hong Kong."

"He's got a fine chest, sir."

"He's well ribbed up, but what's inside? If we have to meet at night, may it be moonlight and may I be first. I shall speak to my agents for giving me tickets for such a place. Now that I am here, I will stay, but I count it a degrading exhibition." He settled himself into his seat, sucked his cigar and stared at Ben.

"The very twin-brother of the half-caste I saw hanged," he growled. "He was one of those women-killers that go about cutting women up." He stared again, with dislike of the entertainment mixed with determination to see it through, now that he was there.

"I'm not sure," he added, "that he did not cut up the women and sell them as dogs'-meat. If he did, it was sheer cannibalism, since they eat dogs there, in some of the quarters. Seven women, altogether, he cut up." He lapsed into silence, gazing over Ben's head into that other scene in his memory of the long past.

Sard turned his attention to the two men in front of him, hoping for more information from them, but Mr. Wiskey was now deep in his pomegranate and Sumecta was smoking a cigarillo. Sard pieced together in his mind all that they had said. "After this fight, which you have arranged, so that the Carib shall lose, you two, with the help of a Mr. Abner, and of Ben Hordano, are going to a party to lay out a Mr. Kingsborough, and abduct a woman, presumably Mr. Kingsborough's wife, for the benefit of a Mr. B. Who is Mr. B.? He is apparently in late middle age, and vindictive. He must be a dangerous criminal, since he has planned this abduction. He must be powerful, because here he is controlling at least four men to do something dangerous while he leaves the country. He must be wealthy or he could not control the men or leave the country. Where is he going, when he leaves the country? They mentioned 'being safe in Santa Barb': no doubt they will all go to Santa Barb; to some part or port of it. There is room enough for them to hide, on that wild coast. At the same time, this is Mr. B.'s self-indulgence, not his real occupation, that is preparing something else, more important. 'The other thing is getting ready.' I wonder what thing. Before they mentioned 'the other thing' I should have said that they were all liquor-smugglers, but it sounds now more like politics of some sort: a revolution here, perhaps. And yet, these men are all criminals; they must be in law-breaking of some kind: liquor smuggling is likeliest. They bring the rum from to leeward, land it somewhere here, carry it across Las Palomas province, over the frontier into Entre las Montanas, where they sell it, at three hundred per cent profit, among the gold-miners. Mr. Kingsborough has the cards stacked against him: I wonder what I can do to help him."

While he was wondering, he turned leisurely round, first to his right, as a blind, then to his left, to see who was sitting in the back row about seven from the end. There were three or four people close together at that point: a young well-dressed native, with much silver in his hat; a sad-faced, thoughtful, middle-aged man, with a goatee beard: neither of those could be "old Abner."

Next to the middle-aged man was a man with a pale, predatory, grim face, having pale eyes, bony cheeks, a beak nose and a slit of a mouth: he seemed likelier. Next to him was a rosy-faced old man, white-haired and bearded, jovial and bright-eyed with good living, like the pictures of Father Christmas: could that be old Abner? The grim man seemed likeliest of the four.

"Bueno; mucho bueno," Mr. Wiskey shouted to the referee, who now came into the ring to examine the boxer's gloves. "You're only one hour and thirty minutes late."

The Master of the Ceremonies now followed the referee into the ring. He wore an evening suit, with a white waistcoat. A large silver disc hung on his chest from a broad red ribbon that went about his collar. He carried a white wand with a cross at its end, like a billiard cue rest. His hair was plastered down into his eyes with grease: he had the look of a retired cut-throat who was also a retired dancing-master: he looked graceful, cruel and fatigued. He explained that the moment was now come when the two great champions would display the splendour of the ancient athletic. The delay, he said, the deeply regretted delay in beginning, could only be described as an insult to such an audience: the people responsible for the delay had been discharged, so that it would never happen again. Now that all was ready, he would introduce the referee, Don Isidor . . .

Don Isidor, a short, thickset, bull-necked, bullet-headed man, with a bronze-coloured face, scarred from chin to brow with a horn-rip, advanced into the ring with a set stage smile, amid thunders of applause. He had been a matador of renown in his day, but had been "unlucky with a bull" and had come down to this. He had something of a style and a tradition about him; a rose in his ear, the walk and swagger of a tenor, and the contest look of a bull entering a ring, looking for a fight.

"And now, gentlemen," the Master of the Ceremonies said, "let me introduce to you the famous El Chico, or the Tierra Firme, and the noble Ben Hordano, of Mexico City, on my left, on my right; now, as I turn, on my right, on my left; champions both; noble exponents of the ancient athletic; gentlemen both, sportsmen both, and, let me add, gentlemen, quite ready both."

He bowed, amid cheers, and stalked out of the ring: a bell gave a broken tinkle and all four seconds hopped out of the ring: the boxers stiffened, looked at each other, the gong banged for time, the men rose, their backless chairs were whisked away by the legs behind them, and the fight began.

Ben came out of his corner looking downwards out of the corners of both eyes. It was difficult for anyone to say what he was looking at or whether he saw what he looked at. He came out with a crouching shuffle, pale, very silent, and very evil. He crossed his opponent, led without style, squared up to him and sparred for an opening. The Carib was a very different kind of fighter. Sard saw at once that El Chico was not only a superb boxer, but the master of Ben Hordano in every way. He smiled and shifted and was sleek with a body of a golden bronze. He played light and landed and got away, then came again, smiling, muttering little mocks in Spanish, and tapped Ben in the face, then warmed to his task and put in some hot ones. Ben came into a clinch, hit the Carib low in the clinch, hit him low again, hit him in the breakaway, grappled with him again and again hit him low. The negroes rose from their seats yelling "Foul!" The Carib grinned, shook Ben from him, punched him hard on both sides of the head, rushed him: they grappled again: he bored Ben to the ropes, they sidled along the ropes, putting in short-arm blows, Ben hitting low continually. When they broke, they paused and feinted, then rushed into a clinch: the Carib had the better of it; Ben came out of it uncertain. The Carib rushed and landed; Ben countered wildly, the Carib drew blood and shook him and followed him up. All the negroes rose again and cheered and cheered and cheered. Ben went into a clinch and hit low and hung on: the gong put an end to the round.

"What do you think of that?" Captain Cary asked.

"Hordano ought to be pitched out of the ring, sir, and the referee with him. I've never seen fouler fighting."

Others thought the same, for at least a hundred negroes surged down to the ringside yelling "Foul! Foul!" Half-a-dozen of the bloods, in sailor-suits, clambered up by the ropes to insult the referee, with dirty words ending in ucho and uelo. The referee seemed not to regard them for a moment: he stalked up and down, looking over their heads. Someone flung a bottle at him as he stalked, it hit him on the side of the head and knocked the rose out of his ear. He changed on the instant to a screaming madman; he picked up the bottle by the neck and beat the bloods off the ropes with it, and then yelled at them in a sort of frenzy of blasphemy till they went back to their seats. He stood glaring down at them till they were quiet, then, with a gesture he resumed his dignity, and told them that as the referee he would stop the bout if they did not behave more like caballeros. "I am the referee and I am Isidor, and no man shall dictate to me nor daunt me. Never had I thought that my fellow-citizens of Las Palomas would try to impose the mob-will upon the individual. On this individual they fail, for I am Isidor . . ."

He broke off his remarks in order to walk across to Ben, to caution him for hitting low: in doing this, it occurred to him that he might seem less partial if he cautioned the Carib, so he walked over and cautioned El Chico also. The time between the rounds had lengthened out to some three minutes with all this, so that Ben was fresh again.

"So," Don Isidor said, "all is quiet, is it not so? This is Las Palomas, I hope, not Europe with her savagery. It is thus that we deport ourselves, with calm, with the individual, with Isidor." He gave a grand gesture to the time-keeper; the gong clanged: the second round began.

The gong had scarcely stopped before Ben was in the Carib's corner on a roving cruise. Like many men, he boxed better for having had his stage fright warmed out of him in the knock and hurry of a first round. He hit rather low still; perhaps with his oblique and downcast eyes he could not do otherwise. He was clumsy but exceedingly strong. The Carib fought him off and made some play upon his face, but lightly as though the bout were a sparring match. Ben's seconds shouted insults at him; the negroes yelled to him to go in and finish the dirty white dog. He boxed on gracefully, grinning alike at insults and cheers: he was playing with Ben. He drove Ben into a corner and clouted him right and left, Ben kneed him hard in the ribs and drove himself out of the corner; turning sharply, he fouled the Carib with both hands, kneed him in the ribs again and sent his right across as the Carib staggered. He was short with his blow; the Carib slipped aside, recovered, rushed and sent Ben flying through the ropes, off the platform, into his seconds' arms. The negroes rose and yelled and sang; knives and revolvers came out on to the laps of the whites. The referee counted five very slowly while Ben climbed back into the ring. The Carib rushed: Ben stopped him: got into a clinch with him: refused to break: hung on to him: wore through the round with him hanging on his shoulder, while the negroes sank back into their seats with a moaning croon. Right at the end of the round the men broke: the Carib came in like a flash, Ben rallied to it, there was a hot exchange: then—Time.

Instantly there came yells of protest at the foulness of Ben's fighting, but the yells this time were from a few, because all saw that it had been the Carib's round. The referee let the protests pass by, turning his back on the negroes and talking about something else in a loud tone on the other side of the ring. He abused a sweetmeat seller for bringing flies into the arena; when he had finished with him he swaggered to the centre of the ring with a phrase:—"It is well known that I am for the sport, the sport English, the sport native, the sport antique, the sport all the time. I am not for the white, I am not for the coloured, I am for the sport: it is well known. Money speaks all languages, is it not so? The coloured man's money is as good as the white's; is it not so? Good, then; money speaks all languages, and I am for all money and all sport."

This because he was well-known, was received with loud applause by the negroes. He ended by calling for some lemonade, sipping it, and making a joke about there being no little bit of good in it.

"I think we need stay for no more Mr. Harker," Captain Cary said. "The white man cannot win, and I do not think it decent to watch the Carib overcome him. Shall we go?"

"Certainly sir, if you wish."

They had risen from their seats and had reached the entrance alley close to their seats, when the gong struck and the two men rose for the third round. Both sailors paused where they stood to watch the start of the round. The fighters were now both warmed to their work, they went for each other hot and hot. Ben came out of an exchange with a bloody lip and looking wild; he clinched, hit in the clinch, was told to break, broke, but clinched again immediately. They wrestled round the ring together, then broke, with the look of strain at their nostrils and blood-smears on their ribs. The Carib feinted, then rushed, Ben ducked, and, as Sard saw, trod with all his weight on the Carib's foot, the Carib tripped, then hit him as he fell, hit him again and fell over him. Ben got up and stood away, but the Carib lay still and was counted out. Sard saw him smile as he lay there.

Sard saw that Mr. Wiskey and Sumecta were standing at his elbow.

"That is what Mr. K. will get to-night," Sumecta said in Spanish; "the right across."

"Or the cross all right," Mr. Wiskey said.

"Will you come then, Mr. Harker?" Captain Cary said. They turned swiftly up the alley out of the arena, while Don Isidor held up his hand for silence. A roar of riot broke out behind them an instant later, when Ben was declared the winner. Sard, glancing back at the door, saw a mob of negroes at the ropes, and bottles, flasks, oranges, tortillas, pieces of water melon and bananas falling in the ring round Don Isidor, who was slipping out of the ring into a phalanx of whites already formed to receive him.

In the fresh air, outside the Circo, Captain Cary hailed a caleche.

"We're well out of that," he said. "I understood that it would be a display of athletics, but it was a very low piece of black-guardism: I call it degrading."

"Sir," Sard said, as they settled into their caleche, "you perhaps noticed the two men in front of us. They were talking in Spanish of raiding a Mr. Kingsborough to-night with a gang, in order to kidnap a woman."

"Kingsborough? I do not know the name."

"He must be English or American with that name, sir: and they talked as if they meant to do it."

"Kingsborough? I suppose they were these liquor-smugglers, going to punish one of their gang?"

"No, sir: they called him Mr. Kingsborough, as though he were outside their gang. I wondered, sir, if you would mind enquiring at the Club, where Mr. Kingsborough lives, so that we could give him a warning."

"I don't know that I want to be mixed up in the business, Mr. Harker. But you say they mean to kidnap a woman?"

"Yes, sir."

"It isn't a very easy thing to do, in a fine modern town like Las Palomas."

"They talked as though it would be easy to them, sir."

"I fail to see how it can be easy, Mr. Harker. I should not like to have to try it, even with all hands. However, what is the time?"

"Twenty minutes to five, sir."

"The tug will be alongside in an hour, and we aren't hove short yet. What's more: I don't like the look of that sky at all."

"No, sir."

"Still, we ought to do what we can. We will just ask at the Club, if this person should be known. But it would be wiser, I should have thought, to go direct to the police."

"Sir, if these people are liquor-smugglers, the chances are that they have bribed the police, or have an arrangement with them."

"That is so. There was a man at the Club the other night who said openly that when he settled here, he asked how he could stock his cellar. They told him that it would be costly, as liquor is against the law, but that he could stock his cellar if he put his order through the chief of police. So he did, and the stuff was delivered. But that was last year, Mr. Harker. They have put in a new Chief of Police since; this Colonel Mackenzie, a Scotch-American: there is no such thing as squaring him."

"Sir, we shall pass the Club on our way to the Palace of Justice. Might we pass word at both?"

"That is so. Heave round, then, Mr. Harker. Just pass the

47

word to the driver. But kidnapping a woman, Mr. Harker . . . I don't believe that it could ever be done. I've never heard of it's being done. What would be the object?"

"Partly the woman, sir, and partly (as far as I could gather) to pay off some old score."

"Well, a man would have to be a pretty thorough-paced scoundrel even to plan a thing like that; but the doing of it is what I don't see. How would it be done?"

"Sir, they said that Ben Hordano would be there, so I suppose they mean to knock her senseless: give her the knock-out blow on the chin and then lash her up, like a hammock."

"No, no, Mr. Harker; men are not like that."

"Sir, Ben Hordano is not a man, but a dangerous animal. The others are the same: they neither think nor act like men."

"Yes, but, Mr. Harker, a woman is not so easy to attack as a man. You ask one of these big policemen: they would rather tackle three men than one woman. I've known it take seven policemen to take one woman to prison: she was a little woman, too; but she kept them guessing and one of them was streaming with blood."

"Was that in England, sir?"

"Yes, in London."

"They are very forbearing men, sir, the London police."

"They know when they meet their match, Mr. Harker; but here we are at the stairs."

"The *Otoque* is in, sir; we have a fair chance of our mail."

"There's nothing much coming to me, that I've any reason to look forward to. The post is like hope, Mr. Harker, best in youth."

"There is Mr. Brentano, from the agents, sir. He has some letters."

"Where?"

"There, sir, to port, talking to a priest."

"Wait one minute, Mr. Harker, he may have some news for us. Ho, Mr. Brentano, were you waiting here to intercept me?"

Mr. Brentano left the priest and came running up to Captain Cary, who had now dismounted from the caleche. Mr. Brentano was a middle-aged, foxy-looking man with an astute mind.

48

"Ah, Captain Cary," he said, "the boatman told me that you had not gone aboard. I hoped to catch you here as you went off. By the way, here is some mail for the *Pathfinder*. There is this priest, a Father Garsinton, from the mining district, who came in, just as the office closed, to beg a passage to Santa Barbara."

"Indeed."

"He has a letter from one of our clients, one of our most important clients."

"Do I understand that he wants to come in the *Pathfinder?*"

"Well; he comes from one of our very best clients, Captain Cary, so if you could manage to strain a point. . . . He is a priest, used to every kind of hardship; you could put him in the coal-hole, anywhere, it would make no difference to him, he would give no trouble. I don't suppose he's very rich, but of course he would pay his passage. You see, Captain Cary, it is a very special case. He is a poor man. He has only a month's leave of absence. He wants to reach Santa Barbara to settle the affairs of his mother, who has died there. He has missed the *Alvarado*. He is an Englishman and his poor sister is in Santa Barbara all alone."

Captain Cary bit his glove, and showed a poor mouth.

"I suppose we'll have to take him," he growled to Sard; "I hate priests: they always take snuff. But I'll have no nonsense about fish on Fridays."

Mr. Brentano led up and introduced Father Garsinton. Sard noticed the priest particularly. He was a big bull of a man, with immense chest and shoulders, a short, thick neck, a compact, forceful head and little glittering eyes. There was something magnificent in his bearing. He was of about the middle age, near that time in life when muscle goes to flesh, but still on the sinewy side of it. At a first glance, his face, which was fresh-coloured, looked wholesome, hearty and healthy; but at a second glance Sard felt that there was something wanting. There was a greyish puffiness under the eyes, and something unnatural, or at least unusual, about the eyes themselves. The man's face was unusual, the man was unusual, he was an odd-looking man, with enormous bodily strength to make his oddness felt. Sard, who had not seen any such Englishman before, realised that a man so odd would choose

49

a way of life followed by few Englishmen. Father Garsinton wore new blacks; he was smart, for a priest from a mining camp; his cloth smelt new; his voice, as he thanked Captain Cary, was soft and gracious, but his eye was sidelong as he spoke, taking stock of Sard.

"Mr. Harker," Captain Cary said, "will you be away, then to make those enquiries, and then follow us on board?"

"Yes, sir."

"If you should hear of those people, don't let them entangle you into delaying. There's a norther coming and I cannot wait for you. I would not like to lose your passage."

"I'll not lose my passage, sir."

"I see the tug's down the quay there, with steam up. Now, Mr. Garsington, have you any gear to go aboard?"

"Yes, Captain Cary, a small trunk and that packing-case."

"That packing-case? That sort of deck-house by the bollard? It looks like a pantechnicon van. What is in it?"

"Two sets of Las Palomas crockery for my sister, with the necessary packing."

"You'll have to pay me freight on it. It will take a yard-tackle to get it over the side. Now we must get a boatman and a couple of Carib boys to get it aboard for us."

Sard in his caleche was by this time turning about to go to the hotel. He paid particular attention to the packing-case, which shone there in new white wood beside the bollard. He thought that it looked big for two sets of crockery, but supposed that the stuff was dunnaged against the sea. He drove to the hotel.

At the hotel, the woman in charge remembered the name of Kingsborough.

"Yes," she said, "a lady and her brother, rather more than three weeks ago; they were here for two nights, on the first floor, in Rooms B and D. Let me see. February the 20th and 21st, it was. They came in on the *Palenque* from San Agostino. They were going to stop somewhere here, he said. He came in for letters a day or two after they left the hotel."

Sard thanked her, turned to the 20th February and saw the names:

Hilary Kingsborough
Margarita Kingsborough $\Big\}$ Br. subjects, in trans.

written by the man in what is called a Civil Service hand. "Here
they are," he said. "Do you happen to know where they went
when they left?"

The woman turned up a register. "No," she said. "They breakfasted here on the 22nd, and then left the hotel. I'm not here in
the mornings, but he said they were going to stop here for a little.
They were taking a furnished flat, the upstairs maid thought."

"Do you happen to know what he is doing here?"

"Writing something for some examination, so someone said.
He was a very young gentleman."

"What was she like?"

"A very nice lady."

"Could your colleague, who saw them go, tell me where they
went, when they left here? I want to give them a message."

"The other clerk won't be here till midnight," the woman said.
"Perhaps you could come back, then?"

He drove on to the Club, much pleased to be on the track of
these Kingsboroughs. There was something odd about the names
of Hilary and Margarita. " 'A very young gentleman,' " he repeated, "and 'a very nice lady.' And there, as it happens, is their
enemy."

There, on the pavement before a café on the water front, was
Mr. Wiskey dancing a Hottentot breakdown to his friends. Mr.
Wiskey's hands were behind his back, jutting out his coat-tails;
his head was bowed forward because of his boil; he was singing
as he danced:

> "O, I'm a lady,
> A Hottentot lady,
> A one-time-piecee lubly gal O."

His friends kept time for him as he danced by clacking spoons
on their front teeth.

Sard wondered how it had come about that a very nice lady

and a very young gentleman had roused the employer of such a crew to take extreme measures against them. He reckoned that it would be quite impossible for him to find these Kingsboroughs and then visit Los Xicales. "The thing has always mocked me," he said, "perhaps all things do, if you think too much of them."

He entered the Club just as the clocks struck five.

"Why, for the love of Mike," the Club porter said, "if it ain't Mr. Harker! Why, sir, how are you? Maybe you'll not remember me, but I was in the crowd with you in the Venturer one trip, 'way back."

Sard saw before him a young man of about twenty-five with a smile which brought him back to memory. It was Richard Shullocker, a young American who had been stranded as a lad by the death of his parents during an epidemic in one of the fever ports. He had shipped himself aboard the Venturer as an ordinary seaman, so as to reach a windward port from which he could sail for Boston. In spite of his age, he had done very well. He had been known on board as the Big Smiled Kid, for his smile stretched from ear to ear and never ceased in any trouble or any weather. Now here he was, prosperous and ambitious, a Club porter in Las Palomas.

"Why, Richard Shullocker," Sard said. "So you are here. I've often wondered what became of you. You're looking well."

"Yes, sir. This place suits me. But I'm through here this month. I've figured out this hotel and club business. I'm going to start business in New York on my own account. And I suppose you are Captain Harker now?"

"No, just mate; with Captain Cary still. And now I want you to help me. Do you know of any man in this Club, a courtesy member probably, of the name of Kingsborough?"

"Why, sure, Mr. Harker. A young fellow, Mr. Hilary Kingsborough. If that's the man, he was in here for his mail only half an hour ago. He's been here about three weeks. He's staying at a place up the coast, General Martinez' place, Los Xicales."

"Los Xicales," Sard said, startled. "That house near the beach?"

"Yes. Colonel Mackenzie hired it for him; the police colonel.

He's staying there with his sister, who is sure one lovely woman; but they're going from here to-morrow, down to Ytá-Ytá."

"Where do they come from?"

"England, I guess. He writes up these old Spanish buildings and his sister draws them. She's just plum lovely."

"I want to get out to them, to give them a warning. I believe that they're threatened by a gang of rough-necks. I'm sailing at six and have very little time. While I go out to them (I know the way to Los Xicales), will you go to the Palace of Justice and ask Colonel Mackenzie to have a patrol along there to-night?"

"Sure, Mr. Harker, I'll go right now. But how are you going to Los Xicales? Not in that shay, I guess, if you're in any hurry. You'd best take my bicycle if you're hurrying. Say, George, rouse up the bicycle for Mr. Harker."

While the negro went into the basement for the bicycle, Sard said that the crowd on Las Palomas beach seemed tougher than formerly.

"That is so," Richard said. "These rum-runners have made it a tough joint. They run rum in and they run guns out. That mush-nosed maggot, Don José, is doing it all, to rouse up trouble in Santa Barbara."

"Don José, that scum, against the Dictator?"

"He ain't called a scum here in Las Palomas, Mr. Harker. This rum-running has made him a very rich man and his stock is away up in G. You'll find that Don José will have another try for Santa Barbara before long."

"I'm bound for Santa Barbara," Sard said. "Would Mr. Kingsborough be mixed up with, or against, the Don José gang?"

"I guess not," Richard said. "One can't ever tell. He wouldn't be *with* them, that's sure: Mr. Kingsborough's a gentleman. But here's your bicycle, and if you're sailing at six, I guess you'll have to roll your tail like the Arab or you'll not make it. Don't you heed your caleche, I'll square your driver."

"One other thing," Sard said. "Do you know a priest, a Father Garsinton? A lone rogue bull of a man?"

"No, sir: he don't come bullyin' around here any."

"Well, thank you for your help," Sard said. He swung the

53

bicycle round and rode off, thinking that he would have to sprint to be on board by six.

"So," he thought, "I lied. The dreams are true. Here I am, led to this house, and by what strange ways. She will be there then, stopping with the Kingsboroughs. Could she be this Miss Kingsborough? But that cannot be, of course; Juanita de la Torre cannot well become Margarita Kingsborough. But let that wait. The dreams are true. She will be there somehow."

He rode through the market-place over a mess of corn-sheath and trodden pumpkin, and away through the North gate to the savannah. Outside the walls there were a few houses, then a few market gardens, then the rolling sage-green savannah to the forest. The road was not macadam but dirt-track, with soft going, after the first mile. The houses ceased with the macadam, then came nothing but a ruined hut or two, and from time to time a stone cross, with a tin mug of holy water, a bunch of tinsel flowers, and an inscription, begging all who passed to pray for the soul of such an one, who had been killed there. Most of these many dead had been killed by Indians in the three dreadful raids of Capa Roja, when Sard had been a little child. Seven stone crosses together marked where Capa Roja had with his own hands martyred "seven most Christian virgins" as recently as 1872. Indian trouble had not ceased there until 1876.

Passing these, Sard rode on up a rise into the wild, mainly upon grass. Las Palomas had shrunk away from this northern tract, perhaps because of these old Indian killings; the savannah was as it had been before the white man had landed, an expanse of grass which seemed always alive from the wind. On a rise, the forest hove in sight, stretching across Sard's track from the sea to the mountains. Clumps of forest stood out in the savannah like bull-bisons in advance of the herd: the sun was in their tops in a way which told Sard that he had not a moment to lose. "Still," he said to himself, "I am going to Los Xicales, to her. Time will not matter beyond a certain point."

Out of the forest a peon in a scarlet serape came loping on a pinto pony. He came with a jingle of plate, for horse, man and trappings were hung with discs and dangles beaten out of broad

54

silver Mexican dollars. He rode, like a part of his horse, with matchless grace and swagger. He had a xicale flower in his hat, which he wore sideways, so as not to crush the yellow cigarettes behind one of his ears. He was probably an estancia peon, but he had the manners of a Master of the Horse to a Queen. "Xicales," Sard thought, "you have come from there. Con Dios, caballero."

The peon gravely saluted as he loped by, thinking that without doubt the English were mad, but that without doubt such was God's will.

Almost immediately after the xicale flower had passed, the track, which had been trending inland (for the advantage of the rise in the Indian time) swerved seaward sharply, so that Sard as he rode had a glimpse of the sailing ship anchorage, and a part of Jib and Foresail Quay where the tug still lay at her berth. "There, Sard Harker," he said to himself, "that has been your art hitherto and now you are a master of it. How much longer are you going to use your life in box-hauling another man's yards around? Not long after you find 'her,' I know, and perhaps you will find 'her' this hour."

The forest glowed in its tops across his path: myriads of its birds came in to roost. "I shall have to sprint all I know," Sard thought, "if I am to reach Los Xicales and be back on board before we sail."

Behind him, from out in the anchorage, but very clear in the quiet of the evening, came a cheer, followed by the chorus of men singing.

"There it is," he said; "they are heaving in already. It must be half-past five already. I must set my stunsails or be done for."

The glow became intenser upon the trees as he drew nearer to them, then, quite suddenly, he shot out of the glow into the gloom of the forest, which struck cold as well as gloom. On his left were pine trees all sighing together, on his right were Turkey oaks all hoary and evil with Spanish moss. They looked like evil Mr. Wiskeys grown bigger. They seemed to thrust out their heads and to wag their beards and to be wicked to the core. Through the crowds of these trees, Sard followed the track, in sound of the beating of the sea, till he dismounted at the lodge beside the gates. Wired to the side of the lodge was a white wooden roofing shingle marked in pale blue letters with the words "Los Xicales." It had a look of having no one there, of being to let. As Sard looked at it, he felt an oppression in the air, as though all the life had gone out of it. "Here's the norther," he said; "and as it is coming on so slowly, it is going to be bad."

Sard propped his bicycle against the gates and hammered on the lodge-door with his knife-handle.

Nobody answered. The door, which stood slightly ajar, let out a smell of stale tortilla. Sard could see little pale ants wandering on the floor within. He hammered again and again and called. Presently a slatternly-young negress, in a blue cotton gown patched with sacking, came up among the pine trees, and grinned at Sard like an idiot.

"O Jesu," she said, "O Jesu!"

"Can I go to the house? Is anybody there?"

"The gates are always locked."

"Yes, but I want to go to the house."

"Tehee."

"May I go to the house, to see Mr. Kingsborough?"

"O Jesu."

"I am going to the house. See that no one steals this bicycle, or you'll be a sick negress, mucha, mucha."

He crossed the fence by the gap (the fence was indeed mainly gap) and set off down the weed-blinded drive under pines which had been tapped and were now either dead or dying. The effect was dismal in that muggy air, but Sard's heart beat high with the expectation of adventure. Beyond all doubt, this was the house of his dream, the dreams were true, and he was going to meet her the very thought of whom made all that inner life of which no one had any suspicion. The turn in the drive brought him within sight of the house. He stood still, at the turning, to take stock of it. Then he went boldly up the steps and rang the bell.

An old white-haired negro, with charming manners, admitted and announced him. In a moment he returned, to say that Mr. Kingsborough would see him, at once, if he would follow. Sard followed, along the hall, which was paved, for the coolness, and grass-matted for ease in walking. The hall was bare of furniture save for an old Spanish chest, painted with the life of St. Dominic, which stood under a window, with its legs in glass jars (against the ants). Like all men accustomed to take bearings, Sard fixed the details of it. It was a long hall running along the length of the house, with doors opening off it, and a staircase at the western end. The old negro major-domo opened a door a few paces from this staircase, and announced him:

"Señor Don Harker."

Sard went in and instinctively put back a hand to close the door. He felt the door as the negro closed it; he was amazed at its weight: it was black maruca wood from the house of some conquistador.

The room to which he entered was a long room at the southern corner of the house. The wall to his right, as he entered, contained a French window opening upon the verandah. A woman stood at the door of the French window, half in the verandah. He could not see her face, since it was turned from him, but there was something about her that made his heart stand still. She spoke as he closed the door:

"I will water the xicales, Hilary," she said, "and come back when you are alone." Her voice rang in his brain like a memory: she closed the glass door behind her, and passed by the verandah steps into the garden out of sight.

Sard turned to his left. A young man had risen from a chair to greet him. Sard looked at him eagerly for some trait or feature that would be like the face he sought, but the face was new to him: it was the face of a smiling young man, fond of fun and ease, perhaps twenty-five years old. Sard envied him the fun and ease, but felt that the lad was a child, compared with himself, who had dealt with the sea for ten years.

"What can I do for you, Mr. Harker?" the young man said.

Sard told what he had heard at the ring-side and described the two men. The young man listened attentively and showed no sign of fear, but seemed puzzled.

"I know nobody like those two men," he said; "and as for any-

57

one called B., or Sagrado B., in Santa Barbara, I know no one of that name nor in that place. We have never been near Santa Barbara."

"Nor met either the Dictator or Don José?"

"Never. I know nothing of either, except the gossip that one hears."

"The danger threatened your sister more than yourself, Mr. Kingsborough. I gathered from what was said that this man in Santa Barbara had a grudge against your sister, perhaps of some years' standing."

"I think that's out of the question."

"There is no other Miss Kingsborough here, or any Spanish lady?"

"Spanish lady? No, nor other Miss Kingsborough."

"They meant your sister, then."

"Yes, but that is impossible. Of course, I am very much obliged to you for coming to warn me. It was very good of you. Do you think that we are in danger?"

"They were a bad two, mixed up with others worse; and we have a saying, "It's better to be sure than sorry.""

"Well; thanks. Only, I must say that I do not understand it."

"I see, sir," Sard said, "that you do not take it very seriously. Well, perhaps it is best not to cross rivers till you reach the water."

"Threatened men live long."

"Not in seaport towns," Sard answered.

"Well," Hilary said, smiling, "what do you think we ought to do?"

"I have passed word to the police to stand by," Sard said. "But you know how much that is worth, among these Occidentales. I would say this, Mr. Kingsborough: take your sister in to the hotel in town, the Santiago, until you leave Las Palomas. I understand that that will be to-morrow."

"You really think that the danger is as great as that?"

"I don't know the danger," Sard said, "only the risk. That is what I should do, if it were myself and a sister of mine."

"Thank you, Mr. Harker. Will you smoke?"

"Thank you, I don't smoke."

"Will you drink something?"

"I don't drink."

"I think you said, Mr. Harker, that you belonged to a ship here?"

"Yes, sir, the *Pathfinder*, sailing now for Santa Barbara. And I must go aboard now or lose my passage. So I will say good-bye, Mr. Kingsborough. I hope to hear some day that nothing has come of all this."

"Is your ship a steamer, did you say?"

"The ship in the sailing ship berths there, about to sail."

"Well, a pleasant voyage to you. And thank you again for coming to warn me. I'll see you to the gate."

Outside, the sun had westered so that the light was off the house. The oppression in the air, added to the gloom of the evening, made the place menacing.

At the angle of the house, the woman was watering the xicales. She wore white gardening gauntlets and a sun hat. Sard felt his heart leap up with expectation. He took a step towards her.

"This way, Mr. Harker," Hilary said, correcting him. "That way leads to the garden."

The woman had turned from them; he did not see her face; she disappeared round the angle of the house.

"Excuse me," Sard said. "But is there no Spanish lady here?"

"Spanish lady?" Hilary asked. "You asked me that before. No. You may mean Tia Eusebia; she's coloured."

"You'll speak to your sister about this warning," Sard said. "And tell her everything that I have told you."

Hilary answered coldly that naturally he would. The thought came to Sard with the pain of a blow that the dreams were all lies, and that once again he had failed to find her.

"Is anything the matter, Mr. Harker?" Hilary asked.

"A little queer," Sard said. "Don't come any further. I'll let myself out. I must hurry. But tell me . . . Are you Spanish?"

"No," Hilary answered, looking at him oddly, "I'm English."

"Right, then. Good-bye. And I hope all will go well."

"Good-bye and thanks."

Sard hurried away, trying to pull himself together. He knew

that Hilary thought him mad or drunk. Hilary watched him as far as the gates: then waved a hand and turned back to the house. "Odd beggar," Hilary thought, "a very odd beggar. I didn't half like the looks of him. He seemed to me to be as mad as a hatter. And asking me if I was Spanish. And whether I kept a Spanish lady!"

At the gates Sard stopped, saying to himself that he must go back and warn the woman. "That boy does not believe," he said; "he thinks me daft; and she is in danger. And beside all that, I must speak to her. I must ask her if she be that one; for I believe she is: I believe she must be. And yet she cannot be Juanita: the name and everything else is changed. Her brother thought me mad when I asked if he were Spanish. Yet she was like enough to her: and then there was my dream. Changed or not, I must know, one way or the other; and besides, she must be warned. She is older and wiser than this boy and she must be warned of the danger."

He knew very well that if he went back, he would meet a Hilary convinced of his madness and not speak to Miss Kingsborough, yet he half turned. As he did so there came from the anchorage far behind him, yet very clearly, a beating of the *Pathfinder's* bells as though for a fire. In an instant's hush after the stopping of the bells there was a shout, which he heard but could not distinguish, followed by three roaring cheers. He knew what it was. The *Pathfinder*, being about to sail, was cheering all the ships in port. The cheering was followed by a carillon of bells and a thunder of cheering, as both anchorages made reply.

"There it is," Sard muttered, "I have twenty minutes before they man the windlass. I'm due on the fo'c'sle head to see the anchor grow. I'll do it yet."

He might have done it, no doubt, but when he reached the iron gates, his bicycle was gone.

Part TWO

HILARY KINGSBOROUGH returned to his sitting-room to think over what Sard had said.

"I didn't half like that fellow's looks," he muttered. "If there are thieves about, he might well be their advance agent come to spy out the land. Besides, kidnapping ladies is simply not done. What rot! It isn't easy to hide a dead body, but as for a living one, it's out of the question. How are they going to get a living woman out of Las Palomas against her will, either by land or sea? They can't do it."

He walked to the window to look out at the port. "All the same," he said, "old General Martinez may have heirlooms and things put away here. Burglars might have got wind of them, perhaps. I'll lock up carefully to-night."

He stood at the window, looking out at the glow. The coast mailboat was at her buoy from San Paulo. She was the *Otoque* that was to take him down the coast on her return journey the next day. The launches ground and hove about her gangway, while the slings of crates swayed up, poised, swung and jolted down among cries and clanking. There was a run of sea in the harbour which had not been there that afternoon; launches squatting on to it under way split it white. A sort of swell seemed to be coming into the harbour from the north. His thoughts were of Sard: but he could not help noticing the swell. "It is all rubbish," he said. "Someone at the Club has sent that fellow here for a rag. These things do not happen. This is one of that bounder Coghill's rises. He is always planting rags on people. What an ass that I was not to see it at once! Now that fellow will be at the Club telling how he scared me. Then at midnight, I suppose, they will serenade us with firecrackers and expect us to let them in and give them cocktails. Well, they will not get."

Presently as he sat reading at his table, he heard the song of men from the sailing ship anchorage. He went out into his verandah to listen. It had gone strangely still and close, he thought; the roar of the chorus came to him over the water as though it were in the grounds. They were only heaving in, but he concluded that they were getting the anchor.

"That part of it at least is true," he thought, "she *is* sailing now: and if he were one of her crew, he must very nearly have lost his passage. Still, those silly devils at the Club would have chosen him for that reason; because he will be gone, out of the way, before the rag is apparent. The whole thing is a rag."

In the closeness he heard, quite distinctly, the words of a song:

"The charming little girl down Tiger Bay."

Then the singing stopped and discomfort grew upon him; it was really very close indeed. At the same time the glow on the masts in harbour died suddenly: all the colour became ashen: night seemed to prepare and advance in the one moment; he noticed the flash of the light on Point Manola. "How dark it is," he thought, "the very instant the sun goes down."

He shivered on his verandah, not from cold but from uneasiness; he stayed an instant longer, half thinking that he saw something stir among the mita shrubs. He turned his glasses on the spot, but decided that he had been mistaken: there was nothing there. "Yet it looked like a face," he said; "like the face of a little evil elderly man, such as Mr. Harker described."

Now that the light was off the bay, the place looked forbidding. He saw, for the first time, how easy it would be to creep up to the house unobserved, and how hard it might fare with them if people did creep up, for revenge or lust. "Of course, it is absurd," he said to himself, "but I will walk round the house before we settle in. I will make sure that that was not a face in the mita shrubs."

He picked up a stick, in case of snakes, and stepped out into the garden towards the shrubs. The world had already taken the night like a garment: the bats and wood-owls were abroad: the frogs in the marsh were singing: the sparks of fireflies burned and died among the dusk. He thrust into the shrubbery to the place which had made him doubt; he beat all round it with his stick. No one had been there; no one was among the rocks beyond the shrubs, nor on the beach between the arms of the rocks. The place was as deserted as it always was at such a time. The ships' lights shone out from the anchorage. He heard some men in a fishing boat a mile away. Nothing there told of anything but quiet and of day telling day; no wind, no sea, no tumult: nothing but night at the end of toil. He could see no footprints on the beach.

In the covert on his way round the house he paused to listen. He heard nothing but the noises of the anchorage: a hail, a clanking of something coming to anchor, the hush and hiss of waves on the beach. Listening intently, he heard the noise of the lesser world: the snake moving; the rat roving; the insect's shrilling. The night seemed all whispering and stealthy; he did not like it. He was glad to see his sister's lit window in the upper floor, with his sister's shadow against the blind. "This will not do," he told himself. "Very likely that ruffian Coghill is watching to see me go round the house. That devil Coghill is always springing his rags: then watching to see how they take. I will work a rag on him before I leave the coast."

When he had walked through the covert all round the house, finding nothing suspicious, he looked into the ruins of the outhouses, where the Martinez' slaves had lived in old time. They were plainly given over to the rats and scorpions; there was nothing suspicious there, except that in one of the ruins there was a faint smell of tobacco, as though someone had smoked there during the day. "And who could have smoked there? Who could have, or would have? No one living here." He could see no cigar-stub, nor cigarette-end, no match, nor sign of smoker; there was nothing there except the memory or ghost of tobacco; it was hardly even a smell, hardly a flavour. By opening his mouth and breathing in, Hilary felt the record of tobacco against his palate. Then, on the wall, he saw a faint luminous streak, which at first he thought to be one of the centipedes which glow with the decay they live in. Looking at it with a light, he saw a match streak. Someone had struck a wax match there, probably during the day, since the phosphorescence still showed. Who could have been there with a wax match? No native, no one employed about the house. "That limits it," he said, "to members of the Club, like Coghill."

When he left the out-houses, he walked along the foot of the perron to the verandah. All seemed quiet there: the night was darker, the stars brighter, and the harbour lights twinkled more, but the sea-breeze was not setting in. "It is a lovely night," he said. "All this rag business is absurd. I will not give it another thought. I will send Ramón, or one of the boys, down to the police, perhaps, for Margaret's sake; but I will see that Coghill is paid for this. What is that white thing on the shingle there?"

The white thing lay on the ground near the steps leading to the verandah, in such a position that he must have seen it, had it been there when he left the house. "It was not there when I came down," he said. It was a large, coarse, dirty-white linen handkerchief with a coloured border.

"This will be Ramón's," he said.

He went into the house, and called for Ramón, but received no answer. At his fourth call, his sister answered over the railings of the floor above: "Ramón has gone out," she said. "He went into the garden five minutes ago, to look for you. Did he not find you?"

"No; nor did I hear him. I will call him."

He went out and called Ramón three times, but received no answer. "It is very odd," he said, "he does not reply."

"Probably he has gone to the lodge; and he is a little deaf."

Hilary came within the house to examine the handkerchief by the lamp in the hall. It was a man's pocket handkerchief with a blue border: in one corner the initials A.B. were roughly stitched with black cotton: the stitching looked liker a laundry mark than a mark of the owner.

"Margarita," he said, "I found this handkerchief in the gravel outside. It is marked A.B."

"It must be Ramón's."

"Ramón's would not be marked A.B."

"Then it must be your friend's: the man who was here must have dropped it."

"He would not have had a rag like this."

64

"Then it's Lotta's; she is the woman at the lodge; feckless enough for any rag."

"What would she be doing in front of the verandah?"

"Dropping her handkerchief. Leave it. She will come back for it."

"I will."

When he had laid the handkerchief upon the shingle, he examined the floor of the verandah for footprints, but found none that he could read. He entered his study somewhat ill at ease. When he entered, he stood still for a few seconds listening intently: then he looked under the table, behind the chair, behind the curtains and into the outer passage. Finding nothing suspicious, he returned, locked the window door and drew the curtains across it.

"All the same," he said, "it is just as well to be on the safe side. It probably is a rag, but, as that Harker fellow said, 'it's better to be sure than sorry.'"

His sister entered the room behind him.

"What are you looking at, Hilary?"

"Just the bay," he answered. "We're in for a storm."

"It feels close enough for a cyclone," she answered. "Who was your friend who was here?"

"No friend of mine. A Mr. Harker, a sailor."

"Had you seen him before?"

"No."

"What did he come about?"

"Just a minute," he said. "If we are in for a cyclone, would you not prefer to go into town for the night? This forest will be a dree place in a gale."

"It will be sheltered here," she said. "I'd rather be in a forest than in a city during a cyclone."

"I'm not so sure," he answered. "These pine trees wail so."

She looked out upon the darkness beside him.

"What did the sailor man come here for?" she asked.

"The sailor? Oh, nothing much. It was some rag of that bounder Coghill's, I think. They said he was planning to get a rise out of us."

65

"Do you mean Mr. Colin Coghill?"

"Yes."

"He went up the coast to San Felipe three days ago. His brother has just died there."

"How do you know?"

"Mrs. Pennington told me."

"Oh, well, it was some other fellow's rag, then?"

"He did not look to me to be the sort of man concerned in a rag. You say that his name was Harker? It seemed to me that I had met him somewhere. His face seemed familiar. Won't you tell me what the rag is or was to be?"

"Yes, Margarita, of course; but it seems so absurd." He told her in outline what Sard had said, omitting anything which might frighten her. He made his tale as light as possible, but he saw that she became very grave.

"Why are you so solemn, Pearl?"

"I was thinking of what you said."

"Do you think that it is anything but a rag?"

"Yes, I do, Hilary. The man who came here this evening was in earnest."

"You did not see him."

"Yes, I did. I saw him in the garden. I noticed him very particularly, because I thought for a moment that he was someone else, a Mr. Chisholm. The only thing which puzzles me is the lack of motive. Why should burglars come here? There is nothing to steal here."

"It is that which makes me think it is all a rag."

"There was a case in Greece last Christmas of English people being kidnapped and held to ransom. We might be the . . . the swag, in this case."

"Mr. Harker thought that the people were not burglars nor bandits, but rum-runners from Santa Barbara. He said that they spoke as if they all knew about us and that a Mr. B., or Sagrado B., apparently their director, had a score to settle with me. I cannot think of anyone of that name or nickname."

"Sagrado B.? Sagrado? The holy or sacred."

"Yes. It means nothing to you, does it?"

66

"Yes; it does, Hilary; at least it suggests something. It came into my mind directly you began to speak of this, and it explains it. You remember how, when you were a fresher, I went to Paris for a year? Well, when I was there, I met a man who tried to make love to me; a horrible man, who practised magic among other things. He wanted me to help him in a rite, and when I refused, he said that he would make me help him."

"What was the rite?"

"Oh, one of the last infamies. It is unspeakable. When we were in Cuba last winter, I heard that the negroes practise it."

"Who was this fellow?"

"He called himself the Holy One. His real name was Hirsch: I don't know what his nationality was: he talked all languages. He was evil if ever a man was."

"That was a good long time ago. He hasn't bothered you since then, has he?"

"No; but he said then that the hour for that rite came once in every seven years, and it is now almost seven years since he made me that offer in Paris."

"Sagrado does mean the Holy One. Do you suppose that this Hirsch would cherish a grudge or a desire for all that time?"

"Yes, I do. I know he would."

"The sailor fellow advised me to take you into town to the Santiago, till we sail. Suppose we do that? After all, it would be wiser. I'll send Ramón up to Paco's for the buggy. We should be in the Santiago by half-past eight."

"It seems like running away. Besides, if we go, we shall be leaving Ramón and his wife, as well as that lunatic Lotta, to meet whatever trouble may be coming."

"No trouble threatens them, apparently. But I will explain it to them: if they wish, they can come with us. All the same, Ramón is a fighter. He was with General Martinez, under Juarez, in Maximilian's time; he will not be easily moved from here. I'll go send Ramón to Paco's; he must be back from the lodge by this time. I'll ring." He moved over to the mantel and pulled the bell.

"Of course," he went on, "if we can't have the buggy, we can walk. If I put on a sombrero and you a mantilla, we should pass for two greasers. We will each take a revolver, of course, but we aren't likely to meet any bad characters before midnight."

"I'm not so sure of that; but I'd rather meet them than stay here for these others."

"The roads are safe enough. Colonel Mackenzie told me that there had been no serious crime for over three months. Las Palomas is reformed. Of course twenty years ago people disappeared every night."

"Where?"

"The quicksand out at Melilla is supposed to hide a good many. Now we'll just take our things for the night and be ready to start. Ramón is a long time answering that bell. I'll ring again." He rang again, then walked to the window and peered out into the darkness.

"You never told me about Hirsch," he said.

"He is not a fit topic for conversation."

"I'm sorry that our happy stay here should end in a scare."

"I am not scared. I am thinking about the people who disappeared. Do you think that any of them were women?"

"Good Lord, no! Don't be distressed, my dear. They were these drunken diggers from Palo Seco at the time of the gold-rush. They were just floating men. Every nation has thousands of them, who cannot settle down. They wander off to sea or to drive cattle, and they get caught in a gold-rush or stuck with a knife in a brawl, or fall off a train or something. They have a run for their money. The solid fellow sticks at home and grows fat and bald and warlike in an office. The floating life has more dash about it."

"If you want dash," she said, "you should give up a planet and try a comet."

"Ramón might try a little dash. I have rung twice. He must be in now. I'll try a third. There; he cannot say that he didn't hear that."

"Listen."

"I don't hear him in the kitchen."

"It is odd that he should be away at this time."

"And on this night, too, Margarita. I will see what he is up to."

68

He went into the corridor calling "Ramón," but had no answer and heard no sound.

"Ramón!"

He went into the kitchen. The light was burning; the table was covered with the preparations for supper; grape-fruit, a dish of limes, mint, the long glasses with the crushing spoons for julep, eggs for an omelette, the patty-pans for hot bread.

"Ramón! Tia Eusebia!"

No one answered, but in the silence the clock ticked and the cazuela in the earthern pot began to boil over.

"Aren't they there, Hilary?"

"No."

"And they left the cazuela on the fire? Tia Eusebia never did such a thing before. Where can they be?"

"They must have gone to the lodge."

"They would never have left these things like this. They would never both have gone."

"They might, Margarita, with an urgent call, for a moment or two."

"What urgent call has there been?"

"We ought to have heard any. Or Ramón would have told us."

"They must have been gone ten minutes. Sudden death alone would make Tia leave her cooking."

"I must go to the lodge to see what has happened."

"Wait for one moment, Hilary; they may be upstairs. Tia may have swooned or Ramón had a stroke."

"Tia! Tia Eusebia!"

"Ramón!"

They went upstairs together, into all the rooms, but the servants were not there.

"They must have been called to the lodge," Hilary said.

"How? Without our hearing?"

"Lotta or one of her children ran to the window instead of coming to the door. We should not have heard that."

"No. And of course if the call were very urgent, Ramón would not have stopped to tell us that he was going."

"Put on a mantilla, then, Margarita; we will go together to the

69

lodge. But before we start, we had better be a little cautious. Those rum-runners may have enticed them out."

"I don't think so," his sister said. "Ramón went out to look for you, while you were in the garden."

"What did he want with me?"

"He did not say. I thought he had something to ask you about supper. I don't believe he ever came in again. I haven't heard him. I believe that he has been out ever since; Tia Eusebia went on cooking, but at last became anxious, and then went out to look for him."

"She would have called."

"No she wouldn't, Hilary. Ramón is rather deaf. She never calls him: she always goes to him. Old General Martinez has trained them both to be silent."

"You're right, I expect, Pearl," Hilary said. "Most mysteries have commonplace explanations. But the question is, what has happened to poor old Ramón? He is an old man and may have had a stroke or a fall, and broken a bone."

"I'm afraid that he may have turned down to the creek to find you and been bitten by one of those horrible moccasins."

"Oh, Lord! Well. Let's get a light and come to look for him."

"We can't, Hilary. See. Tia Eusebia has taken the lantern."

"Well, we will take those old copies of *La Nacion* and light them up for flares. We'll go to the lodge first, for Lotta and her children may be ill or something. You put on this mantilla and I'll just get my revolver from the drawer."

He swathed her in her mantilla, but was rather a long time getting the revolver.

"Buck up, Hilary," she called.

"Just a minute," he answered; "the catch of this beastly revolver seems to have jammed, or something. I can't get it open, to load it."

"Let me have a try."

"I'm afraid it's rusted-in, or something. I ought to have oiled it when I put it away." He brought it to her. She thumbed at the catch, which was fixed tight.

"I'll give it a bang or two with the tin-opener," he said. He gave it a bang or three with the tin-opener, and then again with Tío Ramón's hammer, but failed to release the catch.

"Open, you devil," he said. He gave it a good clout with the hammer and cracked the catch across; a piece of metal fell with a clink upon the floor.

"Now I've done it," he said, "I've broken the beastly thing."

"You were just a little rough with it, weren't you?"

"Yes; but who would have thought the metal would have cracked like that? It would have been dangerous work firing a thing as weak as that."

"You have your pearl-handled pistol."

"Yes, but the worst of it is, I'm afraid it won't take these cartridges. I meant to have bought some for it only this afternoon, but like an ass I forgot."

"Then we haven't any firearms?"

"None that we can fire. We could use them as bluffs. And there's a machete here, that Ramón cuts vines with."

"Very well, then. Take that. Now, light up a torch and let us start."

They rolled up some copies of La Nacion as torches and lit one of them while they examined the outer steps. They called loudly, "Tía Eusebia! Ho, Tía Eusebia!" but had no reply. They came down the steps into the drive, by the light of the flaming newspapers, which Margaret lit one by one as they proceeded. Small things crossing their track, scared by the light, reassured them, since their presence showed that no strangers had passed that way recently. It was dark night now. The shrubbery through which they passed glistened like a lot of eyes. The depth of the wood beyond was so ugsome, that it was a pleasure to them to turn the curve in the drive and see the light from the open door of the lodge.

Hilary called aloud, "Tía Eusebia!" and "Lotta!" but no answer came from the lodge or from the wood.

"There is something not quite right here," Margaret said. "Jorge! Marianela! Even the children do not answer."

"We will soon find what is amiss. Hola! Tía Eusebia! I believe that the lodge is empty."

"That looks bad for Ramón; but we'll soon know."

They both ran to the lodge, calling.

"I'll go in," he said.

"Be careful, Hilary."

"I will, my dear," he said. "If one of these big black marimbas has come in, there'll be somebody dead here."

He rattled with his machete at the door and then went into the lodge. The oil lamp was burning on the table beside a pipkin full of frijoles. The room was empty: the bunks at the side were empty.

"Lotta," he cried. "Marianela! It's as I thought, Pearl. There's nobody here at all. But they've not been long gone; these frijoles in the dish are warm."

Margaret peeped in at the door. "Aren't the children in their bunks?" she asked.

"No, but they've been in their bunks. These blankets are warm still, and the bichos are on the hop, too, still, good Lord!"

"Well, where are they?"

"It's very odd; but it can't be foul play; it is on too big a scale for that: three adults and two children. Come to the door and let us both shout together."

They shouted and yodelled and clapper-shouted for the missing five.

"Now," Hilary said, "anyone within three hundred yards must have heard; even a deaf person must have heard. If they've been within hearing, they've heard us. Keep quite still now. We may hear an answer."

They kept as still as mice on the grass near the gate, but heard no noise at all except the dropping and rustling never absent from the forest at night.

"It's the spring equinox, or near it," Margaret said. "Just listen a moment longer, Hilary; I seem to catch a noise like drums and a guitar, very far away."

"Yes, there is some sort of tom-tom going; it's in the forest, to the west, in that clearing called Los Jardinillos."

"Well, Hilary, don't you think it likely that the negroes have been called to some fiesta of the equinox?"

72

"That doesn't fit it. They would have told us. It's more likely that a priest has come with extreme unction, in need of a guide through the forest."

"No. That doesn't fit it. The man who fetched the priest would be the guide. And the priests here need no guide to any of their flock."

"A revivalist preacher would draw these negroes," Hilary said.

"Not these Catholics, and certainly not without telling us," his sister answered. "It must be one of two things, Hilary. Either there has been some miraculous appearance in the wood, which would draw them out to worship, or these rum-runners have devised something. I begin to be afraid, Hilary."

"I'm not afraid," he said. "Do not you be afraid. Listen a moment. That tom-tom noise seems louder."

They listened, while the thudding resolved itself into the plodding of a trotting carriage-horse coming from the direction of the port.

"A carriage," she said. "It may be Paco with his buggy."

"It's more likely to be Colonel Mackenzie," he said.

They listened, while the jog-trot of the horse drew so near that they could hear the noise of the wheels behind him. A carriage lamp shone through the trees. One of the city caleches came to a standstill before them. The driver told his fare that this was Los Xicales.

Hilary lit a new copy of La Nacion, so that he might see this fare. The man got out of the caleche and came towards him. He was a sleepy-looking man with a face seemingly made of wood. He blinked as he spoke. His speech came from somewhere in the northern midlands.

"Is thy name, Kingsboora?" he asked, "and has oor Mr. 'Arker bin 'ere?"

"Yes," Hilary said; "he's been gone from here an hour and a half."

"Dostha know which way 'e went?"

"No."

"Oor Captain Cary sent me to find oor Mr. 'Arker. Tha see, there's a norther coomin' on. We're in the Pathfinder, sailing.

73

We don't want to wait all night, tha see. Did 'e go back into the town, choom?"

"He went back to his ship, I think," Hilary said. "You must have crossed him."

"That's it, tha see," the man said. " 'E didna coom by t'reet way. Look, choom, if 'e coom 'ere again, will tha tell 'im to coom aboard? Ma neem is Dorney. Now, lad," he added to the driver, with pantomime instead of Spanish, "tak' me back to Jib and Foresail, will tha?"

The driver turned his caleche and carried Mr. Dorney away into the darkness. When the wheels were almost out of hearing, Hilary suddenly remembered.

"We were asses," he said. "We might have gone into Las Palomas with him."

"I was thinking that," she said. "But we couldn't have gone, not knowing about Ramón. I hope that Mr. Harker has not met with any trouble on his way."

"Not he," Hilary said. "He took a short cut and passed this Mr. Dorney on the road somewhere. Let us call those negroes again."

They called, but had no other answer than the distant drumming noise, which seemed to be a part of the tenseness of the night.

"It began with Lotta," Hilary said. "Her handkerchief proves that Lotta came for Ramón. Any folly may have come from Lotta. We have given them a fair chance, now we will go."

"Listen."

"No; there's no one."

It was close, still, tense night, save for the sighing in the pines and that beating, like a heart-beat, from the distant drum.

"Come along, then, Hilary," she said. "We will take Paco's buggy and go into town."

They set out for Paco's estancia. They were both glad to be out of the grounds of Los Xicales. When they had gone about a hundred yards, they stopped and looked at each other.

"We're both thinking the same thing," Hilary said. "We can't leave quite like this, without knowing what has happened to these people. We had better go round the estate before we go to Paco's. Or how would it be if you went to Paco's alone, while I went back to the house? Or wait: I'll walk with you to Paco's, get Paco and the buggy and Paco's son Enrique, with their guns, and then we'll all come back together, search the estate and then go to Las Palomas. Let's do that: come along."

"No," she said. "All that will take time. I'm afraid that Lotta, or one of her children, or her imbecile man, or poor old Ramón, is in extremis somewhere. And our losing time may be fatal. I don't like leaving the estate. I'm not afraid of desperadoes. If they were about, why did they not set upon us when we were shouting at the lodge?"

"I wondered that, myself, at the time," he said.

"Surely it shows that they are not here. Besides, it is full early for desperadoes to be abroad."

"I see all that," he said. "We owe it to Ramón to be sure about him before we leave. We will turn down here, along the creek, and so circle back to the house. We shall have newspapers enough to light us there. But I don't think we shall find him on this side of the house."

"We may find him at the house." she said.

"If he be not there, and if we do not meet him or learn about him within the next ten minutes, then, Pearl, you and I will go off to Las Palomas, by Paco's buggy or on foot. Is that agreed?"

"Yes; agreed. We shall have really done all that we can, then."

"I think we have done a good deal in turning off here for him; but he is a fine old boy."

"He would do more than this for us," she said.

"That is true, he would."

They turned into the path beside the creek. There was plenty of water in the creek and plenty of snags in the water. The current was tearing at the snags with a lashing noise.

"You mentioned a Mr. Chisholm," Hilary said. "Did I ever meet your Mr. Chisholm, or was he one of your Paris friends?"

They had stopped at this point to light a new torch from the stump of an old one. He saw her face blush a little in the light, and her eyes sparkled.

"By George, Pearl," he said, "you are a lovely woman."

"About Mr. Chisholm," she said. "I met him at Passion Courtenay when I was a girl: long before I went to Paris. I have never seen him since. I don't expect that you ever met him. He came with some people called Penger or Penga."

"No. I never met him. And this Mr. Harker was like him?"

"Yes."

"He was a pretty rough customer, if you ask me, that same Mr. Harker."

"I would be very glad of his help, Hilary, if we were to be mixed up with the friends of that Paris man."

"Put him out of your mind, my dear."

"I wish I could, Hilary."

They walked on until they came to a cleared space by the water. A wooden bridge had once spanned the creek here, but it had been swept away in a wash-out. The palings of it stuck out, like ribbones, from an island in midstream. The water went past in a rush, curved out into the sands, and made a bar of seven white breakers as it reached the sea.

"It is from here, on, that one gets the moccasins," Hilary said. "If any rum-runners come by this swampy bit, they'll meet their match."

They went warily forward, lighting themselves with their last copies of La Nacion. They met with no moccasins, but as they crossed the swampy patch by the causeway, the croaking of the bull-frogs hushed for a moment.

"This was the sort of place the Conquistadores landed in," Hilary said. "Cortés landed in just such another, and burned his ships on the beach behind him. When we go down the coast, we will draw the very beach where he landed. Imagine landing like that, a thousand miles from any store, or any friend, in an unknown world. It was a lonely night for those fellows, when their ships were burned and they turned inland to what was waiting for them."

"I would not pity them too much," Margaret answered. "They were there from choice, mainly from greed; nor were they novices at the work. They had also three great advantages, guns, horses

76

and Cortés. The prizes to be won were enormous, and the dangers to be faced only thirst, which was probably chronic with them; hunger, which they must have known in Spain; and death, which they would have had on the gallows if they had not emigrated."

"I see all that," he said; "yet there it is. Cortés came to the difficult new thing and did it. Then four hundred years afterwards, fellows like me appear, who write how Cortés did it and how he ought to have done it. Do you think that we last fulfil a function?"

They had now turned off on their way to the house through the forest.

"Yes, Hilary," she said. "It is even called a kind of wisdom."

Something in her tone made him pause to look at her.

"I don't quite see your point," he said.

"It is a kind of wisdom," she said, "to be wise after the event."

A moment later they came in sight of the bulk of the house looming up among the trees. A light from a scullery window shone directly upon their path, making the tops of the leaves to glisten like silver. As they came to the sight of this window, they both smelt on the instant a flavour of hot bread.

"They've come back," Margaret said. "They have brought a candle to the scullery and Tia Eusebia is making the hot rolls."

"Well, I'm blest," Hilary said. "But you're right; there is Tia Eusebia, taking away the candle."

"I wonder where they have been."

"We shall soon know."

They hurried past the out-houses and up the steps to the door. Hilary knocked. After an interval Ramón and Eusebia opened to them. Both the old servants were flustered. They closed the door carefully behind Margaret and Hilary and then began to tell in swift soft Spanish of the wonders which they had seen.

"We have both been great sinners and thankless for God's great mercies, O Señor and Señorita, but henceforth we shall live in sight of the throne, having been called, having been chosen. O the beauty and the grace and the sweetness that we have known this night. She, Herself, who is all good and grace, looked upon us and blest us. The most blessed Virgin has trodden upon these soils, O Señorita and Señor, and all the Blessed Fellowship will follow where she has trodden, and all the devils will be driven away. And the man with the two heads has gone already from by the blasted pine, and Black Peter with his tongue out has gone, and old Master that used to look sideways with yellow eyes, ran straight away out to sea, where all the lost go, and oh, hallelujah, hallelujah, be Thou seven times blest, O seven times Wounded One!"

"What has happened, Ramón?" Hilary asked.

"O Señor, the woman Lotta is surely a great saint, with all inner perfection."

Hilary hoped that it might be so, but doubted.

"But where have you been, Ramón?" he asked. "We have been to and fro, shouting for you. Did you not hear us?"

"O Señor, yes, but we could not turn to you, having Her before us. The most blessed Virgin was at the Cross of the Stranger near the forest edge. Lotta ran to tell us, and we all ran, and oh it is blessed grace to be so blest as to behold, and oh joy, she looked upon us and blessed us; and oh joy to be set free, and oh bliss to be white who before was scarlet; oh triumph, oh glory; hallelujah, hallelujah!"

"For oh Lord, Señor Hilario, she was there, shining in her glory, in a blue skirt and white lace mantilla, and all diamond glory spangles and hairpins of purest gold, oh hallelujah, come down to set us free from wicked flesh and all damned temptation; and her face shone, and oh her voice, my dear, her voice, it was like a ripple."

"How many were privileged to behold her?" Margaret asked. "Were there any beside yourselves?"

"Lotta and Jorge and Marianela, and we two, Ramón and Eusebia, by special grace, and the two from Los Jardinillos, Pablo Paloverde and his wife; we seven; only we seven of all the world: we seven dreadful deadly sinners; and now we are ransomed and released, and the precious grace comes floating in; oh sing and give thanks; oh sing before the throne, sing the glad happy psalm, knock the timbrel of glory."

Here both the two old servants became possessed by religious

78

excitement. Ramón's words for the last two minutes had been running in a rhythm, now they became almost a song. The two old heads went back, their eyes closed, while their bodies began to sway in a dance, to which their hands kept time. "Oh," they sang,

> "Oh, we are come into the glory,
> Oh, shout aloud: salvation.
> By the cross of the stranger, glory
> Salvation shake the whole world: joy.
> Oh, the blessed Virgin give us glory,
> Glory, oh, fire off the pistols, brothers,
> Little sisters set the bells ringing.
> Burst something, brothers, oh salvation.
> O ho ho ho ho hallelujah,
>   Hallelujah, hallelujah, ho."

They were no longer of this world, nor conscious of it: they went dancing back to the kitchen, with hallelujahs. A jar or pot boiled over as they entered, with an overwhelming wash of sputter and crackle. A flood of smoke shot up from the mess with a smell of burnt dinner. Ramón seized the offending pot and cast it on the floor, singing:

> "Never mind the little things, happy Ramón,
> The little things of this world, happy Ramón,
> For you have seen the joyous, happy Ramón,
> Lady in the blue skirt, happy Ramón.
> But, oh, the Lord, the saucepan burn my fingers!"

Hilary and Margaret watched the dance from the kitchen door. They had heard that miraculous visitations were frequent along the coast and that when they came they filled the lives of those visited for two days.

"So they have seen the Virgin," Margaret said. "They will need us no more to-night. We had better take a few more Naciones and go off to Paco's."

"Yes, indeed."

As he stooped to gather up the pile of newspapers, he heard distinctly a noise of whistling within the closed sitting-room at the end of the passage. A man was whistling "Charmante Gabrielle" in the stumbling way of a man who does not sing well. Margaret heard it at the same time. The suddenness and nearness of it startled them both.

"Somebody in the sitting-room," Hilary said.

As it happened, the sudden startling of the two made an impression on the two ecstatics in the kitchen. Ramón came out of his trance and became, in part, the old butler of daily life.

"Why," he said, "I believe, Señor, that I never told you that a gentleman has called to see you. He is in the sitting-room."

"What gentleman? Who is he?"

"A very old Lutheran padre, Señor. He came to see you a few minutes before you came in."

"A Lutheran padre? What is his name?"

But here Eusebia interrupted with a cry. She had been rocking herself to and fro in a rocking-chair, with her apron over her face; now she sprang up in excitement.

"Oh, be joyful," she cried, "for the holy footsteps. Wherever the blessed feet tread, there come the lovely, lovely flowers. Oh, I feel them grow! Oh, I feel the angels. Catch old Tia, Ramón; give me your hand for the Lord's sake; we will be caught right up to the throne together. Oh, I hear the harps! Oh, I hear the singing!"

"I hear them," Ramón cried, taking his wife's hand. "They sing tirra-lu, tirra-lu, just like the lovely band."

"Come on to the throne, Tio Ramón."
"I am coming, Tia Eusebia."
"There shines the Lord."
"O, the little glittering feet!"
"I see the long white beard of Father Abraham."
"Oh, the Holy Ghost, the Holy Ghost, the Holy Ghost."
"Halle-halle-halle-hallelujah,
 The beauty of the Lord is joy."

"A Lutheran padre?" Hilary said. "That sounds harmless. The only Lutheran padre here is old Skinner, who runs the Sailors'

Mission. He is a very fine old man. Shall we go to him, or leave him and go to Paco's?"

"If it be Mr. Skinner, we must go to him."

At this moment the whistling stopped, the door of the sitting-room opened, and an old man, with a long white beard, moved slowly out to them with the shuffling shamble of old age. He spoke with the voice of an old, educated man, from one of the United States.

"Is this Miss Kingsborough?" he was saying. "Is that you, Mr. Kingsborough? I was not quite sure, but thought that I heard voices in the hall, besides your servants. You will forgive my coming in like this, to wait for you. I see you don't remember me, Mr. Kingsborough; my name is Brown, Abner Brown. You have forgotten that you met me at the Club the other night?"

"I'm afraid I have."

"Well, well, I was one of a crowd; quite a lot went there. We were talking after dinner that night about international crime prevention."

"Yes, I remember the talk," Hilary said. "So you were there?"

"I was there with Colonel Mackenzie."

"It was my first night at the Club," Hilary said. "I was introduced to so many. You must forgive my not remembering you. Margaret, will you let me introduce Mr. Brown: my sister."

Margaret bowed.

"While you talk," she said, "I will see about some food. The household is a little disorganised." There was not much light in the hall, but she looked hard at Mr. Brown and went into the kitchen.

"Come into the sitting-room, Mr. Brown," Hilary said. "What can I do for you?"

"I am an American minister, Mr. Kingsborough," Mr. Brown replied, as they walked back to the sitting-room together. "I am here, engaged in getting information about this rum-running. I was in Colonel Mackenzie's office an hour or two ago, when Richard Shullocker, the club porter, came in, to say that you had been threatened, or warned or told of some risk or other. No, I don't ask you if that be so or no, nor for any details, but I just felt it to be my duty just to look in, Mr. Kingsborough, and I will tell you why. You have a man up the road here, a young fellow, of the name of Paco; Enrique Paco, to whom I owed a small sum for horse-hire. I was driving out to pay this to Paco, and I said to Colonel Mackenzie and to Richard Shullocker, 'I will tell you what I will do,' I said. 'Don't trouble to send out guardias or vigilantes to them. No,' I said, 'for I have to go out to Paco's on a matter of business, and coming back from Paco's, as I pass the gate of their house, Los Tamales, or whatever it may be, I will stop my horse-car or caleche, or country-surrey, and offer Mr. Kingsborough a ride into town.' So now, Mr. Kingsborough, there it is, I have paid Paco; and my surrey, though not exactly a White Surrey, is at the gates of your house, at your service, ready to drive you and your sister in to Las Palomas. You could have rooms at the hotel, for I took occasion to ask that at the hotel, before I came out to Paco's. And I guess you would both feel easier in your minds away from this place, miles out in the forest."

"Thank you, Mr. Brown," Hilary said; "we are most grateful for your thought and for the offer. We were on our way to Paco's to hire his buggy to take us to Las Palomas, as we thought it best not to neglect the warning."

"That is sure sound sense, Mr. Kingsborough, near a seaport town like this. And if you will excuse me the observation, Mr. Kingsborough, your servants, though I guess you hired them along with the house, are not quite in the frame of mind to repel boarders."

"They are not."

"May I ask if it was the Adventist, from San Mateo Obispo, got them into their present state?"

"It was not the Adventist; but they saw a miraculous appearance in the clearing not far from here."

"Then it will be three days before anyone gets an hour's work from them. Oil in the coffee, chilis in the bread, eggs in the shoes —oh, don't I know these soul's awakenings."

Something in the man's tone jarred Hilary. He looked a most benign old man, with a fresh colour, bright eyes and long white silky beard. He had the appearance of Father Christmas. Yet this last remark, about the spiritual excitements of others, struck Hilary as hard and vulgar. He looked at Mr. Brown and decided that here was something hard and ugly about the man's mouth, for all that holy white hair.

"Now. Mr. Kingsborough," Mr. Brown continued, "I don't want even to seem to be in a hurry or to be pressing you. Miss Kingsborough spoke of preparing some food. Well: food is the best remedy yet found for hunger; I'll say nothing against food. But meanwhile, can't I be moving some bags or things for you out to the surrey? Miss Kingsborough will want a warm wrap: the breeze is setting in; and though it is only a mile or two into town, it is going to be cold."

"Oh, thank you," Hilary said, "it won't take a minute to get all that we need."

"No, surely," Mr. Brown answered. "No, indeed."

He sat down away from the light, and dusted his hat with his handkerchief. A restraint came upon the conversation. Mr. Brown felt the chill and tried to remove it.

"It is this rum-running which leads to all the crime along this part of the coast," he said. "This republic is a very nice republic: I don't say it isn't, but it's as slack as one of these republics always is so long after any revolution. The public services are away down. Then that old sinner, the Dictator, Don Manuel, out in Santa Barbara, sees a chance to profit. He can make rum, in his sugar-plantations, which have every natural power just beside them, water power as well as fuel, and all just near the sea, for not any more than five or seven cents a gallon. In a good year I guess he might get it out as low as even three cents for a gallon. Mind you, Mr. Kingsborough, I'm speaking of a low grade of rum. Santa Barbara can't compete with Jamaica, nor with Santa Cruz; but it is rum; it scratches as it glides; as they say. Well, now, say, he makes it at as high as seven cents. He can get it aboard his big power lighters and land it on the coast here at twenty cents the gallon. Then, what with mule teams and palm-oil and what is known here as the underground railway, he can get it up as far as the mines in Palo Seco for half a dollar. Now in Palo Seco he has no opposition, Mr. Kingsborough. No other rum has a geographical chance of coming in. Well, now, in Palo Seco, where I have been, studying this question, he can sell that rum and has been selling that rum for close upon two years, to gold-miners, who care not one jack-straw what they pay nor what they drink, as long as it scratches as it glides. He sells that rum, which cost him, say, seven cents to make and forty-three cents to transport, for from eight to twelve American dollars: yes, sir, two or three dollars the quart. I've seen him do it, or at least his agents. Now that is a good business, Mr. Kingsborough, even allowing for losses, thefts and the squaring of the vicious circle."

"What is that?" Hilary asked.

"The vicious circle is this Occidental police, Mr. Kingsborough. They say a perfect circle can't be squared; but this circle I guess has got a kink in the loop half the way around."

"Colonel Mackenzie is a good man."

"Why, sure, Mr. Kingsborough, he's a wonderful man, but he's not been in the police yet a quarter of a year. Still, that's the business he's up against. It's a business run by old fox Don Manuel, in Santa Barbara, with all the resources of a thriving state to back him. But we are going to have it stopped."

"In your investigations into this rum-running, Mr. Brown, did you ever hear of or come across a man called Hirsch, nicknamed Sagrado or Sagrado B., now living in Santa Barbara?"

"Sagrado, you say?"

"Yes, the Holy One."

"I guess you've got the name wrong, Mr. Kingsborough; there's no holy one in Santa Barbara. I guess you mean Sangrado, a blood-letter. They have a whole alphabet of them. But Hirsch and Sagrado, no."

"I was warned against that man."

"I guess it will be some nickname or gang-name. May I ask who it was who warned you, Mr. Kingsborough, against this man Hirsch?"

"A stranger."

"An Occidental?"

"No. English."

"Of Las Palomas?"

"No."

"Would you recognise him again?"

"Yes."

"Would you describe him to me?"

"No, Mr. Brown."

"Quite right, Mr. Kingsborough; quite, quite right. I was wrong to suggest it. But I would put all thought of there being any Holy One in this business right out of your mind. That is probably a nickname for their headquarters: very likely Don Manuel himself, who prides himself on his religion. No, sir; you've been warned (as I see it) because they think you may be a spy. Anyway without you here they could land stuff on this beach. They have warned several people off the track, up and down the coast, in the last eighteen months. They all had the sense to take the hint. All except one, I think; one did not. He was a good while ago, before you came here. Prince, his name was, Jacob Galls Prince; lived on the coast like you, up at San Agostino."

"What happened to him?"

"He neglected the warning, so then they took steps. The first time he had friends with him who drove them away, but the second time they gave him his pass all right."

Hilary thought that Mr. Brown's tone, when he spoke of the giving of the pass, was suddenly savage. He noticed that Mr. Brown's mouth tightened as he spoke, as though a lid were being snapped down.

"Were the murderers caught?"

"No, sir, there's a lot too much money behind these fellows."

"Are you in the United States Police, Mr. Brown?"

"No, sir, I'm just plain Abner Brown, from Brownstead, Massachuzzits. I'm a minister of Brownstead Light-Arising Church. I'm in this rum-investigation business, because I hate rum like hell. Yes, Mr. Kingsborough, like hell. Maybe you'll think that strong talk for a minister of a church that goes dead against any language that's anyways got a kick. But I guess it's not too strong. Mr. Kingsborough, I believe that if rum were wiped clean off of this planet this planet would just rise up three hundred per cent."

85

"Where would it rise to, Mr. Brown?"

"Rise to the Light, Mr. Kingsborough."

"What do you think it would do then, Mr. Brown?"

"It would enter into a new plane of being, Mr. Kingsborough, which lies just beyond anything we have going now. I guess the prophets saw it: a new world: gee, I guess it's worth working to try to bring. All your dividends and worldly cares just dumped where they belong, and all your spiritual being three hundred per cent pure light."

"It sounds delightful," Hilary said.

"It would be all it sounds."

"Yes, I dare say," Hilary said. "But would it?"

"Perhaps you are not an optimist, Mr. Kingsborough? However, there it is. Meanwhile could you let me know the right time?"

"Two minutes to eight."

"Is your time correct?"

"Correct by the noon gun."

"Two minutes to eight. I must be slow. I make it no more than three and a half minutes to eight." He busied himself with his watch.

Margaret from the kitchen gave a call of "Oh, Hilary!" Hilary opened the door and called back:

"Do you want me, Margarita?"

"Could you come here just a moment?"

Hilary excused himself to Mr. Brown and hurried along the corridor to the kitchen, which was in some confusion. Dark smoke wreathed about the ceiling: the table was still set with some preparations for a meal: there were several broken plates, dishes, sprigs of herbs and limes upon the floor, but the negroes were gone. The place stank of burnt oil; great greasy smuts floated on the air.

"They've gone again," Margaret said. "They have been beyond all bounds. Oh, Hilary, I have had a marvellous time with them. At first they kept going into paroxysms of prayer and giggles, and dropping things on the floor. Then they started behaving like raging lunatics; they upset the oil on to the fire. They almost had the house on fire, but I have managed to beat it out. They danced while I was doing this, so I told them to go out to see their appearance again, which they have done."

"Are you burnt?"

"No."

"I wish I had known that you were having this trouble."

"I'm very glad you didn't. What does this Mr. Brown want?"

"To drive us into Las Palomas. We had better go. He has a carriage waiting at the gate."

"What do you make of him?"

"He's a minister in the Light-Arising Church."

"Do you think he is?"

"Yes. Don't you?"

"No."

"What do you think of him?"

"I didn't like his mouth."

"I don't take to his mouth, myself," Hilary said. "But he isn't a minister in the sense that a priest is a priest. He's a commercial traveller in an intellectual light co., with a bonus of thirty cents a soul."

"Did you meet him at the Club?"

"I can't remember: I may have: I met so many that night. But I think you may put all suspicion of him out of your mind, Pearl, because he comes, really, from Colonel Mackenzie's office. That Harker man told me that word had been sent to Colonel Mackenzie, about our being threatened. Well, this fellow Brown was in Mackenzie's office when the message came. It seems that he knows the Pacos and was coming here to see them anyhow, and so he volunteered to bring us back with him to Las Palomas. He arrived in a buggy (at least he calls it a surrey) while we were down by the creek."

"I am all ready to start for Las Palomas," she said. "I ran upstairs, after you had gone into the room with him, to pack a few things for both of us. They are in handbags on the ledge in the hall. The only question is, shall we not get out here and go alone? I don't quite like this Mr. Brown. I think he's a bad man. His mouth snaps to just like a trap."

"Well, he is old and alone, and I think that he must certainly have been at Colonel Mackenzie's."

"Yes," she said. "It is that which weighs with me. I suppose it is all right; but I'm uneasy to-night: so many unusual things are happening. Oh, whatever is that?"

"That" was the running down of the weights in the old English kitchen clock which had been Tia Eusebia's pride for many years. With a sudden jarring, chirring and dropping noise, these weights dropped themselves, a little door opened, a little man appeared, who jerked himself forward and backward eight times as the bell behind him struck the hour.

"Eight o'clock. What a shock it gave me."

"We can't stay here. This place is on our nerves to-night: we had better go. And I should say, go with this man in his surrey buggy, or whatever it is he calls it. It is two or three lonely miles to town: if he will drive us, all the better."

"I do not feel at ease about it, Hilary. I have misgivings."

"I haven't, because I know now that Mackenzie will be looking out for us. It is all right. Come along."

"Right. Come along."

"Leave the lamp for Ramón."

They left the lamp burning, but turned it down: then they went into the corridor and closed the kitchen door behind them.

The first thing which they noticed on coming into the hall was a draught of air (blowing in from the sitting-room) which was causing the lamp to smoke.

"I say," Hilary said, "I shut the sitting-room door when I came out. Mr. Brown must have opened it. The draught is from there."

"He must have opened the window too," Margaret said. "This is the breeze."

"The window was shut when I left the room."

"Perhaps it blew open," Margaret said. "It sometimes does if the catch be not pushed home."

"The catch was pushed home."

Hilary picked up the two little handbags from the ledge, thinking that this Mr. Brown had a pretty cool cheek to go opening people's windows and making their lamps smoke. He walked along to the sitting-room door, carrying the bags; Margaret was just behind him. He pushed the door open and came well into the room. A gush of air blew past him on the instant, for the window opening into the verandah was wide open. "Come in, quick, and close the door, Margarita," he said. "This window's wide open." Margarita closed the door to save the hall lamp; they were thus both within the room.

Hilary saw at a glance that Mr. Brown had not only opened the window, but had moved the lamp to the corner near the fire-place. "He has a pretty cool cheek," he thought again.

Mr. Brown was standing near the open window, facing them, with his hands behind his back.

"Come in, Mr. Kingsborough," Mr. Brown said. "I see you have done your packing, so we can start right away."

Hilary felt quickly that there was something wrong and deadly. There was that rasp in Mr. Brown's voice and that snap upon his mouth; and besides these things, he stood still, and there was something in his last five words which sounded like a signal, and thirty years seemed to fall from him.

"Yes, sir," he repeated, "we can start right away." His hands came up from behind him with a flash and a bang: something very hot struck Hilary in the chest with a pang and a thud which came together: a little, slow bluish smoke twisted out of Mr. Brown's pistol: Hilary found that he was on the floor. He heard Margarita cry aloud. He tried to rise, but the place rocked so and surged: there was a sort of tight red wave which got into his eyes. Then a lot of people seemed to dance out of the night into the room; they seemed to dance all over him; they seemed to be dancing with Margarita, and there was a smell of a cigar which was pushed red-hot into his cheek. After that, he knew that he climbed to his feet, and that somebody grinned in his face; then the water seemed to fall all off the mill-wheel into a peace-like sleep or death.

Everything seemed to be over when he came to himself again. The dancing was done. Men were going out of the room by the verandah window: they were carrying a great package which moaned and seemed to be moving, much as a fly, trussed up by a spider, will move. He felt a weight in his chest and found it difficult to understand what was happening. Then he realised that the moaning package was Margarita, who was being carried away by all these men.

"All right, Margarita," he said, "I will set you free." The words which he spoke did not seem to be these, because the men laughed. He said, "I'll teach you to laugh," and tried to rise from the floor, but the floor rocked all round him, so that he had to lie down again. He shut his eyes to make the floor steady, but it did not become steady. He tried to steady it with his hands, then it started spinning.

Presently he managed to sit up. A man was looking down upon him; the man's hat was cocked on one side, he was smoking the stub of a cigar and staring at him.

"Mr. Bloody Kingsborough," the man said. "My dear old college pal, dammit. You've no memory of me. You haven't been introduced to me. I'm one of the vulgar lower orders, dammit. Sumecta, my name is. I'm a fellaw, dammit, a rude vulgar low fellaw. And I'm going to cork your eyebrows with my cigar."

He leaped upon Hilary and rubbed the burning cigar along his eyebrows. Hilary noticed that the man wore ear-rings and had a wide mouth lacking one tooth. The man straddled across him and slapped his cheeks and puffed cigar-smoke into his face.

"I'm Sumecta," he said. "And you've got no London police force here. You can't order the horrid man away. Your sister's going to Mr. Holy B, and nothing that you can do can stop us. You won't see your sister again, because the Chief wants her. The Chief wants her."

Another man appeared behind Sumecta: he was a little elderly man with an inflamed face and a dirty rag about his neck, covering a boil.

"Don't try to stop your sister going," he said, "or you'll line an elmwood shell with name engraved. We'll just tample his dags, Sumecta, and then frolly the dusty."

They emptied the cigarette-box and took a drink or two. The little man began to sing a song:

> "Travelling with the lady,
>   You'd best pull down the blind,
> Make it cosy and shady . . ."

He came round the table close to Hilary and danced a little break-down, with two of Hilary's cigarettes in his mouth. "O I'm a lady, a Hottentot lady," he sang. "One time piecee lubly gal, O."

"I'll singe my college pal's lips," Sumecta said. "Baillon de cigare chaud." He straddled down over Hilary, sucked his cigar to a glow and prepared to burn his victim's lips.

"Cut that out, Sumecta," Mr. Brown said, at the window. "Come on here, the two of you. The train's just going." Mr. Brown's beard was sticking out of his pocket, but his white eyebrows were still in place.

The two men followed Mr. Brown through the window, which they closed behind them. Mr. Brown opened it again an instant later, to take a last look round the room. Mr. Brown seemed to have no further interest in Hilary, he neither spoke to him nor looked at him. Hilary to him had been simply something to shove aside and leave. After they had gone, Hilary heard footsteps and voices; presently the light went out; he was alone in the dark. A bat flew about the room after insects; presently it knocked down a tumbler which dripped water on to the floor for a long, long time.

Tio Ramón and his wife did not see the miraculous appearance again, though they waited in the clearing, near the stone, till after eleven. They then walked to Las Palomas, and heard a midnight office at a monastery, then stayed on praying in side-chapels of the church till after dawn. After some more prayer and the offering of all that was precious in their apparel to the image in a side-chapel, they walked and partly danced to Los Xicales. They did not enter the house even then, for they had to compare notes with Lotta at the lodge.

At eight in the stormy morning, they found Hilary lying in a chair in the sitting-room, in pain and fever. In the wild weather Tio Ramón summoned Paco, who summoned Enrique, who sent Lotta to find Miguel, who shook his head, and thought it better to call Enobbio. Enobbio was an elderly Italian with a clear wit;

he at once rode in to Las Palomas and called a doctor and Colonel Mackenzie. By midday Los Xicales was thronged by detectives, who looked mysterious and took a lot of measurements and shook their heads. Their Indian trackers said that there were seven men concerned in the raid and that two were "little Indians"; that five, including the Indians, had come from the beach, while the other two had driven from the north, in a buggy, which had waited at the gate for some time.

After the raid (the trackers said) the men had carried Margarita to this buggy and had driven her away. Lotta, Lotta's children, Ramón and Eusebia, all admitted that they had seen the buggy go past, full of men, and that they had heard a woman among them crying for help, but they had not known that it was more than a joke. They had not noticed where the buggy went after it passed them; but this the trackers explained. It drove out of the forest by the city road, turned to the left, and crossed the savannah to the beach. Near the beach it stopped, five of the men carried Margarita to the water; there, presumably, they found a boat and put to sea. The two men remaining in the buggy drove off to Las Palomas, where all trace of them disappeared.

The rain was heavy before noon: the tracks were rained out.

No further trace or track was found. No more evidence was forthcoming. Enobbio had seen a stranger looking for a lost bicycle; but this stranger was proven to have been Sard Harker, mate of the *Pathfinder*, which had now sailed. Acting on Enobbio's evidence, the police recovered Richard Shullocker's bicycle, but found no trace of Margarita. Hilary's story of the events was not very clear. He could repeat only what he could remember of Sard's story, which he had not much wished to hear, and of Abner Brown's story, which had not told him much. He maintained that the abductors were mixed up with Santa Barbara and with the boxing hall, the Circo Romano.

Ben Hordano was questioned, but his movements on the night of the raid were well known: he had been drunk by six, disorderly by seven, and in jail by eight. One curious thing, which none could explain, was how the man Abner Brown knew that Richard Shullocker had warned Colonel Mackenzie of an intended raid at Los Xicales. The warning had been given privately, in person: no one could possibly have overheard it. Paco and his son Enrique denied having had any dealings (horse hire or other) with anyone outside their hamlet. This denial was backed by sufficient proof.

Colonel Mackenzie, acting on Richard's warning, had sent two patrols to Los Xicales during the night of the raid, but as one had gone at midnight and the other at four in the morning, and both had shrunk from the weather, neither had seen anything suspicious.

In those days there was no direct cable to Santa Barbara. A message thither had to be cabled to the Florida station, thence to Punto Poniente, thence to Tres Dientes, and thence on. The Santa Barbara police declared that they knew of no one known as Mr. B. or Sagrado B., and that if the raid had been carried out by one of the liquor gangs, which seemed possible, those liquor gangs were composed of Occidentales, not of men from the State of Santa Barbara.

Hilary had been wounded in the wall of the chest by an American revolver bullet. He was in bed with his wound for thirteen days. On the fourteenth day he heard the final reports of the police that they did not know where his sister was and that they had no clue whatsoever to her abductors. The story had by this time reached the American and English newspapers. A question was asked in Parliament, whether it were true that an English woman had been abducted by brigands in Las Palomas, and whether Her Majesty's Ministers were making such representations, etc., etc., as would, etc. The Ministers replied that they had heard the report, and that they had every confidence in Her Majesty's representatives on the spot and in the police of Las Palomas.

Colonel Mackenzie, who was newly in charge of that police, had less confidence. He told Hilary privately that many in the Occidental police force were bribed by the liquor gangs, and that in this case they were determined not to help. Hilary asked whether it would be any use to look for Margarita in Santa Barbara. "Do you yourself think that she will be there?" he asked.

"No, I don't, Mr. Kingsborough."

"Well," Hilary said, "we know that the raiders were not Occidentales, and that they took her away by sea. The men at the boxing match said that the raid was planned by a Santa Barbara leader, who had some grudge against us. My sister said that there was one man with a grudge against her. Why should not an international ruffian of that sort, speaking all tongues, establish himself at Santa Barbara, work with the liquor smugglers, and use his gangs to gratify his grudge when he heard of our presence here?"

"That is a theory, Mr. Kingsborough; but remember, that it is very unlikely that members of a gang would talk in public of their gang's headquarters without any disguise whatsoever. If they spoke of Santa Barbara, be sure that they meant some other place. Santa Barbara is a big place, however, with seven hundred miles of coast. However, I had a flimsy from Santa Barbara this morning; here it is."

"Quite impossible Kingsborough lady landed here during past fortnight. Paris Surete report the magician Hirsch committed suicide Monte Carlo, 1894."

"Good God! then, what do you suppose?"

"That we may put aside this Santa Barbara theory as untenable. Let us waste no further time on it."

"What other theory have you? Who would have taken my sister? What motive could anyone have?"

"I do not know who took your sister, Mr. Kingsborough, but I am working and hoping to find out. The motive is obvious to anyone who has had the honour to see your sister: she is a very beautiful woman. That was the motive, as I read the case."

"And where do you suppose she is?"

"I hope to find out and restore her."

"You mean that she has been shipped to some damned tolerated house?"

"Mr. Kingsborough, it is no good thinking thoughts like those: that way madness lies. I believe that we shall find your sister wherever she may be."

"Well," Hilary said, "I believe that she is in Santa Barbara, in spite of all your beliefs, and I shall go there to look for her.

At least, if I go there, I shall be following the only clue there is. And I shall see that mate of the *Pathfinder* and get descriptions from him of those men at the boxing match."

"Unfortunately, Mr. Kingsborough, the *Pathfinder* has not yet arrived at Santa Barbara."

"What; not in a fortnight, running dead to leeward?"

"No."

"She's overdue?"

"No, not yet; but making a bad passage."

"Has she been met with?"

"No. She has not been reported."

"Is there a single thing in this," Hilary cried, "which doesn't go dead, dead against us? I'll see whether the Dictator of Santa Barbara is as helpless as a bribed bureaucracy."

He was unjust to Colonel Mackenzie, but then he was young, very fond of Margarita, shaken by his wound, and new to reality of any kind.

Colonel Mackenzie was sorry for him, but sorrier for a very lovely woman in the hands of ruffians.

Part THREE

WHEN Sard found that his bicycle was gone, he thought that the lodge-keepers had taken it within the lodge. He knocked at the lodge door to ask; getting no answer, he looked within: the lodge was empty, the bicycle was not there.

It was dim in that track through the forest: Sard struck a match to see what marks were on the ground. The earth was still moist from the rains. Two or three matches showed him that someone with long feet had taken two strides out of the road, wheeled the bicycle into the road and had then ridden away upon it. The tyre tracks were firmly printed on the road; the thief was no doubt heavy as well as tall.

Sard had never been heard to swear, either on deck or aloft; he did not swear now. He thought, "I am well paid, for leaving it out of my sight in a place like this. But he cannot be more than five minutes ahead of me, and may be only a minute. If I run, I may catch him."

He took two more matches, carefully examined the tracks and made sure, mainly from the length of the feet, that the thief was a tall negro, wearing boots which needed soling, and that he was riding, not very fast, into the forest, away from Las Palomas. "I'll catch him," he said, "but I'll have to be quick."

He set off at a slow lope along the forest road, thinking that when he reached Enobbio's, if he had not caught the thief, he would have to hire a horse, and gallop back to his duty "I'm running it very close," he said, "but I'll do it yet. If the worst comes to the worst, the police-boat would run me on board, even if she's out as far as the Rip-Raps. I've got half an hour of possible time; if I ride by the beach, thirty-five minutes."

He stopped at the bridge to have another look at the tracks: they were still there, leading on towards Enobbio's; so he set off again, at a quicker pace, through the forest, which was evil all about him all the time. He made good way to the clearing, which shone from the forge fire. A lamp was lit in the inn. Enobbio sat with his wife at a table there, eating frijoles from earthen platters and drinking wine and water from cups of horn. Sard hailed them at the door:

"Good-evening, señora and señor. May I intrude upon your peace to ask: Have you seen anyone ride by on a bicycle?"

"Yes, señor," Enobbio's wife said, "a negro rode by two minutes past."

"It was more than two minutes, my heart," Enobbio said, "for to my mind it cannot have been since we sat down to supper."

"Desire of my eyes," his wife said, "it was when you went to the forge for the bread. When I say two minutes, I do not tie myself to a second, but to two minutes, which the world knows to be a space of time. It was a space of time since the negro rode past. I am not one, as it is well known, like these giglots and inglesas and ayankiadas, whom one sees in Las Palomas, may the Lord have vengeance on them, shameless as they are, even as Jezebel, always painting and purple-powdering and making their eyes to shine with poison; I am not one, I say, like these, to spend my time in noticing each male who passes and in endeavouring to ensnare his soul. No, my heart's affection, Enobbio mio, when a male passes, I thank God that God has created women differently, in such a way that they can regard such passing with indifference. Therefore, when a negro passes or when a white man passes, be he an Emperor of Rome or decked even as a pumper in the fire-brigade, I can control myself, I can think calmly, even as St. Lawrence upon the gridiron, of other things. Therefore, when this negro who so suddenly excites your jealousy, rode past, I did not hasten to the clock of San Agostino, nor yet to my confessor, nor to the Four Liars of Las Palomas, where four clocks together tell each a different time to a different road, to make sure of the precise instant at which he passed. For to me, as one more dowered with knowledge would have known, a negro is but a negro and a passing a passing."

"This, O affection of my life," Enobbio said, "no man dare

question. But, señor, permit us to request you to eat and drink, reclining at your ease upon this chair, so that you may enquire concerning this negro more as becomes you."

"Thank you, indeed," Sard said, "would that I might; but I am pressed both by spur and quirt, and cannot stay. May I ask the señora whether she noticed in which direction the negro rode, when it fortuned that he had the honour to pass her?"

"In which direction, joy of my hearth," Enobbio asked, "did this negro proceed?"

"Sun of my worldly life," his wife replied, "it is said that, at the allotting of talents, the Padre Eterno gave to woman such talents as man would not sensibly feel the need of. Even as, in equipping her with flesh, He allotted to her that rib which man could not use and has not missed, so in endowing her with mental faculties, which some call reason and others soul, He chose those qualities of acuteness which man, though made loutish by their lack, could not, when he had them, use. Thus it comes about that the wife blushes for her husband in conversation before strangers. For, behold, had not the Padre Eterno deprived you of such acuteness, you would have perceived that sitting as I have been sitting, facing the open door, which we have not yet to keep closed (as is our custom, señor, later in the season, on account of the flies) I could indeed perceive the approach of the negro upon the bicycle, coming from the forest towards me, but not without showing indecent curiosity could I tell into which direction he proceeded; nor, as I have said, should I, in any case, have observed, since as it is well known, a road is as a brook, in which one regards what passes, but not what is past."

"Señor," Enobbio said, "beyond the forge there are three ways; to the sea, to the north and to the mines. The negro must have ridden on one of these. Let us examine the tracks, since there is light enough. Is it possible that you should desire to stay this negro?"

"He has stolen the bicycle, which I need."

"Let us, then, be swift," Enobbio said.

The tracks at the road-meet led away to the left, into the forest.

"You see," Enobbio said, "it goes there, this wheel-track, to the direction of the mines. You see, Camilla mia, this thief will be one of the negroes of Los Jardinillos."

"They are indeed a thievish company," Camilla said. "But if the señor be swift, he will confound the thief in the moment of his exultation."

"How far is it to Los Jardinillos?" Sard asked.

"It cannot take long if taken swiftly," Camilla said.

"My love," Enobbio said, "it is the half of a league, or two kilometres. It would take the señor twenty minutes or more, only to the clearing."

"It may well be, my earthly consolation," Camilla said, "that if the señor should walk, or indeed trot, to Los Jardinillos, his progress would not be swifter than a walk or trot. But as my remark suggested, comrade of my earthly trial, if the señor should proceed swiftly, his arrival would be likewise swift."

"Can you lend me a bicycle or horse," Sard asked, "so that I can go in chase?"

"Alas, we have neither."

"Is there anyone here who might lend either?"

"There is no one here with horse or bicycle. I have, by the blessing of God, a small ass; but God has afflicted him with worms, doubtless lest I should become proud."

"Are there many negroes in Los Jardinillos?"

"There are fifty, señor, and no whites. Doubtless you know him who has taken your bicycle."

"I do not," Sard said: "I am following so that I may know him."

Enobbio did not answer this. Sard noticed that the husband and wife looked at each other, with a look as though the bottom had fallen out of their comprehension.

"Assuredly," Enobbio said at last.

"Assuredly," Camilla answered. They looked at each other again. As in a Latin exercise, Sard was conscious of a good many words "understood."

"Assuredly," Enobbio said at last, in a different tone, "the señor will carry weapons?"

"I am a sailor," Sard answered. "A sailor has always ten weapons and a knife."

He saw in a flash that he had no chance of retaking the bicycle that night by himself.

"I am a sailor," he continued. "The bicycle was to take me to the quay, where I must be in all speed. Has anyone here a cart or conveyance to take me there, for money paid, or had I better run?"

"Paco has a horse, which is in Las Palomas this day," Enobbio said. "His son, Enrique, has a mule."

"Enrique is indeed by God's mercy the owner of a mule," Camilla said, "but on this day he is with the mule, packing stores to the railway siding for the miners."

"A railway siding," Sard said. "They might run me to Las Palomas in a truck."

"The rail does not run to Las Palomas, señor. It runs from the mines of Tloatlucan to the seashore here, where barges come for the copper."

"Then I had better run," Sard said.

"Run," Enobbio said, "run to Las Palomas?"

"Yes."

"It is a league and a half."

"Even so. I must be on board my ship within half an hour."

"But you could not run more than a league. Stay, señor, let me consult my wife. Tell me, my heart, is not Miguel stabling horses each night in the old huts near the salt-pans?"

"Who knows what Miguel does? His doings, being modernist, do not concern us, but rather stir our horror."

"It is true. my life, that Miguel errs in mind, but not, my delight, in heart. In his heart he may be the instrument of good. Listen, señor. In less than one kilometre northeast from this are salt-pans near the beach, with huts. Run thither by this track to the right. It is likely that at this time you will find Miguel there with the horses of his occupation. He, for money if not for love, will lend you a horse and ride with you, so that he may lead it back. Say that I, Enobbio, sent you, knowing the goodness of his nature. Thus will you reach your ship in time, and in no other way can you do this."

"You say that it is only *likely* that he will be there."

"He will be there, señor," Camilla said; "he is always there at this hour with his horses: never does he fail."

"You may count quite certainly on his being there and on his lending you a horse," Enobbio said. "I, who am Enobbio, will serve you as to bread and lodging for a year, without reward, should he not be there."

"He will lend assuredly," Camilla said, "to any señor such as the señor whose need is as the señor's."

Sard felt in her speech the insincerity of one anxious to be rid of him: he made up his mind at once.

"Can I reach the seashore by this path to the right?"

"Assuredly, señor. Miguel and the salt-pans are on the sea-shore."

"I mean, can I come at once to the seashore?"

"Assuredly, señor."

"It is not a good path, save where men have gone," Enobbio said. "In fact, it is no path, but what is opposite to path."

"I must risk that."

Sard thanked them both for their kindness and apologised for having disturbed them at their supper. He set off at a fast trot along the path towards the salt-pans. He meant to burst through the thickets to the seashore and then run straight along the beach as hard as he could put foot to it, to the water-front.

"It is a full three miles," he thought, "even by the beach; but with luck I can be there by half-past. The old man will give me some grace, and the police-boat may be there; but I'll do it some-how."

In a couple of hundred yards from the clearing, he put his arm before his eyes and thrust into the bushes towards the sea. He judged that the sea beach would be about half a mile from him and that he would save at least three-quarters of a mile by going by the beach. The thought of passing right under the walls of Los Xicales helped in his decision.

He burst through his thicket into a sort of meadow of tussocks, over which he made good time. Beyond the tussocks the woods began again, shutting out all his bearings, but by taking a departure he kept a straight course, as he thought, from the point where he left the track. Just inside the woods, when he came into them, was a tangle of thorn along which he had to run for a hundred yards before he could find a way through. He came out on to a soft patch, which had harder ground beneath it, though all was covered with the wreck of thorns which the bog had killed. He floundered across it to the other side, which was a rise of red earth covered with pines. He skirted the rise to a point where it was split by a gully, which barred his progress.

Not more than a year or two before, some rains heavier than usual had made all the upper ground a bog. This from its weight had at last torn through the bank beyond it and gone in a torrent of mud and water into a ravine below. All along the sides of this ravine were the rampikes of trees, killed by the stuff brought down, but still standing, sometimes with half their roots laid bare. Not less than fifty of these trees had already been picked and sucked to their bones by the ravin of tropical life. They now stood like a valley of bones come to life. They stood up white in the dusk, waving their arms. Many of them glistened with decay or with vermin shining from decay. On many of them fungus had seized with a greed that seemed to have purpose and plan. One quite near to Sard was a tree grey with death, barkless to the tips and swathed with a sprawl of fungus that was scarlet at its fringes. It was as though the fungus had sucked out all the blood from its victim, except these last drops.

Many trees had fallen into the ruin of the bog and now lay there, submerged or half-submerged in mud. The antlers of their branches were white. Rank things had sprouted out and hoisted themselves up by these prongs. One bulk or stump of a tree which Sard saw in the swamp was covered with xicales, all forward, in profuse blossom, a mass of blue and white, crawled on by gorged flies.

Flowers like enormous flags shot up on firm fleshy stalks among the morass. Some, which were very tall, had whitish blossoms as big as faces, splotched with darkness like faces; these seemed to lean forward and mow at Sard; they were like ghosts, lean and intense, but very beautiful.

All that place of death, thick as death, sickly with the forms and the smell of death, with that evil, low, over-abundant life which brings death, had a sort of weltering chuckle as though it exulted in its rottenness. The water in its pockets droned to puddle below, there was a suck of noise like that of a beast trying to get out, but sinking back.

All this danger barred Sard's path in the worst possible way: it shut him from the beach and from the port: it ran north-west and south-east across his course.

"I'll get across," he said: "I'm not going to lose my passage. Now that I have come this way, I will go this way."

The light was off the place and the sun was down, but it was daylight still. He marked a place in the ravine, below the xicales flowers, where he thought there would be a fairly easy crossing. A fallen tree lay sloped there as a safe approach or step into a pool of water which might be forded or swum. Beyond the pool two great trees lay locked together; they were barkless, like the rest, yet so placed in the mud that Sard judged that he could cross by them, or almost cross, to the further side of the gully. The last two or three yards beyond the trees looked dangerous, but not bad enough to stop him. It was quicker to cross than to go round, which ever way he tried it.

He had no time nor very good light for survey. He made up his mind and went at it within thirty seconds, quoting his sea-proverb of "the sooner the quicker." Blood-sucking water-midges were already at him in a swarm: the drone of their horns called up their reserves: a faint smoke of them was rising. He jumped like a cat from tussock to tussock, scrambled over the roots of the tree on to the trunk, steadied himself, and then balanced like a tight-rope walker down the bole to the water. He saw the whiteness of the pilled boughs in the ink of that pond stretching deep down. He was amazed at the depth of the water. "Better deep water than mud," he said; so in he went with a thrust which carried him across.

He edged along the nearer of the fallen trees, caught a good hold of a bough, felt bottom with his feet, got one foot against the bole, gave a great heave, and was instantly backwards in the water with the broken bough on top of him. He came up with his eyes full of touchwood, and felt something run along his head. He brushed it off into the water and caught his tree again: something ran along his hand; he brushed it off, fearing a scorpion; but instantly other things ran in its place. He shook them off and backed away, till he saw that the things were wood-eating beetles, whose colony he had disturbed. "A scorpion would be a bore," he said.

He trod water while he looked for a better place. He swam in, caught a bough, swung himself up, and instantly went backwards into the water for the second time, with the bough in his hand.

He came up, somewhat troubled, for a third attempt. This time he dodged in under the boughs, laid hold of the body of the tree and hove his weight on to it.

With a sort of flounder of deliberation, the tree moved sideways to his weight, then tilted suddenly as the heavy branches gave leverage, then it rolled over into deeper water, carrying Sard down.

Sard had learned in a hard school to look out, to know when to let go and when to stand-from-under. He went down with the tree as it rolled, right under water, so that he never saw his hat again, but he kept above the tree and emerged when it settled. Very cautiously he moved along its bulk, as soon as it was firm, with the feeling that he was riding a beast whose ways were not to be trusted. He felt it waver in front of him and settled behind him as the submerged boughs went deeper into the mud. There came a sudden crack and drop, as these gave way: the tree soused him to his waist and then steadied. It was just then that he felt vicious pricking bites in his legs as the leeches began.

He stood upon the bole and had "a look-see." The second tree, which was to be his gang-plank to the shore, was now further away than it had been. He could no longer step to it from where he was. "A little more swimming," he muttered: so in he went to be done with it.

The second tree was steady in the mud, but as he neared it, he saw that the yellow-tail bees had a nest in the bole. Away from the nest and dangling from the boughs, there were strings of withered poison-ivy, which he knew both by sight and from experience. He swam inshore as far as he could to avoid these dangers, then scrambled up upon the bole and slipped along it to the roots. A few bees came round him, to make sure, but did not attack; he dodged the poison-plant. He scrambled up the gabion of roots, all tangled and earthed, to look beyond at the banks. As he stood up, the cloud of water-midges settled down upon him: ants came from earth of the roots to bite him: the leeches of the pond bit and sucked.

He had not liked the look of the banks from the other side, but he liked their look much less from near at hand. They were nine feet from him beyond a mud pond of unknown depth. They rose rather steeply from this mud pond, in a bulge of wet, red, oozing mud, which shone and trickled. A few blades of grass grew out of this mud, but not enough to give it firmness. The mass looked to be bulging out to burst. A rain-storm more, or the weight of a body trying to climb it, would bring it all down like an avalanche out of which there would be no rising. The bank of mud was eight or nine feet high: above it there was a shoot of reeds sheathed in pale grey dangling and shining husks. "If I can get hold of the reeds," he said, "I'll be out of this in half a minute; if I can't, I may never be heard of again. That mud looks evil; but the longer I look, the less I shall see. There's a star already."

Looking up from where he was, he saw a blackness of trees above and beyond the reeds. Against the blackness, the pale fluffy flowers of the reeds stood out like gun sponges, with white moths, as big as humming birds, wavering over them: above them a star appeared in a sky changing from greenish to violet. It grew rapidly darker: or, rather, objects became less distinct and the pilled branches more uncanny.

"Come along," he said. He clambered over the roots, hung on by a root which stood his test, and edged out along submerged roots till he touched the mud. It was soft, bulging, full of evil, with neither foot nor hand-hold. "If that should come down," he said, "I shall be gulfed, like that man in the *Venturer* who got under the wheat-tip in the hold and wasn't heard of till we got the hatches off in Hamburg five months later. But with this difference: I shall never be heard of again. The way to get up that mud is to drive in stakes to climb by."

There were many branches ready to hand. He tore a stake and thrust it into the mud. It sank in for three feet as easily as if the mud were something softer than butter. With a sobbing noise, followed by a gurgle, some reddish water, rapidly turning to something black, iridescent and semi-solid, exuded from about it. Sard drove in a second stake above it, with a third above that: at each thrust the bank quaked and water or liquid mud exuded: there was also an ominous sag in the body of the bank. "Neck or nothing," Sard said. He drove in a fourth stake and instantly swung himself up on to the gabion or fan of the roots by which he held. He was only just in time. The fourth stake broke the last strength of the barrier: it gave outwards: a shoot of water spurted it outwards: a swirl of running mud followed the shoot: then it all came down with a crash, which picked up Sard's tree, canted it out to mid-gully, and dashed it against a dam of other trees, on to which Sard was pitched.

He picked himself up and slipped along a tree bole to a hand-hold by which he swung himself up to safety, just as the dam gave way. He was back almost at his starting-point, wet to the skin, mud to the thigh, bitten, sucked and foiled. The long pent-up seepings of the rains poured down from the burst bank before him. "I'm well out of that," he thought, "but I'm going to cross this gully; for it is the short way and I still have time."

He trotted up the gully for a few yards, wondering at the increase in the darkness since he stood there before. It had seemed to him that his crossing had only taken a minute, yet here it was sensibly darker; there were now five stars in the heaven where before was one. He broke a stake and sounded some of the going. It was like sounding the vale of Siddim.

Then lifting his eyes from the mud, he started, for there in the gully was the mound covered with xicale flowers. "There," he said, "I will try it there. I believe that the xicale flowers are a sign. I shall get across there."

At his feet, almost as though prepared for him, was a heap of what had once been a tree, but was now a sodden log easy to break into lengths. He picked up pieces of this and laid or tossed them one by one as steps before him in the marsh; then very swiftly, holding his stick as a balancing-pole, he ran across them to the stump covered by the xicales. To his astonishment, it proved not to be a tree at all, but a rock or sarsen, thrusting from a patch of firm earth in which the xicales were rooted. He edged round it carefully to the gully beyond.

The first two steps from the xicales were over his shoes; his third and fourth, being parts of the same flounder, took him over his knees, but brought him to the pikes of a tree on which he could tread. Branches of this tree served as treads to his going for the next six yards, but beyond those six yards lay ten yards of bog, which he could not clearly distinguish nor test. Here, for the first time, he began to wish that he had not tried his short cut across country to the beach. "All the same," he said, "if I can get to the beach in five minutes, or even ten, I'll do it yet."

He took a swift survey of the bog ahead of him: it did not look easy; but he always held that it is better to be in a difficulty than expecting to be in one. He took a note of possible tussocks in a line, drew a breath, and set off in a hop, skip and jump.

The hop took him to firmish tussock which squelched, but gave him some support for his skip. The skip took him to something very soft with a log about a foot beneath the surface, from which he made his jump. The jump took him into what had looked like grass, but which proved to be weed-covered water: he went into it over his head. He came out again, thinking fiercely of the *Pathfinder's* fo'c'sle-head and of that iron rail over which he ought at that moment to be peering. The soft green grasses gave before him; they stroked his face gently, they closed in at the back of his neck; he felt them caress his body and tremble along his legs and lay enfoldments about his feet. When he thrust out his hands to swim, they sped from him, for they were frail grass and he a strong man; but before his stroke was made, they were back again: he felt them at his chest; they touched his chin: they rose from the water and touched his face. He swam six strokes and then felt for bottom. There was bottom at five feet: he touched it, but it went over his foot; he wrenched the foot clear, but it went over his other foot; he wrenched that foot clear, and, lo, all those soft little frail grasses seemed to come all about him with a whisper, and they were as heavy as lead and as strong as sail-maker's twine.

"Whatever I do," Sard said, "I must not fight these things, but go where they will let me go."

He was not afraid, but very cautious, knowing the power of his enemy. He had once known a boy who had been drowned by waterweed. "He was caught deep down, where they are strong: at the surface they yield."

When he yielded they also yielded; he floated clear; the little soft grasses, fine as flax, unclasped their hands, they whispered about him and let him go. Little moths floated about the water and a bird somewhere in the thickets made a plaintive cry. All that Sard could see was what the bull-frog sees: gleams of water, little starry blossoms on the grasses, ripples like steel, bubbles.

He turned upon his back and swam thus for a few strokes till he slid on to the mud in which the grasses were thickly rooted. He gripped handfuls of the grass and pulled himself forward, but they came from the mud into his hand. When he pressed his foot down, the mud went over it like softness' self. Great bubbles gurgled up and burst about him with the smell of decay.

Sard reached forward till he could lay a hand upon something ahead which looked like earth. It was firmer than anything there; he drew himself to it, and pressed himself up upon it. It gave beneath him, being very like sponge, but it did not collapse, it did not try to swallow him.

"Not much further," Sard said. "A few feet more, and I will be there."

He said these words aloud, for the comfort of hearing a voice. Instantly, from in front of him, came a splash and scutter: things were swimming away from something dark in the water; he could not see what the things were nor the thing from which they swam. "They are snakes," he said, "and here is one of them coming at me."

He struck at it. To his great relief, it gave a squeal and dived from him. "Rats," he said. "They have a carcass here. I'll get out of this."

He saw that the dark thing was a body. His first thought was that it was a man, but groping forward, he was reassured: it was one of the half-wild razor-back hogs which the negroes allowed to stray in the woods there. It had been drowned there some hours before and now the rats were at it.

Sard had his hand upon it as he floundered forward, when the texture of the stuff beneath his feet changed suddenly from mush to something vicious. His feet, sinking into it, were held: the stuff closed over his feet and fastened them: he sank lower down: the stuff caught him round the ankles. He knew on the instant that he had met his match: he was gripped to his death as the hog had been. If he did not get out of that quag in the next minute, while he had his strength, the rats would eat him there before dawn.

He put both hands on the hog's back, pressing it down and himself up. He dragged his right foot up, then slipped sideways to his left, giving himself a nasty wrench. The bubbles gurgled up all about him: they popped with a flapping noise. He hove again, pressing with all his power on the carcase; he got his right knee on to the body, and urged it down into the mud; his left foot came out of the mud; he stood up, balancing, on the corpse, for the next leap.

"If I get into a place like that," he said, "without anybody to give me a purchase, I shall be posted as missing."

He peered ahead; but there was nothing to guide him; all before him was bog: there were pools of water, juttings of mud and grasses growing out of water.

"If I step into that," he said, "I may never step back to this pig nor forward to the bank, but be caught right there. My best chance is a standing leap, to get as near to the bank as may be."

He measured it roughly as nine feet to hand-hold on the bank. He gathered himself for it, swinging his arms, above the unstable corpse which squeezed out the bubbles. He launched himself violently forward into a mess which gulfed him to the waist. He urged himself through this for a foot or two, felt it drag him quietly back, made a greater effort, got a purchase on some grasses, which helped him for another two feet; then he floundered, trampling on stuff which gave beneath him yet came back folding over him. He thrust forward, but his feet were fast; he fell on his face, the stuff surged up over his back. He kept his head up and thrust with his hands and wrenched with his feet. All the fat, weltering, bubbling bog seemed to chuckle at having got him. The bubbles burst in his face: they were as big as inverted saucers and came from the heart of corruption.

"I'm not going to die in a place like this," he said. "Come out of it, port main; up with her!"

The old rallying cry timed his efforts: it was like one man standing the scrimmage of a pack of forwards in football. The bog gave an ounch of release, like a beast smacking its lips. He got hold of something on the bank. It had prickles on it, but it was solid and grew in dryness. Then as he put his weight upon it, it came out of the ground by the roots: a little avalanche of earth and stones came over his head, blinding him for the moment with grit in his eyes.

He could not see; he could only flounder forward with spread arms which availed nothing: the bog had him fast for all his effort.

Then his hand touched a liane brought down by the bush. It was a double liane, tough as flax and as thick as honeysuckle. He caught it and pulled on it, and instantly a great flowering spray of xicale flowers came floundering down from above, into his face. He saw them for what they were. "Xicale flowers," he said, "xicales. I'm going to be saved."

He got both hands deeply into the lianes of the xicales and pulled as he had never pulled, never, on any yard or on any rope. Digging forward into the squash of the bog he found something hard for one foot. "Oh, heave," he cried, as he had so often cried to his watch. "Oh, heave, son, heave; oh, heave and start her; heave for glory."

He found himself half out, with his right knee and side on hard earth and his left leg stuck in the bog. He drew deep breath for a minute, as once he had stopped to breathe when beaten dead by a sail five years before. Then gathering all his powers, he hove "all together," and emerged erect on sound earth, shaking with the strain, and without his left shoe.

"Xicales," he said, "you've saved my life. I knew that you were mixed up somehow with my life; and I'll carry some of you with me in gratitude till I'm laid in my grave."

He picked both flowers and leaves for his soaking pocket-book. His hands shook: he was cold to the marrow and filthy beyond description.

"I'll do it yet," he said. "But first I must make a shoe of sorts, or I shall be lamed."

He cut off his trouser-legs at the knees, with his knife. With one of the pieces, folded fourfold, he made a shoe, and with the other he made thongs which secured it as a sandal to his foot. It was a rough and ready sandal, but it stayed on when put. It was good enough to run on.

He did not think of what the time might be. He roughly judged that he could reach Las Palomas in twenty minutes or twenty-five minutes by running along the beach with all his might. Any waterman on the front would put him aboard: the police-launch would take him. "I can't miss my passage," he said, "I must be on board. I told the old man I would be on board." For the first time he said to himself, "And the old man will give me an hour's grace."

He set off over the headland of the gully under the clump of pines whose blackness he had seen from the mud. It was soft but firm going on the pine-needles; the trees over his head made a sighing which merged as he ran into the sterner sighing of the water on the beach. At the foot of the spur over which he had run, he came to the outcrops of the springs all overgrown with azaleas. They ran all along the foot of the spur, so thick with blossoms that they looked like an unbursting wave which was yet foaming at the crest. Over all the foam of blossom the fireflies glowed and went out, now as many as stars, not few, now like sparks, but always beautiful. Just beyond them was the broad sea-beach, with the breakers only fifty yards away. The sea was coming in, as it will in a shallow bay, in half a dozen long lines, each glowing with mild fire, shining as it neared the sand, then flashing like the moonlight, as the wave burst, then gleaming greenish, and showing the globes of the stars, as it wasted and died out upon the sand.

Sard burst through the azaleas to the sands, which stretched along for a great distance right and left. To his right (seemingly quite near) was a shining, which he knew to be the river near Los Xicales; beyond it, in the darkness of trees, was the house of his dream with one light burning. All a vast expanse of night, the sea-beach, the forest, and muttering water lay behind him. He rushed down to the sea and let three breakers go over him to cleanse him from the swamp and the leeches.

"Now, Sard Harker," he said, "come on, port main, up with her!" He broke into a steady run facing to the Los Xicales light. The pine trees on the spit shut away a view of the anchorage, so that he could not see the *Pathfinder*; he could only hope and put his best leg foremost. "Upon them that *hope*," he thought, "is His mercy." He ran at his steady pace which, as he knew, he could keep for miles.

Thought it seemed so near, that shining on the sands, which he knew to be the river, was a full half-mile away. Before he had gone three hundred yards of it, he saw that the sand just ahead of him was darker and shinier than the sand under his feet. A memory of another dangerous sand, far away on an English sea-coast, shot into his mind on the instant, but the footing failed before he could stop. The sand gave beneath the one foot and let in the other: ooze of water shot up to the surface: he flung himself backwards violently, and got out, but fell, and saw, or thought that he saw, the surface of the sand shaking as though it were laughing at him. He rolled himself clear, then rose and looked at it. "That's a pretty bad quicksand," he said. "I might get through, but from the pull on that foot, I think that it would pull me down. Probably I can get round the shoreward end of it."

He tried, but failed: the shoreward end of the quicksand was tropical bog.

"Very well," he said, "I'll swim round the seaward end. It is only a hundred yards. I need not go far out. It will be something to have the swamp washed off me again." He went knee-deep into the sea, with some misgivings, for the shallows of all that coast are haunted with sand sharks, which come right in to have the warmth of the sand. He splashed as he went, to scare them. He had gone about thigh deep into the water and was just settling down to swim, when there came suddenly an agonising pain in his left foot.

His first thought was, "I'm on a thorn," then, "I'm on a snake"; then, as the pain ran in a long, hot, stabbing streamer up his leg, he knew the truth, that he had trodden on a sting-ray. He hopped out of the water to the shore, feeling all the blood in his foot turn to vitriol and come surging along, as vitriol, to his heart. Most excruciating agony made him fling himself down. He tried to hold out his leg, but that was unendurable torment. He tried to kneel upon it, while he put a ligature above the knee, but the pain made him so sick that he could not bear it. He tried to lie down, but that was unbearable. He rolled over and over, moaning: then staggered up, and hopped and hopped, gasping with pain, until he fell. He had never known any pain in his life, except the bangs and knocks of his profession, but now he tasted a full measure.

Although he fell, the pain did not stop, it hit him when he was down, it grew worse. The cold, deadly, flat thing in the sand had emptied his horn into him. He buried his face in the sand: he dug his hands into the sand. Then the poison seemed to swing him round and double him up. It seemed to burn every vein and shrivel every muscle and make every nerve a message of agony.

He managed to cast loose the wrappings from the foot. The foot no longer looked like a foot, but like something that would burst. In his deadly sickness he thought that his foot was a pollard willow tree growing to the left of the road. He wondered why he was not on his bicycle. He said that his foot was dead, that it had died of the gout, and would drop from his body and never grow again.

All the venom came in pain on to his abdominal muscles; then he felt it come swimming along like little fiery rats round the carcase of his heart. He saw his heart for a moment or two like a black pig caught in a bog; the rats came all round it together, from every side, they closed in on it and bit it, bit it, bit it.

When he came to himself a little, he said something about the stars being too many, altogether too many, for the job in hand. He said that he could not pick up the guiding lights. Then he felt that every star was a steamer's masthead light, and that all those myriads of steamers were bearing down upon him without side-lights. "Their look-out-men are all asleep," he said, "I can't see how they are bearing, and I have no lights at all. I must find a flare and burn them off." He groped for a flare, but found only his wet clothes pressing on his body. "The flares are all damp," he said, "the flares won't burn. It is my fault; I stored them in the pickle-house. They ought to have been in the chart-room with the flags." He wandered off in his thoughts far away from the lights of the stars. He lost all knowledge that he was lying on the sand three or four thousand miles from home. His main thought was that he was wandering along corridors in search of doors. He knew that it was very important to find doors, but whenever he found any, they closed in his face and became parts of the walls.

After a long time he roused himself up, feeling weak and sick. He knew at once, from the feel of things, that it was midnight. A sense of his position came to him. The *Pathfinder* must have sailed: he had lost his passage: he was miles from anywhere: he had lost Richard's bicycle. All these things had happened because of his dream, because of Los Xicales. He sat up, but saw no light in the direction of the house. Over the spit with the pine trees there came a sort of flashing glimmer twice a minute as the light swung round in the tower of Manola point. He was bitterly cold, for besides being wet through, a mizzling rain was falling on him. He was sick and wretched. The closeness in the air was gone; a breeze was blowing the rain straight along the beach. The trees inshore were whistling and rustling: the seas broke as though they were cross, with a sharp smash instead of the relenting wash of twilight. All sorts of little life was scuttering about the sand: white owls, or sea-birds, cruised overhead as silently as sails.

Sard sat up and tried his left leg. It was numb and much

swollen. He could not feel anything in it from his mid-thigh to his toe. It had become as dead as a leg of clay or mutton. When he dinted the flesh by pressing on it, the dint remained.

With a little difficulty he stood up on one leg. He then felt for the first time that he had only one leg, that the other would not act. He could move it, but not bend it; when he put it on the sand, leaned on it, or tried to walk with it, the thing ceased to be his, it neither obeyed nor rebelled, it failed. He was so cold that he felt that he would die. He sat for twenty minutes working to restore his leg. He no longer felt pain in it, the pain was gone, but it was as though the poison had burnt out the life. In some ways he would rather have had pain than this deadness.

"Now I am in a bad way," he said, "for not many come to this beach, and none in this State will wander about looking for me. If I could only reach Los Xicales . . . However, I can't reach Los Xicales this way: the quicksand bars the land and I'm not going to risk another sting in the sea. I can't get back to Enobbio's inn by that swamp. But I might crawl along the beach to that man who has the horses, Miguel, with the good heart, near the salt-pans. He might not be very far: two kilometres. He might take me in to the port, or at least to Los Xicales, where I should be in time, if those fellows were trying anything."

He was suffering much: the leech-bites in his right leg itched like mosquito-bites, but were also hot and stinging; his mouth had fur in it, which tasted like brown paper; he felt that he was dying of cold. His hands, neck and face were swollen from the bites of the midges. His blood seemed to have changed within him to something grey and slow. Worse than his bodily state was the thought that he had broken his word to Captain Cary and missed his passage; "mizzled his dick," as Pompey Hopkins called it.

"She'll be sailed by this time," he thought. "Whatever grace Captain Cary gave me, she'll have gone by this."

He stood up to look about him: he now realised, for the first time, the change in the weather.

The northern section of the heaven was covered with intense darkness. Over the blackness a sort of copper-coloured wisp, like smoke, was driving at a great speed. The blackness was lit up continually by lightning, which burned sometimes in steady glows, sometimes in sharp stabs of light. The wind had risen; directly Sard crossed the sandy pit, it struck him with fury, driving sand and fragments of shell against his face and down his neck. The sea was not yet breaking with any violence upon the beach. It was white as far as the eye could see, as though the heads of every wave had been whipped off and flogged into foam, which shone as though with moonlight from the phosphorescence. Washes of breaker burst and rushed up the sand to Sard's feet, like washes of fire in which all the marvellous shells of which the beach was composed, were lit up like jewels. Far away to the right, out at sea on the edge of the sky, there was, as it were, a shaking wall of white from the sea already running upon the Rip-Raps. He could see it waver, but it never seemed to change. There was a roller there before the last had gone.

"This is the norther," Sard thought. "I hope the old man did not wait too long for me, but got clear of the Rip-Raps before it came on."

He re-bandaged his foot, picked some stakes from among the driftwood, to serve as walking-sticks, and with the help of these set out towards the salt-pans to borrow a horse. He hobbled forward, dead into the teeth of the gale. The worst thing about the gale was the cold. Far south as it was, the wind came down directly from the northern ice-fields. To Sard, who was thinly clad and wet through, it was piercing. He stumbled along against it, keeping his direction by the pale flame of the breakers which roared at his side and flung their fire at his feet.

When he had gone about a mile, he saw the stretch of the salt-pans like a patch of white heather away ahead, distant he knew not how far. It might be a mile, or it might be two miles; no man could judge distance on a sand so flat At anchor, under the head beyond the sand, was a ship which had not lain there when he came to the beach. She seemed to be a small tramp or large coaster, sheltering from the norther. She carried no lights. Sard judged that she had come there to load copper from the mines of Tloatlucan. He knew that there was a pier there, at the mouth of a river, and that the ore came by a light railway direct to the pier from the mine.

He hobbled on towards the whiteness of the salt-pans: a flat road is a long road at best; against a gale it is a bad road.

Nearly all the way a great white bird (whether an owl or some sea-bird, he could not tell) flew above and ahead of him. It seemed to him that this bird shone. Perhaps the poison had upset his eyes, or perhaps his eyes never lost the shine of the sea breaking beside him. In his shaken state, this bird seemed like a luminous swan, guiding him to quiet.

Near the southern end of the pans he saw a shack or stable, facing him. The seaward end of this shack was a small adobe house, with a palm roof. The stable was empty: there was neither ass nor dog there.

Sard listened for half a minute, standing still, at ten paces from the house, while he took stock. The house was closed to the night, yet it had the look or feel of having someone there. Perhaps an animal instinct survives in us from the time when it was important to know if a lair were blank or not.

Sard went no nearer; he hailed the house in Spanish, calling on Don Miguel by name. The place was silent, except for the flogging of the palmetto on the roof, the scutter of crabs and gophers on the bents and the wail of the wind across the salt-pans. Then presently something tinkled within the house. It might have been a revolver cartridge, or a knife coming out of a sheath, or a bottle upon glass. Sard hailed again, saying that he came alone, in peace, from Don Enobbio, with desire to hire a horse.

This time, Sard saw the shutter which covered the window (a space a foot square near the door) move about three inches to one side. He heard no noise, but he was watching the shutter and saw its greyness change to blackness as the wood moved. "I am a friend," he called. "I come from Don Enobbio to Don Miguel to hire a horse. I, a sick man, wish to ride to Las Palomas if Don Miguel will give aid, thus emulating the Good Samaritan."

He heard the heavy iron-wood bar of the door go back in its runners; the door opened about eighteen inches; a young woman appeared, yawning.

"Enrique," she said, "Enrique, back already?"

"I am not Enrique, lady," Sard said, "but a traveller in need of a horse."

"Dios mio," she said, "and I not combed! I thought you were Enrique. Wait, then."

He did not have to wait more than a minute; a light appeared at the shutter; a tin basin or pan was kicked into a corner; then the door was opened, the young woman called:

"Will the caballero enter, then?"

"Enter," Sard thought, "and have my throat cut, perhaps; but I will enter."

He went in, with a watchful eye lest Miguel, who "erred in mind," should be lying in wait with a sand-bag just behind the door. However, Miguel was not there, the young woman was alone in the one-roomed house.

She had lighted a little tin lamp, which had a smoke-blackened glass, broken at the top. By the light of this Sard saw the room to be bare and untidy. The bed was an array of small pine boughs, with their needles, covered with sacks, ponchos and old serapes. The young woman had just risen from her nest there; she was "not combed," as she had said, nor dressed, but hung about, as it were, with a long undergarment torn at the shoulder. She was a plump young woman, just beginning to grow fat: she was very dirty: her long, black hair shone from an unguent; she flung it rakishly back from her brow with the gesture of a great actress. Her eyes were like mules' eyes, black and shining, with yellow whites. Her mouth was exceedingly good-natured. She stood near the door, clutching her sacking to her shoulder with one hand, while with the other she motioned Sard to enter. She grinned at Sard as a comely woman will grin at one whose praise of her comeliness would be esteemed.

The room, which was next door to the stable, had been lived and slept in for some months with closed door and shutter. It smelt of oil, tortillas, frijoles, horses, rats, mice, espinillo, hair-grease, poverty, garlic, tobacco, joss-stick and musk. A sort of mental image of a life made of all these things, all flavoursome and with a tang to them, reached Sard at once through his nostrils, with the further thought that it was not such a bad life, since it left the person both dignified and kind.

He explained that he needed a horse.

"Ay de mi," she exclaimed, "but Miguel is with the horses at the siding beside the jetty, a half league hence. Assuredly he will lend a horse, but it is further on, at the quay, that you will find him now."

"I will go on, then," Sard said.

"But you are wet and have known misfortune. Enter, I pray you, and rest from your misfortune. Ay de mi, your foot has trodden unhappily."

"Not since it has led me to your presence," Sard said. "But thank you, I must not enter. I will go on to Miguel, to the horse."

Something in his tone or bearing or look, something in himself, seemed to impress the woman.

"Assuredly," she said, "the good Jesu comes thus, but must not go thus. Sit you, Sir caballero." She brought forward a three-legged stool, the only seat in the room, and made him sit. "Sit you down till I see your foot," she said. She would have none of his protests, but had his bandage off.

"You have met a snake," she said.

"No; a sting-ray."

"Then you have been in the sea and are of the ship, no doubt; ay de mi, all wet, all wet, what misery." She felt his arm and shoulder and cold hand. "And a sting-ray; often have I seen them, with their horns. There is a negro who can cure such with a white powder; but I have nothing. Nothing but love which is a part of the love of God."

She was kneeling at his side with his foot in her hands, kneading the swollen flesh.

"No," she said, "this is no time for the cure. The poison has killed, but is now dead: the flesh is dead. It takes a day, two days, who knows, after a sting-ray. Then, when the life begins to return, one can help. See now, I can, by God's mercy, do something. I have here a stirrup shoe made long ago, but still of use. I have but the one, for the other was cast out in error as I always maintain; while others, on the contrary, think that Martin took it, Martin the pedlar, the old soldier, who comes round with saints and handkerchiefs. See now, a shoe for a count or duke."

She produced what had been the stirrup-shoe of a count or duke in the days when such things were. It was a sort of wooden-soled slipper, with a sole of wood, and heel and toecaps of cuir-bouilli. The great silver bosses and brackets had long since been wrenched from it. The last user had fixed it to his leathers with wire. The design on the cuir-bouilli was of a coat-of-arms, but eaten away by ants and green with mould.

"See now," she said, fitting it to his foot, "a shoe for a count or duke. You shall walk the better for it. It is a shoe such as might have been made for you."

Her hand rested for an instant on Sard's pocket, from which a draggled silk handkerchief hung.

"Dios mio," she said, "you are count or duke. It is so soft. This is silk of the countess."

She fingered it with a child's delight in the texture. "Is it all like this?" she said. "Truly, if you are not count or duke, you are servant to one."

"That's more like it," Sard said, rising, so as to tread upon the shoe. "I'm a servant, to a limited company. Your shoe, señora, is as water to one dying in the desert. You have been a friend to me in time of need. You know the wise saying, 'a friend to the beggars will never lack guests.' I say, 'May a host to a beggar never lack friends.'"

"The good Jesu comes in all shapes," she answered. "And you are not a beggar, but very much a caballero; oh, very, very much a duke or count. You are English. They say that the English are as ice, and therefore come hither to be thawed."

"That is partly true, señora. I have been melted by your kindness."

"It is also said (though this I do not believe) that no Englishman will kiss a woman to whom he has not been married by the priest."

"That is assuredly true, señora."

"Never, never, never; even if all things conspired: the moonlight, perfumes, music, and beauty such as hers of Sheba?"

"Never, never, never," he said.

"Ay de mi," she said. "But it is said that the English are as Turks, and are married to very many."

"We are as God made us, not as people say, señora; but we remember kindly acts forever, and I shall remember you."

"Forever?"

"I think so."

"That is very caballero. But what is memory? A thought. You have not even asked me my name."

"I was going to ask it."

"You were going to ask it?"

"Assuredly."

"Assuredly," she said. "It is true, then, as they say, that the English are as ice. 'Assuredly.' You said it with a peck, as from a beak. 'Assuredly.' If I were to take a dagger and thrust it into my heart so that I fell dead, you would say 'Assuredly she has driven the point too far. Assuredly she is no longer alive.'"

"Not so," Sard said, "I should not say it. I might think it."

"Would you be sorry?"

"I am sorry for any suicide."

"Your cold ice would not thaw one tear. But, vaya, if I were countess, and lay dead, you would stand like marble and say poetry. Listen: my name, the name I call myself, is Rose of the South: will you remember that?"

"Yes."

"Assuredly?"

"No; faith of caballero."

"Will you remember me, who am that name?"

"Yes."

"It is me, myself, that name. When I was little, I had a sister: we used to play grand ladies out in the sage-brush. She was Lily of the West; I was Rose of the South. She is dead, pobrecita, the Lily: she was of this world, which needs a man, not a woman: pobrecita mia."

"What is your real name?" Sard asked.

"Clara," she said, "Clara of the Salt-Pans, the woman of Miguel, called Miguel sin Nada."

"He is Miguel con Mucha, with yourself, señora," Sard said. "And now adios, and always my thanks, siempre, siempre, siempre. I will return your shoe by Miguel."

"For the love of all the saints in bliss, caballero," she said, "in no way let Miguel suspect that you have talked with me. Ay de mi, we women; we suffer for our hearts. Miguel is of a jealousy that would make proud, being such evidence of love, if it were not such inconvenience. A thought, a turn of the head, a look, and he at once ranks me with those infamous of life, with her of Sheba, and Ysabel, Queen of England."

"I will not let him suspect," Sard said. "And now farewell, and my thanks and again my thanks."

"Stay yet," she said. "Stay yet for one instant. I shall be here sixty years, perhaps, like Caterina La Fea, below, at the poblacion, old, old, and wrinkled like the devil, red-eyed, blind, from sitting in the smoke, sucking bits of meat at last, with her gums. And little children flinging dead rats at her and calling her Witch-Witch. I have had one instant with you; let me have one other; only one; since it has to last for sixty years, you would not grudge me one instant? Then when I am as Caterina, I shall think, ah, but truly I lived, once, at that midnight, when one like St. Gabriel came to my door, and was as a count or duke to me, who am Clara the woman of Miguel."

"Señora," Sard said, "I, too, shall think of you, at times, for whatever years may remain to me; but now I must go, and so I say again, thank you and farewell."

He turned away as fast as he could hobble.

"Stay yet," she implored. "I do not importune, but I do not know your name. Tell me your name. I would think of your name and pray for you in the chapel and before the image here."

"My name is Harker."

"Harker. What does that mean?"

"I do not know: perhaps 'one who listens.'"

"Listens for what?"

"What do people listen for?"

"The sea wind in the heat," she said thoughtfully; "and the crowing of the cock in the night of pain; and, in life, the footstep of the beloved who never comes; or when he does come, goes on the instant."

"Good-bye."

"What do you listen for?" she cried.

"A change of wind, perhaps. Adios."

He turned from her rapidly, but as he turned she knelt suddenly at his side, snatched his hand and kissed it. "Thank you," he said, "but men are not worthy of that, señora." He withdrew his hand and hobbled a few steps away. At this little distance, he called: "I thank you, señora; good night."

He knew that she would not follow him into the darkness: she did not, but he heard her break into a wild crying of tears and lamentation. The last that he saw of her was the grey of her sacking and the pallor of her face, standing looking after him while she lifted up her voice and wept.

Perhaps threequarters of an hour after leaving Rose of the South, when it was (as he judged) a little after two in the morning, Sard saw in front of him the sheds of "the siding beside the jetty." Sard could see no horses, but there was an engine on the line with steam up; a glow was on the smoke coming from its funnel; a glare from its fire made the stoker and driver ruddy with light. The engine was headed inland with a load of trucks coupled to it. Men were moving about between the quay and the trucks, either loading or unloading something heavy.

At any other time he might have wondered why men were shipping copper ore at midnight during a norther, though indeed the jetty was screened from the wind by the high land beyond it. He had no suspicion of these men. He was perhaps stupid from poison and fatigue; he thought that he had reached his rest.

One of the workers came away from the trucks to get a drink at a scuttle-butt. Sard heard the chain of the dipper clink, and the water splash. Then the man spat and went slowly back to work, singing in a little low clear voice the song about the rattlesnake.

"There was a nice young man,
    He lived upon a hill;
A very nice young man,
    I knew him we-e-ell.
To-me-rattle-to-me-roo-rah-ree."

Sard drew nearer, to look for Miguel and the horses. He came
down on to a loop-line, crossed it, and passed between sheds and
shacks, some piles of pit props, fuel blocks and drums of wire rope,
on to the pier-head. A naphtha-flare was burning there to give
light to a gang of men who were handing cases from a launch,
which lay below the level of the jetty, to the trucks coupled up to
the engine. Even then, Sard did not see at once what company he
had come among. One of the men, who had been watching his
advance whistled. A man, who seemed to be in authority, moved
up swiftly and rather threateningly on the right: two other men
came up from the left: the work of the gang stopped. The men
put down the cases which they were carrying and faced Sard in a
pointed manner. Most of them had been humming or singing to
themselves as they worked, but their singing stopped on the instant. More than this, a voice in the launch asked:

"What's the rally?"

One of the men in front of Sard replied, without turning his
head: "Strangers in the house."

Three heads showed over the edge of the jetty, then three more
men sprang up from the launch on to the jetty itself. Sard found
himself facing about a dozen men, with other men closing in on
each side of him. All the men were silent, most of them were
watching him intently, though some peered into the night behind
him. All the men, without perceptible motion, had pistols in
their hands.

"Stop just right where you are, brother," the man on Sard's
right said.

Sard stopped.

"Drop them palos and put them up." The tone rather than
the words made Sard drop his sticks and lift his hands.

"Are you alone?" the man asked.

"Yes."

"Move right down to the edge of the jetty. Keep your hands up."

"I can't walk without sticks."

"Walk him down there, two of you."

Two of them did "walk him down" to the edge of the jetty. Ill as Sard was, the men, their voices and their every action, made him feel that his life hung upon a thread.

He knew, too late, that he had come upon a gang of rum-runners in the act of putting their freight ashore. There was no question of showing fight; he could only hope that they would not shoot him in the back and leave him to the crabs.

He was walked to the hard-wood blinders at the very edge of the jetty. He saw beneath him a broadish stretch of water reaching to the high land beyond. The river bar was noisy at some little distance to his left. Just below him was a scow-launch half full of cases. She was lifting and drooping a little to the motion of the water. A deck hand, sitting on her forward gunwale, was staring up at him. A short, foreign-looking man, with a bush of hair under which gold earrings shone, came out from the covered engine-room abaft all, and stood there, in a glow of light, holding on by the wheel. He, too, stared up at Sard, but went on eating an onion: he did not speak. His eyes were intensely bright: his shirt, which was whitish, with a few coloured stripes, seemed to shine as though it were made of silk.

Sard took all these things in very exactly in an instant of time, but noticed most the man with the bright eyes who munched the onion and stared. The deck hand who was sitting forward pitched a folded tarpaulin over some cases directly below Sard. He did it on the instant, with a backward jerk of his hand. Sard knew on the instant what had passed through the man's mind; that it would be a pity if his, Sard's, corpse should break any of the good rum bottles in falling.

The man in authority called out behind Sard.

"If there are any more of you, who try to lift a finger, over your friend goes."

Sard kept very still; everybody was very still, except for the launchman munching his onion and the clicking back of revolver cocks. The man in authority called out again:

"Go through him, you two."

The two men "went through" Sard's pockets, not like thieves, but like policemen.

"Is he heeled?"

"No, sir; he's got a knife. He's been in the water."

"He'll be in again, for keeps, if he tries any monkey-tricks. Now, brother, answer me and no damned shinanniking. Are you alone?"

"Yes," Sard said.

"Who are you?"

"A sailor."

"What in hell are you doing here?"

"I've been on a sting-ray and came here to get a horse from Miguel."

"What the hell do you know of Miguel?"

"I heard he had horses here."

"Who told you he had horses here?"

"Some people in the poblacion."

The man in authority called to one of the other men:

"Antonio!"

"Si, señor."

"Here a moment."

Sard heard the man go across to the officer. They talked together in a low tone for a minute: Sard could not hear what they said. Presently the officer called again:

"You, brother: turn round."

Sard turned about into the light of the flare, to find himself covered by half a dozen revolvers.

"Do you know him, any of you?" the officer asked.

The men stared at him, then gave their verdict that they did not know him. "No, sir." "Never seen him." "Never set eyes on him." One man, who had been standing aloof, somewhat behind the officer, came forward, to have a nearer look. He was a man of short stature, but enormous breadth of chest. He had sallow face, intensely bright black eyes, a short nose, a mouth of unusual width slowly working upon a quid of tobacco, and both hands thrust forward into deep waistcoat pockets, where they rested on revolver butts. He came forward slowly, chewing his tobacco, with a goodhumoured leer upon the world. There was something in his slouch which was of the very essence of the man: it was his style: his pace à lui: if the world wished to go faster or slower, it might, for all he cared, nothing would make him change. He came to within a few paces of Sard, who seemed to remember that slouch and leer, but could not place the man.

"D'you know him, Doug?"

"Nar."

He winked at Sard with one eye and slouched off to the left, to stand among the other men.

"What's your name?" the officer asked.

"Harker."

"What ship do you belong to?"

"The *Pathfinder*."

"That's a god-dam lie," one of the men said, "the *Pathfinder* sailed last night."

"Will you just stopper your lip?" the officer said. "If I want your dam' soprano in this duet, I'll call it."

"Well, it is a god-dam lie," the man said. "She did sail."

"You hear what this man says?" the officer said. "That your ship sailed last night. What have you to say?"

"I missed my passage," Sard said. "I was ashore, cycling. My bicycle was stolen: I trod upon a sting-ray down on the beach and came hopping here to try to get a horse, to take me to Las Palomas."

"That's a dam' likely tale," one of the men said.

"Py Chesus," another said, "he trod upon a tam sting-ray! Py Gott, he iss a got-tam police-spy."

"Less lip," the officer said. He seemed to debate the evidence within his mind for an instant, then he said:

"What are you in the *Pathfinder?*"

"Mate."

"What were you doing ashore, cycling, when your ship was sailing?"

"I came out to see an Englishman in the house along the beach there."

"What Englishman?"

"Kingsborough."

"Did you see him?"

"Yes."

"Is he a friend of yours?"

"No."

"What brought you to him, then, when your place was on board your ship?"

"I heard that he was threatened by a gang of rough-necks, so I rode out to warn him."

"You did? Did you also warn the police?"

"I did."

This roused a storm among the men: there were cries of "Narker!" "Put it on him, George!" "I set he was a spy, py Gott!" "Hay que matarle!" etc.

"What business was it of yours, to warn the police?" the officer said.

"One would do as much as that for one's countryman, I hope."

"What did the police undertake to do?"

"I do not know."

"Give me the god-dam truth now. Whom did you see at the police?"

"No one. I sent word there."

"By whom?"

"Find out."

At this point, which might have been troublous but for intervention, the Scandinavian interfered. He was a sinister-looking man with a swollen lower lip which drooped. This gave him permanently the look of a gargoyle. He looked, on the whole, like a young devil just after his first night in hell, a little bloated and battered, but thrilled by the way Beelzebub wore his bowler. He came forward towards the officer.

"Mr. O'Prien," he said, "dis feller he wass one got-tam police-spy. What he want de police for? What he come putt in for?

He call hisself mate of de *Pathfinder*, by Chesus. Py Chesus, I don't pelieve one got-tam wort he say, py Chesus. And this got-tam yarn about a got-tam sting-ray. You see, fellers, he iss a spy. Dat's what dis feller is: a spy. He tell de police and get us pinched."

The black-eyed smiling sloucher slouched forward as the Scandinavian warmed to his appeal. His left hand shot out suddenly, caught him on the chest and slung him violently backward. The motion seemed effortless, but the strength used must have been that of a bull, for the Scandinavian went backwards tottering for five steps and then sat down. The other men laughed. The sloucher grinned at the Scandinavian.

"Come off with your folly," he said. "Tell it to the marines but not to the deck department."

The Scandinavian rose up whimpering and rubbing the sore place.

"Py Chesus, Doug," he said, "if you wass not trunk, I make you pay for dat. It's your being trunk saves you, py Chesus."

"Well, I am drunk," Doug said, "I thank God I am drunk. I like being drunk: it's so cadoodle. But let's see this man who says he's mate of the *Pathfinder*. Keep all fast with your enquiries till I've had a go at him." He slouched up towards Sard, with his hands drooped down as before on the revolver-butts in his waist-coat pockets. His whole being seemed to slouch, to smile and to chew tobacco. He seemed to be chewing a sort of cud of tobacco. He seemed to give forth a gospel of slouching, smiling and chewing tobacco. He stood slouched before Sard, a man of immense strength, fearing nothing on earth and capable of any folly and any kindness. Sard could not place him, even yet, but the slouch was familiar; he had surely seen that grin before.

" 'Arker, my bye," Douglas began. Instantly a thrill shot through Sard, for the words "my bye," spoken in that way, gave him a clue to the speaker. " 'Arker, my bye, answer my question, my bye. Who's the captain of the *Pathfinder?*"

"Captain Cary."

"What mark has he got on the right side of his chin?"

"A mole; a dark brown mole."

"Down in the cabin of the *Pathfinder*, what is hung on the starboard bulkheads?"

"Nothing at all, except two canary cages."

"What is the name of that black cat you have?"

"Nibbins."

"What is odd about your fiferails?"

"We have small hand-winches on them (monkey-winches), so that we can get a bit on anything, with two men and a boy."

"That's right enough," Douglas said, "he belongs to the *Pathfinder* all right."

"That's not in question," the officer said. "The questions are, what he is doing here and what he has been doing with the police."

Again there might have been trouble, but for intervention. This time the launch-man interfered. He had finished his onion and had licked his fingers and was now on the jetty close to Sard.

"Meesta O'Brien," he said.

"Avast heaving," O'Brien said.

"Meesta O'Brien."

"I'm dealing with this man here."

"Meesta O'Brien, I wanna know."

"What in hell d'you want to know?"

"I wanna know how long we stay-a here? The capitan-a he say-a to me be back by the six-a bell. Here it come the six-a bell. The whiska still in the launch-a and all a talk-a, talk-a, talk-a and wow-wow-wow with-a the pistol."

"Get to hell out of this!"

"No, I tell you, I not get-a to hell; not for you I not get-a hell; I get-a to hell when I like, what road I like. But the capitan-a, he say-a to me, be along-a the side at six-a bell. Here it come the six-a bell. And all the stuff lie in the launch-a and you talk-a, talk-a. Why you not get the stuff out of the launch? It six-a bell, soon seven-a bell. I tell-a you now, I tell-a all of you. You get-a this stuff out of the launch. Or if you not get-a this stuff out of the launch, I tell-a you what I do. I get-a to hell out of here: see? I go back straight away to the capitan-a. He soon see what for, hey. He know why you talk-a, talk-a. He want to know what-a for."

"Shut your dam' Dago head!"

"You tell-a me to shut-a my head. I shut-a your head. I got-a stiletto, good as your pistol. What for you tell-a me to shut-a my head? Shut-a your own head. You get-a the stuff out of the launch. Never mind you this sick-a man, but get-a the whisk out of the launch. My Jesu, too much-a talk-a talk-a. Get-a the launch clear, see, or I go back to the capitan-a. I cast-a loose, I go, see."

"See here now, Jesus-Maria, mind yourself. I'll clear your launch and you too, in my own time. I'm captain in this gang, and I'm going to be it."

"You are not capitan-a in my launch. I am. And if you not get-a out the stuff, I not-a stay."

Douglas, the sloucher, came forward again, not addressing either Jesus-Maria or O'Brien, but the men.

"Come on, boys," he said, "we've still got some of these dam' medical comforts to sling ashore."

"We'll get the stuff ashore, when we've finished this enquiry," O'Brien said. "I want to know about this man." He turned again to Sard. "What are you?" he asked. "A Protestant?"

"Yes, thank God."

The men cheered Sard for this, not because they were Protestants, but because O'Brien was not. One of the men, who had taken no part whatever in the court of enquiry, but had been sitting on some pit props drinking from a bottle, now came up to Sard and shook his hand.

"Shake hands," he said, "if you're a Protestant. You belong to a blurry fine religion, if you're a Protestant. I'm not, if you understand what I mean, a Protestant myself, if you understand what I mean, but I do believe in crissen berrel, which is as near as the next, if you understand what I mean."

"Come along, George," Douglas said, "we'll get this medical comfort ashore and then we'll have one long cool one on the house."

"Are you a Protestant?" George asked.

"Sure, Mike."

"There's a lot of fellows going about," George said, "if you understand what I mean, who call themselves blurry Buddhists.

I'll shake hands with a Protestant and I'll shake hands with a Mahommedan. It's true they have a lot of wives. I honour them for it. I'd do the same myself if I could afford it. But these Buddhist fellows: I want to tell you about these Buddhist fellows. All right, Mr. O'Brien, if you don't want to listen, you can do the other thing. These Buddhist fellows, they're not Buddhist fellows, if you know what I mean, they're a secre-ciety. That is," he concluded, "if you understand what I mean."

"They're a lot of vegetarians," Douglas said. "But come on, boys, and let's get the stuff ashore."

"You'll not get-a the stuff ashore," came from the Italian on the launch. "The capitan-a tell-a me 'be back by six-a bell.' You not clear-a the launch, so now I go. I tell-a the capitan-a. He give-a you what-a for."

The launch had been thrust clear of the jetty; she lay two boat-lengths away, canted so that the current was swinging her.

"Come back with that launch, you Jesus-Maria!"

The Italian made an obscene gesture and sent the launch at full speed for the distant ship.

"There," one of the men said, "there you are, O'Brien; half the cases not ashore, all because you want to hold a private Old Bailey."

"And I'm going to hold it," O'Brien said. "This man is a police spy and I'm going to shoot him."

"You'll shoot him, hell," Douglas said.

"Not on your life," George said, "not on your life. He is a Protestant, if you understand what I mean. And why is he a Protestant? Because he isn't a low-down vegetarian secre-ciety Buddhist. Because he isn't a Mahommedan. He might have been a Mahommedan. They offered him seven wives, if you understand what I mean, and he scorned the action. 'No,' he said, 'I'm a Protestant,' he said, 'to blazes with your houris,' he said. That's right, isn't it? That's what he said. Isn't it what you said?"

"Now, George Henderson, mind yourself now, or I'll put a head on you which you'll remember."

"You'll put a head on me? Who'll put a head on me?"

"I will."

"You silly blighter, we're not in Ireland here, we're talking religion at El Cobre."

"No, we're not talking religion," O'Brien said; "we're landing rum, and I'm going to see that we land it safely. What is this man but a spy?"

"He's no spy," Douglas said, "he's a sailor like yourself."

"Only he's ate a damn sight less flapdoddle," someone added.

"Well, if he's no spy, what are we going to do with him?"

"Let him have Miguel and the horses and ride back to Las Palomas as he wants."

"So that he can leave word with the police in time to have us headed off at the mines. To hell with him having the horses!"

"He cannot in any case have the horses," said the man known as Antonio, "since Miguel took the horses, some time since, by the footpath."

"He can stay here, then, after we are gone."

"Well, O'Brien, I wonder at you," Douglas said. "Here's a man half dead, as you can see, from poison, and a better fellow, I daresay, than any of us. If we leave him here, he'll be dead before noon, from cold and exposure. He's coming in the cars with us to Tloatlucan, where he can take the branch line to Las Palomas before noon. And meanwhile, boys," he added, raising his voice, "here's a man pretty damn wet and sick; what do you say to dibs all round to give him a dry shift? I say a pair of trousers."

They all said something out of the little they had. O'Brien moved away to talk to the engine-driver. Douglas and Antonio brought Sard the dry shift and helped him to change. "Here's a dry shift," Douglas said. "And I'm afraid they're like a pig's breakfast, a little of all sorts."

"Get on board here," O'Brien said.

"On board, hell," Douglas answered. "This man's not shifted yet."

"I don't give a pea-vren. This ain't Delmonico's, nor Maggy Murphy's. This train's going."

"It's going, hell," Douglas answered.

"Very well, then; it'll go without you."

"Without me, hell!"

O'Brien turned from him savagely, darted forward to the engine-driver and cursed the other hands into the cars. Douglas winked at Sard. "Chief officer's perk," he said. "All the same, we'd better hop it."

The nearest car to them was the last in the train, and empty but for some tarpaulins and rolls of slickers. Douglas helped Sard into it, hove his wet things after him, and was starting to heave himself in, when the train started. A man less strong in the arms would have been pitched headlong, but Douglas clambered into the car, made a warm corner for Sard, covered him up and sat beside him.

"Ambitious swab, that terrier," he said. "How are you feeling?"

"Very grateful to you," Sard said, "for without you, things would have gone hard with me. Who are you? Aren't you Castleton? Weren't you once C.P.F.?"

"Yes. I used to be Castleton, C.P.F. I was a year senior to you," Douglas said. "You wouldn't remember me, for that reason; but I remembered you. You see, I've got a memory which can't forget. I often wish it could."

"I remember you now, of course," Sard said. "But when were you on board the *Pathfinder?*"

"Never."

"But how did you know about Captain Cary's mole; and the cat, and the monkey-winches?"

"Three days ago I passed under the *Pathfinder's* stern, as I went ashore to see my girl. I saw a man with a mole on his chin doing hygrometer at the taffrail. I knew it must be the captain. It couldn't have been anybody else. The cat was fooling about on deck and the old man called it Nibbins. As for the monkey-winches on the fiferail, you were clearing a boat with one of them. I thought it a dam' fine little contrivance."

"But how did you know about the cabin bulkheads?"

"I didn't. The point was that you did."

"Well, you staggered me," Sard said. "I was wondering when you could have been on board."

"It's a dam' easy game, being mysterious, when you've anything at all to go on. Your Christian name's Chisholm, isn't it? I saw you first on 2nd February, 1883. I remember you coming on board, by the tug, when you were a new chum. The chests were hove in on the port lower deck and the lock of your chest was broken by that old fool Goose-rump letting it drop off the slide."

"I remember," Sard said. "You swore at old Goose-rump. You sailed with him later, by the way. What became of old Goose-rump?"

"He went to hell on the Barbary coast."

"What are you doing?"

"Running rum up to Entre las Montanas."

"It must be exciting work," Sard said.

"It's the finest life on earth. That dam' terrier is an ambitious swine, but even he can't spoil it. I count all my life just wasted till I began rousting rum. I've been at it seven years."

"You've got a ticket, haven't you?"

"Ticket, hell. Yes, I've got a dam' fine second mate's ticket, for which I could get four pounds a month and find my own tobacco. Ticket, hell! Watch and watch, when it isn't all hands, boxing another man's yards around. Ticket, hell! At this job I'm pretty well my own master; sleep when I like, get drunk when I like, and see my girl when I like."

"Are you married?"

"Married, hell."

"Isn't it a rather dangerous life? Things may have been slack, but they're tautening up. I hear that Colonel Mackenzie is going to put an end to rum-running. The penalties are severe."

"We've a stronger combination than some think."

"I don't doubt it. The combination is strengthening against you. Two torpedo-boats on the coast would stop you."

"We'd buy them."

"Not with Colonel Mackenzie."

"We'd get them, then."

"How?"

"Put a stick of dynamite in the crankshaft."

"Where do you go with this train of rum?"

"We go right up the mountains with it, till we reach the jumping-off place."

"Do you never have trouble?"

"We have had a certain amount of trouble. There was trouble on the Mesa Line one time. But trouble, hell. You lie still and get your strength."

"Heya, you, Doug!"

"Heya yourself."

As the train jolted up towards the mines, along the bank of the river, a man came catlike towards them, from truck to truck, from the direction of the engine. He hung on somehow by his eyelids, and jangled as he came with hook-pots of hot cazuela slung round his neck. From time to time jolts of the truck spilt the hot broth on to his knees. When this happened, he cursed in Spanish. He it was who called Douglas from his talk.

"Cazuela," he said. "Catch a hold. And here's a hook-pot for the other fella."

"Got any pan?"

"Mucho pan."

Douglas leaned out, took the hook-pots with the care of one well used to guarding an allowance, gave a pot to Sard, and then salved the bread, which was supplied in yellow hot buns split and filled with sausage and peppers.

"That's more homelike," Doug said. "Heave round and eat: it will give you strength."

Sard did not want to eat: the thought of the hot dough made him faint, but he sipped the broth and felt the better for it. He was warm again, there in the shelter of the car under the tarpaulins. With the warmth came a queer feeling in his skin, all altered by the poisons which had afflicted it, that the norther was going to be a bad one. He felt too weak to look at the heaven, but he said to Doug:

"Is it very black to the northward?"

"A bit dark."

"Much lightning?"

"Yes. It has been flashing a little."

"We're in for a bad norther."

"We're in a norther," Doug answered. "But we're running out of it. But you'd better sleep. I'll cant these slickers from under you, for the hands will want them. Now, sleep."

Sard was so weary that he was almost asleep while Doug routed out the slicker rolls. He felt Doug heave a tarpaulin over him and smelt the overpowering sweet rum-like smell of the Lucky Hit being chewed in Doug's mouth; he noticed the stars going out under trails of smoke; then the world ceased for him while the train jolted on.

He woke, or half woke, when the stopping of the train sent all the rear trucks one after the other with a bumping clank into the buffers of the truck in front of it. He did not know where he was and did not much care, being as weak and drowsy as one full of a drug. He noticed that Doug was gone, but heard, as it were far away, Doug's voice saying something to someone about uncoupling the last three trucks. In his drowse he heard men swearing at chains which clanked: then he heard men pushing the truck in which he was a little further down the line. He heard their "O heave! O heave!" and "That's got her. There she goes!" and the sound of their feet padding beside the rails. He heard someone say: "That's you. Leave them there," and then the motion stopped and the feet moved away. The wind seemed to have risen during the passage from the coast, but he could not care. He was not awake enough to care much about anything. He heard in his drowse the noise of engines, steam was being let off, a shunting engine went swiftly by, and above these noises there came at intervals a dull grunting thud or stamp from some machine or pump not far from the railway. Men moved to and fro, and voices called, there was a noise of running water and of wind. Afterwards, it seemed to him that while he was at this place, wherever it was, he heard men running. The thought came into his brain that he was at Tloatlucan, where he would presently get a shift-train to Las Palomas, but he felt that all that would be presently, mañana, not then, not anything like then. He lapsed into sleep again.

In his usual health, he would have been up and out striding on foot to Las Palomas, without waiting for any shift-train, but he was only the wreck of himself, all weak and weary. Perhaps a salvo of guns, a blast of trumpets, or the noise of all three masts going over the side, would have failed to rouse him then. He slept, as sailors say, "dead-oh." He would not have wakened for less than a kick in the face.

Presently, however, he roused again at the battering clank of a train of trucks backing in upon the truck in which he was lying. He roused enough to hear voices and the clank of chain, with the thought that they were doing something with a steam winch, he could not care what. He drowsed off at once into the deeps of sleep into which none but harvesters and sailors ever sink. In his sleep, he became conscious of vibration, as though he were in a berth above the engines in some small steamer under way. It was soothing, or at least not unpleasant, to his mood of feverish drowsiness, to be shaken thus, perhaps he slept the better for it.

For some hours he slept. Gradually, as he came to himself, he found himself listening in his sleep for the bell, so that he might know how much of his watch remained to him. The bell did not strike, though he hearkened after it. He felt cold, and was aware that sprays were hitting the side of the deckhouse continually.

Then, punctually at the "one bell," at the moment at which he would have been called, he roused up wide awake with the knowledge that something was very wrong indeed.

He was accustomed to turning out and being on deck within a minute. He roused up now with one heave, weak, stiff and aching as he was, ready for action. He came to himself, remembering all the events of the night before, and at once took stock of things. He was in the truck, which was jolting along a bad line at about fifteen miles an hour. It was daylight, yet all dim with storm. The hitting on the truck which he had taken to be sprays on the deckhouse was sand, pelting in from the desert. The floor of the truck was covered with a fine layer of sand. A pelt of sand flew over the side of the car continually. As he stood shakily up to see where he was, the sand blew into his eyes, hair and mouth, down his neck, into his clothes, into his lungs. It came on a cold wind in little dry particular pellets. Hard snow coming in a gale has a similar power of annoying and confusing; this had a power beyond snow, of maddening. It stung like hard snow, but after it had stung it did not melt, it remained as grit where it had fallen, in the clothes, the eyes or the mouth.

He could see, perhaps, sixty yards to windward and a hundred yards to leeward of his truck, which seemed to be somewhere towards the end of a goods or freight train. The train was going along a waterless land which was sometimes a scrub of chaparral and mezquite and sometimes a desert, with cactus and prickly pear. Over all this expanse the accursed norther came down like a devil pelting sand, never in any great volume, but in a drift which never ceased. Sard noticed that the side of the next truck to his had already had a kind of polish given to it by the never-ceasing pitting of the pellets.

He knew that the "norther" being as cold as it was, must be blowing from within three points of north. This gave him the train's course as roughly north-west. The sort of glow in the sky, which marked where the sun would be, as well as his own sense of time, always very acute, showed him that it was about eight o'clock in the morning. Reckoning that the train had picked up his trucks between three and four o'clock, he judged that he had been carried some sixty or seventy miles into the desert of Tloatlucan, and that the next stop would be fifty miles further on, in the foothills beyond the desert, where the railway began its climb into the Sierra.

Doug and his brother smugglers had of course gone with their freight on the other fork of the railway far to the west. Looking about in the sand on the floor of the truck, Sard found a hook-pot half full of cold cazuela and two of the small loaves stuffed with sausage. He was glad of these, in spite of their being gritty with sand. When he had breakfasted, he felt more like himself.

As he could neither stop the train nor get out of it he went on with it, wondering how soon he would be able to return. And as he wondered, he took stock of his equipment. He was dressed in a pair of old serge trousers belonging to Doug, a pair of slippers which had been cut down from bluchers, an old flannel shirt, as clean and soft as lint, a blue dungaree jacket, blackened with stains of dried oil, plainly the gift of one of the launch-men, and a tam-o'-shanter working-cap, wanting the topknot, which had once belonged to a sailor in the French battleship *Suffren*. He had his own belt and knife, an old blue handkerchief printed with the legend "A present from Bradford," a paper collar, one sock and one stocking. His own wet clothes, which he had put in the truck, were gone. His watch, his money, penknife, key-ring and "pocket tool chest," a little appliance containing a marler, screwdriver, nipper, spanner and corkscrew, were all gone. He had put them into the pocket of the dungaree jacket, when he had changed his clothes, but they were gone. He had nothing but the clothes in which he stood, his sheath-knife and a little brown pocket-case which contained a few pulpy visiting-cards, some stamps ruined by the wet, a few matches and three crushed xicale flowers.

He had lost his job, his passage, his clothes, his possessions, his identity. He was being carried across the desert into the heart of a continent. What he was to do when he left the train, in order to get back to Las Palomas, was not very clear.

"After all," he said, "there will be someone at the way-station who will let me have a passage back in a truck. When once I am there, I can get along."

The events of the night before seemed to belong to a past life or to another man. He rose up again to take stock of his whereabouts and to see if he could see a train-hand. He saw the trucks forging and jolting ahead. Beyond the trucks, both in front and behind, were the high, closed, yellow, wooden Occidental freight-cars, marked with capacity marks in dull red. The train lurched and jangled along the desert in a ceaseless pelt of sand. The sand was merciless and pitiless, a little and a little and a little. The chaparral bowed a little to it, the cactus seemed to put back its ears. Everything was dry with it, gritty, cracked, burnished. The persistence of its small annoyance told on all things. As the dropping of water wears the stone, so the pelting of the sand wore the spirit. Sard remembered what he had heard of these northers: how the children are kept from school lest they should mutiny, and how men, maddened by that insistent patting, will strike and kill. The thought crossed his mind that if he had to walk back along the track in that pelting, that annoyance of the tiny hands pat-pat-patting on face and hands would be soon unbearable. Even there, sheltered in the truck, it came pat-pat-patting, flying like a little dry-shot over the sides, filtering up through cracks in the bottom, and dancing there, like grains in a spring, till they were flung away. From time to time the dry, quiet pat-pat-patting deepened to a noise of water, with a roaring and a swish, into which the train joggled, lurched, jangled and clanked, and at last seemed to tread down and over-roar.

He had plenty of thoughts to worry him. First of these was disappointment that he had not seen "Her," as he had hoped, the night before; next to this came rage at missing his passage; then came anxiety for that brother and sister in Los Xicales; what had happened to them? Lastly, from somewhere in the background of his mind, the thought came that it might not be easy to rejoin the *Pathfinder*. It was going to be a good deal more difficult than he supposed.

"Hi, ya!"

The yell of "Hi, ya" was repeated from somewhere ahead. It was a shout or hail loud enough to be heard above the noise of the train and of the storm. It was addressed to him.

He stood up, screening his eyes from the sand. There, on the top of the freight-car nearest to the trucks, a train-hand lay. He seemed annoyed at Sard's presence. He yelled at him and motioned to him to get out of the truck. He was a hard-looking man with a swollen face and a kind of vindictive energy. He lay crouched on the freight-car, hanging on with his left hand to the iron rail on the car-roof. In his right hand he had a long club, like a baseball club, which had a leather wrist-thong. He shook this club at Sard and motioned to him with it, that he should get out of the car. He also yelled at Sard in Spanish to ask what he was doing on the train and to tell him to get out of it. As he seemed to be an unreasonable man, Sard smiled at him and resumed his seat. The man crept a little nearer, perhaps to make certain that Sard was alone, and shouted:

"I'll have you out of it before long, my white-faced Luterano with the pip!"

"Will you have me out of it by force, or by your sweet persuasion?" Sard asked him.

"You will see."

"That will be something to look forward to."

"You wait."

"I am waiting."

The man crept a foot nearer, spat towards Sard (not very successfully against the norther) and called him some filthy names.

"I will open your bag," he said, "with my knife, which is used to opening the bags of Englishmen. I will see whether it is true that Englishmen have the tripes of cats, as it is said."

"It is quite true," Sard answered. "They have. May I ask if you are in love?"

"I will soon teach you."

"What does your lady love in you; your appearance or your breeding?"

The man champed with his teeth, bit and worried his thumb as though he were a dog and it a bone, and as it were jerked the worry at Sard. It is a passionate gesture which looks more effective than it sounds. Sard smiled at him. Sard was slightly to windward of the man and could speak to him without effort with the certainty of being heard.

"You will get blood-poisoning," he said, "if you bite your thumb with those teeth."

The man seemed to focus into a pair of flaming eyes; the balls of the eyes rolled upwards so as to leave nothing but glaring yellow, then they rolled down in a frenzy. He opened his mouth, grinned with clenched teeth, hissed like a snake and howled like a hyæna. He spat thrice at Sard, nodded at him, and then retreated along the freight-car top out of sight. Sard noticed then that another train-hand was watching him from the nearest freight-car to the rear of him. This man did not speak, and did not meet his eyes. When Sard looked at him the man dropped his eyelids and seemed to be looking at the ground, but in another instant he was watching again and making a motion that Sard should leave the cars. Sard could not see him so clearly as he had seen the other man, but he made out a look of shiftiness and hardness, a mixture of

142

prison and the boxing-ring, yet tanned, as it were, or coloured with the fineness of endurance. A sort of glimmer of high quality showed in the pitiless evil mug, as in the faces of old soldiers, with bad records, who have been through great campaigns. Sard judged that this man was not an Occidental. There was a look of English or American about him. Then he did not speak nor threaten: he used neither curse nor club, only watched. Presently he caught Sard's eyes and undoubtedly made the motion that Sard should leave the cars.

"Beat it, kid," the man cried.

This seemed so unreasonable that Sard paid no heed to him: he looked the other way.

"Beat it," the man cried. "Pasea."

Sard looked at him; then looked away.

"Hell and Maria," the man said, "if you ain't got a gall!"

Perhaps in normal runs the train-hands on that freighter foregathered for talk, drink or cards in the after car. Perhaps the three trucks in the middle of the train made the journey impossible on this occasion, or it maybe that Sard, the unknown man sitting in the truck, with the look of one able to guard himself, made them think the norther not worth the facing. They did not attempt the journey. The train pounded and jangled on across the desert, in the ceaseless pelting and pitting of the sand. The train presently reached a part of the desert where the wind for some reason had more scope. Perhaps the line there crossed the mouth of some great gut in the distant Sierra. The wind suddenly rose in strength and voice, lifting the sand so that it looked like a smoke into which the train had to butt. "Ai, ai!" it cried, just as it cries in rigging, while the sand came over like sprays. Sard kept well ducked down under a tarpaulin. When he looked up from his place towards his left, he sometimes saw the train-hand watching him. Whenever their eyes met, the train-hand motioned to him to leave the cars. Presently the train-hand grew weary of such foolishness: he shouted something which Sard could not hear, and then beat his way aft, out of sight.

Sard knew enough about the train-hands on these freighters to be sure of evil from them. Hoboes had killed so many train-hands that now the train crews always carried clubs, which they used on any hoboes who were unable to pay their way or to defend themselves. Sard had no doubts about being able to defend himself, but that evil face abaft-all made him wonder how he was to get back across the desert to Las Palomas. How would he fare, he wondered, if the train-hands on the returning train were that sort of men? He realised that he was not now Sard Harker, the mate of a crack ship, but a ragged-looking rough-neck, dirty and unshaven, who would get "the hoboes' deal, a bat on the head and six months' road-gang." He began to have misgivings about his future.

For another two hours the train ran on across the storm. It was running away from the storm, all the time, so that the violence of the wind and the annoyance of the sand both abated. Presently the sand ceased to pelt, the train ran out into the sun, leaving behind it a cloud of sand-coloured storm, stretching up into the heaven, where it smoked like sulphur fumes.

Now on both hands in a winking bright light was the desert of the Indios Salvajes with the Sierra of the Holy Ghost beyond. After the misery of the night and the nuisance of the storm, the beauty of the wilderness was overwhelming. It lay in a half-circle, stretching for ninety miles under the spine of the Sierra. It was all shining, vast, mysterious, lonely beyond belief, empty of any life that was not poisonous and spined and savage. There were patches of chaparral, a few mezquite trees, a few giant cactuses. The most of it was empty shining sand, many-coloured, flitting, sometimes danced over by eddies. Rocks of violent colours rose out of it like the bones of dead beasts. Parts of it seemed to be alive and thinking, other parts of it seemed dead from old time, all parts of it drew Sard like a temptation.

He knelt on his tarpaulin to stare at it. He had known the desert of the sea for a good many years. There men exist by effort and strength, pitting their worth against it day by day. This was the desert of the land, which calls men, not to try their worth, but to consider their nature and their source, and to let all their effort and their strength be absorbed in that contemplation.

He felt power come into him from that vast expanse which bore no life, or almost none, that was not deadly, yet had absorbed for centuries, unshielded, the energy of the sun in his strength.

At about midday the train, which had been running in sight of the Sierra, passed so close under the foothills that Sard lost sight of them. He was feeling rested and well: his leg was still numb, but fit for use. He looked ahead along the line. There in an opening of the foothills a couple of miles away were the houses of a settlement. They were adobe houses, some of them limewashed, under a roll of foothill which bore the marks of silver-mining. There was a white church with a red-tiled campanile pierced in the Mission fashion for three bells. Sard could see that there was a station here. Something made him look back suddenly behind him. He was not in any danger, but from his perch in the after car the hard-faced man was watching him.

"Beat it, kid," the man shouted. "Beat it like hell." He signed to Sard to leap from the car on the desert side. "Kid," he cried, "this ain't no kid glove foolishness. You wanna beat it just like smoke."

Unfortunately, Sard had heard of men shot while trying to "beat it" from a freight car. He did not want to beat it, but to explain his presence and get a lift back to the coast. Besides, with one leg numb from poison, it was not easy to beat it while the train was moving. The train-hand shook his head much as Pilate washed his hands; he moved aft along the cars out of sight again.

The Occidental train-hand, who had promised to look at his tripes, reappeared for an instant to make sure that he was still there. He showed his teeth at Sard and made a motion of cutting open a waistcoat with the upward sweep of one hand. The train slackened speed so that Sard could hear the clanging of the bell on the engine. Looking out, he could see the population of the town sauntering to the station to watch the train come to a stop. She curved in to the platform, which had been made there some years before for a President's visit. Only the engine and one car could draw to the platform at one time. On the end of the station building the name of the place, Tlotoatin, was painted on a plank. The train stopped.

As she stopped, Sard laid hold of the truck side to swing himself out. At that instant, the train jerked forward and then backwards violently, so that he was pitched down into his truck. He was out of the train just three seconds after the train-hands.

To his surprise, neither of these men made any movement towards him: they stood watching, while a squad of soldiers followed their officers out of the rear cars. The officers and men wore the grey uniforms and green tejada-de-burro caps of the Nacionales. The officers plainly knew of Sard's presence on the train. They came straight towards him with drawn revolvers in their hands. One of the officers was an elderly captain, fat, pompous, slow-witted, and with a face like a slab of something: the other was a little thin dapper lieutenant, with legs like pipe-stems cased in tight patent-leather boots to the knees. Sard knew at once that these men were coming back to barracks after being escort to a consignment of silver from the mines. He saluted the officers, who did not return his salute: on the contrary, they seemed indignant at his saluting. A couple of soldiers covered Sard with their rifles.

"Who are you?" the captain asked.

Sard told him.

"So. You speak Spanish. What are you doing on the line?"

Sard told him.

"A likely story, eh, lieutenant?"

"Very likely, my captain."

"You know the law against trespass on the line?"

"No, captain," Sard said.

"That is false," the captain answered; "since you know Spanish, you must know it."

"I am English, and do not," Sard said.

"That is false," the captain answered. "You are not English. You are French. Your cap proves it. You are a deserter from the French ship which called here."

"If there be any English or Scotchman here," Sard said, "or any American, I can prove that I am English."

"We desire no proof, since we need none. You were on the line, that suffices; without papers, which clinches it. You are arrested."

"You had better not arrest me," Sard said; "in spite of my clothes, I am an officer, equal in rank to yourself."

"Enough words," the captain said.

"By many, too many words," the lieutenant said.

"At least," Sard said, "you can telegraph to the British Consul at Las Palomas about me, or send me to him."

"It is not for you to prescribe our course of action," the captain said. "You are arrested. Your case will have every consideration. Meanwhile, to the barracks."

"To the barracks: march," the lieutenant added.

If he had resisted, perhaps if he had said another word, they would have shot him and pitched him down a disused working. Sard knew that the silver escorts were apt to shoot to save trouble. He judged it best to submit. "They are cross from the sandstorm," he thought; "soon they will have lunched; then they will listen to reason; or I can get word to some Englishman, or to the Consul." Like all sailors, he had the utmost contempt for soldiers; to be jailed by soldiers was a bitter experience.

The guards fell in on each side of him; two men came behind him with fixed bayonets; the officers brought up the rear with drawn revolvers; the captain called "March!" As they set out, the Occidental train-hand darted two steps forward and crouched to screech some insults. He mocked, showed his teeth and jeered at Sard, making again the gesture of the stomach-ripper. "You get him," he screeched in English, "you get-a your bag cut. A te te . . . ucho!"

Just a couple of paces beyond this screamer, the other train-hand stood, twirling his club as though puzzled. He was looking hard at Sard with a face made of broken commandments: Sard expected a bat on the head from him as he passed. He did not get it: the man dropped his eyes as before, and spat sideways as though dismissing the thought of Sard. They passed out of the station enclosure to the town, which was crowded with inhabitants, who had either come to see the train or were now coming to see "the bandit." Most of the citizens were mestizos or Indios. Sard looked in vain for an American or English face. He heard the comments passed upon him.

"An English bandit who robbed the silver train."

"That a white so sickly should have so much blood!"

"Ha, dirty thief, to the gallows!"

"Ho, Englishman, it is not so easy to rob our silver: we are not your Africans from whom you may rob gold."

"Englishman, the garota: cluck-cluck!"

"They say he killed seven before being taken."

"He? An Englishman? They were asleep, covered in their blankets. He stabbed them sleeping."

"Hear you, he killed seven, sleeeping."

"Let them kill him, then. We have enough of these whites at our doors without Englishmen."

The barracks were close to the station. The party marched into the patio of the barrack buildings: the heavy maruca-wood gates were closed behind them. The place looked as dingy as a prison and as mean as a workhouse: it smelt like a cesspool. One end of it, the men's end, was two storeys high and covered with scaling plaster, the sides were one-storey adobe buildings which had been limewashed once since they were built. The left side of the square seemed to be officers' quarters, for it was screened by a verandah. On the side opposite to it were stables, kitchens, and a sort of barton where two charrucas were housed.

"You will be imprisoned till you can give an account of yourself," the lieutenant said. "Take him to the cells, you men."

"I am perfectly ready to go to the cells," Sard said, "but I wish to let the English of this town know that I am here."

"This is not England," the lieutenant said, "but the Occidental Republic, where the English, the Irish, and other accursed gringoes have no voice, save when they mew like cats for the charity of our leavings. Your presence shall be explained to such English as may be here. The brothel-keeper is English and the town-scavenger Irish. There is also a Scotchman in the road-gang for murder. Such are the places of your race among the Occidentales."

"We do the things most needed," Sard answered. "Next to begetting a new race."

"For half a peseta I would blow your brains out."

"Any Occidental would do murder for half a peseta."

148

"You will find, my dog, that we do justice for nothing."

"So America thinks."

The lieutenant whirled right round upon his heel, a complete circle. He gurgled in his throat, thrust his revolver-butt into his mouth and bit it, so that marks showed upon the wood. His face turned black with rage: he stamped with his feet so that Sard expected his little brittle pipe-stems to snap.

"Remove him to the cells," he said, as soon as he could speak.

"I am going to the cells," Sard said. "Remember that you have been warned that you are jailing an officer and will be held responsible." He turned his back upon the lieutenant and followed a corporal through the barton to a yard beyond. In this yard, which was fenced with a high adobe wall, tiled at the top, were the cells. The corporal unlocked the door of one of the cells and motioned to Sard to enter. Sard cast a glance about the yard. He noticed all down the western wall a line of bullet marks about breast-high. He had seen similar marks on walls in Santa Barbara: they marked executions.

"Enter, then," the corporal said. The cell was dirty, but the dirt was old dirt.

"Look," Sard said, pausing at the door. "Will you, or one of your men, send word to the engineers of the mines that I, an Englishman, am in the cells here?"

"Assuredly."

"At once, can you go or send at once?"

"Assuredly."

"I will see that you are rewarded."

"Assuredly."

"Send to the chief English or Scotch engineer at the chief mine."

"Assuredly," the corporal said. "Meanwhile, enter."

Sard entered and was locked in. The corporal opened the grating in the door and said: "How am I to be rewarded for this sending to the engineers?"

"You shall be rewarded when they come."

"Who will reward me?" the corporal asked; "will it be yourself or the engineers?"

"It will be myself."

"Truly, then," the corporal said, "since it will be you who will reward me, when the work is done, it must be you who shall make it worth my while to do it. How much then? A hundred pesetas?"

"Not a penny piece," Sard said, "till the engineers are here. Then indeed you shall be rewarded."

"There is a very wise proverb," the corporal said, " 'Paid first never grieves.' And yet another proverb says, 'Will-pay is a fine bird, but cash-down sings.' "

"There is yet another proverb," Sard answered, " 'The fed hound never hunts,' " and another still, 'Penny-pouched is promise-broken.' "

"These are English proverbs," the corporal said, "and do not concern me. Show me at least the colour of your money, or no message will go."

"There is another proverb," Sard said, "which says, 'Grudging greed gets not.' "

"Adios," the corporal said, "grudging greed will get no food nor drink; no message to any engineer; nor blanket at night, if blanket be needed." He slipped the shutter across the grating and moved across the yard, back into the barton, leaving Sard alone. The cell was empty of any furniture. It measured about seven feet each way. Its roof sloped down from about eight feet at the door to six feet at the back. The floor was earth, the walls adobe, the roof ceiled with plaster, European fashion, against tarantulas. The cell was lit by the omission of one block of adobe just under the eaves at the back. Sard could just see out of this hole by standing on tip-toe. He saw a patch of sandy soil which had been channelled and pitted by people wanting sand; rats were humping about in this among refuse tipped there from the barracks. Beyond the sandy strip and distant about 120 yards was the railway, with its platform, water-tank, fuel-heap, and the legend

Tlotoatin.

Beyond this was the desert, reaching to infinity, where violet rocks gleaming with snow merged into the shimmer of the sky.

150

The shutter of his door was pulled back: a private soldier peered at him through the bars.

"See," he said, "you want a message taken to an engineer?"

"Yes," Sard said.

"Which engineer?"

"Any English engineer. There must be some."

"Yes. There is one, Mason, at Chicuna Mine."

"Can you go to him? Will you go?"

"Yes."

"Will you tell him of me and ask him to come here?"

"Yes. Listen. That corporal is a fool. He is put on to ask money by the lieutenant."

"Indeed."

"He is a greedy one, the lieutenant. But one who will squeeze his feet will bleed his mother, as we say. And to ask money of whom God has afflicted . . ."

"You, who ask no money, shall be well rewarded."

"I ask no reward," the man said. "God forbid that I should make profit from distress. One thing only I would ask: that you lend me your coat, so that I could leave the barracks, since in uniform it is forbidden."

"Truly I will do that," Sard said.

"If you will pass it through the bars," the man said, "then I will put it on and hurry to the Chicuna Mine, so as to be there before the whistle blows. It will blow for dinner and siesta in a few minutes now."

Sard knew that the siesta hour must be very near and that the moment was propitious for the finding of a fellow-countryman. He had only been a few minutes in prison, but already the thought of being locked up through the siesta when he might be outside, made him anxious for the engineer to be there.

"Give to the engineer this card," he said, "and urge him hither at once; any engineer who speaks my tongue."

"There is a penalty," the man said, "if we are caught outside the gates in uniform."

"What penalty?"

"That of the thumbs."

"Still, in this coat," Sard said, "you could surely pass out unobserved?"

"They will not catch me," the man said; "and if they do (though they will not), it will be well worth while, since to help the afflicted can never be a sin. This will I always maintain."

"Surely right," Sard said, stripping off the old and oily jacket. "But here is the disguise for you; this coat. You had better take the cap as well."

Sard could just make out that some other soldiers were in the yard not very far away.

"Is it safe?" he asked. "There are men there who may see you take the coat. Will they betray you, if they see you?"

"Never," the man answered. "They are my brothers, set there to watch for the corporal."

"Take then the coat and cap."

The soldier cast a glance about him, to see if it were safe to take them; then he slipped them through the bars and under his coat. "Wait yet, one moment," he said; "should you desire food or drink, I would buy some, if you would give the penny. I mention this, because otherwise you will have neither food nor drink."

"Thank you, I need neither food nor drink," Sard said, "but only the engineer, as soon as you can bring him."

"Right, Excellency," the man said. "And now it will be necessary that I close the shutter."

"Right," Sard said. "And thank you."

The man closed the shutter. "I will start straight away," he said.

Sard heard him move away to the other soldiers, who were standing in the shade of the wall.

"I have the coat," he said proudly to his comrades. "And not only that, he said, 'You had better take the cap as well.' I had asked for the coat as a disguise, thinking it the limit that I could ask, when, lo, he himself says, 'You had better take the cap as well.' "

There came a roar of laughter from the soldiers.

"Cap and coat too?"

"Yes; and it was he himself who said, 'You had better take

the cap as well.' And I had not thought of the cap. Never once should I have dreamed of it. But he himself thrust it on me, 'Take the cap as well, O take the cap as well.' 'I beseech you,' he said to me, 'take the cap as well.'"

"It is a French cap, Martin," one of the soldiers said. "The Little Twig-Legs remarked of it, that it is a French cap. Thus we have the Paris fashions at Tlotoatin."

"Mind" (another said) "that the French cap do not bring within itself the French crown."

"This Englishman is more innocent than Joseph."

"Wait, Martin," one of the men said; "did not this Englishman offer you money?"

"Money? Why, he has no money. I, who watched his face, know well that he has no money."

"No money and no coat and no cap."

"Stay yet," one objected. "He handed you paper, as I myself observed. Was not that money?"

"It was this, which I was to give to an engineer."

"What engineer?"

"One Mason, of the Chicuna Mine: such being the names which came into my head. He asked, 'Is there an English engineer?' 'Truly,' I said, following my inspiration, 'there is Mason of the Chicuna Mine.' 'Give him this, then,' he said."

"What is it?"

"I know not. Writing. He had several like it."

"Is it English money?"

"No. The English use only gold."

"Accursed Lutherans, and that they steal!"

"I think that the writing is the symbol of a secret society to which all these dogs belong," one of the soldiers said. "These symbols they pass to each other by messengers to give warning of their accursednesses."

"Tear it up then."

"Meanwhile," Martin said, "I will with this coat and this cap to Eustaphia; madre de las putas that she is, even she will assuredly give me one twenty-five for them."

"They are old," a soldier objected. "She will not give one

twenty-five, but one five, or one ten, not a Portuguese milrei more."

"One five or one ten. They are of European weaving and will last for many lives. But to market."

As the soldier passed Sard's door, to market the coat and cap, he called out, with a fair imitation of Sard's voice and accent:

"Take then the coat and cap. You had better take the cap as well."

As a blow, which would have been pleasanter than an answer, was impossible, Sard kept silent, though his thoughts were bitter. In about ten minutes, Martin returned triumphantly. He passed close to the cell-door, so that Sard not only heard him, but smelt the fragrant reek of the hot tamales and annis brandy, which he had bought with the spoils.

"See," he said, "she being glad with brandy gave me one-forty."

"One-forty; is it possible?"

"Let us, then, into our room, away from corporal and Little Twig-Legs."

"Stay yet," one soldier said. "Shall we not give a tamale and a tot of brandy to this Englishman?"

"He has refused it," Martin answered. "He refused it with scorn, almost with insult. 'I need neither food nor drink,' he said, 'only the engineer, who is my sole passion, now that my wife has fled with the lodger.'"

Sard would have been very glad of a tamale and a drink of water, but neither was offered. The men moved off and closed a door behind them. Soon after that, the hooter-whistles blew at three different mines. A trumpeter, taking the time from them, blew a call in the patio of the barracks. For a few minutes Sard could hear the shuffling of many feet, hurrying to those calls to dinner and siesta. "No one will come to me now," Sard said, "for three hours. I am locked in till they choose to remember me, and nobody who knows me knows where I am." He tried the door which was locked, as well as barred across: the upper and lower panels of it were metalled. He tried the walls: they were made of a kind of adobe which had been furnace-burnt: they were brick. The roof he could not easily reach, except at the back of the cell. The floor was of clay, which had been puddled and beetled.

Of all these four barriers, the floor seemed to him to be the most easy to remove. He hung the handkerchief, "A present from Bradford," over the grating in the door, lest some spy should pull back the shutter. When he had done this, he knelt down close to the back of the cell, took out his knife and began to dig bare the lowest courses of adobe.

His knife had been given to him years before as a keepsake by his second in the port main; it had been with him in his first voyage in the *Venturer*, and ever since, in all his sea-going. It had not been taken from him by the soldiers, because they had not expected that any man would carry a weapon where a sailor carries his knife. They tapped his side, breast and hip pockets, but not the middle of his back. The knife was of the common type of sailors' sheath-knife. He had cut nicks on the handle, a nick for every passage completed between port and port; thirty-six nicks altogether. The sheath was not the original sheath, but a gift from a sailor called Panther Jack, who had made it for him in the *Pathfinder* out of an old boot. The knife-blade was worn away to a thin crescent of steel by repeated sharpenings at the grindstone. It was as good a knife as a man might hope for in work aloft, cutting stops or ropes' ends, but it was the poorest kind of trowel. In his eagerness, he put too much weight upon it and snapped the blade across about an inch from the handle.

He was disheartened by this, but continued to scrape till he discovered that the pounded clay on the floor had been laid on a spread of pebbles set in mortar. The mortar was queer stuff, very hard near the pebbles, but soft between them. It took Sard one hour to clear out three pebbles. Under the third was an iron bolt, or nail, the length and weight of a marline-spike. It had been bent a little. In its day it had had a good deal of battering. It was rusty, but very well fitted to be a punch to drift out other pebbles. Using a pebble as a mallet, Sard was making good progress when a low voice called him:

"Kid!"

"Who's there?" he asked.

"Say, Kid, don't make any noise, but come right up to the hole there."

Sard came cautiously, half expecting a missile through the hole. He saw that the hole was blocked by a man's face, which so shut out the light that he could not recognise it.

"Say, Kid."

The face swung away from the hole, for the stone on which the man was standing slipped a little. Sard recognised the ugly-looking train-hand who had watched him from the after-car.

"Say, Kid," the man repeated, as he clawed back into position, "you wanna get quit of here, or you'll line the cold-meat cart."

"I'm trying to get quit," Sard said.

"Well, you wanna try pretty dam' hard. You was on the silver line and you ain't got any plunks, I guess."

"No."

"Well, you wanna get out before sundown, sport. These silver-escort guys, they'll keep a man till sundown, to see if he'll pay to be let out. If he can't, they bring him into the yard 'for exercise' and shoot him full of holes. If any question's asked, they say they shot him while he was trying to escape. What the hell did you stay on the train for till she pulled up? I gave you the flag to beat it, and you put your dam' hoof right on it."

"I thought you were going to shoot me," Sard said. "Anyhow, I could not have jumped from the train, because my leg is queer."

"Hell!" the man said. "You ain't got ten plunks?"

"No."

"I mean, sewed away anywheres, against an emergency?"

"I haven't a penny."

"Because if you have ten plunks, you're up against your emergency, don't you make any mistake."

"I haven't a farthing."

"Hell!" the man said, "I was cleaned out at pinochle myself, only last night, by that dam' Dutchman. Hell!" He climbed from his perch, readjusted his foothold and clambered back.

"Dam' that Dutchman's soul and that dam' Las Palomas Pilsener." He seemd to be busy with his hands and eyes: soon he spoke again.

"Say, Kid, you gotta get out-a here. Watch-a doing? Digging?"

"Yes."

"Is the roof ceiled inside? I see it is. Hold on, then, till I have a try."

Sard heard him heave himself up on to the roof, where he seemed to lie prone, working busily, with very little noise, for ten minutes. It was still siesta time, but Sard judged that someone in the barracks might see or hear at any moment. Mutterings, mainly curses, came from the man on the roof, with the scraping and raking of tiles. For all the attempt to keep quiet, a good deal of force was being used; soon pieces of tile went slithering down the roof with what seemed to Sard a devilish tumult. Then the man seemed to get a purchase on a key-tile and wrench it this way and that, with the noise of a riveter's yard. Sard felt that any sleeper within a hundred yards must be roused by the racket. Worse followed, for the tile broke; some of it flew off into the yard and smashed upon a stone, the rest bounced on the roof and then slithered down it and off it: the train-hand cursed it and its parents.

One of the soldiers, who had been sleeping in the barton, came into the yard, looked about him, saw the man on the roof and challenged.

"What are you doing?" he asked.

"I'm mending this dam' roof. Remediando this dam' teja."

"Who told you to mend the roof?"

"The capataz and also the teniente."

"Is that true?"

"Yes, my brave, it is true. Go you and ask them if you don't believe me."

"What do you say?"

"Go you and ask them, if you do not believe."

"They did not say so to me, that the roof should be mended."

"See here, brother: they said so to me. Do you get that? To me, that is me here, they dicoed that I should mend this dam' roof; and I'm mending it; and when it's ended, you can have the dam' bits to scratch with."

"Bueno," the man said, after a pause. "Esta bueno."

"I guess it is bueno," the train-hand muttered. "It's pretty dam' bueno, if you ask me."

He went on working. Having cleared away two tiles, his task was easier, because he could get at the pegs in the heads of the course below them. He cracked each tile at the peg by a smart tap, then shook it clear and piled it to one side. Presently he wrenched a couple of laths away, beat violently downwards with them and knocked a foot of the ceiling into Sard's cell. He had begun his work with some precautions against noise: he now took none. A second soldier came yawning out of the barton. He stood staring with his mate at the breaking of the tiles.

"What is he doing?" he asked.

"Mending the roof."

"Verdad?"

"Verdad."

"See here now," the train-hand said to Sard, "can you ketch aholt of these laths and give a swig down on them?"

"Yes."

"He is talking to the prisoner," the second soldier said to his comrade. "He ought not to talk to the prisoner."

"Assuredly he ought not."

"And what was I saying to the prisoner?" the train-hand answered. "The prisoner was talking to me. He was complaining that I broke his siesta." He bent his head down, as though speaking to Sard. "You say you'll complain at having your siesta broken; complain to the capataz. You'll complain hell. I'm doing my duty in mending this roof." Then under his breath he added in English: "Two more swigs like that and she'll make hell-gate on the flood. Heave, Kid, you can git more purchase on it than I can."

Sard could get purchase on it, by leaping up, catching at a lath or at the plaster, and tearing it down by his weight. The noise of the wreckage falling into the cell gave the two soldiers some uneasiness. They looked at each other at each fall, with comments.

"He is making much mess."

"Assuredly."

"Do you think that it is all right? What?"

"That is what I ask."

"I heard no word of the mending of this roof."

"Nor I."

"I half think that I ought to report it."

"Such is half my thought also."

"Assuredly, if aught should happen that should not . . ."

"Then, indeed . . ."

"Suppose, then, that you acquaint the corporal . . ."

"Yes; but if all be truly well, if the roof be entitled to this mending, then shall we be like him who, fearing the burglar, shot the priest."

"If it be not so entitled, on the other hand, what then?"

"Then, indeed . . ."

The train-hand judged that this conversation had reached a danger-point. He started a counter-topic.

"My aunt hell," he cried.

"What is it?" the soldiers asked.

"Good Sarah, watch the devils."

"Watch what?"

"Say," the train-hand said, in an excited tone, "Pronto now, where does this ceiling end? At each end of the building, isn't it?"

"Yes; but why, what has happened?"

"Get you within doors, then; one at each end; quick now; take sticks. Do as I tell you; quickly."

"Yes, yes; here are sticks; what are we to do?"

"Into the building, one at each end, quickly now. It is rattle-snakes curled up here, twenty at least. Get in. I'll drive them down to you. There is a reward, half a peseta a rattle. One at each end, now. And watch. I'll drive them down to you."

"Watch where?"

"Where shall we watch?"

"At the ventilators. Quick, quick, or they'll be gone. Get down and kill them as they crawl out. It will be ten pesetas each."

The men did not know where to go, but realised that they were to be indoors, watching the ventilators. They had picked up laths from a bundle lying against a wall. After a half a minute of confusion, turning this way and that, they did as they were bidden, they ran indoors, one at each end of the building.

"Shut the doors behind you," the train-hand cried, "or they'll be out into the yard."

The doors were slammed to.

"Now," the train-hand said to Sard, "now, Kid, hump yourself. Get a holt of this rafter and out, pretty P.D.Q."

Sard leaped to the rafter, caught it, drew himself up to it, got an arm over it, got his head above the roof and saw the station and the desert, both beautiful with freedom. The train-hand gripped him by the belt and hove upon him. With a wrestle and a struggle he got his other arm over a rafter, then his knees; he was on the roof top.

"Beat it, Kid, like hell," the train-hand said. "Here's Twig-Legs."

Sard just saw that someone was entering the yard from the barton. He did not stay to see who it was, but shot himself off the roof into the waste with one heave. He swerved to his left under cover of the barrack wall and "beat it" as his helper had bade. His helper hurled bits of tile into Twig-Legs' face, then flung himself off the roof and "beat it" in the other direction.

Sard turned at the angle of the barracks into a sandy street of adobe houses, some of which had white canvas screens spread across their stoops. The street was like a street of the dead in the siesta. A few dogs, the exact colour of the sand, lay in the sun as though killed by a pestilence. Sard dodged their bodies, darted down a lane to the right, and found himself barred by a wall, which was topped by spikes. He got hold of a spike, swung himself up and scrambled over, into a graveyard in which the dead seemed to be coming out of their graves.

The rats and dogs snarled at him as he crossed the graveyard, the skulls looked out at him, the hands clutched at him. He went across the graveyard and out of it, by a gap where the wall had fallen, into a lane. He turned to his left, ran along the lane for about fifty yards and turned sharply to his right into a street of detached houses, some of which had palms growing in boxes at their gates. He walked along this street for a little way, listening for pursuers but hearing none.

"I must find out if they're after that train-hand," he said; "I must find that train-hand and thank him."

He listened intently, expecting to hear a tumult at the barracks, but all was still there. He brushed the plaster and tile dust from his clothes. He regretted that he had no hat: not even "A present from Bradford," which he had left screening the shutter on the door of his cell. He remembered suddenly three cases of murderers arrested from having lost their hats at the scene of their crimes. He remembered another case, from the time of the Terror in Paris, of a man saved from the guillotine by having a hat thrust suddenly upon his head, while he waited his turn in the dusk and rain at the place of execution. When his turn came at the end of the batch, he was judged to be one of the spectators and passed by.

"I'm suspect without a hat," he thought, "and I am also guilty of train-trespass and prison-breaking. But I'm not going to beat it from here till I know whether that man has beaten it."

He turned to his left, walked along another sandy road of silent adobe houses and sleeping dogs, and soon reached a road which he recognised. Far down it, a quarter of a mile away, on the left, was the barrack entrance, with its flag-pole, bearing the green-grey-blue tricolour of the Occidental Republic. Opposite Sard, as he stopped to reconnoitre, was a pulperia, with a hoarding on its roof. It was this hoarding which was familiar; he had noticed it while he was being led to the barracks; it bore a legend which he could now read, in translation:

Palace of Pleasure.
Look. The biggest Glass in Tlotoatin. 5c.
Beds for Knights, Artists, Travellers.
Beans. Beer. Wine. Beds.

"Beans, beer and a bed," Sard thought, "how good those things are, and how lucky they are who can afford them. Well is it called a place of pleasure, if that is the kind of life they live here.

I begin to understand the phrase now: 'he hasn't got a bean.' And at this time yesterday I was mate of a crack ship."

From a mine to the westward from him there came the blare of a hooter, giving warning that siesta was nearly ended. Other hooters took up the blast, till the place rang with echoes coming back from the hills. Now from some of the houses workers came half awake, like sailors coming on deck, buttoning their shirts. They went slouching off towards the mines, rubbing their eyes.

A man came yawning from the door of the Palace of Pleasure. He had a straw-broom in one hand with which he pretended to sweep the doorstep. Half his face was covered with one hand as he yawned. It was the train-hand.

"Say, Kid," he said, "step inside here."

He stepped inside and shook the man's hand and thanked him.

"Aw, come off," the man said, shutting the door. "Come in here." He led the way by a dark passage past a flight of stairs. Sard heard the rustle of skirts and smelt scent; looking up suddenly, he saw the heads of two women looking over the stair-rail on the landing above. One of them coquettishly sucked her cigarette to a glow as he passed, so that he might see her face the better.

The man opened a door into a room which had a bar at one side of it, and a long table, with benches, at the other. The bar was closed by a grating. Two men were asleep on the benches with their heads drooped on their outstretched arms; they were breathing heavily from purple faces: "Feeling their siesta doing them good," the train-hand called it. A third man, powerfully built, with a mottled olive face, brass earrings and a purple neckerchief, was sitting at the table eating with his knife. He had a small slab of something pale upon a dish in front of him. He shovelled flakes of this on to his knife-blade and then shovelled them into his mouth. He was a noisy as well as an untidy eater, being still a little in drink. He seemed displeased at the entrance of Sard: he dug his knife-point twice into the table, as though into someone's body, and he said nothing, which was unusual in a land where all at least offer to share their food and drink with the newcomer.

The train-hand took Sard to the end of the table away from the other three and sat him down.

"Say, kid," he said, "you wanna beat it right out a here."

"How about you?" Sard asked.

"Me?"

"Yes, you. You broke prison. You helped me to escape. You flung a tile at the officer, and some of those men must have recognised you, since they came in on the train with you."

"I'm not lying awake any," the man said. "I'm one of the boys. But you ain't. What in hell you doing here? That's what gets me."

Sard told him.

"Where you wanna get to?"

"Las Palomas."

"How're you going to get?"

"Could I get a ride on a freight car?"

"No, sir. The only freight cars from here is silver cars. There's not much these 'Tale guys mind, but they mind their silver. You'd be shot, sure as hell."

"Could I get a job on the train, shovelling coal?"

"Nit."

"Why not?" Sard asked.

"Cut the train right out of your thought," the man said. "The freight cars ain't going to be healthy to you. My mate Antonio will remember you."

"Very well, then; I'll walk along the line."

"Hell, Kid," the man said, "it's a hundred and seven miles, desert all the way; and anyone seeing you on the silver line would shoot you sure as hell."

"What am I to do then?"

"You could get a job in the Chicuna mine, sinking the new shaft. But I guess you'd have to stay a fortnight, before you touched your wad: they always hold back the first week. After that you could go in on the cars to Las Palomas. No, you couldn't neither. You have to stay another week, or six days. They ain't only but one train a week. They call her the Flying Fornicator or the Hop to Whoredom. I guess she's about rightly christened."

"I can't wait," Sard said, "I must start back right away. I'll walk it. If I can't walk along the line, I'll shape a course of my own across the desert."

"Watcha going to eat? Watcha going to drink? Kid, you can't do it. Besides there's snakes in the desert. Even the Jackarillers didn't cross the desert from here. No, Kid; cut it right out; and go up to the Chicuna to-morrow before the whistle. It will be the quickest in the end. Here's the boss; he'll tell you the same."

The boss came in with a demijohn and funnel; he had been doctoring cider with red pepper to serve as whisky for the later drinks of the evening. He was a very tall, fair-haired, sandy-moustached man, with a cold and evil blue eye. He carried a gun in front as well as one in a hip pocket. He nodded at the train-hand and cast an eye over Sard. He was in the business which brings men much into touch with the broken. He summed up Sard at once as being "on his uppers," or penniless.

"Pitch," the train-hand called. " 'Low me to introduce my friend. What did you say your name was, Kid?"

"Harker."

"Mr. Harker. Mr. Pitch Hanssen."

"Pleased to meet you," Pitch said: he did not look it. He put down his demijohn and funnel upon the bar, and stood there, looking at the company.

"Pitch," the train-hand said, "Mr. Harker wants to get to Las Palomas. He ain't got too much money; so I say he'd better put in a fortnight at the Chicuna. What do you say, Pitch?"

"He wants to get to Las Palomas?"

"Yes, or the coast," Sard said.

"I guess you'd better inform yourself, sir," Pitch said. "There's only two ways of getting to a place; you know that as well as I do."

"Pitch," the train-hand said, "this gentleman's a friend of mine."

"If he'd like to order anything," Pitch said, "he'll be a friend of mine. But if he ain't got any dough, or is the dead-broke bum I take him to be, I'll ask him to take a walk. This is a place for men who can pay their way and can afford hats. Are you going to order, Alonzo?"

"Yes," Sard said. "I am."

Although his leg was numb from the poison, he could still move like an athlete. He slid from his bench to the landlord in one motion.

"I'm going to order you to mind how you talk to me."

"Order me hell," Pitch said. "You'd best order yourself a hat, you low-down hobo. Or order yourself a shave, while you're at it. And now take a walk to some place where you can buy. Get out of it."

He did not pull a gun, probably his guns were not loaded, but he poked up his left at Sard's face, as Sard had expected he would. Sard on the instant cross-countered with his right to the point. Pitch slithered sideways along the bar, fell, rolled over on the floor and lay quiet.

"Carai!" screamed the man with brass earrings, "Hijo de la gran puta. You dog-assassin of English!" He flung his knife at Sard with the backward flick from the wrist which "takes a year to learn," so the bad men say. Had he flung the knife before screaming, Sard would have had the point through his throat, but the scream warned him; he had time to dodge. The knife stuck in the bar. Sard pulled it out. The two men at the table woke up. "Rough house," one of them said.

"Cut out your dam' row and let us sleep," the other said.

"Carai, carai, carai," cried the man with brass earrings. "I'll give you dog-assassin with the bottle." He came across the table at Sard with a bottle, knocking over one of the sleepers as well as a bench. Floundering in this wreck, he himself fell, cursing. There came a scurry of swift yet heavy steps on the floor above.

"Beat it, Kid," the train-hand cried to Sard. "Here's the missus." He held the door open for Sard, who slipped through it to the front door, which was already open. He was moving swiftly, but had a glimpse as he fled of a monstrous woman, with an inflamed and frowsy face, who was floundering downstairs to him, calling him to stop. Something cracked the woodwork of the door to his left and something banged to his right: the woman was shooting at him.

He reached the street, turned sharply, ran round the house, scrambled over a low wall into an enclosure, and ran along it, while the pursuit grew loud behind him. At the end of the enclosure there was a wall, which he climbed. As he climbed it, there came cries of "There he is!" and bullets struck the wall and the earth beneath it. He dropped into a second enclosure. At the end of the enclosure there was a house, at the door of which a man lay in a chair taking his siesta, with a gun upon his knees. The man woke up as Sard reached him, and at the same instant the pursuers reached the enclosure wall and opened fire. Sard slipped past the man in the chair into the house. He said, "Excuse me," as he passed, and slammed the door behind him. There was a door on his left; a woman opened it, asking him, in Spanish, what was the matter. He said, "It is the washing, Madam," and slipped past her and up the flight of stairs. On the upper floor were three children, who screamed when they saw him. He called out to them, in Spanish, that their mother was bringing them some sweets.

He tried a door, which was locked, and another door, which opened into a shuttered room; he then ran up to the next floor. There was a door opposite the top of the stairs. He opened it, and found a young man lying on the bed, taking his siesta. The young man's slouch hat was on the floor; Sard picked it up and put it on. There was no sash to the window of that room, but closed, green, jalousied shutters. He unhooked them, took a hurried look out, and found to his great joy that there was a fire-escape. He went down it, hand over hand, and reached the ground as the young man looked out, and asked him what in the blazes he was doing. He did not stop to answer, for he was collared, on the instant, by the man who had been sleeping in the chair. Sard back-heeled him, sent him flying and reached the garden gate, just as the woman and the three children came out of the door with a couple of dogs.

He got out of the garden gate with the dogs at his heels, and ran along the road, hearing the pursuit increase, as the men from the Palace of Pleasure joined in. He turned to his right, then sharp to his left, then again to his right, the dogs following him and joined now by three or four pariahs, which had been sleeping in the sand. The last turn that he made was into a blind alley. There was a wall at the end of it, overhung with trees. He leapt for a branch, but the branch broke in his hand, and he came down into the midst of the dogs. He sent them flying with a few blows, scrambled up the wall and down on to the other side. On the other side there was a woman sitting in a rocking-chair, knitting. "For the land's sake," she said, "for the land's sake, young man, this ain't no right of way. Go back the way you came."

"I'm going back," he said, and ran on.

"George! George!" the woman cried, "get you gun quick; there's a rough-neck come through the garden."

Somebody inside the house answered, "What's that you say, Anna?"

Sard called to the man, "There's a rough-neck murdered Mr. Davis; I've got to break it to the widow."

"Stop him, George," the woman said.

The man tried to stop him, and got one on the jaw which he remembered for a long time.

Sard got out into a road which led quite clear of the houses into the wilderness of the foothills. There was a sort of trail leading up the hill, through a sparsely-grown jungle of brushwood. He took his chance of snakes and dodged into the brush and zigzagged through it, keeping uphill all the time. At the top of the cañon, half a mile from the town, he stopped for a moment, but he heard people as well as dogs, so he set off downhill into a gully.

At the foot of the gully there were great rocks among which a little river ran. He ran upstream in the water for about a hundred yards, so as to puzzle the dogs, and then scrambled out of the water up a great rock. At the top of the rock there was a recess filled with dry sand and screened by boulders. In the sand were the fresh footprints of a wild cat, but Sard judged that wild cats are less dangerous than men, and flung himself down to get his breath.

In a couple of minutes he heard the dogs at the water, and the voices of men, encouraging the dogs to hunt. He judged that there were at least eight men up with the hounds, and others joined them. He could hear their conversation as they walked up and down, and poked among the rocks.

"He's the silver bandit who broke gaol at the barracks this afternoon."

Another said, "He nearly killed Hanssen at the Palace."

Another said, "Mother Hanssen reckon she hit him with one of her shots; leastways there was blood under that wall."

Another said, "He took to the water all right, but these dogs don't seem to get the scent any."

Another said, "Well, he must have gone upstream, because if he'd gone downstream, they would have got him."

Another said, "He can't have much breath left in him, the clip he has been going. Like as not he's got in among these rocks here; maybe he's listening all the time we're talking."

Another said, "The hell he ain't got much breath! He goes over the darned ground like a darned cyclone."

Another said, "Come, Peppy; come, Toto; I'll just take this couple of dogs up along this further bank, and you get on upstream and see if we can't pick up where he's landed."

A voice came from amongst the bushes: "Say, boys, did you get him yet?"

They said, "No, we ain't got him yet, but we guess we're going to get him."

"I guess I'm going to get him too," the voice said. "He come into my room, when I was having a lay down, and sneaked my hat right off of my pillow."

"Well, come on," said another, "and we'll get him and the hat."

They went splashing up the stream, and then presently all the dogs burst into a frenzy of barking. He heard cries of "They're on to him! Come on, boys, they're on to him; he can't only be but a little ways ahead."

Sard heard the hunt pass upstream and gradually grow fainter towards the head of the gully. He lay still for about half an hour.

He heard some shouts and presently the footsteps of men returning, some distance up the stream.

"It's very odd where he's got away to," one of them said.

Another said, "It's my belief he never got away, but just lay quiet somewheres. Back in town is the place to look for him, if you ask me."

Another said, "That's right. You know that time the dogs went on like they was crazy; it's my belief they was on a panther, not on a man at all. It was somewheres around here we lost him, and it's somewhere around here we'd find him again."

"Well, the scent's cold now," another said; "and not only that, the dogs have forgotten what he smelled like. Besides, the trail's been all trodden out. We'd best get back to town."

"Well, I ain't going back to town," said the young man, "not without my hat I ain't."

"Well," another said, "no one seems to me to be able to describe the fellow. You saw him, kid; what was he like?"

"I wasn't only half awake," the boy said. "He was a great big fellow, an ugly fellow, and Pop says he was a big fellow; and he ain't got no coat, only just pants and a shirt."

A man said, "Well, kid, even if he were to spring up right among us now, I guess you couldn't say it was him. Maybe he's gone downstream after all."

"Well, I guess I'm going to get my hat," the boy said; "no cheap skate ain't going to pinch my hat and get away with it."

"That's right, kid," said a man, "you get him, and when you get him, soak him good."

They moved away downstream all together, beating with their sticks as they went, to scare the snakes. Presently they were out of earshot, down the stream. Sard lay very still, waiting for darkness. He heard the hooters from the mines blowing for six o'clock. The light by this time was going from the river-bed, but from where he lay he could see the brush shining in the sun at the top of the cañon. He was very weary of lying still. He said to himself, "They've gone, it'll be safe to move, I might be starting now."

He was on the very point of rising from where he lay, when a

169

rifle was suddenly fired, not twenty yards from him, on the other side of the river. It was a repeating rifle, followed by a second shot an instant later. He heard something snarl, and a man's voice cried, "Got you, you son of a gun!"

Another voice said, "Well, was she a painter?"

The other said, "No, a wild cat, and she's got her nest hereabouts. Maybe we could find the kittens. She's got her nest somewhere among them rocks, the other side of the water. I see'd her little tracks, where she's hopped from stone to stone, so as not to get her feet wet. See here."

"What's she carrying?" said one of them. "Is it a rabbit?"

"Not it; it's a woodchuck, I guess."

"Are you sure she's dead," said one man. "I've known 'em to play dead, so as to get a bit of their own back."

"She's dead," said the other. "See here. Pretty poor, too; skin's no good, but I guess I'll take her along. If we'd got dogs, we'd have them kittens out. See here, the tracks lead this way. Here's the place she crossed. My, that's a pretty good lep! But where did she go, after this? That darned bunch this afternoon have trodden out all the signs. She's gone somewhere up them rocks, and it's in among there, most likely. If you'll give me a leg up, I'll go up and have a look round."

"Hold on a minute," said the other; "it ain't too light down here. I guess I'm not going to poke around in any cavern when this cat's mate may be about. The toms are as bad as the shes, and if it's up there laying for us, I'd guess we should know it. We'll come around in the morning and bring a couple of dogs."

"Now come on, man," said the other; "the tom'll have hidden the kittens to-morrow morning. Finish the job, now we're at it. Give me a leg up."

"I guess I won't," said the other. "These cats blinded old 'Lije Goldschmidt. He went after 'em into a place where he couldn't see, and they fair tore his face off him."

"Funk!" said the other man.

"I guess I am a funk," said his friend; "but I don't want to sit at any street corner holding a tin pan for pennies, the way old 'Lije done, for the rest of my days. But I'll come along to-morrow morning, and I'll bring a shot-gun, which is a sight more use than the thing you're using."

"Well, if you don't care to come," said the other man, "I'll do it alone. You take my rifle and hand it up to me when I'm up."

"No," his friend said, "I ain't going to be a party to no such foolishness. If you want to get your eyes clawed out, you can. Even if you got your rifle up there, you couldn't see to shoot. It's just darned foolishness, and I'm not going to stand for it. We've got the she, after waiting long enough, and the whistle's been gone this half-hour. Take what we've got and come on, and we'll come again in the morning."

The other man growled a little at his friend, but, at last, picked up the dead cat and turned homewards up the gully. They stopped every now and then to complain of the steepness of the climb, then their voices ceased to sound.

It was fast falling dark and the stars were already bright above the gully. Sard cautiously rose, wondering whether the cat's mate were thereabouts. He was very stiff from lying still. It was cold down there among the rocks and he was faint from want of food. He scrambled down to the water and drank. After groping about for a little while, he found the woodchuck, which he brought along.

He scrambled up the cañon on the side away from the town. It was very steep, the scrub was full of prickles. Presently he reached the top and saw a wilderness of scrubby foothills stretching away for miles, as it seemed, into the Sierra. Behind him, whenever he turned, he could see the lights of the town, and hear the dull thumping of the machinery and the noise of the band playing in the Plaza. On his right was a vast sea of ghostly paleness stretching away for hundreds of miles into the sky, where crimson faded into a kind of green. In the green, here and there, the tops of mountains made jagged marks. The stars were bright in the heaven. He looked up to the eastward stars, with the thought that by rights he should be in his ship, watching these stars, four degrees to the eastward from where he was. He realised that there was no reaching the coast by the railway line.

"I'll go eastwards," he said. "Among these foothills there must be some trail by which I can reach the coast."

He had several matches remaining to him. By the help of two of these he contrived a little fire, at which he cooked the wood-chuck, by toasting collops of it upon skewers. It was not as juicy as rabbit, nor so rank as ferret, but something between the two. He saved some of it for breakfast next morning. Then taking his bearings from the stars he set out to walk to the coast. He knew the trend of the coast from the charts; it was all in his favour. If Las Palomas were one hundred and seven miles from him, he reckoned that he might reach the port of San Agostino in ninety miles. He judged that he might do it in four days.

At the end of two hours of walking, he entered a sheltered valley in a high state of cultivation. He burst through bushes into a track, which led, presently, to a settlement, where the people were already asleep. He could see the little grey-tiled houses scattered, at intervals, among orchards. Dogs barked at his approach. The smell of oranges came to him on a warm breath of wind. He found himself walking between two orange fields. He could see great globes of the fruit among the dark and shining leaves. Some oranges had fallen and lay beneath the trees. He took some and ate them, skin and all, as he walked. At the end of the village or community, the fruit was thicker on the trees, and he was plan-ning to step into one of the orchards to take some oranges when two men with guns stepped from underneath the trees, and called to him to stop.

"What are you doing here?" they said. One was a European fruit-farmer, the other a native servant.

"I'm walking through," said Sard.

"Walking through? Where to?"

"San Agostino."

"Where's that?"

"On the coast," he said.

"On the coast? How do you expect to make the coast from here?"

"Walk there," Sard said.

"Walk? Hell!" said the farmer, "you've come along orange-pinching. You walk to hell clean out of here, or you'll get lead into you so mighty darned quick, that you'll think a cyclone's struck you. Now get out, and don't stop to pick no flowers till you're past the end of my plantation."

Sard walked on along the trail; the two men followed him at a distance of about a dozen yards, until he was clear of the plantation. The trail led on uphill out of the valley. It seemed to go on interminably, winding up the foothills, but remaining a track, apparently a good deal used. At about eleven o'clock that night the track swerved to the left towards a northern valley, which Sard judged to be useless to him. A sort of track or trail led on in his direction. Though he did not know it, the track was one made in the course of centuries by animals going to drink at the brook below. He followed it for about half an hour and then came out on a lonely hillside, from which he could see no sign of human habitation except the glare in the sky above the mining town, now many miles away. He could see little but mountains, most of them covered either with scrub or with pine trees. A kind of ghostly glimmer stood out into the sky in front, from those peaks of the Sierra which ran into the snow. In the sandy soil among the sage brush all round him there were little scurryings and squeakings from the gophers. Far away, he could not tell how far, it might have been miles away, he heard the howling of solitary wolves, a noise more uncanny than the crying of owls and more melancholy than lamentation.

High up there, in the foothills, the wind never ceased. It stirred the sage brush continually, so that the whole hillside seemed filled with footsteps and the noise of people pushing through the brush. He could go no further for that night, but scooped himself a place in the sand in a sheltered nook of the hill, out of the wind. There he covered himself up and slept.

All through the next day he held on across the foothills through the sparse-growing sage. He was already in the wilderness, for the hills were waterless even so soon after the rains. He saw no sign of man all through that day, except once, when he had a view of the desert far below with a train, trailing under smoke, going to the west. As he was still fresh, he resolved to march without food this day: this resolve he kept. He found no water anywhere until towards the evening, when he struck an animal trail which led him to a dripping rock. In the pan of water below the rock the carrion of a wolf lay. He stayed at the rock to catch the drippings till his thirst was assuaged: then feeling like a new man, he went on till he could go no further. This was a good day compared with what followed. He made good some twenty miles of his course. He slept on the ground where he stopped; but slept ill owing to annoyance from the ticks.

After some hours he rose up as a sailor will, knowing that his watch was at an end. It was about a quarter to four. He felt uneasy, and sitting up in his shelter, he heard horsemen close to him. He heard the muttering of voices and horses wrenching at the brush. After listening intently, he decided that what he heard was neither men nor horses, but some other thing, he could not tell what. He remembered now that some weeks before, on board the *Pathfinder*, he had talked with an Occidental, who had come on board on ship's business, about these very mountainous tracks in which he was wandering. He remembered that the man had said, "No one goes there, even to prospect for metals. They are bad places where bad things happen." He remembered, too, stray bits of talk or of reading about these mountains, how nobody really knew them, except a body of men known as the Jacarillos, a tribe of most savage desert Indians, to whom all the most savage of the native bandits fled. These men, alone, were supposed to live in the Sierra, and when Sard sat up in the cold morning, hearing that muttering all around him in the dark, he judged that a war-party of the Jacarillos was passing that way.

Then he thought that that could not be so, because no frontiersman, and certainly no desert Indian, would speak when on a war-party except by signs. There was something there that he did not understand. He crept very cautiously towards the noise, and presently was able to peer between boulders, at the hillside whence the noise came. It was not perfect darkness; he could see an open space where the brush was low. In this space, moving about exactly as though they had dropped something, which they were trying to pick up or hoping to find, were some gigantic men. One of them was standing not far from him. He was not very tall, less tall, perhaps, than Sard himself, but in bulk and bigness like a gorilla. They were going slowly over the ground in a suspicious way, muttering to each other. They were uneasy about something for which they were looking. Sard felt that they knew that he was there, and that they were looking for him. Then he felt that though they were men, they wanted some of the senses of men; they were like some race of men born blind, who felt for their enemies by some sense which men no longer have. They went slowly over the ground across which he had certainly passed some hours before. They seemed to feel the ground and lift samples of it, then they muttered remarks about the samples. One of them, away to the right, the one furthest from Sard, seemed to be the captain. When this man reached the point where Sard had stumbled on his way to his lair, he paused and felt the ground and gave a little cry, at which all the others hurried to him. Sard could hear their mutterings and a discussion going on among them. Evidently they had come upon his trail and were puzzled about it.

For a few moments the thought of dealing with a race of giants was unnerving. He saw how such a race would live in that land in the great caves of the limestone, coming out only at night into the wilder places of the hills, taking their prey and going back before dawn. Then he thought, "They cannot be men, they must be bears. But if they are bears, it won't be any better. They can only be grizzly bears who attack any man on sight."

He kept still as a mouse for half an hour, while the bears loitered about and muttered among themselves and rummaged in the earth and seemed to find food, though he couldn't think what. One of them came lumbering quite close to where he crouched. He saw him stand and look up at the stars, in an attitude exactly like that of one of the seamen in the *Pathfinder*, at the wheel. While he was standing thus, he seemed to be conscious of some scent that was not usual. Sard could see his head tip up and down in an attempt to get the stray wafts, to give some certain evidence, one way or the other. He moved away a little and repeated the process, and then moved back, moving with his head exactly like a questing hound and peering sometimes in Sard's direction, yet not seeing him. At last he seemed to be satisfied, and went shambling off to his fellows. They moved off into the thickets and he saw them no more.

When he felt that they were out of earshot and smell of him, he turned his back upon that place and went on through the scrub up a hill that went up and up, yet never came to any summit. He must have walked for about two hours when he stopped suddenly, hearing a woman singing. It sounded like an Indian woman with a very sweet voice, singing one of the tuneless Indian songs. A little listening showed him that it was not a woman, but a little hidden spring of water, gurgling from a pipe to a trough. The air came with a waft of sweetness upon his face, as of azaleas in blossom and oranges in fruit growing together in a thicket.

He said, "There's a house here." He called aloud in Spanish, "Is anybody there? I am a friend. Is anybody there?" In front of him he could see this thicket, which smelled so sweet, all starred either with blossoms or with fruits. He knew from the look and feel of the place that it had been made by good people and was good, and that the people were there, watching him, to see what he would do.

"I am not armed," he said. "I am an English sailor going to the coast. Don't turn your dogs at me, but let me have shelter."

Nobody answered, but he felt quite certain that the thicket was full of people looking at him.

He said, "Don't shoot. You see I put my hands up. I am alone."

He went forward to the thicket and there saw that there was no one, only a profusion of creeping flowers that looked at him like eyes, out of the darkness of the hedge. It must have been years since anybody had lived there. The hedge, which had been planted, had gone back to jungle. He walked round it till he came to what had been the gate. There he could see within a little ruined chapel with one bell. As he came through the gateway in the first of the dusk, a bird, perhaps an owl, which had been perched beneath the bell, flew out with a cry. Her wings struck the bell, which jangled a little. It was exactly as though Sard had rung the door-bell. He drew his breath and stood still in the court, wondering who would answer the bell.

It was still not more than twilight, but birds were stirring in the scrub, and colours could be seen. Some blue birds with orange breasts came wavering down among the bushes, tore a few petals apart, from wantonness, and flew on, talking to each other.

Sard stepped across the courtyard and looked in at the deserted chapel's western door. It must have been built very soon after the Conquest. It had been deserted for perhaps half a century, which in that dry climate had not been enough to destroy it. The roof had gone, except over the altar. From the wall-plate of the falling roof great strings of flowers hung. Many flowers and grasses had sprouted among the stones. Just over the altar a bough had thrust through the wall, and had blossomed there with a white clustered blossom which smelled sweeter than honeycomb. The wall above the altar had once been painted in fresco. Most of the paintings were now gone, but Sard saw, as it were, the heads of men, eagerly looking upward. To right and to left of the door within the enclosure there were marks in the earth which showed where the mission huts had once stood. But monks, converts, mission, and the very memory of their dealings were utterly gone. Sard might well have been the first man to have stood there, since the mission ended. It ended in pestilence, he thought; nobody was left alive here for the mission to save. He judged that the pestilence which had destroyed the mission might still be there, in the air, the earth, the water. Yet the place seemed good, it was unvisited, it seemed sheltered, and there were no scorpions nor snakes.

He lay down in the shelter of the altar, and instantly fell asleep. He had not slept long before he became aware that somebody was calling him by name from infinity far away, in a voice which was familiar and yet strange. The voice called, "Harker! Sard Harker! Sard!" from a distance so great that it seemed like another continent. He knew, in his sleep, that the voice wanted him to wake. He woke and sat up and found it still twilight there in the chapel, with the stars not yet gone from the hole in the roof. No one was calling, the blue birds were back again, tearing the blossoms, no call had disturbed them. He thought, "I wonder whose voice that was. I seem to know the voice"; and while he wondered, he fell asleep.

In his sleep he saw the owner of the voice, a boy called Peter Maxwell, who had been dead eleven years. He saw Peter, not as he had ever known him, but eager, like the faces in the fresco. He knew that Peter had some message for him, yet could not say it, having no longer any human tongue or any use for human thought. He saw Peter leaning out of the altar wall from the place where the branch was blossoming. Peter was stretching out his right hand to him, but what he wanted he could not tell. He cried out, "Peter, old man, is that you?" and in his gladness at seeing Peter so near, he woke up and saw the blossoming branch shaking, as though someone had brushed it by. It was daylight, but not sunlight, as he rose up. No one was there, no one had been there; the birds were still tearing the blossoms, uttering little cries. No man could have been within a mile of them, probably no human being was within ten miles, and yet he expected to see Peter Maxwell.

"Peter," he said, "Peter."

When he saw that there was no Peter, he thought, "That was a strange dream. Peter Maxwell has been dead since 1886. He died of yellow fever in the *Cliomene*. Yet that was Peter in my dream."

He walked round the little enclosure. There was nothing to alarm him, except the sense that he was more alone than he had ever been in his life. He was weary from his tramp and his hard day. He returned to the chapel and presently slept again. This time he slept for some hours, but towards noon, at about the time when his watch would be drawing to an end, he was aware that a trumpet was being blown and that armed figures were there, wanting him to go. With a little effort he cleared his eyes, so that he could see these figures. There were three: two women and a man. The man was standing between the women and raised above them. He was standing on the altar blowing a blast upon the trumpet, and the notes of the trumpet came out like flames, so that Sard could see them as well as hear them. The women were looking at him with faces so calm that they could not have been mortal, yet when they saw that he saw them, their faces became alive and incredibly eager. They both turned to him and bent to raise him, and with their free hands they pointed at the trumpeter, who shone in all his being and pointed the way to go, and blew upon his trumpet a blast like a cock-crow: "Get you gone out of here, get you gone out of here!"

In his dream Sard called to the trumpeter: "What is it, Peter, what is it? What is it, you great spirits?"

But the women faded from him, Peter faded from him into the wall, but he could still see the shining trumpet and notes like flakes of fire falling all around him. The trumpet dwindled slowly and resolved itself into the blossoming branch that had grown through a crack in the wall. The figures were gone, the fiery notes had vanished, only as Sard stood up he smelled very faintly a smell of burning. He walked to the altar and felt along the wall. It was a wall of perishing plaster. No one had been there. He went out into the enclosure, and as he passed through the door, he smelled again the smell of burning. "Get you gone out of here," he repeated. "Get you gone out of here! What is that smell of burning?"

Once long before, far out at sea in the Pacific, he had smelled a smell of burning during the night-watch and had reported it to his mate. The mate said, "Yes, you often smell that here, at this season of the year. They are burning the scrub on the mountains four hundred miles away." He thought of that remark now. Looking out of the enclosure at the thickets beyond, he saw a faint trail of smoke curling among some dwarf oaks.

"I believe this scrub's on fire," he said. "I'd better get me gone out of here, or I'll be burnt like a rat in a trap."

As near as he could judge, the wind was blowing from the north-west, and his course was to the east of north. If the scrub were on fire, as he supposed, he would have to get across its path. He left the enclosure of the ruined chapel and set off further up the hill to a clear space among the scrub, where he could see. The foothill on which he stood looked like a moraine across the track of some ancient glacier. From the top of it he could look right up the valley down which the glacier may once have flowed. The wind was blowing straight down this valley, driving a line of fire behind a wall of smoke, which was beaten down below the tops of the dwarf oaks. Suckers and snakes of flame ran out along the sides of the valley and over its summit. From time to time these suckers seemed to die out, but others always leaped up in front of them. It was advancing in a ragged line, coming pretty fast, with a crackling, hissing, sighing noise that sounded very terrible. Sard judged that it might be, at the furthest, a mile from him. It died down and glittered up like a living thing. At that distance it did not look like a raging fire, but it was laying all things dead behind it.

Sard could not see how far it stretched on the side towards which he was going, but he judged that he would have to hurry to get round it, so he set off at his best pace along the ridge of what might have been the moraine. As he went along, the air thickened with intensely bitter smoke from the burnt bush. Little floating fiery particles came flying past and settled on his clothes. Every now and then some streamer of flame would blow down on something dry, set it on fire and blow out. He ran for about ten minutes, mostly uphill, and he reached the top of that side of the valley to which he ran. He found that on the other side of the hill the ground tipped very sharply down into a rocky chasm. Beyond this rocky chasm, which contained water, was a hillside covered with scrub, blazing like the Day of Judgment. There was no possibility of getting round the fire. He was shut in on that side, and he hadn't time to get back. His only chance was to get down to the water.

There was a place where the crag had fallen in a scree of big pieces of stone. He scrambled down this towards the water, but the scrub burning on the other side of the stream was so bright and hot that he had to cover his eyes as he slithered down. Quite close to the lip of the water there was a big shelving stone, worn smooth by floods. It was so hot from the blaze that he could hardly bear his hand upon it. He slithered into the water from it, just as a flame seized the scrub upon the opposite bank, and scorched it into nothing.

In a minute the fury of the fire had passed, and it was running up the hillside away from him, leaving a blackened earth, covered with glowing stalks, which hissed and sighed. It went on, he could see it running up the hill, licking down the scrub and leaving blackness. The wind blew over the burnt tract, bringing soft ash, little fiery particles, and a breath as from a furnace door.

Sard clambered out of the water, which was brackish and quite unfit to drink, and set off upon his course again. He walked, like Satan, on the burning marl, in a desert which had been grim before, but was now terrible. He followed along the course of the chasm for half a mile, and came out above on to a sort of tableland of rock, where the fire had ceased. He paused here to take his bearings, and noticed, for the first time, that a house or hut had been destroyed by the fire, close to where he stood. It must have been almost the last thing burned; so he went to it, thinking that perhaps somebody had been burnt in it. On a sort of shelf at one end of it was a skeleton of a man, gripping a crucifix. It might have been there fifty years. The only other remains were a couple of earthenware ollas of a good size. These were Indian pots of a dull yellow colour, with decorations of black and red. One of them had a thong about its mouth, and had been used as a waterbucket; the other, which was still covered with its earthenware lid, contained parched corn, shrivelled to the dryness and toughness of split peas, but still food. There was nothing to show what the man had been. He was tall for an Indian; the crucifix seemed against his being a miner or prospector. He may have been some hermit, or contemplative.

Sard removed the ollas into the open. After a little search he found the spring where the hermit had got his drinking water. He made a fire and cooked what was left of the woodchuck with the parched corn, and took his bearings while the meal was cooking. In front of him the path of the fire still ran on along the valley. It was already far away, running in little bright flickers of flame, under driven-down smoke. To his left, on the line of his course, there was a mile of scrubless desert of sand and rock, without even a cactus or a prickly pear, stretching to the rocky bulk of the Sierra. By the Sierra, in the direction in which he wished to go, was a chasm or cleft or cañon, it could hardly be called a glen. It ran into the very heart of the hills, for a mile or two, as far as he could see, but beyond it there were crags with pine trees, and beyond those more crags, and beyond those, crags with snow and more crags. To his right he could see very little. Foothills shut in the line of sight on that side. Wherever he looked there was no sign of the works of man, there was desert, rock, desolation and death. Between sixty and seventy miles of unknown country still lay between him and the coast. With some tough tendrils which had escaped the fire he contrived slings for the two ollas. He was now equipped with bread and water for two days.

As he judged that the chasm or cleft would give him an easier path into the hills, he set off towards it. As he drew near to its entrance, it looked like the entrance to hell. He remembered that he had read somewhere, or somebody had told him, that the Indians dreaded these clefts in the mountains, and said that unspeakable things lived in them. Now as he drew near the mouth, he heard far up the cañon something like a voice, which was not a voice, crying in the heart of the rocks. It was a strange, metallic cry of "Ohoy!" The echoes repeated it. It was no beast that he knew. It was not like a beast. It was like the voice of the rock itself. He stopped at the very mouth of the cañon, trying to think what that voice could be. It was not any human voice, and yet it had a human ring. It was not the voice of any beast, and yet it came, as it were, from the strength of a beast. It could not be the voice of a bird, no bird could be big enough, and yet there was something birdlike in its tone. If it were not the voice of a man, beast or bird, what could it be? Though it could not be a bird, it was likest to a bird; there was something spiritual and birdlike about it. It gave him the impression of some giant bird, some bird of poetry, some phœnix or roc, crying from a full heart. Then in its deeper notes it sounded like the voice of some giant who was beating on an anvil, and crying as he struck the blows, "Ohoy!" At these times it came with a pure metallic clang, which thrilled him to the marrow. He stood still to listen to it. Whatever it was, it came from some living thing, it had not the rhythm of any machine. It was not any drill or pile-driver beating into the heart of the rock. Sard's mind offered many suggestions, one after the other. Now it was like some great bell, but it was not a bell. Now it was like some ringing true blow struck by a gigantic tuning-fork, or like the blow of an axe upon a gong, or like the drilling of some gigantic woodpecker into a musical wood. He could not think what it was. It was not sorrowful nor joyful nor terrible. It was great and strange. It came from the heart of the wilderness of rock, miles from any human dwelling. It was like the rock speaking. Into his mind there came again those words which he had read or heard, "The Indians do not go into the Sierra, nobody goes into the Sierra; there are strange things in the Sierra which do not want to be known."

He asked himself whether he were not delirious and imagining this noise. But it rang clearly and made an echo.

The cañon was paven with clean dry desert sand. It led into the heart of the hills. The side of the mountain had been snapped asunder there and torn fifty yards apart. Sard could see a great black boulder midway up the cliff, on his right hand, and its other half on his left hand. He saw the patterns of veins and lines, where they once had joined each other. It needed some little resolution to go on towards that noise, but he repeated his proverb, "A danger met is less than a danger expected," and went forwards toward it.

There were no tracks in the sand, perhaps no human foot had trodden that path for fifty years or five hundred years. "Here," he thought, "I may come upon some unknown beast or bird or race of men or giants, for there may be anything in a place like this." Half a mile up the cañon he stopped, for in front of him the walls of the cañon drew together, and there at each side of the chasm the rock had been hewn into a semblance of columns, a hundred feet high. Drawing a little nearer, he saw that the heads of the columns were carven with the heads of monsters which were crushing human skulls between their teeth; blood seemed to be flowing from their mouths; blood spattered the columns; as he drew near, he could hear it dripping on the rocks below. The noise of the great bird, or whatever it was, had been silent for some time; now he heard it much nearer and with a new note, not of joy nor of sorrow, but of laughter that had no feeling in it. Sard stopped; he felt his hair stand on end, while his heart seemed to come up into his throat and thump there till it was as dry as bone.

"All the same, I'll go on," he said; "there's no going back. That thing knows that I'm here. If I've got to die, I'll die, and I may as well get it over."

All the time the great figures on the columns seemed to chew their quids and the blood spattered down upon the rocks.

"They're only those streams," he said, "with iron ore or with red pigment in them, and they've led them in channels to those figures' mouths. That's all it is."

It was all that it was, but in the dusk of the cañon and of the day, to one very weak and weary as well as feverish, it was enough. He walked boldly up to the feet of the figures. They stood in blood, like butchers, and the red water splashed Sard as he stood there. Though he had expected much, he had not expected what he saw. The two great columns stood one on each side of a narrow pass, not more than four feet across. Within the pass the cañon widened out again, but not very far. On both sides of it the rocks had been carven into gigantic shapes. It was an avenue of the gods, all of them terrible; they seemed to turn their heads and look at him; the wardens at the gate seemed to turn round upon him after he had passed them. Into his mind, from some forgotten book or speaker, came the phrase of what the Indians in that country had said of these old temples, that their gods come to life at dusk, and are alive all night, and live on men. They seemed to gnash their teeth and lick their lips, and to tremble as he drew near.

He would have thought nothing of it had he had so much as a dog beside him. A lunatic, even a village idiot, would have seemed a comrade and a backing to him. But he had to face it alone. He backed into the rock of the pass and tried to reassure himself, but he kept telling himself, "It was one of these things whom I heard singing. They do come to life at dusk."

Then he said, "It isn't so. If these things were beautiful, I would fear them, but they are not, and there is nothing in them that I will recognise as gods. These things are all over this land: I have heard of them. I'll go on, and if they kill me, they'll get little glory by it."

He went on, and as he went a strange moaning music seemed to wind from one god to another. It was the wind striking sharp angles in the rocks at the chasm top, but it sounded like the song of the figure of Memnon in Egypt. Just in such a way should the thoughts of the gods pass to each other, without a movement of the lips.

"Those Indians spoke the truth," he thought, "when they said that the gods speak in music from dusk to dawn."

At the head of the cañon was a small stone temple, high up at the top of a flight of steps. The columns and the walls were brightly painted with images of terror and of power, in war and triumph. Bats were flickering out from the temple door. They were the first living things that he had seen since he entered the cañon. They made him feel that he was coming back to life, after walking in the kingdom of death. As he went up the temple steps, which were as perfect as when they had been laid down, centuries before, the voice of the bird, or whatever it was, rose up from somewhere in the mountain not far ahead. It rose up with a new note, it was like laughter with exultation. He could see nothing because the temple shut away all that was in front of him, but he heard above the noise of the laughter the clanking as of enormous wings, slowly rising from the ground and gathering power and moving away and away.

As he entered the temple there came a great rush of many hundreds of bats, whirling past his ears into the air. He passed between walls of carven and painted figures, which were still sharp and bright in detail. He went through a first room, as long as a cricket pitch, into another, which was pleasant with the sound of water. A pool had been cut in the rock in the midst of this great room; water spouted into it from the tongues of grotesque heads. At the end of the room there were stairs leading up to an altar made of a piece of black obsidian chipped to a point. At the back of this altar there were rooms filled with the murmur of pigeons.

These rooms must once have been the priests' dwellings. They were now dovecotes for the blue rock-pigeons which flew out, on his approach. He clambered out after them on to a terrace cut upon the rock of the mountain for two hundred yards by a people who had no explosives save the will of their rulers. There was no green thing in sight, nothing but rocks and sand. The rocks were of every savagery of splinter, of savage colours, bright blue, yellow, red and black, all spiked and toppled and tumbled, and only brought into order upon this terrace by the unknown priests of dead gods.

He took what he could of the eggs of the rock-pigeons, then shaped his course and went on into the wilderness, until his way was barred by a cliff across his path, eight hundred feet high and more. He walked along it for over a mile, but found no scaling place. At the end of his walk the cliff bowed over so as to make a shelter or cave. Here in some remote time some forgotten tribe had built up a house for themselves by piling a wall of stones without mortar, between the hollow and the light. The path of these men still led to their entrance, a hole in the wall, just big enough for a small man to crawl through. Sard did not dare to try to enter by that door for fear of snakes. There was a sheltered place among the rocks where he lay down to rest. He fell into a deep sleep, and slept until the cold woke him. He felt something pressed against his chest which had not been there before. It was some snake which had crawled there for the warmth. Very cautiously he moved his stiff arms, until he could fling it from him, and leap up in the one motion. He leaped clear of it, and then leaped clear of the place.

It was then about four in the morning and intensely cold. The snake was perhaps too sluggish to attack. He was too miserable with cold to stay longer there. He ate a little of his food, and went on along the face of the cliff, until he found a place of fallen rocks where it was possible to climb.

It seemed to him that he had gone for hours out of his way trying to find a path, and that already he was weaker than he had been from want of proper food and rest. He knew now how easy it would be for him to die up there in the Sierra; why, he might wander for days trying to find food or drink, the way out or the way back. He knew now that he might have been wiser to risk the silver escorts, and follow the railway across the desert.

All that day he wandered on among the mountains, far to the west of his proper course. The crags of a great snowy peak were like a wall upon his right hand, they seemed to edge him off to the west at every point. He would walk for a mile and then think, "Now I can get across to the eastward," but always when he had scrambled up the screes, he would come to some cliff which he could not climb. He saw no living thing in all this day, except two little birds running among the rocks, and the eagles quartering in the heaven.

At last as he wandered, he saw above him a gash or chimney in the cliff. He scrambled to its very foot and looked up it. There was a percolation of water down the side, which he tasted and found sweet. The rock was very rotten, but he saw that it was a way up this cliff. As it was a possible means of getting back to his course, he set himself to climb it. It took him an hour to reach the top, and as he scrambled up to safety above it, the thongs of his ollas broke, and both jars dropped to the bottom of the chimney and smashed to pieces there.

He found himself on a great heave of rocky mountain which went on to a pine forest. Beyond the pine forest the main crags of the Sierra rose, covered with snow. They were blindingly bright in front of him, rocks as blue as steel and ice as white as death, a wall between him and the sea, which he would have to climb.

At about sunset, when he was entered into the pine forest, he smelled suddenly a smell of smoke. It was the smoke of burning pine-cones or pine-needles. He judged that it came from a little fire, because he so easily lost the scent. He turned towards it, thinking that even the most savage of mountain Indians would be less terrible than that loneliness. Sometimes he lost the scent, then he cast about like a dog, until he picked it up again. Presently he was almost certain that he heard a moan. It seemed the fitting speech for such a place. He went towards it, and soon heard the moaning pass into something much more savage, a cursing and a calling down of vengeance. After a minute of violence, it died again into grief and mourning and lamentation.

He went towards the noise and came round some great rocks on to a scene which he remembered until he died. There was an open space there with the tracks of men and horses on the sandy floor of the pine forest. Someone had kindled a little fire there, and the ground was littered with bits of tamales. Beyond the fire, swinging so that his feet were sometimes covered by gusts of the smoke, a dead man hung from a pine branch. At the foot of the tree, crouched and moaning, was a woman. She was rocking to and fro with her grief. From time to time she stretched her arms abroad and cursed and screamed in a kind of rhythm or poetry of hate. Then the grief again became too strong for her, and she moaned and lamented. One of the dead man's slippers had fallen into the fire and lay half burnt there. There was a paper pinned upon his chest, with the word "Traitor" drawn on it with a burnt stick. The paper was a coarse paper bag which had once contained chewing tobacco. The man was quite dead; he must have been hanging there since noon. Both he and the woman were Pardos. From the tracks near the fire it was plain that about twenty had been at the hanging. It was the act of justice of some gang. It was a shock to Sard to find man as harsh as that desolation.

The man was of middle stature, very broad and powerfully built, with a big, broad, rugged face and grizzled curly hair. His arms, which had been bound in front of him, were knotted with muscle. Sard cut him down and laid him on the ground and cut loose his hands. He saw that the man had been shot after being hung. He did what he could to compose the body, and asked the woman if there was nobody near at hand who could help to give him burial. The woman did not answer, she was possessed with her grief and continued to rock to and fro, crooning, moaning, and sometimes bursting out into cursing. He asked if there were any place to which he could take her. He motioned that she should go home, and offered to take her thither. At first she did not understand. At last it seemed to enter her head that he was trying to take her from the body or to take the body from her. She rose up, foaming at the mouth, snatched a knife from her belt, and stabbed at him; then stood snarling and cursing at him, while sobs shook her and tears ran down her face. He did not like to leave her there in that wilderness, but she was not in any mood to let him help her or even to know that he wished to help. He asked if he could carry the body for her to the settlement. He was standing at some little distance from her, speaking slowly and distinctly, so that she might understand what he was saying. At the end of his speech he was almost certain that somebody laughed. Glancing sharply to one side, he was almost certain that somebody slipped behind one of the big pine trees.

"Who's there?" he called. He leaped to one side and caught sight of somebody behind a tree. He saw that behind this person, at some little distance, were two women. They seemed to be negresses. Their faces were covered, and they seemed to be the slaves of this hiding man.

"What are you doing here?" the man said. He spoke the English of an Occidental who had lived for some years in an American port.

"Trying to reach the coast," Sard answered.

"Well, you want to be getting on. There's nothing here that concerns you," the man answered. "You'd best pull out for the coast."

"Which is the way to the coast?" Sard asked. "Is there no trail that will take me there?"

"Trail? Hell!" said the man, "find your trail yourself. Beat it."

"I want to beat it," Sard said. "Can you tell me if I can get across the Sierra, going eastwards from this?"

"No," said the man, "you can't. You must go south-eastwards from here, keeping along the line of those peaks there, and after about ten miles you'll find a gap that they call the pass of Hermita. That's the only pass in all that range."

"Can I reach the coast from that pass?" Sard asked.

"You'll find out what you reach when you get there," the man said. "Now beat it just like hell, or you'll reach nothing this side Jordan."

Sard glanced for just one second or half-second at the two veiled women. They had not stirred during the talk, but in the half-second of his glance he saw one of them start, and in the same half-second he knew that he was in danger and leaped to one side. It was all over in half-a-second, but in that half-second the man had fired from behind his tree. Sard heard the revolver bullet go past him. He dodged to a tree, then away to another tree, then to a third. The man dodged after him, firing whenever he saw a target. The shots came very near: Sard turned and ran.

He went on running for a quarter of a mile, till he was over the brow of the hill. Here he turned at right angles to his track, and ran along the rocky hillside into a glen which had once been wooded with pines, but had been burnt out half a century before. Spikes of charcoal, twelve or fifteen feet high, rose from the ground all over the hillside, like an army of witches. He dodged through this wood and went through it diagonally, keeping uphill. When he reached a bend in the hill, he lay down for breath. He could see no trace of man nor any trace of life, nothing but wilderness, rocks, burnt sand and burnt pikes of trees, the sun looking at it all with indifference, bringing no life to it, and the wind from the icefields floating over it, bringing death.

Sard looked away to the south-east, where the man had said that there was a pass. He could not be sure, and yet it seemed to him that at about that place the hills did seem to fall down into a kind of saddle, as if there might be a pass. Elsewhere he could see nothing but a line of crags, neither sign nor prospect of a pass.

"I may as well die there as in another place," he said. "Why should the man have lied, when he meant to kill me the next instant? But my only chance to get across that pass is to go now as fast as I can put foot to earth, before he can get there first with his gang to head me off."

Tired as he was, he set out for that gap or saddle in the Sierra. He went cautiously, taking care not to expose himself upon skylines. Presently the sun went down. He went stumbling on, in the night, keeping his direction by the stars. At about midnight he could go no further. He reckoned that he must have done ten miles. "In the morning," he thought, "as soon as it is light, I shall see this pass." There was a brook of water coming down the mountain where he stopped. He was guided to it by its flashing and its tinkle. He came to it and found it slightly brackish but drinkable. He drank a very little, and bathed, cold as it was. In a little flat space near the water he found a patch of grass. It was little better than hay, but there were some green blades pushing among the dead, and he ate some for his only supper.

Then he slept and dreamed that he was in the lazarette of the *Pathfinder*, surrounded by food, barrels of prime mess beef, barrels of prime mess pork, tanks of new ship's biscuits, hot out of the oven, casks of split peas, cases of raisins, jams, preserved meats, cheese, butter and pickles. In his dream the steward of the *Pathfinder* came to his elbow and said, "I've put your coffee in the chart-house, Mr. Harker, and I've cooked you a few of those rock-cakes that you like." Then he woke and found himself in the desolation, in the grey of the dawn, with a few blades of grass for his only sustenance. But there in the stream below him was a little clump of plants, bearing still the pods of the seeds of the season before. They were not pods, they were ears, and it was a sort of grain. Most of the grains had been shed abroad, but out of the whole clump he harvested one handful, which he ate almost grain by grain with the husks. They were tasteless but left a slightly bitter after-taste. Hungry as he was, he saved a few with some of the grass for his dinner. It was perhaps five in the morning when he gathered the grain, and only six when he set out to find the pass.

He had not gone very far into the wilderness of rock in which he was before he realised that he was not likely to find any pass. For centuries the great crags of the Sierra had scaled their husks on to these slopes in the heats of the summers. It was a world of tumbled stones, blocks, crags and pinnacles, many of them polished into strange forms by the dancing of the sand about them. He was at that point at which the peaks seemed to come down into a gap or saddle, but he was shut from it by cliffs of a hundred feet, too steep for him to scale. When he had first set out in the morning, he had feared lest his enemies should be waiting for him there, but when he saw the rocks, he knew that no man would be there except himself. Yet he felt sure that there must be some way through the mountains there.

He wandered on, trying to find some point in the cliff which he could scale. With boots nailed in the soles, he might have tried these crags, but he was wearing only the cut-down Bluchers which had been given to him before he left the coast. In these it was quite impossible for him to climb. They slipped aside from under him. This was the first day in which hunger became a torment to him. It had been present in him ever since the first day, but now it possessed him. At about midday he came to a little lake where there was a dead tree growing out of the water. Out of the tree came a piercing and terrible crying from a hawk that seemed to be warning him away. Terrible as the noise was, it was still companionship in that silence. It was something to see and to hear a living thing. The hawk had no fear of him. He walked to within twenty yards of the tree and the hawk looked at him and cried. Presently it rose and circled round and sank away upon the wind, leaving Sard utterly alone. He drank of the water of the lake and pushed on up the hillside to a point where the cliff seemed scaleable. Here as he went he heard noises that made him think that multitudes of men were at work in the mountains near him. There were noises of footsteps and of voices, noises of tools beating upon metals, explosions and the rumblings of machines.

It was now midday, and even at that season the sun had power to loosen stones from the cliff-face. Little stones were falling all round him with little rustling patters like stealthy footsteps. Sometimes a bigger stone would fall, bound for a few feet, and dislodge some other stone. Sometimes little trails of earth and stone came slithering down. Higher up on the great crags boulders fell at intervals, thundering like guns and sending echoes. It was like the laughter of demons.

He reached the summit of the crag and saw beyond him another steep ascent leading to another wall of rock. This ascent was paved with rotten stone, into which his feet sank over the ankles at each step. It was rock made rotten by frost and sun, and it broke like clay under his feet. The sun burned upon his back as he walked, and wind from the icefields blew sand into his face. He persevered until he reached the cliff beyond, only to find that there was no climbing it. It rose up sheer and the point seemed to overhang. When he tried to scale part of it, the foothold and the handhold gave way beneath him. It was stone that had ceased to be stone.

In the heat of the day he learnt that there was no pass there across the mountains. The man had misled him, to bring him into a desert from which there could be no escape. There was hardly any sign of life in all that wilderness, except a few evil-looking shrubs about a foot high, so armed with spines that they seemed all teeth. He had read somewhere that all things in the desert are deadly. These shrubs, the hawk, the asp basking in the sun, and the scorpion beneath the rock, were the only dwellers in that waste.

He made up his mind that there was nothing for it but to go back over his tracks and start again at the pine trees. Evil as the men there were, he felt himself drawn towards them, not from companionship nor from a longing for his kind, but by the thought of the bits of tamale and beans which had littered the ground about the hung man. He plodded back across the field of rotten rock, scrambled down again to the lake, and was amazed to find how little that distance was in returning which had seemed so vast in the going. He bathed and drank out of the lake, found some shelter among the rocks from the wind and the sun, made sure that there were neither snakes nor scorpions there nor any nest of hornets. He repeated the sailor's proverb, "He who has water and sleep has no cause to grumble."

He slept until the sun went down. He was wakened by the crying of the hawk. Rousing up from his lair, he saw the bird perched on the tree with his wings spread, crying what seemed to be a curse upon all that desolation. Hope suddenly came into Sard, for perhaps there was a nest with eggs within the tree. He had been too tired to think of it before, but now the very thought gave him life. He shook with excitement. He went out and swarmed up the tree, found a nest, and though the hawks beat at him and struck him with wings and talons, he took the two eggs, each bigger than a duck's egg and of a mottled reddish colour. In the nest was half of a large lizard which the hawk had brought thither. At other times he would have shrunk from such meat, but now he judged that if it would nourish the hawk, it would nourish him. He ate it with the eggs and wished that it had been ten times its size. Having sucked the eggs, he broke and licked the eggshells. He found that he was not thinking of the wilderness. His thoughts were almost continually in a little English country town, at a grocer's shop, where there were boxes of eggs at the door. He kept thinking of those boxes of hundreds of eggs together, perhaps a thousand eggs in one shop, and of rounds of cheese, weighing a stone apiece. But the eggs were what stirred him most.

Thinking of these eggs, he stumbled and scrambled back over the eleven miles of rock to the pinewood. From his childhood he had been accustomed to take bearings wherever he went, and he had little difficulty in finding his way. In the moonlight he saw the tree with the cut rope still dangling from the bough. Under the tree was the body of the dead man, which had been roughly buried where Sard had laid him. His feet stuck up out of the earth, one bare and one slippered foot. Sard did not think of him, but of the bits of tamale that had been scattered there the day before. To his intense joy they were there still; altogether there were enough bits of tamale and bean pulp to outweigh a ship's biscuit. Hungry as he was, he determined to save half of his find for the next day. He thought, "I depend on a bandit's hanging for to-day's food: to-morrow I need not expect to be so lucky: 'it is not always May': still, 'God will provide.'"

He followed the tracks of the bandits till he heard a wolf howling, with a dog answering him howl for howl. Presently, as he went on, he heard horses squealing at each other: he smelt horses. Next he heard a man singing in a shrill falsetto, with many shakes, to the twangle of a guitar.

Following the noise in the moonlight, he came to a flat pan or gully through which a brook, that had made the gully, still passed on its way to the sea. The hills came closely about the pan, giving it shelter from all gales: this (with the water supply) had made it desirable to the Indians in old time.

The Indians had long since gone from it. It was now peopled by the outlaws who had done the hanging in the pine-barren:

their tracks led into it; their voices sounded from the midst of it. Sard made out a line of huts stretching irregularly across the pan on the line of a track or trail. The falsetto singer was in the midst of the pan, dancing as he sang. Men were sitting about at the doors of their huts, talking, or at least uttering remarks.

"Such, indeed, is life."

"Between Sunday and Monday there is ever midnight."

"She, being a woman, is, as one may say, a woman."

"The gringos, the accursed: is there anything more accursed?"

"Good wine, good water and good sausage: truly three good things."

Sard heard these things uttered with all the dignity of a Solomon pronouncing judgments. Dogs were nosing about among the huts, picking bits of tamale. Sard felt that it would be wiser to move boldly down to the village than to stay skulking in the brush till a dog nosed him. He walked boldly down into the gully and passed at the back of the first huts straight into a lover with his lass. Both cursed him under their breath, but were too much interested in themselves to heed him. He muttered an apology as he escaped. A few huts further along the line he came to a corner where an old ruined adobe wall jutting from an occupied hut made shelter for him. He settled into the shelter, meaning to wait till the men were quiet, when he hoped to be able to find food or a pass, perhaps both. He knew that he was in the presence of men who would cut his throat if they found him, yet he listened to what was going on with enjoyment.

Two or three men were sitting on the other side of the adobe hut; they were engaged chiefly in silence, which they sometimes broke with speech, but more often by spitting. The wind blowing from them brought Sard wafts of cigarette smoke.

"Was that someone passing at the back of the house?" one asked.

"No," another said. "It was some dog."

"To me," another said, "the noise was as of a pig."

"A pig or a dog," the second replied; "when I said that it was a dog, I meant that it was not a Christian."

They talked for a while about different kinds of Christians, of which there seemed to be four sorts: themselves, the ricos, the rojos, and the gringos. There seemed to be something not quite-quite, something not of the sincerest milk of the word, about the last three sorts. They talked about pigs when they had finished with the Christians.

"Never will I be as the gringos," one said, "who will eat of pig, even though it be nourished upon their grandmothers."

"My uncle, who lived not here," the second said, "being indeed from Havana, a city of Cuba, sold certain pigs to certain sailors who were gringos. These pigs these gringos greedily ate; their eyes shone, my uncle said. Yet were those pigs, pigs that had eaten many Christians."

"Lo, now," the third said, "it is not pigs who eat Christians, but witches, the accursed ones, who take the shape of pigs that they may eat: this also only gringos do."

"Yet are the gringos fools," the first answered. "There is Anselmo, who spoke with one but yesterday. Hola, Anselmo, come tell us of the gringo with whom you spoke upon these mountains. Hither, Anselmo. Listen, you, all of you, that you may die with laughter at what Anselmo tells."

There was a pause while Anselmo came to the group: there were greetings of "How so?"; then the first speaker spoke again.

"Anselmo," he said, "these have not heard of your meeting with the gringo upon these mountains. Tell them, then."

"Ah," Anselmo answered in the voice of him who had shot at Sard the day before. "It is thus; if you will see. I was in the mountains, in the pine-barren, where lately a justice of the people was achieved. I, sauntering there, considering many things, since it is my nature to consider, beheld suddenly a gringo, beastly even beyond the nature of such. For a moment I thought, 'Lo, now, a prospector.' Then I saw from certain signs that he was neither this nor that, but an Americano, a Tejano, an Inglés, what matter? This one (I also saw) was lost, as such always are if ever they leave a marked road.

" 'Good day, sir,' I said; since it is ever my custom to be courteous. What, we are not brutes nor Luteranos, I hope; we can be civil one to other. Civility, as they say, costs nothing, yet makes many debtors. I, therefore, did not spit at him as one without faith. 'Good day, sir,' I said, 'I trust that you are well, that your señora is well, that your honoured parents preserve their health, even at their great age.'

"He rolled his eyes upon me like a cow dying of thirst. The gringos have the eyes of cows rather than of men. 'Tell me,' he said to me, 'the way out of these mountains.'

" 'Truly, sir,' I said, 'you who bring civilisation to our savageries will not so soon leave us. Stay, I entreat you, to dine, or at least to sup, or to sing thus to the piano as do the women of you gringos. Yet, since you must leave us, continue,' I said, 'a day's journey north-eastward, till you reach a place where all the rocks are rotten. There you will find a path over the mountains, good for men, excellent for beasts, having grass, inns, a road, good air, good water and good bells, gravel soil and Holy Communion.'

"He was a big man, even for an Americano. He wore no boots, but slippers, such as women wear."

"So you sent him to the rotten rocks," the others said. "But did he go, Anselmo? He surely did not go?"

"Americanos believe all that they are told," Anselmo said. "He either went to the rotten rocks or to another place far from me, which was my desire in speaking to him. Since there was nothing to be had from him, then plainly it was my task to be rid of him."

"Long live Anselmo!" the man said. "So he went to the rotten rocks without question. Thus is it to be a gringo!"

"Without doubt he will be at the rotten rocks, dead?"

"Without doubt."

The man laughed at this: presently the youngest of them said:

"You say that he had slippers such as women wear? Would it be worth the while to retrieve the slippers for Mariquita?"

"It would not," Anselmo said. "This man was outcast from the gringos, unable to live even their easy life. His slippers were not women's slippers, but the wreck of boots cut to that size. He was in all respect ruined: moreover he was lousy."

They continued to talk of gringos for some little time, though the thought recurred to the youngest of the men that Sard's body might be worth the rummaging: he asked Anselmo whether Sard had "a belt of the Americans," or at least "a pouch for tobacco, such as he had seen."

"No," Anselmo answered. "This gringo had nothing: even the crows will have nothing from him. Had he had anything, I, Anselmo, would have had it: as it was, let the vultures give Anselmo thanks."

They talked on, of gringos, gringo women, the women of the district, the recent cock-fights, the ingredients of sausages, the natures of parasites, etc., etc., till Sard, lulled by their drawling low speech, fell asleep. He was in a dangerous place, but danger will not keep men awake so well as love or grief. Besides, few stop to identify a sleeping man. He slept as a sailor will sleep, like a dead man. In his sleep, some two hours later, he shifted about, so as to detach a piece of adobe from his shelter. It fell, with a little clatter which he half heard through his drowsiness. Unfortunately, it roused a little dog within the hut; the dog began to bark. Sard sat up at once, wide awake; his movement knocked down more adobe; the dog barked louder: a man within the hut cursed the dog; but the dog, aware of Sard, would not be silent.

"Listen," said the man in the hut, "be silent, Chaco. Listen; there is someone there."

"Who would be there?" a woman asked. "It is but a dog, prowling for bones."

"I do not know who may be there," the man answered, "but it is no dog, since dog will answer dog with barking."

"It is some drunkard or some pig of the poblacion," the woman said. "Come here, Chaco; down, dog; quiet!"

Unfortunately, Sard in rising to his feet stirred Chaco to bark louder.

"Your drunkard or your dog or your pig," the man said, "these are likely excuses, are they not? Where are my boots?"

Sard heard him drag his boots to the bedside, muttering.

"What then do you expect to find, Andrés?" the woman asked.

"You know well what I expect to find," Andrés replied.

"Indeed I know no such matter," she answered, "since the expectations of a husband are beyond the wit of wives. If you will tell me, then shall I know."

"Know, then," Andrés answered, "that I expect to find Martin, your lover, who taps here, like a second Pyramus, and shall die here in his sin, like a second Chico the Blanco."

Sard did not wish to be the second Chico the Blanco; he slipped up the line of huts as swiftly as he could. He slid round the corner of a hut, under its eaves, into the grey of the wall. He was hardly quiet there when Andrés came rushing past looking for Martin.

"Stay, Martin accursed," he cried; "we have accounts to settle, offspring of a dog." He ran, cursing, along the line of huts.

The village or poblacion had not composed itself to sleep: it was perhaps always ready for a row. Sard heard a general rushing to doors, as the inhabitants came to see the fun. Some boys brushed past Sard, who joined them.

"What is it? What is it?" the boys asked.

"Andrés seeks Martin, to kill him," Sard answered.

"Andrés is killing Martin," the boys cried. "Come, boys, Andrés has killed Martin." Sard found himself in the midst of a crowd of men, women and children, hurrying up the line of huts. The crowd stopped towards the end of the line where Andrés was beating with his knife-hilt upon a door.

"Come out, you Martin," he was crying. "I will have thy liver as a bake meat, yea and I will mince thy heart and eat it with red pepper, without grace."

There was a general edging back of the crowd at this, to get out of the line of fire from Martin's door: Sard edged back too, till his back was against a hut wall. He could see Andrés' wife at her hut door, peering after her husband. All waited for Martin to answer the challenge: Andrés even waited for a reply: none came.

"So, scum of a Martin," Andrés continued, "half-breed of a toad and a heretic, you justly fear my vengeance. See, now, brothers, this Martin, before I take his skin to be my bed-mat, makes his last prayers: he confesses, he sues for mercy. But I am not one to grant mercy till blood has flown on my front teeth. So come out, Martin, offspring of a dog, till I crack your marrow-bones with nutcrackers and take your marrow for boot-grease."

Suddenly the door of Martin's hut was flung open and a woman faced the madman.

"Who is it calls Martin?" she said. "Who is it couples a fine name with the filth of a drunkard's ravings? You, Andrés? I thought no less. Martin is away, as is well known, or by this your tongue would have been tied round your neck with your own entrails, dog of a drunkard. Away, accursed one, trouble not the houses of the honest. But when Martin returns, then he shall know of this, Andrés, and then, Andrés, shall you be squeezed in the press till we know if your blood be wine or oil."

Sard expected that Andrés would at least reply, but there was silence. Martin's wife took up the word once more.

"And you people of the town," she said, "have you nothing better to do than to watch the antics of this fool? Go, every one to his house, or Martin shall deal with you, even as with him."

There was silence again for about thirty seconds, then three or four of the children, who had been on the outskirts of the little crowd, edged sheepishly away. They were followed by others. Sard had no time to dodge or hide; any movement of the sort would have betrayed him. He stood where he was, somewhat bent and peering towards Martin's hut, with his left hand shading his face and eyes. Half-a-dozen people, children and grown-ups, passed him on their way to their huts. They looked at him rather hard, but no one spoke to him. A man and boy, as they passed, looked perhaps harder than the others. After they had passed, Sard heard the man ask under his breath:

"Who was that by the corner of the house?"

The boy said, "Old Ortiz, I thought. Good-night, Ortiz."

Sard answered and muttered good-night. As he spoke, a couple of lads, who were running, jolted into the two friends and jolted Ortiz out of their minds. Up and down the line of huts people went home and closed their doors. Martin's wife stood at her door, looking at them. The last to pass was Andrés, who went shambling past, muttering and twitching. Sard heard him mutter, "With my good knife I would have laid him low, I would have laid him low."

Now from Andrés' hut came the cry of a woman:

"Where is that creature calling himself a man, to whom the church has bound me in matrimony, who suspects me of infamy? Where is this Andrés, who from the blackness of his heart asperses the whiteness of my honour? Let me see him that I may cast his foul calumny in his teeth. Is it for this, O dog of all the dunghills of Spain, that I redeemed thee from thy life as hangman's boy and made thee a knight-at-arms?"

Those who had not gone home hurried to watch Andrés receive his wife's eloquence. Sard saw Andrés enter his home, but then something made him look up suddenly. He saw that Martin's wife, who had come a few paces from her door, was looking at him with curiosity. It was bright moonlight; no one who looked at him could fail to see that he did not belong there.

"Well, I'm caught now," Sard thought. "It's neck or nothing now. Well, the straightest way is the quickest."

He walked straight up to her.

"Madam," he said, "I'm not a spy or the police, or anything. I'm lost here in these hills; will you help me out?"

She looked at him for some moments. "Go further up the line," she said, "the third hut from here is empty. Pass in there and have no fear."

She closed her own door in his face, and Sard did as he was bid. The third hut from hers was empty. He went into it. At some early time there had been a mud wall across the hut, dividing it into two. This had fallen into a pile of loose earth. Sard got behind this pile and thought, "Well, here I am; and if that woman lifts a finger, my throat will be cut on this doorstep, and that little beast, Chaco, will lick my blood."

He waited; each minute seemed an hour. At the end hut of the village the man still sang to his mandoline, in his falsetto voice, a poem of intolerable length and folly, which Sard recognised as a rhymed romance of the early 17th century. Footsteps passed up and down outside the door. Once three men came to the door and stopped there, muttering in low voices for two or three minutes. They were smoking cigarettes and spitting. One of the men was carrying harness, which clanked.

One of them said, "Well, sooner or later that's what it'll have to come to."

And another said, "We can count on you then?"

The other replied, "Well, come here, come on inside here; I'll just give you my reasons."

He had his hand on the door-latch and the door eight inches ajar, when the other said, "No, not in there, thank you. There are tarantulas in there. Come on up along."

They moved away. Then for a long time Sard sat there, thinking of what they had said: "There are tarantulas in there." He heard a queer, regular, clicking noise in one of the corners, two or three yards from him. It was a little dry, slight clicking noise, rather like two wooden skewers being tapped together. Someone had told him, years before, that tarantulas click their mandibles together before they attack. "That's what it is," he thought, "it's a tarantula in the corner."

He kept himself breathlessly still, and then suddenly he heard a little light pattering. There was a swift, flurrying scutter along the floor, a shrill squeal, something leapt and fell across his feet and writhed away squealing. He heard the thing, whatever it was, rat or mouse, trying to shake itself free in the corner of the room. The squeals soon died to a whimper and the whimper to a sigh, as the tarantula in the darkness sucked his fill. Sard presently heard the corpse sink down, as the insect moved away. He waited with his feet drawn up under him and his hands covering his throat, lest the insect should want more blood and come to him for it.

The time went slowly by, the man with the mandoline ceased his song, somebody who wished to sleep cursed a howling dog until it came indoors. But the wolves out on the mountains crept nearer. From time to time one would cry his cry. Whenever this happened, the dogs in the huts whimpered and were uneasy. Everybody, by this time, had gone to rest in that village of outlaws. Sard thought that it could not be long before the woman redeemed her promise.

Then from somewhere up above he heard the sound of drunken singing, which became louder as the singer came down into the village. Sard presently picked up the words of the song, which

202

was one of the romances of the Moors in Spain. As the drunkard entered the village, every dog in every hut flew to the door barking with all its strength, in spite of the curses and boots of the owners. The drunkard paused outside the row of houses and cried in a loud voice, "Here I am, old Pappa Peppy, and I'm as drunk as I want to be. Come on out, Martin, Tomás, Ramón, Espinello, for I tell you I'm not Pappa Peppy, but an avenging angel of the Day of Doom. I'm the Lord's second coming and now I'm come." And at this he let fly with two revolvers at the doors of the huts, in succession. Drunk as he was, he had extraordinary precision. The bullets thudded into the doors as though he were running a stick along palings.

"Come, Tomás," he cried, "and I'll shoot the white out of your eye. Come, Ramón, and I'll see the colour of your blood; for I'm Pappa Peppy, and I'm as drunk as Noah when he got home."

There came another volley. Sard noticed that none of the bullets came into his door. He thought: "This is that ruffian's hut, he'll presently come in here to sleep." The drunkard went to another hut and beat upon the door with the revolver butt. "Come, out, Ramón," he said, "and let's shoot, man to man."

Sard heard the voice of Ramón: "Take another drink, Pappa Peppy, and let us shoot in the morning, for now I'm sober, and how can a sober man hope to shoot like you?" A bottle seemed to be passed through a cautiously opened shutter, and Sard heard Pappa Peppy say, "You're a Christian gentleman, Ramón. All I ever wanted was a drink, and now I've got it."

Sard heard him take a drink and then come unsteadily to the door of the hut where he lay. He fumbled at the door, opened it, and stood groping there, feeling along the wall as though for a ledge where matches and candle stood.

"The lamp's gone," he said; "th' only lamp I ever loved all gone. They all turn from Pappa Peppy."

He came fumbling along the wall into the hut, and then went fumbling back and shut the door. Then he said: "Well, I've got box o' matches. First of all, I'll put the nice brandy up in the corner. I've got a box of matches somewhere. I tell you I've got a box of matches and then I'll show them. They aren't going to fool Pappa Peppy."

Sard heard him creep back to the door, holding on by the wall, and heard him say: "I'll just kneel down very carefully and I'll put down the brandy there, and I've got a box of matches somewhere. I know I've got a box of matches somewhere. The man who says I haven't got a box of matches, I'll shoot the white out of his eye. Who says I haven't got a box of matches? That's the sort of skunk they are. They daren't say it to my face, not one of them. Of course I've got a box of matches."

He proceeded to empty his pockets in the dark, muttering over each thing. "What in the name of all the saints is this? Bit of a cigar. What in the—oh, bit more cigar. That's a bottle of peppermint, all broken. Ugh! the glass is all broken." A reek of peppermint liqueur filled the little hut. "No good looking for them in that pocket," said the man; "there's cigars in this pocket. There goes the box of matches. I knew I had a box of matches and it's gone on the floor."

The box of matches jerked out of the pocket and fell very close to Sard. The drunkard went down on hands and knees, diffusing a warm breath of peppermint liqueur and aniseed brandy. Sard felt as though he was to leeward of one of the Spice Islands. The man began to grope for the box of matches, patting with his great hands and breathing with difficulty. "I know the box of matches isn't far," he said. "It's very stormy to-night. In a wind like this one had to go miles out of one's way. Oh, the wind's roaring, the wind's roaring! And well it might roar, for I'm not Pappa Peppy, I'm the Day of Judgment. I'm the Day of Judgment, and I'm dawning and I'm coming up over the mountains now, just like blood, and if I lay my hands on that box of matches, they'll be the first thing I'll blast. I'll teach 'em to fool the Day of Judgment!"

Presently he paused in his search. He had missed Sard by half inches two or three times. Presently Pappa Peppy stopped not more than a yard from Sard and said in a little, cold, clear voice, "Lord pity the poor sailors on a night like this! That's ten times I've been round this room looking for that drink. It's been witch-craft. I can see you here, and well I've known you were here all the time, and I know you're doing it with your witchcraft, you black beast. I've watched you doing it, but you needn't think to scare Pappa Peppy. He's the Lord's, he is; he isn't one of yours. He's a lily for the pure to look to. He fears not Satan nor all his minions. Ah! here's the bottle. I knew I'd come to it, if I kept to the south far enough."

Sard heard the cork drawn from the bottle and the gurgle as he drank raw aniseed brandy.

"That was what I wanted," said Pappa Peppy. "A man like me who takes a lot out of himself has to put it back or go under. And I'll have another like that—ah! I'll have another like that. And now I can lie down on the floor without holding on, and let the storm roar itself sick. I don't care, I don't care. To-morrow when I get hold of that box of matches, I'll show it what I think of it."

The bottle dropped from his hand. It must still have been a third full, for as it rolled away some liquid gurgled out of it. Pappa Peppy gurgled in sympathy or in tune, and composed himself to sleep, sitting up against the wall. He passed into a drunken unconsciousness almost at once, breathing with dreadful difficulty, being in fact at the point of strangulation, through his throat pressing against his collar. After two or three convulsive gasps, he shook himself out of his dangerous position and lapsed sideways. "There'll be death upon the sea this night," he murmured; "I've known gales, but never anything like this." After this he slept and the village slept.

It must have been full midnight when the door opened suddenly and the cool night wind blew in from the desert. The woman was there. "Come, you," she said.

Pappa Peppy groaned and fought with his drink. Sard rose up and came to the door. The woman had a little leather bag full of food for him and a leather-covered gourd full of water.

"If you go past the houses," she said, "and follow up the cañon, to the end, you will come out below the icefields. In all my living here I have only heard of one man who has ever crossed those fields. His name was Gonzalez: he lived a hundred years ago. He crossed them and reached San Agostino in five days."

"It's San Agostino that I want to reach," Sard said.

"Go then," the woman said, "and may you have that man's luck. He was my grandfather. But know this: you're in the land of the bad men, the land of Red Sleeve and the Jacarillos, and not one other soul for thirty miles would have done what I do, not one other soul."

"Tell me your name," Sard said, "that if ever I get among my people again, I will think of you with gratitude until I die."

"We have no names in the Jacarillo country," she said; "but if ever you come to some church in Christian country, say a prayer to the Virgin for Juanita of the Bolson. And now go."

She was herself gone on the instant and flitted back like a thief into her hut. Pappa Peppy gurgled in his sleep and cried, "I'll deal with you if I can get at you!" and then cried, "O God!" and moaned. Sard knelt down, picked up Pappa Peppy's box of matches, took his two pistols and cartridge belt, loaded both pistols, slung his provisions over his shoulder, and set out with a pistol in each hand from that city of the Jacarillos.

Fifty yards from the huts, he entered the cañon, now stealthy with the noises of the night. Near the mouth of the cañon a sentry lay asleep within the ring of his rope which screened him from snakes. Sard crept past him on tiptoe, but need not have taken such precaution, since the man slept like the dead. Not far away, something large, grey and silent, probably a wolf, which had been creeping up to steal the sentry's food, glided into the sage brush.

In another fifty yards the trail turned upwards into the hills, out of sight of the gully. Sard went on as hard as he could put foot to ground for three hours. Then coming suddenly round a corner, walking rather carelessly, thinking that he was quite out of the reach of pursuit, the faint smell of smoke crossed his path; immediately he was in sight of three mud huts by the side of the road. He was reassured an instant later by seeing that two of the huts were ruined. There came a rustling from within the third; a hideous old Indian woman came out. She might have been any age from a hundred and twenty downwards. They looked at each other in the grey light in the heart of the wilderness. She mumbled something in reply to his question, but any wits she once had had long since gone.

Sard pointed to the snowy peaks below the stars in the sky. He asked in Spanish, "Is there a trail across the Sierras?" He made signs of a trail and of mountains.

Some memory lit up intelligence in her faded mind. She laughed. "They all go over the mountains," she said. "All the young men go into the mountains. That's why all the mountains are white, for all their bones are on the mountains. Your bones will be white on the mountains. I live up here among the mountains and I can hear them. All the round white skulls come rolling down the mountains. She ran into her hut and returned with the skulls of three white men. "They all rolled down the mountain," she said, "for they are Indian mountains, and the white men know much, but they don't know about the mountains. By and by I'll have your skull. I'll put him in the ants' nest to clean and I'll keep him on the shelf."

Sard hurried away from her, but for about half a mile she followed him, hugging the skulls. He pushed uphill as hard as he could go, but in the stillness of that glen he could hear her voice for a long time, saying that his skull would roll down the mountain.

There was now no trail, but he fixed his course straight to the frozen crag, which gleamed above him against the sky. Dawn found him still pushing onward and upward in a trackless wilderness that seemed to bear no living thing. When the sun rose, he found some shelter among the rocks, where he might defend himself if attacked. He expected that the Jacarillos would trail him as soon as it was light enough to see tracks, and that with ponies or donkeys they might well be on him before noon. In this he was unjust to the Jacarillos: they did not trail those whom they judged to be already doomed. In his shelter he ate, drank and then slept; he did not wake until the setting sun shone through a crevice among the rocks on to his face. After eating and drinking he set out again into the Sierras.

All littleness was gone from the mountains now. His world was one with the elements, the sky, great stars, and gigantic crags, silent except when now and then there came a roar from something breaking in the glacier, or the thunder of a boulder falling. The moon rose to light his going up a slope of rock, which seemed curtained by other slopes of rock. Here he laid down one of the revolvers which he had taken from Pappa Peppy. He laid it on the rock beside him. Instantly it slithered down, gathering small stones as it went, till it was thundering down the rocky slope far, far below, with an avalanche about it. He saw it flash and presently heard a report, and realised, as he had not realised before, that he might have slipped like the gun and gone gliddering down among the boulders in the same way.

At about midnight he reached a ledge of rock, where he slept until daybreak. When he woke he saw what he took to be three cloaked Indians, sitting on the ledge beside him. He sat up and looked at them. They withdrew their heads from their blankets. They were no Indians, but vultures. They looked at him with interest and without fear. He spoke to them, they muttered a little and moved uneasily.

"So you're waiting for me to die, are you?" he said. "I'm not dead yet." They craned and sidled with their bald heads. "Get out of this," he said, smiting at one. It went sidelong off the ledge, and the others with it. They beat with their wings, recovered their poise, and sailed out into the air. An instant before, they had been squalid, stinking, huddled creatures; now they were floating in the majesty of beauty. Two hovered at a little distance from the ledge, the third rose above it in a short spire. He had never seen any bird of prey circling at such close quarters. He watched the great pinions soar up above him, while the others hovered away and mewed and cried. Suddenly the bird above him launched itself down upon him and beat him with its great wings, so that he was almost over the ledge. Instantly it was up in the air and repeated its swoop. It came down sighing and struck and hissed at Sard, and immediately the two birds who had been waiting, swooped and struck at him. "So you're going to get me down into the valley and pick my bones," Sard said. He lay flat down upon the ledge, face upwards, and drew his other revolver. The bird came down on him again, crying and smiting. He fired; the bird went up, poised, went up a few feet further, beat with its wings, mounted yet a little further like a towering partridge, then crumpled up and dropped. Sard saw it strike and roll and lie still. Its companions swayed away to look at it and then descended to the body.

Sard looked down and wondered how he could ever have climbed that crag at night without falling. He knew that he could not go down it by daylight. He looked at the crag which rose up above him from the ledge, and felt that he could not climb it. He had reached a point from which he could neither go nor come. He ate and drank and then thought, "Perhaps when I'm rested I will be able to try this rock. If not, I shall end here."

He slept on the rock until the beating of the midday sun became unbearable. He twisted to an angle where his head could lie in some shade, and slept again. He was aware in his sleep that some-one stood upon that ledge and told him to come on. He sat up, looked at this figure and knew that it was only partly human. In his dream, or fever, it seemed like the spirit of the *Pathfinder*, fierce, hard, and of great beauty. He told himself, "This is all nonsense. The *Pathfinder* is a ship, she has not even a figurehead, but a fiddle-head; this is a woman."

But the figure said, "I am the *Pathfinder*. I can find a path for you." She lead on up the rock and Sard followed. He could see her in front of him; he followed where she trod. There was a great star above the crags. The crags were thick with greenish ice, the star shone upon the ice, till it glittered like a crown. Sard said, "I'll put my hand on the crown of the mountain."

At daybreak he came out on a wild place near a brook.

There was grass there whistling in the wind. There was a little bird somewhere, not far away, crying a double note that sounded like a curse, continually repeated. Sard drank of the brook, sheltered from the wind and slept; nor did he know when the woman had passed from there. Afterwards, he was puzzled about that part of his march; sometimes it was in his mind all blurred, like the events of a fever, sometimes it seemed the only reality among things dreamed.

When he woke he was out in the snowfields. He thought that he had reached the summit, but he found that he was only on the top of a small shoulder. Beyond and above him were crags, sprinkled, heaped or overwhelmed with snow, some of it dirty from fallings of rock, some of it violet from shadow, the rest of it glittering. There was no sign of any living thing. If he looked up, there were peaks glittering against the sky; if he looked down, there were glittering snowfields, crags and chasms.

He could not see the country from which he had come, because greyness was hiding it from him. Grey shapes, like the leaders of a herd, were moving into it. A herd of mists followed their leaders, so like oxen that he expected them to bellow. They jostled on in myriads till all the lower slopes of the mountains were blotted out. Soon a sea of mist washed all about those miles of Sierras; the peaks stood out of this sea like islands. "If that sea rises," Sard thought, "I shall be drowned up here. I must move while I have light."

He had his direction from the sun. He pushed on, now up, now down, over snow of every degree of rottenness. He had a little food left in his wallet. He guarded this, but slaked his thirst with snow and chewed upon a piece of his belt.

In the evening it began to blow bitterly cold with a small snow. In one of the whirls of the gale he found himself upon a piece of a made road. He could hardly believe his eyes; but there was no doubt: it had been made by men. It had been cut out of the side of the crag; the crag at its side had been carven with the figures of the gods. A tall god with his tongue transfixed by a bramble was pouring libation on an altar; beyond the altar was a door leading into the crag. As he stood there, the sun shone out through a rift to light the eyrie he was perched upon. Used as he was to heights, it made him sick to think of the will that had spent men, like water, to hew that rock at that height. The sun shone into the doorway. Looking within, he saw two figures upon a throne. They sat side by side, holding each other's hands. They were staring straight at him.

"Yes," he said, "what are you? Who are you there?"

Peering in, he saw that they were the bodies of a king and queen who had been buried there in that mountain tomb, perhaps centuries before the Spaniards came. He crept into the tomb to look at them. Once the door of a slab of stone had been mortared flush with the face of the crag, but it had fallen like most of the road that led to it. The mummies sat side by side, holding each other's hands. Masks of gold still covered their faces. The masks had, no doubt, been modelled on the dead faces and preserved likenesses of that king and queen. Both were tiny; they looked like children to Sard. They were the rulers who had driven men up the mountain to make that road. All about the walls were paintings of the lives of those two.

"Ah," Sard thought, "he was a king and when he died the kingdom fell to pieces. She knew that it would be so, so when he died she killed herself."

The sun, which had been shining. was now suddenly blotted out again. A cloud of intense blackness seemed to rush out of the heaven to engulf the crag. The air was filled with crying and small snow. Sard sat there in the darkness and fell asleep at the feet of the king and queen.

He woke often, because it was so cold. Whenever he woke, he heard the gale full of bells tolling, or voices crying to him: often he answered them. Once or twice he went to the door to answer voices; but no one was there except the gale, full of small snow. He wondered if he were alive, or if this were death; not final death, but the leaving of the body which is the prelude to it.

In the morning the wind dropped: the snow ceased: the storm went bodily off across heaven like an army that had been beaten, in a sullen mass, with rearguards of sulphurous smoke followed fast by the angels of heaven with light. The sun followed hot upon it with fire, till presently it was far, far away, engaged upon the southern horizon.

As Sard came out into the sun, he saw a name cut or scratched upon the lintel of the door of the tomb. The letters were lastingly but rudely graven by a strong illiterate.

Gonzalez Medina.

1795.

"Gonzalez Medina," he said. "That woman's grandfather. The only man who ever crossed these mountains. Here I am upon his track. If he blazed his trail thus, I may still find my way out."

The finding of that blaze was companionship to him all that day, which was a hard day, one of his hardest.

*   *   *   *   *   *

One of the worst of the hardships was the knowledge that all was not well with the *Pathfinder*. He had put so much of his virtue into that ship, that she was almost part of him. He felt that things were going wrong on board her. Sometimes, as he struggled on, he knew that someone was in his place, making evil, and that Captain Cary wanted him. He kept thinking that Father Garsinton had brought the evil.

He could not remember Father Garsinton clearly, yet he stayed in his mind, like a blur of evil.

*   *   *   *   *   *

Long afterwards, in thinking over his climbing of the Sierra, some things came back into his mind as pictures or dreams or happenings; he never knew really which they were. Often it seemed to him that at this point in his journey he heard a beating of pans and the murmuring of bees: he saw bees swarming and a big Spanish woman beating pans to make them settle. He asked to be allowed to beat pans; afterwards he hived the bees into a straw basket.

Then the woman suggested that he should drink some honey drink, and took him to a house where she and her husband, a much older and much yellower person, gave him drink in a strange cup and asked him what he saw after he had drunk.

He said, "I see a path leading upwards."

They said, "Go along the path. Now what do you see?"

He said, "I see a little house at the end of the path, shining as though it was made of some white metal."

They said, "Is the door open?"

He said, "No, the door is locked."

They said, "Go and put your hand on the sill of the door and see if the key is there."

He said, "It is there."

They said, "Open the door and go in."

He opened the door, but inside all was darkness with a smell of carib leaf which choked his throat and made his head stupid.

They said to him, "What do you see?"

He said, "Nothing but a brazier burning carib leaf, which throws out a thick smoke which chokes me."

They said, "No; but to right and left of the brazier what do you see?"

He said, "Two pillars and a person bound to each pillar."

They said, "Look well; who are the people bound to the pillars?"

He looked with all his strength into the thickness of the smoke. It was agony to him not to be able to see clearly, but he said, "One is Juanita de la Torre and the other is myself, and we are being choked by the smoke."

They said, "It is not the smoke, it is something coming from the brazier."

Then from the brazier the little tongues of flame, writhing among the carib leaves, changed to red snakes which were arms and hands that came twining about the throats of the two bound figures. The fire in the brazier glowed into the likeness of a human soul with the face of Father Garsinton, who laughed and said, "I crush you lesser spirits as a sacrifice to my master."

Then all became dim with carib smoke choking and stupefying, but the words, "I crush you lesser spirits" were repeated many times, while the house, the honey-cup, and the Spanish man and woman faded and disappeared.

*　　*　　*　　*　　*　　*

Soon after this he climbed a spine of rock, expecting to find on the further side a dip of snow with a higher spine beyond it. To his amazement, there was no such dip nor spine; but the slope of the mountain falling below him into a different world. On this ocean side of the Sierra there was no desert. Instead of a chaos of rock blasted by the sun to rottenness, there were heaves of hill flinging their waters to the forests. Forests covered the valleys like a fleece. In places where there was no forest Sard could see little white houses. The smoke of a train ran like a caterpillar along the valley beneath the foothills. Beyond the foothills **was** a dark mass, like a bar of metal, yet not like a bar of metal, because it seemed to be alive, it gave Sard the thought that it trembled: it was the sea.

Far away, on the brink of this darkness, was a smudge or cloud in which some chimneys stood like stalks. The smoke merged into the air so that a tiny golden dome glittered: it was the cathedral in San Agostino. Almost at once, quite clearly, though faintly, in some chance channel of upper air or freak of sound, the chimes from the dome reached Sard. It was a familiar Spanish chime to which Sard always put the words of the poet:

> "Gloria in las alturas,
> Cantad in vuestra jaula, criaturas."

Worn, footsore, more than half-starved as he was, he could not see his goal nor hear that chime without "singing in his cage." There was his desired haven, within how many hours of march? He could not tell how many hours; perhaps very many hours; but no matter what his pains were, he felt sure that having seen his goal, he could reach it.

Going down was like soul's delivery after the toils of the last days. In a few miles he was in the timber, going down a glen of great trees towards a smell of honey which came thickly upon the air to him. Sometimes he missed it for a few yards, but it always returned on the next gust. Sometimes it brought to him memories of tea in England, but more often the intense memory of a picnic at Yapavai, where he had sat near a field of the yellow melilotis hovered over by countless blue butterflies.

At the end of the glen he came out on to a heave of the hill, where he found the cause of the honey scent: eleven great trees lay broken on the ground.

Nine of the eleven were hollow from the ground to the upper branches. In all these, for perhaps centuries, the wild bees had nested, till now many hundreds weight of honey lay broken or spilt upon the ground. Over this, in some places, the bees were still flying confusedly, but by this time most of them had gone with their queens to new shelters. Gorged bee-eaters sat on neighbouring boughs. Some small mountain bears boldly foraged in the tree-boles. They clawed out great paws-full of comb which they plastered into their muzzles in spite of the stings. Sard found a piece of broken yellow comb the size of a bath-sponge. On this he fed with thoughts of the prophets fed miraculously in the wilderness. After this, the miseries of the wilderness fell from him as though they had never been. Perhaps the honey had in it some drug of excitement or of comfort. He wandered on happily, feeling sure that all his troubles were at an end. He bathed in the pool of a mountain stream on the banks of which wild strawberries grew so thickly that the ground looked like the foot of a red hawthorn tree after a storm in June. After this he went on through a forest of big timber which grew on easy slopes with little undergrowth.

The moon had risen before he came to any trace of men. He came to a clearing and followed wheel-tracks downhill till he saw the lights of huts. Men in the huts were beating tin pans and singing:

> "Is that Mr. Riley
> Who sets such a styley?
> Is that Mr. Riley who keeps the hotel?
> Is that Mr. Riley they speak of so highly?
> How d'ye do, Mr. Riley, are you doing quite well?"

As he came to the door of the first hut, a man who was tapping out his pipe there, hailed him:

"Hello, sport! where in hell do you come from?"

"Over the mountain."

"Mountain, hell! Are you looking for a job?"

"No."

"Doing it for a bet, then?"

"No. Trying to rejoin my ship."

"Hell!" the man said. "Here, boys, here's a son of a gun come across the mountain, trying to rejoin his ship. Come in, son, and have one on the house."

* * * * * *

At noon the next day Sard was in San Agostino, washed, shaven, fed, reclad, and with money in his pocket. He walked in the crowded street, listening to speech, hearing the bells. Shops were full of food, drink, shoes and clothes; women were looking into shops; work was going on; men with places in life were filling them.

He had no place. He knew now how little a thing will put a man out of a place, into the wilderness beyond, where to be at all is to be an outlaw.

He stopped on the steps of the Consulate to look at the ships in port: among them was the big English steam yacht, the Yuba, which he had seen in Las Palomas, as it seemed in another life. A man hailed him by name.

"Hullo, Harker!"

It was Billy Binge, his old captain of the main.

"I say, Harker," he said, "are you ashore here? Yes? What topping luck! Could you take the Yuba to Santa Barbara?"

"Yes."

"Sir James has sacked his old man for crooking his little finger: going on the jag, in other words. He wants a new old man, muy pronto, and the worst of it is all the masters on the beach here are out at elbows."

"So am I," Sard said.

"Only in your gear," Billy said. "These other fellows are in their souls. I can vouch for you personally. So if you really can take her, come along, I'll fit you out a bit and then I'll take you to Sir James."

"One minute," said Sard. "Have you heard anything of an abduction case at Las Palomas?"

"Abduction of Miss Kingsborough?" Billy said. "We've heard nothing else. She's been carried clean away."

"Where to?" Sard asked.

"Search me," Billy said. "Some damned trader in Eve's flesh; but there's a fine old breeze about it. Now come along."

"What brings you to San Agostino?"

Sard told him in few words.

*　　　*　　　*　　　*　　　*　　　*

216

Billy Binge's recommendation was sufficient; Sir James engaged Said to command the *Yuba*. She sailed late that night, up the coast to the Recalde reef to take some dredgings. After a few days at the reef, she sailed for Santa Barbara, where she arrived at noon just nineteen days from Sard's going ashore at Las Palomas.

Sir James stood at his side as he brought the *Yuba* into Santa Barbara harbour.

"You've not been here recently, Captain Harker," he said. "You'll not know the place; it's a different place: almost a different city. They're making this place the Athens of the West: I say *they*, but it's really *he*, the Dictator, Don Manuel. Look at the cathedral; there'll be nothing so beautiful in the New World when it's finished. Do you see your ship, the *Pathfinder?*"

"No, Sir James, she isn't in the sailing ship berths."

"That is unfortunate for you," Sir James said, "as I suppose it means that she has both come and gone; but it is fortunate for me, for I hope it will mean that you will come home with us in the *Yuba*.

Part FOUR

AS soon as Sard was free, he went ashore to see Messrs. Wrattson & Willis's agents. He was puzzled by the *Pathfinder's* not being in the port. She could not be overdue, he thought, in just dropping down to leeward. She might have come and gone: in which case he would have missed her by a few hours. "More probably," he thought, "she has gone down the coast to Otorin to complete her cargo. I'll find her there."

At the agents, as he asked for his letters, one of the managers of the firm, a tall, alert inscrutable man of about thirty-five, a Mr. Waycock, heard his name.

"Are you Mr. Harker of the *Pathfinder*," he said, "come into my office, will you? I want to speak to you. Sit down here: the cigars are at your elbow. You don't smoke? You're the first sailor I've ever known who could say that. You know, Mr. Harker," he said, "I heard that we might expect you apart from the *Pathfinder*. I had news of you from a man with whom I have business dealings, a man called Douglas Castleton."

"Has he been here?" Sard asked. "Where is he?"

"Isn't that a little like asking where is the curlew?" Mr. Waycock said. "It is best, perhaps, not to ask where Mr. Castleton is. I understand that he is not here at the moment, but away again on . . . well . . . on a business journey."

"What news of the *Pathfinder*, sir?" Sard asked.

"The *Pathfinder!*" said Mr. Waycock. "Haven't you heard? She was wrecked last week on the Snappers. She's a total loss."

"On the Snappers!" Sard said. "How on earth did she get there? Are all hands saved? Is Captain Cary safe?"

"You've not heard then," Mr. Waycock said. "Of course you couldn't have heard. No. all hands are not safe. They had pestilence on board. Captain Cary is dead. He died some days before the ship went ashore."

"Dead!" Sard said. "But he was well when I saw him. How did you hear this?"

"We had a cable from Port Matoche where the crew were landed," Mr. Waycock said. "Here it is. It gives just the bare facts, but if you come here to-morrow morning at nine o'clock, the crew will be here with Mr. Dorney. Mr. Hopkins is still in hospital. The rest will be coming in this evening by the mail. You can see them here in the morning. Here's Dorney's cable as far as it goes."

Sard looked at the flimsy.

"I'm glad Captain Cary didn't lose her," he said. "But how did they put her on the Snappers?"

"Well, she came down on both knees like a riderless horse," Mr. Waycock said. "They had a fever on board. I don't know more than that."

"Yes," Sard thought to himself. "I know the kind of fever they've had on board, Captain Cary dead and myself not there, Hopkins ill and Dorney who can't navigate, a man who doesn't hold with sights but can foodge a day's work, as he calls it."

"Are they bringing Captain Cary's body, sir?" he asked.

"No, he was buried at sea," Mr. Waycock said. "A fine seaman, Captain Cary—of the old school, that is. Of course his day was over. He couldn't have held his own much longer. It's just as well as it is."

"Yes," Sard said bitterly. "He didn't lose her and he hadn't got the sack. But he wasn't wanted and they let him know it. You must excuse me, Mr. Waycock. I have been with Captain Cary for ten years. I must go out and think of it. I will come in the morning."

At the door as he was going out, he said, "One other thing, Mr. Waycock. Douglas Castleton is mixed up with a very queer company of men. I suspect that some of those men were concerned with abducting a woman, a Miss Kingsborough, from a house in Las Palomas. I have reason to believe that the men in that abduction came from Santa Barbara here and were going to bring Miss Kingsborough here to some Mr. B. or Sagrado B. who runs a rum-running business and is plotting revolution against the Dictator here."

"Oh, but I think you're quite mistaken about that," Mr. Way-cock said. "Our friend moves in very queer company, but not in company of that sort at all. Besides, Miss Kingsborough has been found. The case was reported in the press a week or ten days ago. She was taken by bandits, not by rum-runners. She was held to ransom. I think I could find you the account in the paper. I have got it somewhere here. She was in a mining town quite close to Las Palomas, a place called Tlotoatin."

"Tlotoatin!" said Sard.

"Yes, do you know it?" said Mr. Waycock.

"I have been there," Sard said.

"Oh, here's the 'Humanidad,'" Mr. Waycock said. "Here's the account, 'Miss Kingsborough found.' Cost her £400." He pointed the paragraph to Sard, who read:

"Miss Kingsborough Found.

"A cable from Las Palomas confirms the rumour, which we quoted in our columns yesterday, that Miss Kingsborough has been restored to her friends and relatives. Yesterday the agents of the British Consul visited the place appointed by the bandits with the sum demanded for the lady's ransom: £400. Great reticence veils what took place at the meeting, but the bandits were men of their word and Miss Kingsborough was set free. A press agent who interviewed her late last night declares that she is looking none the worse for her adventure, and that the bandits treated her with courtesy. Thus ends a nine days' wonder, and thus, as we hope, will end the campaign of calumny which the Occidental press has waged against the police of Santa Barbara ever since Miss Kingsborough's disappearance. The criminals of this atrocity were not natives of this State, but Occidentales, living on the scene of their crime. Let the doves of Las Palomas change their ways before they accuse others of being wolves."

"I'm relieved to find that she has been found," Sard said. "So that ends that."

"You see," Mr. Waycock said, "this is five or six days ago."

"Did you ever hear the nickname B. or Mr. Sagrado B.?" Sard asked, "in connection with rum-running or plotting against the Dictator?"

Mr. Waycock had a broad, smooth, pale face, tranquil, like the face of an image of Buddha.

"I know no one with such a nickname," he said, "and there is no rum-running from Santa Barbara. There may be rum-running from the coast far to the west, six hundred miles from here, where the rum is made, but none from here. This fiction of the rum coming from Santa Barbara is made by the Las Palomas police, Mr. Harker. And as for plotting against the Dictator, you meant, I suppose, the Don José faction. Who would shoot the Dictator to put Don José in his place?"

"Don José would, for one," Sard said.

Mr. Waycock laughed. "He hasn't that reputation in Santa Barbara," he said.

Sard suddenly felt that he was in the presence of one of Don José's backers.

"One thing, Mr. Waycock," he said, "if Douglas Castleton isn't plotting or fetching rum, what brings him to Santa Barbara?"

"He comes for letters, Mr. Harker; twice a year he comes to Santa Barbara for letters."

"If ever he wants lawyer's counsel or a gaoler's bribe," Sard said, "remember that I will pay for both as long as I'm alive."

Mr. Waycock considered him with just the flicker of a smile.

"Very good, then, Mr. Waycock," Sard added, "I'll come in the morning at nine." He went out into the street. "Captain Cary dead," he muttered, "the *Pathfinder* gone and Miss Kingsborough found. Well, that ends that."

He found himself at the bronze of the Bajel Verde on the beach. He gripped it with his hand, suddenly overwhelmed with grief. His captain, the old extra-master:

'John Craig Cary, of the ship *Petrella*,
Thunder-ship and stand-from-under fella,"

was now a new hand, at sea in death, with perhaps no one to
teach him the ropes. The *Pathfinder*, who had found so many
paths, where no paths showed, would now find no more. She
would be jammed on the reef in the glare, while the rollers would
surge over her, climbing her stern, rising, rising, rising, then
thundering down, blue, then green, then blinding, all day long,
all night long, till she broke.

"I've had enough of the sea," he said. "It takes a man like Cary
to master the sea. Then the day after he goes, the sea smashes all
that ever he made, as though it had never been."

Everything there reminded him of Captain Cary. The bronze
on which his hand lay marked the very place where the Heroic
Six had made their stand at the Green Boat. He had seen them
there. He had been with Captain Cary in the cross-trees of the
Venturer, watching the Heroic Six hiding, creeping out and firing
until their cartridges were all gone. He remembered Captain Cary
stamping and cursing when the boat patrols put out.

"There, boy," he had said, "now they will be destroyed. Their
retreat's cut off. But fly down on deck, boy, and pitch the coils
of the buntlines over the sides, so that, if any of them does reach
the ship, he'll be able to get on board."

He had done this and in the dusk of that bloody day one of
those buntline ends had caught a strange fish, Don Manuel himself, now the Dictator.

"Yes," Sard thought, "it was Captain Cary who saved Don
Manuel and by doing that he made this port the Athens of the
West."

Two hundred yards further along the new front towards the
city was a strong shelter made of white Otorin marble. Something
was displayed within it upon a bronze pedestal. Sard went in to
see what it was, because it seemed to be a ship. It proved to be
a big model barque flying the house flag of Wrattson & Willis:
Sard recognised her instantly as the *Venturer*. On each side of the
supporting bronze was a medallion portrait of Captain Cary, with

an inscription in Spanish, which Sard translated thus:

> "In eternal gratitude
> To Captain John Craig Cary
> And the officers and company
> of the English Barque Venturer,
> For their nobleness to the ruined in the Noche Triste."

Under the inscription was a list of the Venturer's company, divided into watches, just as it had been in that long ago time. The list ended with the boys of his own watch: "Adam Bolter, Charles Crayford, Edward Grant, Chisholm Harker." Under his own name were two lines of verse:

> "They gave their safety, shelter, friendship, bread,
> To me who had a price upon my head."

Sard was overwhelmed. "So," he thought, "here is Captain Cary's monument. I wonder if he knew of it; he never mentioned it. I hope that he knew of it. He must have known of it."

The model had been made in England by skilled craftsmen working under someone who had known the Venturer intimately. Little special matters, such as the make of the truss of the fore-yard, the lead of the braces, the design stencilled on the deckhouse, the use of brass pins in the poop fiferails, all showed that one of the old Venturers had been engaged in the work. "Flackwell, the bo'sun, helped in this," he thought, "there is Flackwell's gadget of the broom-rack in the bo'sun's locker."

By this time the sun was behind the Sierra; the ships were dim against the bay and men were hoisting the riding lights. Sard could hear the blocks creak as they swayed them up. He went along the water-front to the end, and then climbed the great white marble staircase, between the lines of orange trees, to the Plaza of the Martyrdoms. He had never ceased to be amazed and exalted by the beauty of the new work. That stair, ten years before, had been palm-stems pinned into the earth like the rungs of a ladder. Now it was all Otorin stone, white and exquisite, with marvellous busts of the martyrs at intervals along the balustrades: Carlotta, Jane Jennings, Pascual Mestas, Celedonio Vigil, Agapito

Chavez, Luciano Sisneros, Inocencio Chacon; then Carlotta and Jane Jennings again, with those five of the Heroic Six who had been killed in the bay. The faces leaned from among the dark green of the orange trees. In the groves behind them there were fountains.

He reached the Plaza at the top of the stairs. There at least the Houses of the Last Sighs were as they had been. They looked dingy and evil in that place of brightness: they looked as if they would not have any life of their own until all the lights were turned out. They were inhabited still, for a little smoke came from one of the chimneys. Sard wondered that anybody should live still in them; but he had heard that they were let at cheap rates, being supposed to be haunted, and that they were to stand thus, unpainted, till the last of the Don Lopez faction, Don José and one Rafael, had been shot there like their victims.

There were three houses together, a big one in the centre, flanked on each side by a smaller. On the wall of each of the smaller houses, at breast-height, were the chippings of bullets, under the legend, painted in white,

Hic ceciderunt.

He did not need to be told that, for he had seen the prisoners dragged thither to be shot after Don Manuel's defeat. He had seen two or three hundred men shot there by the Lopez faction. He had watched it all from the *Venturer's* cross-trees: batch after batch, volley after volley: not men only, but many women, and some children. He had seen the accursed Reds drag their victims out of houses. It had not been the suppression of a rising, but a massacre of all whose virtue shamed them.

Hic ceciderunt.

He could not see the words without a prayer, that those who had fallen there had found peace, and that those who had killed them there might find justice.

There was another white temple-like structure in the Plaza, a round roof upon columns of marble, which sheltered musicians. In a European city it would have been a "kiosk" or a "bandstand";

here it was a lovely work of art, which took away the breath by its grace and fitness. Some musicians were moving away from the shelter, having finished their playing: the crowd which had been loitering or lounging about the music was now breaking up. Most of it was setting towards a theatre which stood under bright lights on the southern side of the Plaza. Sard went with the crowd, with a feeling which he had never known before, that to be with many people, in bright light, is a satisfaction, an excitement, a consolation.

Outside the theatre doors were the bills of the play, which gave yet another shock to Sard.

> " Theatre Jane Jennings.
> Numancia,
> by Cervantes.
> Tafoya. Archuleta. Vizcarra."

Theatre of Jane Jennings, playing a poetical tragedy by Cervantes. Why, when he had come there in the Venturer Jane Jennings was alive there, a byword, a most notorious bawd, the talk of all the fo'c'sles in port, infamous herself and the cause of infamy in others. Adam Bolter had been to her house and had talked and drunk with her. "A big, fat, black-haired woman, with a hooky nose: she was always either swearing or singing lullabies." Now for her heroic defiance a simple people had made her a heroine, a national heroine. All that was evil in her had dropped from her, like rags or lice, leaving only something noble. He felt the nobleness. She had had her throat cut there in front of those dingy houses rather than do a dirty thing. Now her memory was kept alive in that place, as one whose fineness alone counted; the rest was rightly forgotten. She had come from Bermondsey and had been a bawd; now there were marble busts of her and a theatre named after her in a capital city.

He paid tribute to her memory by entering her theatre. He heard Tafoya, Archuleta, Vizcarra and their companions speak the verse of that great soldier-of-fortune. But he could not heed the tragedy.

His mind was full of what he had heard in Mr. Waycock's office.

"What does it all amount to?" he kept asking himself. "I met a girl, many years ago, who altered my life for me: all my time has been a dream of her. Then in my dream, hearing those men at the fight, I went to warn some strangers; for they were strangers, name and nation different from hers. I warned them. I might just as well have held my tongue and gone on board; they did not profit by my warning. Now the girl who did not take my warning is safe and sound with her friends, while my friend is dead, my ship is on the Snappers a total loss, and I myself am alive only by miracle.

"What does it all mean? Some power, with fore-knowledge and other knowledge, wanted me out of the *Pathfinder* and got me and kept me out of her by the only means which could have done it. With me away, the Captain dies and the ship is lost; then I am allowed to rejoin the ship's company. Why should I have been wanted away, save for evil, since nothing but evil came of my going? The *Pathfinder* was doomed, so the man who could have saved her was taken out of her. That ass Pompey and the foodger Dorney were left to play hell with her and well they seem to have played it.

"I was lured out of the ship by the appeal to the softest thing in me. By stooping to the lure, I have made a pretty mess of things: the ship lost . . .

"It all comes from my love for that girl. Even if it be madness, or folly, or delusion, all that love has been very real, it is my intensest thing: and the intense things cannot lie: they are the only true things. Jane Jennings' intense defiance was the true woman speaking: all the rest was only mistake."

The tragedy came to an end with the blowing of a trumpet for the great who had died. Sard moved out with the company into the Plaza, which was now lively with the city's amusement. He went to a little table in front of a café, and dined there, listening to selections from Gluck's "Iphigenia." He faced the music; the Houses of the Last Sighs lay to his left.

When he sat down at his table, before the waiter took his order,

226

a man in uniform appeared with a pencil and a printed form. Sard's name, nationality, ship, duty, station, lodging and other particulars were asked and noted. "Such is the law," the man said. "In every eating-house and hotel in Santa Barbara. It prevents unpleasantness."

Sitting there in the light, among the crowd, listening to the music, was a pure pleasure to one who so few days before had been starving in the Sierra. Sard could not feel that "unpleasantness" was near that happy place: all seemed so happy. Long after his dinner was at an end he sat there sipping coffee. His waiter, a big brawny Spaniard with a good-humoured cynical face, pointed out the Houses of the Last Sighs.

"It was there, Señor, that they shot the martyrs on the Day of Troubles. See, Señor, the bullet-marks. Never will those houses be cleaned, or painted, or rebuilt, till the vengeance has been paid; thus has our Dictator vowed. When the debt is paid, they shall go; until then . . . thus."

Sard knew more about the martyrdoms than the waiter, but in politeness he edged his chair aside, so that he could see the houses. The two outer houses were closed, with dark green jalousied shutters over every window. The central house, the largest of the three, had no shutters, but the windows were blinded and blank. The big windows of the ground floor were also shaded by the green, iron turtle-back of a verandah.

"The houses are dead," he said.

"No, Señor," the waiter said, "they are inhabited. A poor sort of people live in them. See, there, a padre enters."

The houses were about forty yards away, under brilliant electric light. Sard saw a big, muscular priest walk with the air of a king up the steps of the central house. He turned at the door to survey the Plaza below him. Even at that distance his attitude and gesture gave the idea of domination. He seemed to dilate there. He looked like a lion conscious of supremacy. His pose seemed to say, "You canaille exist and die and rot, but I am above these things."

There was something familiar in the man's presence, strange as it was. That pride and power of bearing seemed familiar to Sard:

he felt that he had seen it before. As the priest entered the house, Sard thought that he reminded him of Father Garsinton, who had begged a passage in the *Pathfinder*.

"He was like that Father Garsinton," he thought. "And it is strange. . . . Sailors would say that it was the sky-pilot who brought her on the Snappers. I did not hear about Garsinton at the office. Waycock never mentioned him, though of course he would not concern Waycock in any way."

"Tiene," he said to the waiter, "that priest who entered, do you know his name?"

"No, Señor; nor himself. A poor sort of people live in those houses. Without the priest they would be poor indeed. 'They have but birth and death,' as we say; with a priest, these will suffice a man."

"Do you know of any people called Garsinton in that house?"

"I know no one there, Señor."

"After all," Sard thought to himself, "it can hardly be Garsinton. He will be coming here in the *Recalde* with the rest on a Consul's order. He can hardly be here yet. Even if it were Garsinton, his story of the wreck would probably be worthless. I suppose Pompey or Dorney will lose his ticket over this wreck, but the fault will be with myself and my dreams."

He ordered more coffee. He talked to the waiter about events in Santa Barbara. The man said, as Waycock had said, that there was a little rum-smuggling from the western coast, in that immensely remote part known as "beyond Caliente." He said that "things" were settled now in Santa Barbara. "Revolution, Señor," he said, "what is it? A grand name for bad manners. What overcomes all revolution? Art. And art Don Manuel brings here. Regard the cathedral . . . the western front not faultless, but what spirit. . . . Then, too, the opera. I, a poor man, have my fill of opera, I sing in opera . . . in certain choruses. . . . All this Don Manuel makes possible. Great things are shared by all here; this gives security."

Sard presently rose, thinking that he would take a turn about the Plaza and then to bed. It seemed to him that to work in a city like this, where great things were shared by all, would be happier, than working against the sea, which shares nothing, permits little and surely takes all in the end. "I must make a new start somewhere," he said, "on a new foundation since the old has come to grief. Since the old ends here, the new had better begin here."

Though it was easy to say that the old had ended, his mind was full of Juanita de la Torre, as he crossed the Plaza to the jut of land called Cachopos. On this jut, completely covering it, was the nunnery of Santa Alba, whose votaries kept the Cachopos Lighthouse. Sard had heard of these nuns. He walked to the end of the Plaza to see where they lived. He could see little more than the body of their church, the walls of the conventual buildings and the pharos with its slowly revolving beam of light. Twice in each minute, the beam as it came round fell for five seconds upon the unfinished spire, tower and pinnacles of the cathedral, making them glow as though they were living creatures.

Sard watched its coming and going for some minutes. He had grateful thoughts of the women who kept that light. He turned slowly back into the Plaza, feeling utterly alone. He found that the café where he had dined was closed. The tables and chairs had been stacked away together at the edge of the pavement; his waiter had gone. Sard took a seat at another café nearer to the Houses of the Last Sighs; he ordered coffee and sat there watching the people. All were going home now, for the amusements were done: it was almost midnight. Among the last to pass across the Plaza near Sard was a little old figure of a woman, who carried a mandoline case and music. Something about her seemed familiar to Sard. Her name and state came back to him in a flash: he rose and bowed, saying:

"Señorita Suarez."

She came nearer to him, looked at him hard, but could not recognise him. She was sixty-five. She wore black and yellow lace upon her head; her face was yellow as gold, wrinkled as shrunk cloth; her hair was iron grey, done in ringlets, her nose was like a hawk's beak and her eyes like coals.

"Señorita Suarez," Sard went on, "I was in the Venturer, years

229

ago, in the Days of the Troubles. You were on board for some days, with other ladies of The Blancos."

"Ah, yes," she said, "sad, sad days in the *Venturer*. You have seen that we remember?"

"Yes, indeed."

"And you remember me? I cannot remember you."

"How should you?" Sard said. "I was but a boy then, and, unlike you, did not make lovely music."

"Ah, yes," she said, smiling, "always I make music."

"Señorita," he said, "for the sake of old times, will you let me offer you refreshment?"

"That, no," she said: then, in English, "No thanky."

The talk did not seem successful, so Sard said:

"We were lucky in the *Venturer*. We saved Don Manuel for a great future." The old woman drew back as though he had insulted her or wounded her to the quick.

"For a great future?" she said, swelling like a cat about to spring. "For a great future? I trust, yes, for a very great future; for an execution so great that all this city, this bay, the mountains and the islands of the sea shall be black with people come to watch it. Let him live, Lord, to taste the greatness of that future, the Lord-with-us, the padre Pipi. You, sailor, dog of the tides, who caused us the contamination of his presence, and cursed this city with his life, speak not to Jenny Suarez of dons and futures, he, the accursed, whose footsteps press blood out of the stones." She spat towards Sard in the vehemence of her hate (she did not do it well) and went shaking, muttering and clicking past him, and so away down the great marble stairs.

"I suppose she was a Red," Sard thought, "become a Red since Don Manuel became Dictator. I thought that perhaps Waycock lied about the Dictator's popularity."

When the waiter brought him his coffee, he asked whether Don Manuel were much loved.

"Very much, Señor."

"Since when, and why have they named him padre Pipi?"

The waiter looked round in alarm.

"This Plaza is Blanco, Señor," he said.

"What of it?"

"Perhaps, Señor, you know little of affairs here. Let me then warn you, as a native, never to make use of that name. It is a Red name, Red as the grid of hell, where I yet shall see those Red accursed roasting. We of the Whites call him the Grande. And truly he is Grande. He is the Lion of the Faith, Grandissimo. Yet even that name, in certain parts, among certain people, it is not prudent to speak aloud."

"It is very true," Sard answered. "Truly a man digs his grave with his teeth, but assuredly he cuts his throat with his tongue."

"Assuredly."

"Viva Don Manuel," Sard said, "to the great race the great ruler."

"Amen, indeed, Señor."

"When will you close?" Sard asked.

"At one in the morning, Señor; lo, now the day passes."

One of the bells of Santa Barbara very sweetly chimed for the hour. Instantly, from all over the city, other bells began either to strike or to chime till the air was trembling with sweetness of sound which melted into the midnight and made it deeper. Some of the ships in the bay made eight bells: a clock in the House of the Dying Sighs struck: it was midnight. Now while the deepness of a tenor bell was toning, there came, from Cachopos, perhaps a quarter of a mile away, the exquisite song of the nuns of Santa Alba at their midnight office. Sard was spellbound. All the night had ceased to be of men and folly: it had become suddenly a thing of stars and flowers and of the joy of the soul in her God.

The coming of the midnight seemed to be a signal that the life of the town should stop. It seemed to bring everybody home, so that in a few minutes the Plaza was almost empty and so quiet that one could tell the passing feet: the small, belated woman hurrying: the guardians in couples slowly patrolling, pausing to try if doors were locked.

Then, from one of the streets leading to the Plaza from the northward, there came the singing of drunkards. Sard hoped at first, from the noise that was made, that the drunkards were foreigners; but they were two English reefers, both sillily drunk, followed by a third, who, being sober and much younger than the others, was trying to pilot the drunkards down to the landing-stage. They were trying to sing some fragment of grand opera which they had heard that night: they made a bestial row, "between the bull and the cat."

Sard eyed them to see who and what they were: the two drunkards were from a small barque in the bay: the sober boy, to his amazement, was Huskisson, a first-voyager from the *Pathfinder*. Huskisson, a *Pathfinder*, running the midnight with these two night-owls, within an hour or two of landing, and not ten days from Captain Cary's death. Sard stiffened and waited.

The drunkards bowed low to Sard, laughed, lurched across to the door of the centre house of the Last Sighs, and banged upon it with their fists. They shouted a song as they banged.

> "Beautiful Rosey-posey,
>   Ever I think of thee,
>   I love sweet Rosey-posey
>   And sweet Rosey-posey loves me."

One of them called to the waiter to bring them some vinos; the other, a short, squat, sub-nosed lad, whose name was Crockums, did not like the waiter.

Crockums: You darned mañano Dago, fetch the vinos, intende, or I'll smash your papish chops. You want to forget, you ain't in no vatican, now, nor yet in any rancheria. Come on, Paggy, and pitch this feller over the bubb-banisters.

Paggy: No; he's not a genelum; never fight with a feller's not a genelum; never fight with a genelum's not (singing) "A captain in the how-d'ye-do brigade. How de do? How de do? I'm a captain in the how-d'ye-do brigade."

Here Huskisson, who had not yet recognised Sard, but was terrified of arrest for disorder, interrupted:

"Look here, you fellows, don't make this row; we'll have the civil guards on us in a minute."

Crockums: Make this row?

Paggy: Who's making any row?

Crockums: We're not making any row, you young pup; go and lap milk in a tea-joint.

Paggy: He talks like my female aunt.

Crockums: I've torn a man's trousers off for less; dammy, the sea's that refined nowadays it's chronic.

Here the waiter appeared with the three little tin cups of Santa Barbara claret.

Crockums: He shan't have any vinos now, because he told us not to make this row.

Paggy: All the more for us.

Crockums: Drink hearty, Paggy.

Paggy: Salue.

The two of them drank each one vino; then shared the third.

Paggy: Hold your tumbler, Crockums.

Crockums: Go easy.

Paggy: It's only this red vino.

Crockums: You're giving me more than my share.

Paggy: They give one the purser's gill here: two thimbles and a thumb.

Crockums: Here's how.

Paggy: Here's health, wealth and unity.

As soon as they had swallowed the wine they put down the cups, breathed deeply, turned, rushed at the central door, beat upon it with all their strength singing "O come let's kick the door in," to the tune of Adeste, Fideles. At the second stanza they changed the words to "Let's fling the table through the doorway," seized one of the tables and prepared to do as the song bade. The waiter interfered with "Ho, Señores, that, no. The tables, no. The song, yes, but not to break the tables."

Crockums: What do you want, steward?

Paggy: He wants to be paid for his vinos.

Crockums: How much for your vinos? Combien de money?

The waiter: Tres pesetas.

Crockums: Tres pese . . . ? tres pesetas?

The waiter: Si quiere usted.

Crockums: Who the hell are you calling a keeiary usted? Hold my coat, Paggy. I'll have this blighter's blood.

Here Huskisson interfered again, saying that the waiter had only said, "If you please."

Crockums: I'll please him. My mother isn't going to be called a keeairy usted by any dam Dago on this coast. There's your keeairy usted in your teeth.

He seized the tin cups one after the other and hurled them in the waiter's face; then he and his Paggy upset a table apiece, screamed aloud, and ran yelling down the marble steps towards the port. Sard turned to the sober reefer.

"Huskisson."

"Sir."

"What were you doing with those two?"

"Helping them to their ship, sir."

"Don't you know that you belong to a crack ship?"

"Yes, sir."

"Why disgrace her, then, by going about with a pair like that?"

"I was trying to save them from arrest, sir."

"Where are you sleeping to-night?"

"At the Sailors' Home, sir."

"Very good, Huskisson, now sit down and eat an ice with me and tell me of Captain Cary's death."

Huskisson sat down and began to cry.

"Avast heaving, with the tears, Huskisson," Sard said kindly. "Tears won't help anybody. Just take your time. Eat your ice and then we will walk to your Sailors' Home and you shall tell me everything as we go."

This is Huskisson's story:

"After Captain Cary left you ashore in Las Palomas, sir, he waited for you a long time. He wanted to be sailing, for it was looking very black and he was anxious for the ship. After an hour or so, he sent Mr. Dorney ashore to look for you. Mr. Dorney didn't come back till after eight. He said he'd been out to a house for you and that you'd started back by another way before he got there. Captain Cary was upset by that. He said he hoped you hadn't got into any trouble. He said to Mr. Hopkins, 'I don't like staying any longer. The ship's not safe here in a norther and the glass is dropping like a stone. Still I must leave word about Mr.

Harker.' So he sent the boat in again to leave word at the police about you, sir. The swell was setting in very heavy indeed when we went ashore, but coming back we were very nearly swamped. When we got back, Captain Cary said that there was nothing for it but to leave you ashore. He was very much upset about it, sir. He said, 'I wish I had not let him go, but I felt it my duty at the time.' And that padre fellow, Father Garsinton, the passenger, said, 'Whatever one feels to be one's duty, is right, depend upon that, Captain Cary.' Captain Cary said, 'I'm not so sure, sir,' and told Mr. Hopkins to man the windlass.

"We were well out of Las Palomas, sir. We were the last to run for it, all except the *Mondovo*, and we heard since that she drove ashore.

"It was after the sea had gone down, when we were well clear of the Serranas, that the trouble began.

"It began the third day out, just when everything seemed settled in for a quick run. It began with quite a little thing, sir. The geraniums in the cabin were all found withering. They all died within a few hours: Captain Cary thought that the steward had given them salt water by mistake. Well, that passed over, sir, and we thought no more of it. But then, the next day, there was something wrong with one of his canaries; something the matter with its throat. The steward said he thought it must have the pip. It kept straining with its head as though trying to clear its throat. And in the course of the day the others fell ill with the same complaint. Captain Cary supposed that some poisonous seeds had somehow been packed in their bird-seed: anyhow they all died. Mr. Dorney told us that Captain Cary was very much upset at the canaries dying. He had always counted on his geraniums and canaries for a bright cabin, and you know, sir, they had been lovely little singers.

"Captain Cary seemed out of sorts that night during the first watch. He said something to the helmsman, who couldn't understand what he said. I was near at the time, time-keeping, and I couldn't understand either; he spoke so thickly. Then the next day he fell really ill. He came down to breakfast dragging one leg and making a noise in his throat as though he was trying to swallow or trying to speak. He couldn't do either; he couldn't eat nor drink nor say what was the matter. At first they thought that something was stuck in his throat, but it wasn't that. Mr. Dorney said he thought it was hydrophobia, and Mr. Hopkins thought it was more like lockjaw. There didn't seem to be much pain, but he was frightfully distressed. He kept trying to explain what was the matter or what should be done, but nobody could understand what he said, and it weighed upon him frightfully that people couldn't understand him. Mr. Dorney said he cried.

"They tried to get him to lie down, but he seemed worse, lying down. He was very much worse next day. You see, sir, he was an old man. He'd never been ill before and the worry of not being able to speak or swallow or sleep broke him up.

"Old Jellybags went aft to be near him in case of a call that night; so as to give the steward a rest. Old Jellybags was in a blue funk about it, because we all thought that it was hydrophobia and that he'd be bitten. Still, he said he wasn't going to let any da . . . I mean any O.S., sir, look after Captain Cary, while there was anyone in the half deck to do it.

"We helped him shift his bed aft. We envied him having all night in. Wolfram saw him at the beginning of the first watch; he said that Captain Cary seemed quieter. I suppose that that was about a quarter past eight.

"The steward peeped in on them at coffee-time next morning. He didn't like their looks, so he called Mr. Hopkins. Captain Cary was unconscious, but still fighting this thing in his throat; and poor old Jellybags had caught it: he couldn't speak nor swallow, but seemed trying to clear his throat. I can't explain it, sir, but it was horrid to see: they felt it so."

"What was the passenger, this Father Garsinton, doing," Sard asked. "Most priests in the tropics have some knowledge of medicine; couldn't he help or suggest something?"

"Yes, sir. He said that he had seen nothing like it. He examined the patients and said that their hearts were very fluttery. He said that the poison must have come on board in the air, from the norther, the day we sailed. He said that it must have come from some very poisonous place away up north, where there is no sun to kill germs, and that it came in at the skylight.

"He said that it must have come in at the skylight because the first things it attacked were the geraniums just under the skylight, that then it attacked the canaries, close to, and then spread to Captain Cary, who was so often there, and from him to poor old Jellybags.

"Mr. Hopkins said, 'We're certainly carrying some tropical disease, it's in the cabin where the Captain and Old Jellybags have been sleeping. We'll sulphur out all the cabins.'

"So we sealed all the cabins, both fo'c'sles and both deck-houses and sulphured them out. Then when we unsealed them, we mopped them all over with carbolic solution. We reckoned that that must have disinfected the ship.

"Next morning Mr. Hopkins was down with the disease, just the same symptoms and this fluttery heart.

"We could find nothing like it in our medical book, but Mr. Dorney worked out a dose for a weak heart; but you see, sir, they couldn't swallow. When we tried to dose them they seemed to choke. Mr. Dorney said all along it was hydrophobia they'd got. You can understand how we felt about it, sir.

"The next day the steward went down with it just the same as the others. That was one of the worst of all the things, sir, because with all these people falling sick, one of the chronometers ran down and something went wrong with the other. You see, sir, it had been in the infected cabin."

"Rot, boy," Sard said, "a chronometer couldn't pick up infection."

"Well, sir, perhaps it can't, but that was how we felt about it when everything in the cabin got poisoned.

"And then that morning, sir, poor Captain Cary died in the room where he was with Jellybags. He hadn't said anything that we could understand since he had fallen ill. You can imagine what we all thought, sir; we all knew what Captain Cary was. We buried him that afternoon, sir. It was dead calm and hazy and blazing hot. Mr. Dorney read the service and just as we put poor Captain Cary into the sea, that little black cat came out of the cabin, and it had the disease. It dragged one of its legs and was fighting in its throat and its coat was all staring. It came to the grating where Captain Cary had lain and mewed. Mr. Dorney said, 'My God, the cat's got it.' I don't think anything scared the men so much as that cat coming out; there was a regular growl; and they growled a good deal too, because Mr. Dorney took the service instead of the padre. Mr. Dorney said that he was acting captain and it was the captain's place to read the service; marriage, christening or burial. The crowd didn't like that at all, nor did the padre; but Mr. Dorney said that they'd 'joost have to loomp it.'

"Poor old Jellybags died the next day.

"Then we got a slant of wind which lasted for three days: the disease never seemed to do much when the wind was stronger than light airs. Then the wind died out and it came on thick, just as we were expecting to pick up Cape Caliente. It was blazing hot, with mist, just when we didn't know where we were. Then the disease came on again: the poor steward died and the poor little cat died, and the padre seemed very queer.

"Then Sainte Marie, the French A.B., who had helped to bring out the steward's body, went down with it. He was the first man forward to get it, and, of course, he got it by coming aft. And now everybody was terrified, not only at the disease but at being shut up in the mist and lost. We hadn't picked up Cape Caliente and we were all afraid we'd been caught in the southerly set and put to the south of it on one side or other. We couldn't tell where we'd got to. We tested the water alongside to see if we were near the mouth of the Santa Maria, but the water wasn't brackish. We'd hands aloft looking for high land. From time to time we hove the lead, but it's all volcanic water there, sir, just like the bottomless pit. It was like being under a curse. One of the worst things was that when the padre went queer he kept intoning the burial service. It was dead calm and very hot, with the sail slatting and all the gear jangling and the ship's bells tolling as she rolled.

"Then about dark that night the wind freshened a little. We got her to lay a course about west-north-west. She made as much as two knots for the first couple of hours, though it was still thick. We had the fog-horn blowing because we hoped to get an echo if we were anywhere near the high land. Just before midnight we heard breakers on the lee bow. Mr. Dorney put her about and kept her on the other tack for a couple of hours. Then we heard breakers again on the lee bow. Mr. Dorney put her about again and took a cast of the lead and got volcanic rock at 125 fathoms. Then the wind dropped and it came on very thick. We had all hands on deck waiting for a call and from time to time we heard the padre, sometimes fighting with this thing in his throat, sometimes calling out the burial service. It went on like that, sir, for some hours. Sometimes we had a few stray slants of air and then they would die away again. At about 3.30 we heard breakers on the port bow and then breakers on the starboard beam. Mr. Dorney said we must be among the Chamuceras. Anyway, we were embayed. I don't think Mr. Dorney had been off his feet for two days and two nights, sir. We drew clear of these breakers, and it was just beginning to grow light when we heard breakers again on our starboard bow and then breakers on the port bow and then the wind died on us, sir, and there wasn't a breath. Suddenly the padre appeared on deck in red socks and with a red tamash for a loin-cloth. He stood at the poop rail, laughing and cursing, and then the fog cleared away, and old Holdfast, the Vancouver man, who was in the cross-trees, sang out, 'Land, ho,' and the look-out man shouted, 'Breakers dead ahead, sir.'

"Mr. Dorney sang out to let go both anchors, and one of them, at least, was let go. Somebody sang out, 'Weather main brace,' I suppose, to lay the main yards aback. Most of us ran to the weather main braces, and I was on the rope and we were just beginning to haul, when I saw something white rise up on our own weather bow, and then she went crash on to something and knocked us all off our feet. She got up just as we did and seemed to look around and wonder what was happening, and she lifted clear of whatever it was and seemed to jump out of it, but perhaps it was only the broken water that gave me the idea that she did, for then she ran fairly on to it with a crash which tore the boat's skids clean off and pitched her fore and main top-gallant masts right out of her like bitten-off carrots."

"Were the men aloft killed," Sard asked.

"No, sir, they were warned by her hitting the first time. After that second crash she didn't strike again, she only worked down into where there were great breakers all round us. Then the fog went as though by magic and it was daylight. We could see everything when it was too late, Cape Caliente, Port Matoche, and all the coast as far as the Cow and Calves. We were on the Snappers, seven miles west of Caliente. Mr. Dorney had been thinking that we were among the Chamuceras, thirteen miles east of her.

"Well, sir, we could take stock of how we were. She was lying over on her starboard side a little and about a foot or two by the stern. We judged that she was ripped pretty well open, for the water was over her 'tween decks. And now that it was too late the wind began to freshen and she began to grind where she lay. Mr. Dorney furled the sails to ease her and got the boats ready for hoisting out, and by the time the boats were ready she was grinding down at each swell with a noise like ice cracking on a lake, and the sea all round her began to come up in a kind of syrup from our sugar.

"By eight o'clock it was no joke to be on deck. She was pounding and breaking the sea. Mr Dorney decided to abandon ship. He hoisted all her colours first, house-flag, ensign and number, and then he got off three of the boats. I went in the bo'sun's boat. Just before Mr. Dorney's boat was put over the side, while we were lying off watching, there came a great big swell, which passed underneath us, of course, but it caught the old *Pathfinder* fair and gave her a great yank over and everything in her seemed to fetch away over to starboard with a bang, and the next swell went right over her all along. It was just all they could do to get that last boat over.

"Well, that was the end of it, sir, we'd a bit of a job to make Port Matoche, for the wind freshened into one of those local northerly gales which they call Arnottos. But we landed everybody and we took the sick up to the hospital. Mr. Hopkins and the A.B. were both much better when we left Port Matoche. The padre, Father Garsinton, was quite recovered. He came on here in a coaster so as to save a day while we were waiting for the mail. The doctor said that we had got some tropical infection on board, he didn't know quite what; he said it was like medellin throat, but he had never known cases fatal before. We were all fumigated and had our clothes baked, which spoiled all our boots."

"Did the *Pathfinder* break up?" Sard asked.

"Yes, sir," the boy said. "Mr. Dorney, Wolfram, the Bos'un, and Sails went out in a shore boat after the Arnotto died down, to see if they could salve anything from her, but they found only her fo'c'sle and fore-peak wedged on the rocks and the fore-mast still hanging by its gear. She had broken short off, they said, just abaft her fore-hatch and the rest of her was gone down into over 100 fathoms. They said that the worst of it was that she was within a ship's length of clearing the Snappers altogether. Another hundred yards would have fetched her clear."

"You aren't allowed a hundred yards, nor a hundred inches, in our profession," Sard said. "A ship is either afloat or ashore, and that's all there is to it."

By this time they had reached the door of the Sailors' Home.

"Here you are at your inn," Sard said. "Now go up to your berth and turn in, and don't run the town with flash reefers again. You can't do them any good, and they may do you great harm. Cut away to bed, and tell Mr. Dorney at breakfast that I hope to see him at nine in the morning at the agent's office."

After he had dismissed the boy, Sard walked back to the Plaza, to think. He sat again at his table, sipping coffee, while the waiters about him prepared for closing time. "Medellin throat," he kept thinking, "dead of medellin throat; Captain Cary dead and the ship thrown away on the Snappers."

There came the tramp of feet upon the stairway: men were marching to the Plaza crying strange cries like cheers. The waiter at his elbow touched him and muttered under his breath "Cuidado."

Sard looked up suddenly. Men in the green and silver uniforms of the Guards came up the staircase into the Plaza: they drew up in three little squads of four men each. They carried rifles with which they stood on the alert. After them marched two officers, who came to Sard, jingled the spurs on their heels, clicked and saluted. Sard rose, returned the salute and waited.

"Captain Chisholm Harker?" one of the men said.

"I am Harker, not Captain," Sard answered.

"His Excellency, Don Manuel, the Dictator, desires to speak with you." They jingled, clicked, and saluted and went. A great man stepped from the stairs into the Plaza. Sard knew him at once; indeed no one could fail to know him; there being only one such man alive. He was a grand man, with beauty and power in every line and gesture. He was dressed in spotless white and girt with a green sash. He wore the great white Santa Barbara hat of white macilento straw. He stood still, surveying Sard, for half a minute; Sard stood bareheaded surveying him. Very slowly and reverently the Dictator removed his hat, bowed to Sard and stood bareheaded before him. He said no word, but stood there bowed. Sard wished that it might end.

The Dictator advanced suddenly and spoke in English with fierce interjections of Spanish.

"Por Dios, Captain Harker," he said, "I have waited all these years, knowing that you would come. When I heard that you were ashore and at the Plaza I could hardly endure to wait. So, give me your hands: no: both hands: so: how are you?"

Sard mumbled that he was well and glad to see the Dictator well.

"Yes," the Dictator said, "I am better than when last we met. You remember the time we met, on board the Venturer?"

"Yes, Your Excellency."

"I, too, I do not forget. Listen, all of you; this man is one of those who saved me in the Noche Triste. I was ruined: I was a beggar, what? Love killed, ay de mi; friends killed, hope killed. Myself wounded, exhausted. Those swinery had a price upon my head: two thousand English pounds. These men in the Venturer they took me in; they defended me. Those swinery were rowing harbour-guard for me. These men in the Venturer drew me half drowned from the sea and stood between me and death."

He paused for a moment muttering words which were customary with him when moved: some were prayers for Carlotta, the rest curses on her killers.

"Yes," he muttered, "the swinery; but they paid with their life's blood, all but that dog, Don José, and that dog, Rafael. They wetted those stones of horror with their tears, those swinery."

"There was a boy in the Venturer," he continued, "what you call reefer, in what you call the half-deck. He brought me in the dusk a suit of serges and a shirt and said, 'Better luck next time, Señor.' What was that reefer's name? Hey?"

Sard growled that reefers generally answer to the name of Smith.

"Not this one," Don Manuel said. "Por Dios, Captain Harker, it was you did that charity, you, then a boy. In the dusk, you remember, by the deckhouse, under the chocks of the boats, I know not the right name of it: you remember? Por Dios, I remember.

"Yes, yes, yes, por Dios; never will I forget. £2,000 to give me up, and I all in rags and bloody and shaking, with nothing but my personal charm, what?

"Ay de mi, one is slow in being grateful, too slow; but always in life the present is so full, the past drops, fades. I have watched for all old Venturers. I read all ships' papers for names. I have watched and waited for you. 'Everything comes to him who waits,' you say. Many things come; not everything, some things come not again. Ah, Harker, youth comes not again; thank God, what? Dead love comes not again."

He was silent for a full half minute, thinking of the dead love. When he spoke again it was very gently.

"No, dead love comes not again, Harker mio. You never saw her, Carlotta mia. That was where they killed her, so some say: others say there: I shall never know. She was not like me, one of power, but one of exquisite life.

"Lopez, Jorge, Zarzas and Don Livio. Jorge, whom they called Pluma Verde, and that other dog, El Cuchillo. Ha, those woman-killers, they repented. Listen. Lopez cut his veins in prison, but not enough: no, he was alive. He and El Cuchillo and Pluma Verde and Zarzas and Don Livio they all came up those stairs on their knees and kissed where she died before they were shot. Ay de mi, Carlotta mia, pobrecita. It was sweet, but it did not bring her back.

"It is with me now as with the slave: I work that I may not

think. God prisons us all in sorrow of some sort, so that we may seek our escapes. I seek, now, only one escape. Don José's throat in my hands, and Rafael's throat in my teeth; then, then, then will she be paid.

"But, Harker mio, old Venturer, my great kind benefactor, I want such men as you. This Santa Barbara is great, great; there is no place like it on earth: only I want men: I have brains, plenty, but only two hands. I want hands like yours. Will you join me? Choose your work, what say you, and be with me. What would you like?"

"I'd like to congratulate you, sir."

"What for? My fortune?"

"No, sir, your gratitude."

He was pleased with the answer. "Ha, yes," he said, "the ingratitude of a king. But it is often hard to be grateful to individuals: it is easier to be grateful to the world.

"I see you are not married, Harker. You, too, have sorrowed.

"But it is now early. I have to rise early to a special Mass at our friends of Santa Alba yonder. I shall have but a short watch below. Come, then, Harker mio, to coffee with me at seven, at the palacio; you will have thought, then, what we may do together. So, then, I shall expect you."

He took Sard's hands and shook them; then he stood back, as though stepping away from the life that he enjoyed into the loneliness of monarchy. Majesty seemed to come upon him like a garment; for the purple, like other habits, may be assumed. His guards clicked, saluted, and fell in. They were all men from Encarnacion, from the old Encinitas estate, where they showed as relics a hoof of Alvarado's horse, set in silver, the sword of Vasco Nuñez, and a piece of the script of the Gospel of St. John.

They passed down the marble stairs, uttering the cries which Sard had heard as they came up.

"They cheer the dead, Señor," the waited explained, "they cheer the Heroic Five and Señora Jennings and the Pobrecita, whose images they pass."

The bells chimed for one in the morning: all shops and cafés

244

in the Plaza closed. The waiters came from within, dressed in their old coats, with turned-up collars; their feet passed away, some to the old town, some to the north, till the town was almost silent. A cat or two went stealthily or swiftly across the Plaza. A little brown owl flew across crying a note that was querulous and sad. Out in the harbour, some watchman whose clock was slow made two bells.

Sard stayed in his chair, wondering.

He had no wish to sleep: he only wanted a new direction for his life. He was going to strike at life until he found one. "I will stay here," he thought, "till I can see what I can do."

He had thought of many ways of life as desirable, after he had once held command at sea. Now his old desire of command was gone. He wanted no more of the sea, but to come ashore and begin anew, without any dreams to mislead him, nothing but the work to do and the honour to earn from it. Why should he not come ashore, to bear a hand under Don Manuel? Great things were being done there: a great state was rising.

Thinking over all this, he had the fancy that someone, or rather not someone, something, was watching him from the central House of Sorrow. It became more than fancy with him that something evil, like a vast black cat, was watching him there. He turned to the house, to face it, whatever it was, but could see nothing there, save the green verandah, the windows blank and sightless, the walls morphewed with scaling. Then the central door opened, a man came out, locked the door behind him and then stood surveying the Plaza. As Sard was the only person there, he stared at Sard, who stared back. He was a shortish, very strongly made man, with the rangey boss movement of a young bull on pasture.

There was something dangerous about him. He tossed his head back, which flashed his earrings and emphasised the raffish sideways cock of his hat. There was something familiar about him: he reminded Sard of that "flash townee," Sumecta, who had sat with Mr. Wiskey at the boxing-match.

The man strode off the doorstep on to the pavement. He gave his hat a further cock, still staring at Sard, almost with challenge, then he pulled a coloured handkerchief from a side pocket and blew his nose at Sard. As he drew the handkerchief something glimmered out with it and fell into the dust of the gutter. The man was plainly Sumecta, and the blowing of the nose was as the range-bull's bellow at a rival. Sard tilted back his chair to watch him. Sumecta advanced to Sard, who waited for him, humming.

"You're out here kind of late," Sumecta said.

"Am I?"

Sumecta sharpened his tone. "Have you got a match?"

"Yes." There was a pause: the two men watched each other. Presently Sumecta said: "Can I have the match? I'd like it."

"Would you?"

"Yes."

Sard went on with his humming but kept an eye lifting lest some other waif of the night should come. Sumecta took a half-step nearer.

"For two pins," he said, "I'd bash your face in."

Sard went on humming, but drew two pins from the lapel of his coat and offered them.

"What d'you mean?" Sumecta said.

"Two pins. There was going to be bashing."

"You're a funny dog, aren't you?" Sumecta said. He edged away from Sard but kept his eyes upon him. He had the flash cock to his hat, a mouth with a tooth gone and a swollen nose. He edged away with his eyes on Sard till he was off the Plaza and going down the stair. Sard edged his chair a little round so that he might follow Sumecta as he went. When Sumecta was out of sight Sard swiftly and silently stepped aside in case Sumecta should rush back for a sudden shot. But no shot came, Sumecta was gone: his steps were dying away. Sard was alone again.

Being alone, he stepped swiftly to where the glimmering thing had dropped into the gutter. As he had expected, it was a door key: he picked it up. "If he had been reasonably polite," he said to himself, "he should have had it. As it is, he shall do without it. And now, if I'm to be at the palace at seven I had better be off to turn in."

He had pocketed the key and turned to the head of the stair on his way to bed, when he heard someone hurrying to the stair-foot.

For the moment, he judged that it was Sumecta come back to shoot him, but a glance showed that it was a much younger, slighter man. He came running up the stairs, looked about the Plaza for someone, and hailed Sard with: "Oh, your Excellency?" It was Hilary Kingsborough.

"His Excellency has gone, Mr. Kingsborough," Sard said. "He has been gone about half an hour."

"Curse," the young man said. "But who are you who know my name? O, you are the Mr. What's-his-name, who warned me that night. Where has His Excellency gone, do you know?"

"Back to the palace to bed."

"Curse. They told me there that I should find him here. I've been hunting for him and just missing him ever since I landed at ten o'clock. I must find him."

Sard was struck by the high, shrill, feverish excitement of the young man's speech; his face was gaunt and burning: his body wasted.

"Let me come with you," Sard said, "I'll find you a cab, I'm afraid you're ill."

"Ill?" he said. "This thing is tearing me to pieces. Those devils shot me and took my sister. And I can't find her, Mr., sir, no one can find her."

"But she was found," Sard said. "She was found at Tlotoatin. I read it in the paper here, only a few hours ago."

"The paper was a damned lie," the young man cried. "She isn't found. We've no trace nor track of her. Good God, they are all in it, police, press, politicians, and I can't get a word of truth, nor any clue of where she is. You said that they talked of Santa Barbara? For the love of God, now Mr. What's-your-name (I can't remember names), those devils whom you overheard, tell me the truth now, they said they were coming here."

"Mr. Kingsborough," Sard said, "they did. What is more, one of the men, whom I overheard, came out of that door not ten minutes ago."

"What? You'll swear that?"

"I don't swear. He did. He went down those stairs, you must almost have met him."

"Then Margarita may be in that house?"

"I don't think that that can be," Sard said. "It's not very likely, is it?"

"Likely?" Hilary cried. "What is likely? She has disappeared and every power, here and in the Occidental, is behind the swine who took her. I've come here to see the Dictator, and I want you to see him, too, Mr., sir. Tell him that you know that they are a Santa Barbara gang and that he must find her."

"All right I will," Sard said. "I was to see him in a few hours' time, but I will go to him at once instead. Only look here, Mr. Kingsborough, I have seen this Dictator. Since I have landed I have seen both himself and his police service. It is hardly credible or possible that Miss Kingsborough could have been brought here without the fact coming to his knowledge."

"That is what I am saying," Hilary said, "he is in it, with the gang, and so I'll tell him to his face."

"Mr. Kingsborough, he is not that kind of man. Be assured, he is one who will help you in every way."

"He will," Hilary said. "Why did his filthy press print that lie, that she is found? He is this rum-smuggling business, as everybody knows. He is in the smugglers' power; he has to let them do what they please. My sister may be in that house: very likely is! Well, I am going in, to see."

"Wait just for a minute, Mr. Kingsborough," Sard said. "You've been shot, you say; you are still ill. We have a Minister here who will have that house laid bare for us almost within the hour. We will find a cab and drive to the Embassy and have the house searched in the proper manner."

"The proper manner," Hilary said. "I don't know of any proper manner with blackguards of this sort. Why should you try to keep me from saving my sister, you might be one of the gang yourself."

Sard was about to answer soothingly, seeing the young man's distress and nervous exhaustion, but as he opened his lips there came the cry of a woman from within the central house. It was the cry of one in despair. It rang out clearly and fully for an instant, then was stopped suddenly as by a blow or a gag.

248

"You heard that?" Hilary said. "That was my sister's voice. She is inside there."

"Listen a moment," Sard said, "wait."

"I'm not going to wait," Hilary answered. "Wait for what? Till they've killed her?" He was half-way to the door, when Sard stopped him.

"Look here," Sard said, "this may be the key of this door; the man dropped it. We'll go in, if it is. Are you armed?"

"No; are you?"

"No," Sard said, "but I'm used to rough houses. Are you?"

"No."

"Well," Sard said, "there's only one rule in rough house fighting, and that is, be first. Come on."

*   *   *   *   *   *

They crept to the door of the house. It looked more solid, close at hand. It had knopped iron plates across it: the fanlight was barred: the windows to each side were covered with old iron rejas. The house behind it was as silent as the grave. For a moment Sard thought of calling a civil guard, but put the thought from him, "I'm my own civil guard in a seaport town; besides, this gang is certain to have squared the police." Both men listened: Sard tried the key.

The key fitted and turned. Very gently, lest the door should be upon a chain, Sard moved it ajar. He peered in. There was a smell of some gum or incense, like the smell of sweet leather. There was an ample hall, dark as old leather, with patches of light from the windows. He saw then what he had not suspected from without, that the windows were of an opaque glass. He edged into the hall, followed by Hilary. They stood together, inside the door, listening intently. Sard felt along the door to make sure how to open it. "It's a latch door," he whispered. "We'd better close it."

"No, keep it open for our retreat," Hilary whispered.

"Too risky," he answered. "It might slam to, or be noticed from outside, or make a draught that would be noticed inside."

"Better have a line of escape," Hilary said.

"We'll prop it, then," Sard said. "Or will you stand guard while I explore?"

"No fear," Hilary answered, "I'm going to find my sister."

"Come on, then," Sard said. "We'll prop it."

There was a mat just within the door. He lifted an edge of this so that it kept the door pressed to, but not shut. Hilary took a step into the room and stumbled on the well of the mat. He gasped out "God!" and then shook with a laugh which was noiseless but hysterical. His stumble crashed in that stillness like a shot. Sard squeezed his arm to steady him: then they both listened: then Hilary whispered:

"I hear a sort of scratching noise."

Sard heard it too, and thought, at first, that it was the fidgeting of feet, then made sure that it was not that, nor yet the brushing of leaves upon a window, but some noise which he could not yet explain: it might be nothing but the breeze upon a ventilator. It was a constant flutter somewhere to their left; it came no nearer.

"It's all right," Hilary muttered.

"Seconds out of the ring," Sard answered. "Come on, now. Time." He could see almost nothing. He groped about the hall. It was soft to the feet with a closely-woven grass matting. He moved eight paces to his right and touched a wall or screen of wood: "wood panelling," he decided. It ran from the front of the house into the house: it seemed to be the boundary wall of the hall on that side. He groped along it to the end, but found no door, nor any break in the panelling. A table stood near this wall; it bore a metal tray containing a visiting card nearly as big as a postcard.

Sard took the card and listened. He heard Hilary at a little distance breathing like a roaring horse. Sard wished that he would make less noise with his breathing. He crept across to him and told him so.

"You're snorting like a horse yourself," Hilary said.

"Have you found any door?"

"No. There's no door on this side. Only a row of pegs for hats and a rack for whips, but the whips are gone."

"Is it all panelling?"

"Yes, panelling; with two chairs."

"The door will be at the back then," Sard said. "Come to this wall at the back. What is that thing on the wall?"

"It looks like a painting," Hilary said.

"It is a painting," Sard said, "but the paint is running on it. And it doesn't smell like paint."

"Is there no door?"

"None. None that I can see," Sard whispered.

"Let me see," Hilary answered.

He peered close to the wall and groped along it with his fingers. There seemed to be no door there. It was panelling, as at the sides. High up in the centre of it was a trophy of a horned beast's head: it looked like a giant goat's head; something odd had been done to it. The smell of sweet leather was much stronger at that end of the hall. There were figures painted on the panels, at both sides of the trophy. The paint was trickling down the wall.

"Someone has been burning carib leaf," Hilary whispered.

"There must be a door," Sard whispered back. "Only it is let in flush with the panels. We must strike a light."

"Go ahead then," Hilary muttered.

At that instant there came a little suck of air, Sard's propping gave way before it, the hall door shut to with a crash.

"I say, you are a pearl of a door-fastener," Hilary said.

"Hush! Watch for a light."

They watched; but no light showed and no sound came.

"Nobody stirring," Sard said; "the breeze is rising. We must leave the door. Look there."

"What?"

"A man looking in at the window at us."

"Can he see us?"

"Not possibly."

"Who is he?"

"I can't see."

"Is he a civil guard?"

"He's not wearing a helmet."

"Do you think he can be coming in here?"

251

"No. He would come in if he belonged here. There, he has gone. He was only some passer-by."

"It's an odd time of morning for a passer-by," Hilary said. "There. It is striking two."

"Look here," Sard said, stooping down; "I've guessed the secret of this wall. It has no door; but it slides in grooves to and fro. They seem to have oiled the runners. I'm going to strike a light to see which way the thing runs. Hold this twine: it is tarry. I'll light it. It will make a candle."

He took a small hank of roping twine, lit it and held it to the wall. "Look here," he said, "at what is on my hands: blood. This which I thought was oil is blood. There can be no doubt of that. They have spattered blood all over this wall here."

"They have killed her, then!"

"Not they. This is not the blood of a murder," Sard said. "Look, it is splashed high up on the wall. It has been flung from a cup at those images."

It was undoubtedly so.

"This seems to be a pretty devilish place," Hilary said.

"We will shame the devil before we leave it. Now come here, behind me, Mr. Kingsborough; dig your fingers into this panel; that's you. Now, heave; heave and start her; oh, heave! handsomely, handsomely; she is moving."

The heavy panel of the wall slowly slid away to their right. A waft of the smoke of burning carib leaf came into their faces, so that they tasted rather than smelled it. It was sickly to taste and dizzying to breathe. Sard stopped heaving at the panel and peered into the opening which they had made.

They were looking into a large room, which ran further back (that is, away from the Plaza front) than they had expected. There were some upright things, they could not see what, in the middle of the room; all very dim. To the right of these there was a brazier glowing faintly with charcoal on which carib leaf had been crumbled. Sard, who was nearest to the opening, felt at once that there was somebody there. His dream of the mountains came back to him with a shock. He called in a low voice:

"Miss Kingsborough!"

252

Her voice from the middle of the room answered faintly:
"Yes."

"Margarita!" Hilary cried.

"She is tied to these uprights," Sard said, as he pushed into the room. He could dimly see that she was there.

"All right, Miss Kingsborough," he said, "we will soon have you out of here."

"I'm here, Margarita," Hilary said.

Sard reached back for his knife, which he had replaced at San Agostino. It was a small but very strong sheath knife without a guard. Margarita spoke from her stake.

"Oh, be careful, Hilary! There are Indians here."

"All right, dear," Hilary said. "We've found you now. We won't let the Indians hurt you."

"Good Lord," Sard said, "she is chained and padlocked as well as tied. Never mind, Miss Kingsborough, we will set you free."

He took the chain, so as to bend the hasp of the padlock, but it was beyond his strength.

"Have you a hairpin, Miss Kingsborough; perhaps I can pick this lock."

"No," she said. As he felt along the stake, he found her hair all loose about her. He felt the foot of the stake. It was an unbarked bole of a tree dug deep into the earth and tamped well home. She was chained to it at waist and ankles.

"Catch hold of the stake, Mr. Kingsborough," Sard said. "We may be able to heave it right out. Sway with us, Miss Kingsborough. We will give the word."

He and Hilary got their arms about the stake and hove and hove again, with no more result than to make the stake tremble: it was like trying to pull down a growing tree.

"We'll save you, Margarita," Hilary kept saying. Sard could not clearly see how they could save her without a cold chisel and a mallet. He struck a match and lit another twist of twine, which burned for nearly forty seconds. He saw Margarita's white face and great eyes, a strange room of a triangular shape, with a throne at the apex, another bole or tree, a few feet from them, but nothing which could serve as a weapon or a tool.

"Look here," he said, "I must fetch in the police. Here's my knife, Mr. Kingsborough. You stay here on guard while I run out and fetch some guardias."

"They'll all be bribed," Hilary said.

"No police can be bribed to this point," Sard answered. "I'll have them here in three minutes. Cheer up, Miss Kingsborough."

He listened: all was still in the house.

"It's all right," he said, "I'll be back in five minutes."

He hated leaving them, but there was nothing for it. A piece of carib leaf settled in the brazier with a little sigh.

"I'll go then," he said. "Look out."

He crept out of the room and across the hall. When he was near the door, he stumbled on something which had not been there on his first journey.

As he stumbled forward over it, he heard Margarita call, "Look out, Hilary; the Indians!" He heard Hilary gasp, as though struck, and cry out, "Ah! would you?" At the same instant, as he himself rose from the floor of the hall, someone most active tackled him from behind, with a strangle-hold round the throat. He swung himself forward and hove the strangler off his feet, but did not make him loose his hold. He stumbled again on the thing on the floor and someone came at him from in front. He hit out and landed on a body, but somebody new caught him by the right arm and gave it a twist which nearly broke it. He hit one or two bodies and faces, but they were all Indians; it was like punching india-rubber; they hissed their breath in through their teeth and came on again. He reached the door; he got hold of the latch, but the door would not open. He got hold of the strangler's arm and wrenched it against the iron of the door. Then somebody thrust him sideways; he stumbled on to somebody who was crouching; then, immediately, he was down, with three or four of these wild cats on top of him. In his rage at being brought down, he hit hard, but they were too many and seemed to see in the dark. He was mastered, bound, blindfolded and gagged. Then a couple of them picked him up like a sack and ran him along into the inner room. A man asked in good Spanish, "If the lad were dead?" An Indian replied, "That he still breathed." They hove Sard against the upright bole. Though he writhed, he was helpless: he felt like a storm stay-sail made up for bending; they chained him there. He heard Margarita wail. Then an Indian— perhaps the man whom he had wrenched against the iron—hit him hard in body and face again and again and again.

Presently he stopped, and there was silence, save for a rustling, as though snakes were gliding away. Then a light appeared, some-one laughed with satisfaction and twitched the bandage from Sard's eyes.

Sard saw before him the Father Garsinton who had asked for a passage in the *Pathfinder*. It was he, unmistakably, but changed indeed. He now wore a scarlet robe wrought with symbols, which gave him the appearance of a cardinal of the Middle Ages. He gave to Sard the impression of an overwhelming power devoted resolutely to the practice of evil. There was cruelty in every line, with enormous strength (and grace) to give the cruelty its part in the world.

The man snickered as he looked at his victims chained to the trees before him. He walked a few yards to and fro with his head up, smiling; he stretched his hands and a light came into his eyes. It was exactly as though he realised those gestures of freedom which would most hurt his prisoners. The face had been made hard and evil by the devil, but it had also been made tired. The flesh was puckered at the eyes; there was some loose flesh form-ing under the chin; the mouth was a shade out of condition. The scarlet skull-cap no doubt hid hair beginning to be grey or thin. The great want in the face was the want of horns sprout-ing from the brow; with those he would have been a complete devil.

"Well," Sard said, "our friends know that we are here. You had better let us go before they come to fetch us."

"You lie," the man said. "Your friends do not know that you are here."

"The Dictator of this Republic knows that we are here," Sard ventured.

"The Dictator of this Republic is my good friend," the man replied.

"My Consul is not; neither is my Minister," Sard said. "You will find this kidnapping trade a poor one."

"How?"

"By our friends."

"You will find night burglary and knight-errantry poor trades, before your friends find you, young man. Who are you?"

"Undo these chains and I will show you."

"You are a sailor; an English sailor, who missed his ship at Las Palomas," the padre answered. "You are one of these ship's dogs who run loose in foreign ports. A slave by day, a drunken criminal by night."

"Less of a criminal than a dirty, foreign, woman-torturer."

"I take you burgling; in the fact, sailor. What is your name?"

"A better name than yours."

"Your name is Harker. My name is the Holy One."

"I thought you looked lousy enough for a saint."

"Do you know the laws about burgling in this land? We may kill burglars. We do kill them. Every day a corpse of a burglar is flung out. You have seen such. They are often sailors, unclaimed three days, then buried. I just tell you now, that your corpse will be flung out of here, in a little while, when I have finished with you. I shall not keep you long, but it will be before your friends come here, never fear."

"You had better hurry up then," Sard said, "for they will be here in ten minutes. And you had better not boast too much before witnesses of the crimes you plan."

The man stepped swiftly up to Sard and slapped his cheek. When he tried to slap the other cheek, Sard, as a boxer, was too quick; he snapped at the hand and bit it; the man wrenched himself free.

"The trapped rat bites," he said. "Very well."

He did not seem to mind the bite, though it bled. He seemed to pass into a state of contemplation in which the body did not matter.

"Do you know what I am?" he asked. "I am the priest of evil. This triangle in which you stand is the temple of evil. These gallows posts to which you stand are the altars of evil. I am going to offer mass to evil, of bread and wine. Do you know what bread and what wine?"

"You drunken, dirty ass!" Sard said. "Mr. Kingsborough, who was here with me, has raised the town by this. You will be taken out, scrubbed with sand and canvas, and then jailed; so hold on all with your folly and let us go."

"Mr. Kingsborough did not escape quite so easily, honest sailor," the Holy One replied. "We are Dagoes, as you call them, here, not Englishmen; not Gringos; we are not sentimental in our earnest. Mr. Kingsborough paid the penalty of burglary. You, Madonna, lovely Margarita Kingsborough, will tell you. You saw what happened to your brother. Tell him."

"I heard him groan from a blow, Mr. Harker," Margarita said. "Then, when the lights went on, I saw him lying dead on the floor; the Indians dragged him out."

"Correct," the Holy One said. "He is dead. And you are helpless. Your fleet can't help you, nor your Minister, nor your Consul, nor your State, nor any other of those things you believe in. You are in the hands of power. You are elements for power to sacrifice. You, man, are bread; you, woman, are wine; and I shall sacrifice your bread and wine, your blood and honour, your life and your chastity."

"I knew a dirty talker like you once before," Sard said. "He was a Portuguese babu on the mother's side; his father was the port of Goa. He fell into the slime once at low tide; but even without that you could not tell him from filth."

"I leave you to prepare yourselves," the Holy One said. "I go to prepare myself for communion with my god, the god of evil, who will come down here, to eat of the bread and drink of the wine." His head went back as he spoke, and his eyes lit up (they were light-brown rolling eyes) till they were like the eyes of a beast that sees in the dark. He began to pray as he stood; his head went even further back, till they could hardly see his lips moving; then he began to chant:

> "I am a body and a hand that wait
> Thy power, O Evil; use and make me great
> With lust and thirst for blood until I shine
> Like goat for rut, like wolf for murder, thine."

He moved off, swaying to the rhythm of his song, and possessed by his thought: he turned to look at his captives as he passed, but there seemed to be no speculation in his eyes, only a glare, such as the petroleuses have, in their eyes, in revolutions, in the days of frenzy. He passed out of that door through which the body of Hilary had been dragged. Sard reckoned that doors led out of the central house into the houses on each side. He made the note in his mind, "the man controls two houses; perhaps three; there may be twenty or thirty of them, living here." The door clicked to behind the Holy One; Sard was alone with Margarita.

"Mr. Harker," she said, "does anybody know that you are here?"

"No," he answered. "It was false."

"Or that my brother was here?"

"Nobody knows. And it is my fault. I ought not to have let your brother into this house without the police."

"Why did you?"

"We heard you cry out."

"I cried because I saw that I was near the street," she said. "They were bringing me in here from inside there. I hoped that someone might hear."

"We did hear. If we shout now, someone may hear."

"At this time in the morning?"

"It is worth trying. Help! help! help!" he shouted. "Police! Murder! Help us here! Help! help! help!"

"It is useless," she said. "When I cried, they drew the doors across; these doors are sound-proof."

"Let us save our breath for the present," he said. "The streets are deserted now. We will shout later, when there are more people stirring."

She did not answer immediately; she thought and he knew that she thought, that there might not be a "later" for him. He put a strain upon his bonds to test them. His legs were tightly lashed, his arms were secure; his body was chained to the stake and that chain was racked.

"Mr. Harker," Margarita said, "is there any chance of the men of your ship coming to look for you?"

"No," he said, "next to none. My ship is lost. People may enquire for me presently."

After a silence Margarita asked:

"Did my brother say if the police were searching for me?"

"Yes, indeed, Miss Kingsborough, you are being sought for everywhere, and the police have been warned."

"Have you any faith in the police?"

"Yes," he said, "indeed, yes."

"But if the police are competent," she said, "then how do you account for our being as we are?"

"The wicked have their day," he said.

He was fearful lest this should be disheartening to her. He hastened to add: "They will get you out of this, Miss Kingsborough. I shall be asked and searched for at seven o'clock, only five hours from now, by the Dictator himself."

"What Dictator is that?" she asked. "Where is this place?"

"In Santa Barbara," he said. "The Dictator is Don Manuel. Did you not even know where you are?"

"I have known nothing of where I have been since they dragged me out of the house after you had warned us. They put me into a boat and then into a ship, where I was a prisoner for a fortnight. Sometimes we were at sea and sometimes in anchorages. I knew from the sun that we went south and west; nothing more than that. Then three nights ago they landed me and wheeled me here, bound, blindfolded and gagged, upon a stretcher in a sort of ambulance. I knew from the noises and smells that we were in a city. Someone stopped the people who were bringing me and asked what was the matter. The woman said, 'She has had an accident, poor thing.'"

"You had women guards, then?"

"Oh, yes, two."

"Surely there were some decent men among the smugglers who

were willing to help you: for instance, a man called Douglas?"

"The only men whom I have met have been those who carried me away out of the house, and those who are here, the Indians and a terrible negro."

"But about this man in red," Sard said, "I know him only as Father Garsinton; he seems to be the head of the business; but what is his aim?"

"He worships evil," she said.

"Yes, but what does he hope to gain by all this?"

"To increase the power of evil in the world."

"But he is not young," Sard objected. "He is grown up; he is even elderly."

"He is a devil," she said.

"I have heard of boys in cities thinking these thoughts," Sard said, "but never grown men. And why does he single out you?"

"He has always wanted me," she said. "He always said that he would have me. He told me years ago that to-night should be the night: now it is. And now he has killed my brother."

He heard her weeping and saw tears running down her steady face.

"Oh, no, no," he said, "do not weep; do not cry like that."

"I cannot help it," she said. "I loved my brother."

"He loved you too, dearly."

They were silent for some minutes, while Sard tried again to shift his bonds. When he spoke again he had good news.

"Miss Kingsborough," he said, "I have to break this news to you. Your brother is not dead. He is alive. He has just crept into the room behind you."

"Don't make any noise," Hilary said. "For heaven's sake don't make any noise. I've been knocked out. I'm dizzy and sick."

He came up between them and sat down upon the floor.

"Oh, Hilary," she said, "you are covered with blood."

"Yes, I know, dear. O Lord, I do feel queer! They have all gone upstairs, the people here. Cheer up, Pearl, my darling, we'll soon have you out of this. The only question is, how to open the padlocks."

"Have you any keys?" Sard asked, "or anything like wire for a pick-lock?"

"No," he said, "I'm afraid I have nothing; nothing at all." He bowed himself forward where he sat and propped his head in his hands; a few drops of blood trickled over his fingers. Sard saw that he was on the brink of swooning.

"Mr. Kingsborough," he said, "will you look about the room for a wire or a tool or something?"

"Wait a moment, will you," Hilary answered. "It's silly of me. I'm afraid I'm going to faint." He fainted, then came to himself, then saw the blood on his hands and fainted again. Presently he hove himself up into a sitting posture and said that he had never felt so sick in his life.

"Shut your eyes," Sard said.

"Yes, you say 'shut your eyes,' but my head's all gone. I'm as sick as a cat. I say, would you mind bringing me some water?"

"I'll bring you water," Sard said. Margarita was crying. "I'll bring you lovely water. Only, you see, your sister and I are locked up here, chained. We want you to unchain us."

"So I would," he said. "But I cannot stand this smell of incense. It takes all the strength clean out of me."

"Hilary," Margarita said sharply, "Hilary, turn round. Look at that shelf on the side of the wall there. Is not that water in a glass jug there?"

"It is water," Sard said. "Look, Mr. Kingsborough. It is water. Get to the shelf and splash yourself."

"It is water," Hilary said. "I don't know about getting to it."

"You can get to it, Hilary dear," Margarita said. "Crawl to it and then you will reach it. Oh, well done, Hilary; how splendid of you!"

The sick man crawled on hand and knees to the wall. He leaned for a moment there and said, "I can't reach it."

"Rest and gather strength," Sard said.

"Hilary," his sister said, "crawl to that little table in the middle of the room. You will be able to push that to the wall and then climb to the water."

"Yes, I will," Hilary said: "only I must wait for a moment, for this sickness to pass."

He stayed there huddled against the wall, with his eyes shut, for two or three minutes. He looked liker a dead man than a living. At last he moved forward from the wall and slowly crawled to the table. The table was liker a large old English stool than a table. When he reached it, he drooped forward over it as though he would never have the strength to rise.

"Take your time," Sard said. "Do not try to lift that stool, but push it before you while you lean on it. So. That is you. Not too big a push at a time: take it quietly."

"Oh, I do feel so sick!" Hilary said.

"No wonder. You've had a bat on the head," Sard said. "You are a marvel to be moving at all, but go handsomely; there's always time; always lots of time; no rushing. Now wait; rest; gather your strength again."

He waited, leaning on the stool, while the others watched him.

"You are nearly there," Sard said. "One more little effort and you will be there. I think your brother's a hero, Miss Kingsborough, to be doing this, in his state."

"You are wonderful, Hilary," she said. "Now forward again."

The sick man thrust the stool before him almost to the wall.

"Stop there," Sard said. "Do not push it further under the shelf. Now you are almost there: all that you have to do now is to heave yourself up and reach the jug. Steady yourself against the wall."

Hilary with an effort hove himself to a kneeling posture on the stool. When there, he found that he had pushed it too far underneath the shelf. He could not see the jug, but saw instead that he would have to lean somewhat backward, clutching to the shelf with one hand while he groped for the jug with the other. The thought of doing this unnerved him, he made no attempt for a minute.

"It is just directly over your head," Margarita told him.

"Yes, I know where it is," he answered, "only getting it is the problem. However, it is water."

"It is lovely water, which will take away all your faintness."

"Yes, by George, it will! I can tell you I want it. I'm going to get it."

"Good. Well done."

He steadied himself as cautiously as a tightrope-walker. He placed one foot upon the stool, swayed, steadied, made an effort, caught the rim of the shelf and stood there.

"Splendid, Hilary! You've done it."

"Good man."

"It's on a tray," Hilary said. "I can't reach the jug, it's too far in. But I've got hold of the tray."

"Pull the tray towards you. There; it is coming."

"Now catch hold of the jug."

"Oh, take care, take care; mind, Hilary!"

"You'll have the whole thing down."

"Oh, Lord!" Hilary said.

In his weakness, as the tray reached the edge of the shelf, Hilary slipped, failed or fell. He tipped the tray over as he dropped; there was a crash and a breaking of glass and a gurgling of liquid.

"I'm sorry, you people," Hilary said; "I was afraid that that would happen. I'm too weak to do this kind of thing: now it is gone."

"No, no, it is not," Margarita said. "Wet your handkerchief in it, then drink that, or mop your forehead with it."

"Well thought of," Sard said.

"I say," Hilary said, "this is not water: it is that what's-its-name, the white brandy these fellows drink."

"Drink some, drink some, then."

"I'm drinking. I say. You may say what you like. It makes me feel a different being."

"Splash your brows with it."

"I will. And I will save this. There's about a tumblerful. And, good Lord, I say, I say!"

"What? What have you found in the tray?"

"Bunches of keys. Look here. Two bunches of keys. I may be able to unlock your padlocks."

"Try your sister's padlocks first."

"No, no," Margarita said, "try Mr. Harker's padlocks first. He is a man. He can help."

"Your sister first," Sard said. "I'll not be set free first. And as for helping, I have not helped anyone, so far as I can see."

Hilary tried the keys in the padlocks of his sister's chains. He tried eleven without success; then, at the twelfth, the locks clicked back and the chains could be cast aside. She was still bound to the pillar by a thong of hide. "I cannot undo this knot," Hilary said, "my fingers are too weak."

"Gnaw it open with your teeth," Sard said.

Hilary sat down and sipped some brandy.

"I wish you would not upset me," he said. "I feel as sick as a dog, and the very thought of taking this stuff in my teeth is more than I can stand."

"Sorry," Sard said. "What you must do is, pick up a piece of broken glass with a sharp edge and saw it through with that."

"Good," Hilary said. "I can do that."

As he bent to pick up the glass, it seemed to all three there that men were muttering just beyond the doors. They heard no words distinctly, but voices spoke, feet shuffled: the noise, whatever it was, died away almost at once: all was still again. Hilary sawed through the hide, so that Margarita was free. She took the keys and began to try them on the padlocks of Sard's chains. She unlocked his hand-chains with the third key, but could not fit the leg-iron padlock until the last key of all. They cast loose the last of the chains, Sard was free. He picked up the chain, which was of a one-inch link, stopped a bight in it for a handfast, made an overhand knot in each end, and then swayed it to and fro. "Now we have some sort of a weapon," he said. "Now we will see whether we cannot get out of here."

"Pearl," Hilary asked, "do you know whether we can get out from here into any yard at the back of the house?"

"There is a yard at the back of the house; I have seen it. There is a shed in it, with a great dog," she said. "But even if we reached the yard, it would not help. There are houses beyond."

"Let us keep to what we know," Sard said. "We know the way to the Plaza, and in the Plaza we may meet people who will help us. We must slide these doors apart and make for the front door."

"I agree," Margarita said.

"Each have a sip of brandy," Sard said.

They each took a sip, then took their bearings and moved to the sliding door.

"The light is going out," Hilary said. The light suddenly dimmed to half its strength.

"All right," Sard said. "That means that it is half an hour from dawn. They cut off the light at the power-house."

"I was afraid that it meant that we were discovered," Margarita said.

"Not a bit of it," Sard said. "It's the custom in the port. Now, Mr. Kingsborough, we'll soon have you and your sister out into safety. Catch hold of the door here. Dig your nails into it. Quietly, now. Are you all ready?"

"Yes. Yes."

"Then, when I give the word, heave back. All together, now. Heave!"

They hove: it trembled a little, but did not give.

They hove again and again, but there was nothing for them to catch hold of: they could only hold by the tips of their fingers: the door trembled, but did not give. While Sard searched for something that would give them a purchase, the light went out.

"We can't shift this panel," Sard said; "we must try this door at the side."

He opened it and peered beyond it into a dimness in which there was a flight of stairs.

"Come on," he whispered. "There's no one here."

They crept into the dimness. There was another door beyond the staircase. They went through it into a darkness in which they groped.

Suddenly Sard trod upon somebody, who caught him by the leg. "Look out! Get back," he cried. Somebody grappled him as he spoke, so that he could not get back with the others. A light suddenly shone out to show him a big buck negro coming at him. An Indian, who had him round the hips, brought him to the ground.

Sard shook himself free, rose to his feet, hit somebody hard, and at once was clinched by the big negro. "You've not got me yet," he said. He hit him on the ribs and kicked his shins; the negro got him by the throat.

"I got yuh, honey," he said.

The Indian whom he had kicked aside, caught him by the leg again. By a violent effort he flung himself free, and hit the negro on the jaw. The negro grunted, ducked and came on: two or three Indians leaped in, like cats. Sard hit one over the heart, so that he fell, then the others got him down, and snarled and spat over him, and called him evil names. They trussed him up as before with strips of hide. The negro held him by the throat while they did it.

"I got yuh, honey," he kept saying. "I sure got yuh."

When he was lashed up like a hammock, the negro slung him over his shoulder. An Indian, the man whom he had knocked down, followed just behind, digging Sard in the legs at each step with the point of a knife. The negro carried Sard back to the temple and chained him to the pillar from which he had escaped. Two Indians came up to Sard and pricked him with their knives.

"Gringucho!"

"Hay que matarle."

"Si, hay que."

"Hijo de puta."

Presently the negro carried Margarita into the room and chained her to her pillar. When he had done this, he lit a cigar and puffed the smoke into her face; then thrust his face into hers, and said, "Ah love de white woman," and kissed her. Then he looked at Sard, blew some cigar smoke into his face, and said, "Yuh hit me on de jaw. Bimeby I come back and buhn yo eyes out with my segah."

After this he and the Indians disappeared, closing a door behind them. Father Garsinton entered from the angle of the room.

He was dressed in his scarlet robes and carried a lamp, which he placed upon the low stool from which Hilary had reached the jug. He then went to a small aumbry, drew out some dried carib leaves and flung a few upon the brazier. The stuff sputtered and threw out profuse smoke, the smell of which was both sickly and stupefying. He seemed to breathe it with pleasure. At last he turned to his victims, looked from one to the other, and spoke.

"So," he said. "My mice. The cat has played with you. And did you taste the pleasures of hope? Did you feel safe at last? Know, my little mice, that I watched while you hoped. So you would not try the back yard, because of the dog? Why, the dog is stuffed. And so the Dictator will search for Mr. Harker? That is to be expected, but he will not search here, where so much of his wealth is planned for. Still, you enjoyed your little hopes."

He drew nearer and seemed in some strange way to grow bigger. It was as though the evil which he served had entered into him and taken possession.

"And now," he said, "put by hope. Evil is stronger than hope; or faith; or charity; or strength, you; or honour, madam. What do you say, sailor?"

"I wish I had you with my hands free."

"Oh! What would happen then?"

"A cleaner world."

"Cleaner?" Sagrado said. "A cleaner world? My friend, I serve the purpose of this world, which is not cleanliness, but triumph. You, with your cleanliness, wasting the energy of men in being clean. Pah, you two sickening things; one clean, the other chaste. Which of you does the more harm, with your beastly ideals?"

"We had a man in the fo'c'sle once," Sard said, "who spoke just the same kind of thing; only there was some excuse for him; he'd been brought up in a brothel. The men took him on deck and scrubbed his mouth out with sand and canvas."

"I do not use those methods," Sagrado said. "But I have my own methods of correcting false philosophers, as you shall see."

He returned, almost immediately, with something tied in a native frail. He laid it upon the floor, then brought the small table or stool and placed it facing the two victims, between them and about one yard from each of them. They could see the carib leaves in the brazier glowing and unglowing and writhing like live things on the charcoal. Then Sagrado unlaced the native frail and drew from it a shell-shaped bomb, which he placed upon the table. He adjusted the fuse with great care and then turned to his victims.

"A fifth part of an hour," he said, "is twelve minutes. In twelve minutes, precisely, this bomb will explode. It contains a quarter charge, which will suffice. What the bomb leaves, I and my ministrants will then take, to the utmost."

He lit a twist of bijuco bast in the brazier, and then with the flame set fire to the fuse. It burned for one second, then changed to a glow, as Sagrado softly blew upon it. It glowed rather redly and the glow showed a black mark which at once began to creep, though very, very slowly, along the unburned fuse. Sagrado blew out his lamp and disappeared out of the room. The two victims saw nothing but the veins in the leaves in the brazier and the black mark charring along the fuse in front of the fire which charred it. Already a small piece of white ash, like a cigar-ash, fell from the burnt end of the fuse.

"Do not look at that fuse," Sard said.

"I cannot help it," she said.

"Yes, you can help it. Look at me. Can you move at all?"

"Hardly at all. Can you?"

"No."

"Tell me the truth," she said. "Do you think they killed my brother?"

"I could not see," he said.

"I suppose they will kill him. And I suppose this bomb will kill us."

"It must injure us," he said.

"How long have we, before it bursts?"

"Ten and a half minutes."

"Supposing one of us should escape?"

"We had better have no false hopes," he said. "We're not likely to leave this house alive."

"I meant only this," she said: "the survivor might take a message. Is there any message that you would care to trust me with?"

"You might explain to my aunt, old Lady Crowthorne, in England. Would you care to trust any message to me?"

"To my brother, if he be alive," she said; "and to my father—he is really my stepfather—Hardy Kingsborough of Passion

Courtenay, in Berkshire. Can you remember that?"

"Passion Courtenay?"

"Yes. Why? Do you know it?" she asked.

"I should think I do," he said. "I've gone there every year, when I have been in England, for the last fifteen years."

"With whom do you stay, then? Oh, this is happy, to hear of home now, here."

"I do not stay," he answered. "As a rule I go over for the day, and then away in the evening. You see, I know nobody there, now: in a way I never did. I go to the inn near the river, the Hunt and Hounds; then I go on the river, and away by the evening train, the 7.13."

"I expect we have passed each other," she said.

"Very likely," he said. "Whereabouts do you live there, Miss Kingsborough? Could you describe it?"

"Yes. For the last ten years we have lived at The Murreys, which you may not know, but must have seen, if you have been to the Hunt."

"I know the outside of your home very well, then," he said. "It's called The Murreys from the mulberry trees. Whenever I go on the river there, I land in one of the fields below your house and walk from the river to your garden wall. The field is called Bridger's Peace; do you know why?"

"It means the piece of ground where the bridgers camped when they built the bridge in the fourteenth century."

"I thought it was the other kind of peace," he said, "the 'Peace which passeth all understanding'; which it has always been to me."

"It is a beautiful place," she said; "and the thought of it is peace now."

"Yes," he said.

"It is going on, now," she said, "under this same night; the water is going on under the bridge."

"Ah, to be tied," he cried, "lashed foot and hand!"

"Why did you land in our field?" she asked.

"The field is mixed up with my life; I have to go there. In a way, that field and house have been all my life. The sea has only been something to wrestle with: that is not enough."

"What have the house and field been to you, then?" she asked.

"It would be mean not to share with my companion," Sard said; "you are linked with the place too. It is all strange, and your being here at the end is almost the strangest: you, the owner of that place, and I, just the trespasser and worshipper. Fifteen years ago I was taken to a picnic there. I don't believe in chance. But it seemed just chance that I went there. We didn't know the people, but they wanted a boy to fill up a side at cricket. Anyhow, I went. Some people called Penga took me.

"But I was quite out of it. I was the youngest there. They had two elevens without me, and I didn't know a soul there except Dick Penga, and he had had the swot of bringing me and thought me a child, besides.

"There was a Spanish lady, a widow, there with her daughter, who was of my own age. She was out of it too.

"I could always talk Spanish, so I talked to the girl. In a way, we were children; but it was not any childishness to me. That girl altered my life. She has been my life ever since, all the life that mattered: the rest was only ropes and weights."

"You saw her again, then?" Margarita said.

"No," he said. "I've never seen her since, nor heard from her. You see, she was only there by as strange a chance, almost, as I. She came from Santo Espirito, in Andaluz, in Spain. I wrote to her there, but I never had an answer: of course, she would never have written to me.

"I went to Santo Espirito as soon as I could; but that was eight years later. Nobody knew of them there. The place had all changed in the interval, for they had begun to work copper there: it was a mining town."

"What was the girl's name?"

"Juanita de la Torre."

"Would you know her again, do you think?"

"I thought that you were she when I saw you at that window at Los Xicales."

"I am she," she said simply. "I am Juanita de la Torre. My mother married my stepfather the year of the picnic. He met her at the picnic for the first time. Four years later we went to live at The Murreys. We took the name Kingsborough when mother married: we've been brought up as English ever since. Margarita is my second name; I took to that, because the English cannot pronounce the other."

"I can, Juanita. Ah! no, no! do not look at that fuse. I will tell you when to prepare. We still have four minutes."

"How can you tell?"

"I've kept watches nearly every day and night for ten years. I can tell time within a minute or two. And to think that we met at Los Xicales and never knew! I was misled by your name. Why did you not speak? You heard my name."

"Remember I did not know your name," she said. "I have always thought that your name was Chisholm. I never once heard you called Harker. You were Chisholm to me."

"Ah! I was afraid of that," he said. "You never got my letter?"

"Never."

They were silent for a few seconds; in the stillness some ash dropped from the fuse with a feathery fall: down in the town a cock crowed.

"Strange," he said. "There is a cock crowing. I cannot hear a cock crowing without knowing that I have an immortal soul."

"It is a live cry," she said.

"It is like a trumpeter trumpeting the graves open. It's the cry the dead will rise with.

"Ah!" he cried, bitterly. "And the living are rising with it, and going out to their work, while we are lashed here like stay-sails. Oh, if I could only heave this pillar down!" He swayed from side to side, but was too tightly lashed: there was no stirring that tree bole tamped in four feet below the floor.

"It's no good," he said. "I am caught. And if I had not been a hasty fool, I could have come here with guardias and set you free."

"Don't think that for an instant," she said. "They were going to cut my throat if there were any rescue. 'We shall all die together,' he told me. It's death to him to be caught here, but he was determined that I should die first. Guardias would not have saved me."

"I haven't done much," he said.

"You have done everything," she said.

The red glow on the fuse suddenly changed to yellowish; a little flame sprang up out of the glow: it wavered like a candle-flame.

"The thing is going to explode," she said.

"I think so, it is bad fuse: it is burning."

"How long have we?"

"Perhaps less than a minute."

"Could you sing something?"

The flame in the fuse suddenly brightened and lit up the room. He turned to Margarita and saw her great eyes fixed upon his.

"Here comes the burst," he said. "Stand by."

The flame steadied, then began to shoot higher with a steady sputtering hiss till it was a foot high and scattering sparks.

"Keep your eyes tight shut," he said. "And remember it may just as easily cut our chains as us. Here she comes."

The flame changed its colour to a dull red, which smoked; it sputtered more loudly, then lessened, sank down and went out.

"Wait," Sard said, "wait: it may be a delayed fuse." He counted up to seventy-three, slowly. "No," he said. "The fuse has failed: it is not going to explode."

The light appeared at the door at the apex of the room: Sagrado came in and looked at them.

"First the pleasures, then the miseries of hope," he said, "to make the victims despair."

"We do not despair," Sard said.

"Do you not?" Sagrado answered. "No; perhaps not yet. But you will."

"A butcher's sponge, like you, won't make me."

"We shall see."

"A man would be unclean," Sard said, "even for spitting at you."

"Unclean?" Sagrado answered. "There are various conceptions of cleanliness, but all have to do with consecrations and devotions. I am called unclean by you, who serve men, who are a servant in a ship. Other flunkeys serve the state. I am myself, unspotted from these flunkeydoms and slaveries. If I serve, I serve evil, the master of this world."

"It is something," Sard said, "to have a master as dirty as the servant."

"It is much," Sagrado answered, "to have a power commensurate with your philosophy."

"I have not seen any power in you yet," Sard said.

"No?" Sagrado said. "Yet I stand free, while you are bound, you and your romantic one. Which of us has the power, Margarita?"

"He has," she answered. "And you know it."

"I do not know it," he said, "nor do events show it. I wanted you in my hands by a certain day: there was nothing that you wanted less. Yet you came to my hands, to the very moment planned. This sailor or second mate, if I understand him, has wanted you for fifteen years: there was nothing that you wanted more, if I overheard correctly. Are you in his hands, or arms, or in mine? Which of us has the power over you?"

"He has," she said. "And you know it."

"If you will not see truth, you must learn truth; and you too, my sailor. . . .

"You, as I understand it," he said, turning to Sard, "were for saving her from danger in Las Palomas. Did you save her? . . .

"Did you save your ship from danger? Why, do you suppose, did I go in your ship amid all that I most despise? Your ship, I say, but I mean your owner's ship, which you were bought to keep afloat: you, a man, being slave to a thing."

"The thing obeyed its slaves," Sard said.

"For a while," the Holy One said. "For a while it gave satisfaction; the slaves earned a dividend for their employers. But then I came, I, the Holy One, who am appointed by my Master to bring down all this order which he most loathes. I came to that ship to lay her low, as an offence, and to smite her brains with numbness. They were slave-brains, thinking of nothing but of keeping their prisons clean. Their one joy was the pothouse, their sole art the music-hall; their religion, what was that, you who reckon yourself their leader?"

"Their religion is to risk their lives and mortify their flesh in order to bring bread to their fellows," Sard said. "In doing that, they make iron swim and dead-weight skim and the dead thing to be beautiful. Show me a finer religion, you who are already carrion for the want of one."

"They had no religion," Sagrado answered. "They were slaves who made pennies for pot-houses while their work made pounds for peers. I, the Holy One, came among them, and scattered among them the seeds of terror. Would that you had been there, my second mate, to watch that terror growing; the geraniums, the birds, then one by one the brains; I, with a little drug, putting my hand on the heart of your so boasted machine. It was a work of art, my second mate, a symphony of horror. I drew out what notes I wished, I struck what chords I loved, and the instruments which I disliked, I destroyed. Your Cary, I destroyed. I numbed him and killed him. With my own dose, in his own stronghold, I gave him Death."

"You weren't allowed to bury him," Sard said.

It was a shot which went home. Plainly, the burial of Captain Cary by the murderer in the priest's clothes would have given a relish to the crime.

"No matter," the Holy One answered, controlling his face, "I shall bury you, when I have done with you."

"You haven't done with me yet," Sard said. "And I owe you for Captain Cary."

"Your owners owe me for the ship."

"Perhaps I may pay that too."

Sagrado walked to the throne in the apex of the room; he seated himself and appeared to consider. Sard knew that he had touched the beast to the quick by his remark about the burial. He followed it up with:

"Mr. Dorney read the service very well, I understand. You did not numb his brains, I gather."

"He has few to numb," Sagrado answered. "But I am thinking of what you said about payment, and of you paying me. You think yourself capable, do you, of standing in a contest with me?"

"I would do my best, the city scavenger being absent."

Sagrado laughed, yet seemed still to be considering: he swayed a little to and fro.

"Yet it is absurd," he said. "It would be no fair match."

"You are older," Sard said, "that is true, but you are fresh. I have already fought twice this night."

"I had not heard that," Sagrado answered. "I heard that you had been beaten: did you refer to that?"

"Yes," Sard said.

"That was not in my mind," Sagrado said, "when I wondered at the fitness of the match. The issue is not between Master and servant, but between the civilised world and its Destroyer. You are disgusting to me, but not important enough. You are not master of your destiny. You are a part of the scum of life, which is active for another (though without religion) and worried for another, though without purpose. And your talk is such as one would expect: it is prejudice based on ignorance, just like your press. Your sports, your muscle, your fair play, all these catchwords which you repeat when people ask you for intelligence, degrade men. Shall we say that they are the barrel-organs played loudly that men may not know of the degradations done to manhood?"

"You may say what you like," Sard said, "the sewer of your mind is probably better fluent than stagnant."

"I see what you are," Sagrado answered, "the prop of it all, the sergeant, the second mate, the curé, the schoolmaster, the petty officer." He strode up to Sard and boxed his ears. "Pah!" he said, "you have no foundations, you paltry thing. You talk about manhood, probably, and reckon yourself a man; not a gentleman, of course, for that not even you would pretend, even at sea, but a man, no doubt. You, a preacher and a slave; who cannot know what manhood is. I will tell you what it is: it is the attainment of power and the use of power. Old as I am, I will show you. You shall stand in the wrestle with me. Esclavos!"

At his call the group of seven Indians entered. Sard saw them in the light now; seven wild animals, with a light in their eyes from the desire of blood: they had faces without mark of mirth or pity. At a sign from Sagrado they cast loose Sard's chains.

Sagrado cast off his scarlet robe and stretched his arms.

"You are free," Sagrado said. "Come, then, to the test. Why do you not come?"

Sard hesitated for a second, thinking that one of the Indians would surely knife him when he moved. He felt that he had reached his end, and that this was how he was to die, shut up here with wild beasts in the presence of his love. He glanced at Margarita, and stood with dropped hands, letting the blood run into his numbed arms again. He meant to hit Sagrado before he died.

"The preacher hesitates," Sagrado said.

Sard glanced again at Margarita; her look made it all worth while.

"I don't hesitate," Sard said. "But keep your slaves from me."

"You are meat for the sacrifice," Sagrado answered, "they will not touch you."

"Time, then," Sard said.

He rushed at Sagrado and landed with both hands upon a guard which he could not break. Stepping back, he trod into an Indian, while another Indian lurched into his side. There were Indians all round him; a sort of net of Indians. Sagrado came at him and gripped him; he clinched and drove in short-arm blows at Sagrado's ribs; an Indian tripped him, and Sagrado got a better hold as he staggered. Sagrado was as strong as an ox and quick as a wild beast. Sard was a strong man, but this was a bull-bison of a man. He wrenched an arm free and struck with it; an Indian parried the blow; Sagrado changed his hold and pinned the arm: it was like fighting with an octopus. Indians, stooping down, snatched at Sard's ankles. Presently Sard tripped and fell: Sagrado brought his shoulders to the mat.

"You see," he said, "you are down. Give in."

"I won't," Sard said. He struck Sagrado's mouth and flung him aside. He rose to his feet, as Sagrado rose swearing and savage. He had cut Sagrado's lip on a tooth, and Sagrado's mouth bled.

"You shall pay for that," Sagrado said.

Sard struck him again on the mouth and saw the blood quicken in the cut; he struck again; the Indians caught his arm, Sagrado pinned it and closed with him. They swayed to and fro, while the Indians struck him in the lower ribs, trying for the death touch. Sard felt Sagrado's fingers squirming free for a death-touch, which he did not know and could not guard. The death-touch came. A deadly weakness turned all Sard's strength to water. He went down and felt his life die away, and then ebb partly back. He knew that he must rise, and tried hard to rise, but he was down, he could not rise.

In a few seconds he tried again, but now Sagrado had him by the throat. "Not so," Sagrado said. "You are beaten. Try that again and I will break something."

"I'm not finished yet," Sard said.

"Yes, you are," Sagrado answered. "But since you doubt it, there goes your arm."

With a swift jerk he snapped Sard's arm against a fulcrum, and then twisted the broken bone so that Sard cried and swooned. Sagrado waited till he had recovered and then bound him to his pillar.

"You see," he said, "you thought yourself a man. You make a poor show in the hands of a man. Do you admit that you are beaten?"

"No."

"You are beaten, by one twenty years older than yourself, and in the presence of your lady-love, who is now my lady-love. Those friends of yours, who were coming, are somewhat overdue. I've beaten you and chained you to your pillar with my own hands. Do you admit that I am your master? Answer, dog; reply, my second mate. For I am your master. The lion has caught his meat; the bull has won his heifer. And now the rites shall begin."

He said something in Indian to the slaves, who brought forth properties from an inner room. They brought robes, rings, a crown, a sword. Then the negro appeared bearing an altar of an evil design, which he set to Sagrado's hand. The Indians brought forward the throne.

The negro held the robe for Sagrado.

"I put on the garments of a king," Sagrado said. "It is the

colour of power. It was woven by a woman who killed her son and lived in infamy till she was hanged."

"Your sister, I presume," Sard said.

The negro held the rings to Sagrado, who put them on his fingers and on his thumbs.

"These rings," he said, "are beaten from your Christian chalices, and reconsecrated to your Master's master."

The negro held the sword to Sagrado, who took it, kissed it and held it to his heart.

"This sword," he said, "is the steel of the guillotine of revolution which slays, unjustly, the shrieking innocent."

The negro laid hands upon the crown.

"See the crown," Sagrado said. "The gold that men betrayed for, the diamond that women whored for, the ruby that men murdered for, the lead that took life, and the poisonous metals which destroy life."

The negro, advancing, crowned Sagrado.

Sagrado sat still for a moment upon this throne. Once again Sard had the impression that something evil flowed into the man to make him bigger: he seemed to dilate and glow with an increase of personality.

"Take now the oil and the wine of evil," Sagrado said, "and anoint me to the worship of evil."

The negro anointed and asperged Sagrado, with some intoned words of ritual which were in no tongue known to Sard. The Indians had heaped carib leaf upon the brazier, which poured forth stupefying smoke. The negro began to chant a hymn with a rhythm which seemed to go between the marrow and the bone. Whatever it was, it stirred the Indians. They were standing three and three on each side of the throne: the seventh fed the brazier. They sometimes marked a rhythm with a stamp and a catching of the breath: their eyes became brighter and brighter, and turned upwards till they were absorbed within themselves. Their tongues licked to and fro as though they were lapping blood. Sagrado rose to his feet and drew his sword.

"Now," he said, "I draw the sword of evil for the deed that

crowns evil." He advanced to Sard and pressed the point of the sword upon his throat.

"Do obeisance to evil," he said, "and you shall live."

"Apply to the marines," Sard answered, "not to the deck department."

"Do obeisance to evil," Sagrado said, "and your lady-love shall be spared."

"I will not be spared," Margarita cried; "I defy you!"

"You dirty lunatic," Sard said, "do your damnedest."

"You have not said one thing yet," Sagrado said; "that you would rather die a thousand deaths, etc. . . . Do you say that?"

"Yes," Sard said.

"You shall, then, die a thousand deaths. And you shall beg life from me before you die the third." He turned to the negro.

"Anoint this beast for the sacrifice," he said.

A tremor of excitement passed through the Indians. The negro cut away Sard's shirt so as to bare the throat and heart. Then he poured the stolen wine over Sard's head. Sard shook the drops from him and glanced at Margarita, who was thinking of him, not of herself. She gave him her love in a look. An Indian came to each side of Sard: each held a pointed knife to his cheek, so that he could no longer see Margarita, only know that she was there, and gazing at him.

"Crown the beast for sacrifice," Sagrado said.

The Indian came forward with a wreath of white flowers which had been drenched in patchouli; he crowned Sard with it and the Indians laughed and clapped their hands. The negro thrust it down upon Sard's brow, so that the thorns in it drew blood, which slowly tricked into his eyes and dripped on to his chest. Sagrado laughed. He paused for an instant as though gathering evil: again he seemed to swell. He held the sword in both hands, with his thumbs uppermost, pointing straight at Sard. For a moment he stared at Sard along the line of the blade; then his head went back and his eyes turned upward in invocation.

He cried aloud upon the evil of the ages and of the day and of the hour to descend upon him. It seemed to Sard that the house filled with a murmur as though the evil obeyed his call.

He heard, as it were, wings, and, as it were, voices, and knew that death came with them.

"I feel you," Sagrado cried, "I know you, I obey you. I offer you this beast in . . ."

The murmur of wings and voices grew louder. In their greed for blood the devils beat upon the door: their teeth snapped like shaking chains. The Indians laughed, clapped their hands and moaned: "Ahi! ahi! ahi-a-hé!"

Then from the hall somewhere behind Sard came a woman's scream of "Danger! Look out!" which was stifled in the throat as by a blow or a gag. Someone seemed to be heaving on the sliding panels and banging on the door behind the throne.

Sagrado laughed with a high, clear, inhuman cry:

"With all my strength and will and spirit," he cried, "I offer you the life of this beast in . . ."

There came a crash both behind and in front of Sard: there was a deafening bang: someone fell over the brazier, which upset. All the stinking and smouldering carib leaf rolled from its metal pot. The room at the instant filled with men: they were all in green and silver. Sagrado whirled about to face them: one of them with a rifle beat the sword out of his hand: it broke below the hilt and fell in two pieces. After the crash, there came a silence so great that the double tinkle and clatter of the broken sword was memorable. The ball of carib leaf broke open, smoking violently: wisps of gunpowder-smoke drifted past. Sard could not imagine what had happened: all that he saw was so tight and red; but one of the Indians was lying on the floor, hardly moving. The men in green and silver were covering the rest with rifles. Behind the riflemen Sard saw the white but interested faces of Paggy and Crockums.

There was deep silence for nearly half a minute. Then somebody flung open a door which brought a gush of pure air into the foulness. An officer who had Sagrado covered with a revolver trod out the carib leaf under his feet. Two guards advanced, struck Sagrado suddenly on the wrists, knocking them together, then instantly twisted the twitch or cuero about them and wrenched it taut. Sard thought, "I have often heard that they put the twitch on criminals. They can break a man's wrists with it, so they say. Now there it is, actually done, before my eyes. They have him at their mercy."

Sagrado neither spoke nor struggled. He was like one drugged and unable to speak through the drug. He thought no more of Sard, but plainly did not yet know what had happened. The negro had turned whitish under his colour: the Indians moved no muscle.

The Dictator strode through the guards and spoke.

"So," he said, "a nice, pretty Christian scene of play! And Harker mio, my benefactor. One turn deserves another."

Guardias kept flooding into the room. They sorted themselves into couples, who advanced, each couple, to an Indian, put the cuero on him and dragged him aside. The Dictator with his own hands beat and tore at Margarita's chains. A chief of guardias, who had keys about him, unlocked the padlocks; the chains clanked to the floor, Sard and Margarita were free. The two reefers were white and subdued, but both were kind and helpful. They brought chairs for the two victims, and then, after a little search, brought water in some bronze bowls and mopped their brows. "You're among friends, Miss," they said. "No one shall hurt you." "You're all right, sir," they said to Sard; "you'll soon feel better. It's all right now, sir; those devils are all cueroed up."

When the Dictator had helped to restore the two victims, he turned to the guards. "Take those Indios and this negro out into the Plaza for the present," he said. "Leave this leader of theirs. I wish to examine him."

When the last of the eight had been removed, the Dictator turned to Margarita.

"Miss Kingsborough," he said, "I'm glad to be able to say that your brother is safe. He will do well enough; but I have thought it better to have him to my palace for my doctor to overhaul. Presently, when my carriages come, you shall join him.

"And now I will a little question this atavist, this throw-back, who has so nearly destroyed my Harker. Bring this creature to the light."

The man who held the twitch brought Sagrado forward. Sagrado seemed dazed still, but in his dream he was unwilling to be seen; he shrank from the Dictator and bowed his head into his robes.

"Let me see him," the Dictator said. "Hold up his head to the light. So, tear away that crown."

A man flung the crown to the ground: Sagrado was displayed: he turned white, but became more himself. The Dictator looked hard at him.

"We have met before," he said.

"We have had dealings," Sagrado said.

"So, it is Rafael Hirsch returned; one more who has not yet paid me for Carlotta. Are you not Rafael Hirsch?"

"If I were fifty Rafael Hirsches," Sagrado answered, "you would not be paid for Carlotta. You will carry that wound to your death, and no son of yours will carry on your work here. Killing her has kept you sterile at least."

"Good work is fruitful of itself," the Dictator answered. "My work is my son and my daughter. My people will inherit from me. So, Rafael Hirsch, we who once talked of magic together, see where our magics have led us."

"The game is not yet over, Manuel."

"The game is never over, Rafael Hirsch, never, never, never, whether in its mercy or in its fire. Have you anything to say?"

"Not with words," Sagrado said.

"Not with deeds," the Dictator said. "And yet, one thing you can say, one thing you know which you can tell me. Upon what spot of these accursed stones was she of whom we spoke bestially murdered?"

"Shall I have life, if I say?"

"You are not judged to death yet."

Sagrado seemed to consider this in all its bearings, while the others watched him. A kind of hope kindled on his face for a moment; he even smiled: then he studied the Dictator's face and smiled again, more bitterly.

"I think you would like to know that, Manuel," he said, " 'pretty damned bad,' as they say. You will not know it from me. But I do know it. What is more, Manuel; I heard what she said, before the knife-point touched her throat. Shall I tell you what she said?"

The Dictator made a sign with one hand: Sagrado was removed. A guardia's hand upon his throat made his telling of what she said unintelligible, furious as it was.

The Dictator crossed himself and remained in prayer until the noise of feet and of raving were shut away by the door.

"So," he said. "So passes the pride of power, into madness which brings a judgment. I knew that man as a scholar of strange things . . ." He paused and then continued in English:

"But you would like to know what brings me here, so like the Deus in the play. You must thank these two reefers here: Mr. Paggy and Mr. Crockums.

"Your brother, Miss Kingsborough, was left for dead in this house. He was not dead, however. He managed to crawl to the wall and there broke a window. Mr. Paggy and Mr. Crockums happened to be in the Plaza when the glass broke. They were in a state familiar to young men: a romantic state, of pining for romance. They thought that some woman was imprisoned here against her will. Hearing Mr. Kingsborough's tale, they ran for help.

"Now at that very time I was coming to the Plaza, on my way to Santa Alba, where I wished to meditate before Mass; for often in meditation light comes. These reefers ran into my party only a hundred yards from here. I, hearing their story, sent at once for the guardias of the ward, while I surrounded the house with my guard. At the back of the house I found a man whose ways I do not like, one Sumecta, whom I detained.

"I thought at that time that I was dealing with things common-place, but directly I had made an entrance into the back of the house, I smelt the carib leaf. When I smelt the carib leaf, I smelt devilry. For remember, Harker mio, I am a son of this land, where the devils are strong, and come much into human affairs. In my youth, for which God has punished me, I sought their help, so I know who uses carib leaf and when and why. So I come in, I and my guards.

"Truly, if the reefers had not been prompt and I not where

I was with my party, we should have been too late. However, we were in time. Now Harker mio, taste here this brandy. You are very white."

"My arm is broken, sir," Sard said.

"Facundo," the Dictator said to an equerry, "see that the carriages, when they come, stay in the street at the back, not in the Plaza. See also that a doctor be there."

When the equerry had gone, the Dictator turned to Margarita.

"Lady," he said, "what shall be done to these devil-worshippers? Doom or mercy?"

"I should have been glad of mercy a few minutes ago," Margarita said.

"And you, Harker mio, would you kill them or not kill?"

"Twenty minutes ago I would have killed them," Sard said. "Then I fought with that man and did not win. I would not have others do what I could not do myself."

"And you, the reefers?" the Dictator asked.

"They ought to be hanged, sir," Paggy said.

"I don't know, sir," Crockums said, "I don't know about their being hanged. I don't know what laws you may have, nor what they deserve, according to your laws."

At that instant, from without, there came a shattering volley of rifles, which made all present leap. While they stared at each other, plaster and glass pattered and tinkled down somewhere outside.

"That," the Dictator said, "is what they deserve according to my laws. Nor are my laws savage, seeing that I live in the South, where things bite worse and poison is more fell than in the North, where even the Devil is cold-blooded. So, they are gone where justice is less fallible than here; there they will receive, no doubt, the surplus which we, in our human weakness have failed to give.

"But come, enough of them: they are dead. I hear my carriages. We will leave this place of devilry, for breakfast at the palace. You reefers, too; you have deserved it: I will explain to your captain. Come, then."

An equerry entered and saluted:

"Your Excellency's carriages are now in the street without," he said.

"Good," the Dictator answered. "Santiago, y cierra España. Miss Kingsborough, I give you one arm; but the other I give to Harker mio."

"Your Excellency," Margarita said, "Mr. Harker only has one arm, and that is mine."

"Better still," the Dictator said. "Now I may have your persuasion to offer him a crutch; or shall we say a rest?"

Both Sard and Margarita had been dazed by the doings of the morning. Sard, who had been cut, battered and bruised, was weary from fighting and in pain from his arm. He was not able to speak. He felt like one who had had an immense day's work, which was now done and well done. Margarita was at his side; that was a happiness; his dream had come true; that was a marvel.

The carriages moved out into the light of the dawn through the white-blossomed thorn-tree avenue which led to Cachopos. The sun was just clear of the sea: the birds were going out and the flower-sellers coming in. Sard had Margarita at his side and the Dictator and a doctor opposite. The little white pennons of the lances of the escort fluttered like butterflies. Off Cachopos, a lofty English barque was coming in on the last of the breeze. She stole along like a ghost, white to the trucks, with a roll of brighter white at her lips which she seemed to stoop to drink. From the church of Santa Alba there came the exquisite pure sound of singing.

The carriages swung away from all this towards the palace, which shone above them among the forest. Behind it, far away, were the mountains, peak upon peak, some of them forested, some snowy; one, with a brow of crag, streaked with cataracts.

The Dictator pointed towards the sea, now shut from sight by many snowy branches. "That is shut from you, now, Harker mio," he said; "but when one door shuts another opens. Here is all this land waiting for you. To me, this land has only given work; to you, I see, it has already given all things; let me then add work to those."

"When my arm is mended," Sard said. "But your Excellency will have to ask my wife."